AMERICAN
JUDAS

A Novel

AMERICAN JUDAS

SFK
PRESS

Mickey Dubrow

To Dot and Reuben.

CHAPTER I

Saved Through Faith. The words were hand-carved into a mahogany sign with a gleaming walnut stain. Fit for a Vacation Bible School, it hung above the entrance gate to a remote outpost. The camp sat on a flat plain surrounded by electric barbed wire fencing and snipers in concrete guard towers. Just inside the gates was a flagpole with a New Glory American flag—the United States of America flag with a white cross instead of stars. The flagpole was dwarfed by a giant cross made of white steel beams, mud splattered at its base.

A military helicopter landed in the empty parking lot between the entrance gate and the train tracks that ran parallel to the camp. Missioner Grace Lim jogged from the gate to greet Federal Deacon Freeman Wingard as he departed the aircraft.

"Welcome to Camp Glorious Rebirth, sir," Missioner Lim shouted over the blender whine of the helicopter blades. "Sorry it couldn't have been under better conditions."

Wingard removed his suit jacket and draped it over his arm. Sweat stuck his shirt to his back. He hadn't expected the summer heatwaves to reach the Rocky Mountains, and he wondered how Missioner Lim managed to appear cool while wearing her standard-issue Hedge Protection blue windbreaker over a dress shirt and tie.

There were no campers or counselors in sight, only missioners and camp guards. Bright colored murals of biblical scenes filled with people and animals that looked like they had been flattened by a steamroller were painted on the sides of the barracks. The vanilla scent of nearby Ponderosa pines was almost completely obliterated by the stench of rotting vegetables.

The camp guard stationed outside the men's barracks shouldered his rifle and saluted Wingard. After he returned the salute, Wingard gazed at the majestic mountain range beyond the camp walls before entering the barracks alone. The stifling heat was like climbing into an oven. Wingard mopped his forehead with a handkerchief.

Walking between two rows of cots, his footsteps echoed off the walls. The smell of death grew stronger as he approached the end of the row. Wingard swiped at the flies buzzing around his head. At his feet was a pool of blood. Its iron tang stung the back of his throat. Above him hung the dead man, his neck broken by a noose made from a twisted bedsheet. The foul odor from his emptied bowels made Wingard gag, and he covered his mouth with his handkerchief.

The suicide victim was former congressman, Chip Randall. His body was rail-thin. Chip had loved good food and had always been twenty to thirty pounds overweight. Wingard used to tease him by poking his bloated belly and inquiring as to when the baby was due.

It was too much. He needed fresh air. Wingard stumbled to the window, but it was nailed shut. The heat squeezed him like a vise. He returned to the body. Though never the athletic type, Chip had climbed up to the crossbeam over his cot. Hanging apparently wasn't enough for him. Blood trailed from his gouged wrists to the puddle on the floor. A few remaining drops dripped off his fingertips. Wingard spotted a bloody nail on the ground next to Chip's cot.

On the crossbeam next to the noose, Chip had written, "If we say we have no sin, we deceive ourselves, and the truth is not in us. John 1:8," using his finger as the pen and his blood as his ink. Wingard stared at his best friend's bloated face. He used his handkerchief to wipe away his tears.

Chapter 2

ANNOUNCER: A blessed morning to you all. It's 8:30 a.m. and you're listening to NCR, National Christian Radio. Now the news.

U.S. armed forces have toppled the Muslim government in Somalia. This is the latest victory in Operation Ultimate Crusade. A White House spokesman reports that American humanitarian forces have begun to baptize the Somali people and estimates that the entire population will be saved within a year.

Popular singer and actress Bobbi Sue Sunshine has turned down an offer to play a non-believer in the hit TV series *Jesus Loves Me, Don'tcha Know*. Bobbi Sue said her faith in Jesus is too strong for her to portray a non-believer, even though the producers of the show promised to have her character accept Jesus as her Lord and Savior by mid-season.

The New England Blessed have accused the San Francisco Crusaders of praying after the game started. This is in violation of league rules, which states that the two teams may only ask for our Savior's guidance before the opening kickoff when both teams pray in unison, so as to avoid either team gaining an unfair advantage.

Former Congressman Chip Randall has died at the age of sixty-four. Randall was the one of the authors of the CHRIST Act. Randall rose to national attention when, while introducing the CHRIST Act on the floor of the House of Representatives, he said these words:

CONGRESSMAN RANDALL: Mr. President, tear down this wall between church and state.

ANNOUNCER: As of yet, there has been no official White House statement about former U.S. Congressman Chip Randall's passing.

Coming up, *The Pauly Pilgrim Show*. His guest today is Federal Deacon Freeman Wingard. But first, these messages.

COMMERCIAL VOICE TALENT: It's the question no one wants to ask. Is there a loved one in your family who has lost their way? Do they challenge Jesus' plan for this great country of ours? Have they openly spoken out against the wisdom of our anointed leaders to guide us to the greater glory?

All is not lost.

A short stay at a Savior Camp may be just what that loved one needs to regain the ecstasy of Christ in their heart. As the good book says, "Submit yourselves therefore to God. Resist the Devil, and he will flee from you. James 4:7."

The Savior Camps are not just for lapsed Christians and those afflicted with the disease of homosexuality. They also cure drug addicts, adulterers, Satan worshippers, and Liberals.

Is your faith in God strong enough to report a morally lost family member to the police, your local federal clergyman, or an official member of the National Church of Christ?

Turn in that backslider. Someday he'll thank you.

ANNOUNCER: And now the show hosted by the man some have called the fourteenth apostle. Pauly Pilgrim!

PAULY PILGRIM: A blessed good morning and welcome to *The Pauly Pilgrim Show*, I am your host Pauly Pilgrim. My guest today is a true man of God, Federal Deacon Freeman Wingard. He oversees the Department of Hedge Protection, which keeps our nation secure from the many threats we face both physically and spiritually. Thanks for taking time out of your busy schedule to join us, Deacon.

DEACON WINGARD: I feel blessed to be here, Pauly.

PILGRIM: The CHRIST Act, an acronym for Christian Households Rising in Support of Truth, declared Christianity as the official religion of the United States of America. This Sunday, a grateful nation will celebrate its tenth anniversary. Can you believe it's already been ten years since it passed?

WINGARD: It's amazing how far we've come in the last decade, but the CHRIST Act was only a symbolic gesture. The Twenty-Eighth Amendment, which repealed part of the First Amendment, made it possible for Congress to establish the National Church of Christ. That, for me, was the official beginning of The Greatest Awakening.

PILGRIM: It has been nothing short of miraculous to see how the country blossomed once the American people allowed the Lord Jesus to be their Commander-in-Chief. As I used to say, once you put Jesus in charge, everything else will fall into place.

WINGARD: I'm sorry, but there's something I need to talk about. As you've probably heard, Chip Randall, the author of the CHRIST Act, died this past Sunday.

PILGRIM: Yes. A tragic loss.

WINGARD: He was one of my dearest friends. We worked closely together when we both were in the House. We had our disagreements. He was more associated with the New Apostolic Reformation in their quest for Christians to claim the seven mountains of culture. I was more of a Christian Reconstructionist. I wanted to see Biblical law replace human law. But we both understood that Christians are biblically mandated to control all earthly institutions until the second coming of Christ.

PILGRIM: Which is why the CHRIST Act was so important.

WINGARD: I agree. But over time, Chip came to believe that the CHRIST Act was a mistake. He said he had opened a Pandora's Box and now the entire country was cursed by what he had unleashed. That's why he was sent to a Savior Camp. With thoughts like that, he needed to be saved. I think it's important that the public knows how Chip died.

PILGRIM: He had a history of heart trouble. It's not official, but I heard that Jesus called him home by stopping his heart.

WINGARD: Chip Randall didn't have a heart attack. He hanged himself.

PILGRIM: But ... Deacon. White House sources. Sunday's celebration.

WINGARD: I went to the camp. I saw for myself. Chip died by his own hand.

PILGRIM: Do you realize what you're doing? You're tarnishing the reputation of an American hero.

WINGARD: I respectfully disagree. Chip may have eternally separated himself from God, but I still love him. The best way I can honor this great man is by telling the truth.

PILGRIM: Well, I can see my producer waving at me, which means it's time for a commercial break. Deacon, I don't want to keep you away from your busy schedule any longer. Thank you for joining us today. When we come back, I'll reveal the government's latest predictions of when we can expect the Second Coming. Don't go away, your summer vacation plans may depend on this report.

CHAPTER 3

The late-afternoon sun cast long shadows. The streets were nearly deserted. Despite the depressed state of the Bethesda, Maryland business community, Seth Ginsberg wasn't worried about being mugged. Theft was a Big Ten offense that carried mandatory life imprisonment, and it was legal for anyone to carry a concealed weapon anywhere the Good Lord told them to carry it. Whether it was God or guns that had reduced the crime rate, Seth had lost count of the number of times he'd heard TV pundits argue over which firearm Jesus would have preferred. He carried an unloaded gun in the range bag slung over his shoulder.

Seth came to a cluster of chain restaurants and gas stations. The Second Amendment Shooting Range was on the next block. Putting his foot on a fire hydrant, he pretended to tie his shoelace as a car drove by. The car pulled into a Boston Market parking lot. Seth took out his phone and removed the battery.

He resumed walking toward the shooting range, but then turned left into an office-building complex. SPACE AVAILABLE signs filled the windows. Lawns were choked with weeds, and weeds poked through cracks in the sidewalk. Seth's echoing footsteps reminded him of last-man-on-earth movies.

Once he was deep into the office park, he slipped between two buildings and zigzagged his way through a maze of side streets designed for when maintenance crews still went about their business out of sight of upper management. Moving as quickly as he could without breaking out into a run, he eventually came to a loading dock and sat on the steps.

Sweat trickled down his back as he caught his breath. He listened. At first he heard nothing, but then he could make out the hum of the generators feeding the empty structures, the distant rumble of traffic, and the occasional bird singing.

Satisfied he was alone, Seth tried to open the door even though he knew it was locked and would set off a silent alarm. He stared at the security camera mounted in the corner of the loading dock door until he heard a distinct click. He opened the door and entered the building.

Inside, the room was dark and smelled of diesel fuel and mildew. A flashlight shone in his face, and Seth held up a hand to shield his eyes. The flashlight blinked off and the overhead lights flickered on. A pudgy man in dark slacks and a dress shirt with the sleeves rolled up stood in a doorway at the other end of the room. Seth nodded at him.

"Hey, Howard."

"Seth."

"Did you see the game on Saturday?"

"I'm sorry to say I did. All that crap about the Blessed losing because the Crusaders prayed after kickoff? Please. As long as the Blessed keep Binkowski as their starting quarterback, they don't *have* a prayer of winning."

Once Seth crossed the room, Howard turned off the overhead lights and used his flashlight to guide them to a service elevator deep inside the dark office building. Howard picked a key from a crowded key ring and put it into the control panel. The doors opened. Seth stepped inside alone and pressed a button.

Red exit signs provided the only light on the seventh floor. Dim as it was, it was illuminated enough for Seth to find his way to a conference room. Sand covered the floor, a tradition handed down from the crypto-Jews during the Spanish Inquisition, who put sand on the floor to muffle the sound of their feet. There were no windows since the room had once been used for video presentations. Rows of seats faced a long table. On the table were stacks of prayer books, a cardboard box filled with *yarmulkes*, and a portable ark. Inside the plain cabinet was a Torah, the congregation's most precious item.

People milled about and talked quietly among themselves. Rabbi Leah, a tall woman with piercing blue eyes and long frizzy gray hair, broke away from a couple and approached Seth.

"Where were you last week?" she said. "For two nights we didn't have enough for a minyan."

Rabbi Leah was the respected spiritual leader of this secret synagogue, but there were times when she could be a pill. Seth did a quick head count and counted twenty including himself and Rabbi Leah, twice as many as necessary for a minyan.

"Last week there were too many people on the street," Seth said. "I had to bail and go to target practice. I was lucky to make it in today." He set his range bag in a chair, pried open a false bottom, and pulled out his blue velvet *tallis* bag.

"I'm sorry," Rabbi Leah said. "Whenever anybody doesn't show up, I always think the worst."

Along with praying to a shared deity, a religious congregation was a family. But since they worshipped in secret, congregants went by their first names only. Seth knew nothing about the other members. If he passed one of them on the street, he pretended he didn't know them.

Seth noticed that Sam and Esther weren't here. He remembered how strange it had been when Esther was pregnant. Normally, people gushed over a pregnant woman, but none of the congregants had even acknowledged her swollen belly. Then one day Esther wasn't pregnant. No one asked her if she'd had a boy or a girl. And now, she and Sam were missing. Seth felt guilty for snapping at Rabbi Leah. She was worried about him, just as she was worried about all of them.

"I'm sure Sam and Esther are fine," Seth said.

Rabbi Leah's eyes widened. Seth wondered if he'd said too much. She turned away from him, went to the long table, and stood next to the Torah ark.

"It's after sundown," Leah said. "We should begin the service. Grab a siddur. I have yarmulkes for anyone who doesn't already have their own."

People lined up to take a prayer book, and the men each selected a black skull cap from the cardboard box.

Seth unzipped his tallis bag. He took out his yarmulke and placed it on his head. He then took out his prayer shawl, held it up, and quietly recited the prayer embroidered along the collar band. He kissed both ends of the prayer before swinging the tallis over his shoulders like a cape.

Rabbi Leah led the service. She sang softly. At times, Seth had to strain to hear her. The building was in the middle of an empty office complex, the room was too high for anyone on the street to hear, and there were no windows, but still the fear of discovery hung in the air. Rabbi Leah ended the service with a prayer that everyone in the congregation be safe and in good health.

As a safety measure to avoid detection, congregants left the building at fifteen-minute intervals, either alone or in pairs.

Rabbi Leah approached Seth while he was folding his tallis. "Do you mind waiting toward the back of the line tonight?" she asked. "I was hoping we could talk."

"Sure," Seth said. He stuffed his folded tallis and yarmulke into his velvet bag.

They sat in the front row facing the ark.

"I wanted to apologize again for the way I spoke to you earlier," Rabbi Leah said. Seth started to comment, but she waved him off. "I know how dangerous it is to come here."

"I'm no braver than any other member of the congregation," Seth said.

A couple interrupted their conversation to say goodnight. Rabbi Leah stood and gave each one a hug. Though she was older than Seth by at least ten years, Rabbi Leah was the type of Jewish woman his mother had wanted him to marry instead of the Catholic girl now waiting for him at home. The couple left, and the rabbi turned her attention back to Seth.

"There's something I've been meaning to ask you," she said. "Don't worry. I ask all the congregants this question."

"What is it?"

"Why did you decide to join us?"

Seth kneaded the velvet bag in his hands. It was a good question. He could answer it without revealing specific information about himself.

"I grew up in an observant family," he said. "Though after my bar mitzvah, I pretty much stopped going to services except for the High Holy Holidays."

"How did your parents react?"

Seth could feel the old ache of his parents' disappointment. He'd been their favorite, easily outshining his older brother until he decided he didn't want to be observant.

"They weren't happy about it. My mother didn't say anything, but

my father constantly gave me a hard time about not keeping kosher and dating non-Jewish girls. He once asked me why I didn't go to services. I told him that I didn't believe God graded us on attendance."

"How do you think God grades us?" Leah said.

"According to what's in our hearts. By how we treat others."

Rabbi Leah smiled, but Seth couldn't tell if she was agreeing with him or amused by his ignorance. He didn't mention that his parents' disappointment in his lack of observance was nothing compared to how they reacted when he told them he was converting to Christianity, how his father accused him of driving a knife into their hearts.

"Does your wife know you come here?" Leah said.

The question made Seth nauseous.

"How did you know I was married?" he said.

"You should have taken off your ring if you wanted to keep her a secret," Leah said, pointing at his wedding band. She held up her hand to show her own wedding ring. "My husband knows I'm here."

Seth didn't have to answer her question. Jews weren't required to confess their sins to Rabbis.

"My wife doesn't know I'm here," Seth said.

"You need to tell her."

Seth stared at the portable ark with the sacred Torah inside. "Why did you decide to join us?"

"No one has ever asked me that before." Rabbi Leah played with the ring on her finger.

"It's only fair," Seth said. "If we tell you then you have to tell us."

"I could've gone to Canada," Leah said, brushing a strand of hair out of her face, "but I had to stay and do this. It's like you said. God doesn't grade us on attendance. Jews come together to worship because we need each other."

Chapter 4

Church bells rang loudly. And kept ringing. Maggie Ginsberg rolled over in bed and shook Seth.

"Get up already," she said.

"Little more sleep," mumbled Seth. He reached over and pressed the snooze button on his phone. The bells stopped.

It was too early for the sun to begin leaking through the edges of the curtains, so the bedroom was comfortably dark and cool.

"Not the snooze button," Maggie said. "I won't be able to sleep knowing that those damn bells will start ringing again at any minute. God, you are the worst about getting up in the morning."

"Phone only comes with two alarms. Would you rather hear 'Amazing Grace'?" Seth said.

"Why can't you get up the first time the alarm goes off?"

"Hate mornings."

Seth turned onto his side and wrapped his arm around Maggie's waist. She nudged him gently with her elbow.

"I don't have to get up for another hour," she said. "But you need to get up now or you're going to be late. Again."

Seth responded by placing his hand over one of Maggie's breasts and giving it a playful squeeze. Maggie pulled the covers up closer to her face, but she didn't move his hand.

"Seth," Maggie said. "Come on. I really cherish the hour I have the bed to myself. Get up."

"You don't like sharing the bed with me?"

She reached back and patted his hip.

"I love sharing a bed with you. I just don't want to be awake when I don't have to."

Seth rubbed his groin against Maggie's rump. She could feel that part of him waking up.

"You can't be asleep," he said. "Otherwise you wouldn't be talking so much. Since we're both awake and I'm probably going to be late anyway, why don't we take advantage of the hour before you have to get up?"

Maggie smiled. "I can be persuaded. Do you have any condoms?"

"Got one left. Getting more this afternoon."

"Let me pee first."

Maggie threw back the covers and headed for the bathroom. Seth removed the lower drawer of his nightstand and slid out the false bottom. He pushed aside his Star of David necklace, took out his last black market condom, put it on the nightstand, and replaced the drawer. Seth heard the toilet flush and the water running. Maggie preferred to brush her teeth before sex but never complained that he didn't.

Before getting back into bed, Maggie stripped off her t-shirt and boxer shorts. Seth pulled off his underwear. They embraced, enjoying the warmth of each other's body. Seth loved the combination of Maggie's black hair and blue eyes, but he loved her dimpled smile the best. He tickled the nipple of her left breast with his tongue.

"Now do the other one." Maggie giggled when Seth complied.

Their kisses grew from playful to passionate. Seth rubbed the base of Maggie's back as she stroked him. When Maggie was ready, Seth ripped open the package and slipped on the condom.

"I'm home," he said as he entered her.

They were moments away from orgasm when determined knocking on the front door of their townhouse interrupted their lovemaking. Maggie dug her fingers into Seth's shoulders.

"Don't stop," Maggie said.

"I have to," Seth said.

"They'll go away."

The steady knocking changed to banging. Seth pulled out and frantically searched the floor for his underwear.

"I have to go see who it is," Seth said. "It might be her."

Maggie rolled onto her side.

"Calm down," she said. "I'm sure it's nothing serious."

Seth threw on his robe, went downstairs, and squinted in the front door's peephole. He hurried back upstairs.

"I was right," he whispered. "Darlene's here."

Maggie broke the third commandment.

"She's authorized to make surprise visits," Seth said as he put on sweatpants and a faded Yale sweatshirt. "But she's never done one before. Do you think something happened?"

"If we were in trouble, it wouldn't be Darlene at the door," Maggie said. "You have to stop letting her freak you out."

"We don't have time for this discussion. I'll let her in. Get dressed and please, first chance you get, make some coffee."

The banging stopped when Seth reached the top of the stairs. He paused, thinking that she had left, but then the banging began again in earnest. Seth rushed to the front door. "Oh, it's you, Darlene," he said. "For a moment there, I thought I was under attack from Muslim terrorists."

Darlene Thomas tugged at the jacket of her maroon business suit and turned so Seth could clearly see the FFV patch stitched to the jacket's shoulder.

Darlene cleared her throat. "As your Federal Faith Verification case worker, I am authorized by the state of Virginia to inspect your home at any hour of any day at my own discretion to verify the authenticity of your Christian conversion."

"Nobody locks their door these days," Seth said. "You're welcome to enter my home any time you please."

"I wanted to make sure you were decent." Before Darlene entered, she looked over her shoulder and said, "Thank you. You've been most helpful."

Seth peered out the door and saw his neighbor, Larry Bruner, standing on his front porch with a Bible in hand. A mere sliver of space separated the porches of their row houses, which were typical homes for young families in the Alexandria, Virginia neighborhood. Ever since Larry had returned from Savior Camp, he'd spent hours on his front porch reading Bible verses aloud or staring off into space. Seth wondered what Larry could have told Darlene that she found so helpful.

"Morning, Larry," Seth said.

"As for the one who is weak in faith, welcome him, but not to quarrel over opinions, Romans 14:1," Larry said.

"Sorry, I have to go inside. Got company."

Seth found Darlene in his cramped living room. Family photos dominated one wall, and Darlene flitted from frame to frame, leaning in so close that her breath fogged the glass panes.

"Is this you?" she said, pointing at a photograph of Seth as a young boy, his curly hair sticking out from underneath his baseball cap. "How old were you in this picture? Seven? Eight? My, my you were so cute."

Seth resisted the urge to point out she had seen this photo many times before and always made the same comment. Any bad attitude from him would go down on his record as evidence that he wasn't filled with the calming spirit of Christ.

"I was six," he said. "I'm wearing my T-ball Tigers uniform."

Maggie entered the room. She wore the T-shirt she'd slept in and a pair of jeans. Seth was relieved to see she had put on a bra. Even though she was in her own house, Darlene could claim Maggie lacked the proper modesty of a Christian wife.

"I just put on a pot of coffee," Maggie said. "I know you want some, Seth. How about you, Darlene? Fancy a cup of joe?"

"No thank you," Darlene said. "All I need to get me going in the morning is to sing a song of praise for the Good Lord. Gives me enough energy for the whole day."

Seth's brain screamed for caffeine. He followed the deep aroma of coffee brewing in the kitchen. Darlene and Maggie tagged along behind him.

"I have it written down in my paperwork, but remind me," Darlene said. "Where do you go to church?"

"N.C. 58 on Union Street," Seth said.

Seth poured himself a cup of coffee and took a grateful sip. He drank it black. He didn't like sugar and milk to get in the way of the caffeine rush. He poured a cup for Maggie.

"You like your F.C.?" Darlene asked.

"We like our federal clergyman very much," Maggie said, taking a carton of milk out of the fridge. "Reverend Mike's sermons are so inspirational."

"It's nice how you can see the back yard from your kitchen." Darlene gestured toward the floor-to-ceiling window that made the small space seem slightly larger. "Tell me about the tricycle. Are you expecting a precious gift from Jesus?"

Maggie and Seth stared at the red tricycle in the middle of their fenced-in yard as if noticing it for the first time.

"That belongs to our neighbors' child," Seth said. "We let him ride in our yard because it's safer than riding on the sidewalk. His mother is worried he might dart out into traffic."

Darlene put her fists on her hips. "When are you two going to get busy and start raising children of your own? I know you make enough money so that your wife can stay home and raise the kids. The Lord says we must be fruitful and multiply."

"We haven't been blessed yet," Maggie said. "But it's not for lack of trying. In fact, we were trying to be fruitful when you knocked on the front door."

Darlene leaned toward Seth and sniffed.

"That explains why you smell like a cat in heat," she said. "You're not doing anything to impede the will of the Lord to your wife's womb, are you?"

"Of course not," Seth said.

Darlene narrowed her eyes at him and then pointed at the area rug on the kitchen floor. It was decorated with chickens and fruit.

"This is a nice rug you have here. You ever pray on it?"

Maggie rolled her eyes.

"Muslims use prayer rugs. Seth was Jewish before he converted."

"My momma called Jews *Jesus Killers*. What were you before you joined the National Church?"

"I was Catholic. We invented religious persecution."

"Wife!" Seth shouted. "Still thy tongue!"

Maggie jerked her head back as if she'd been slapped, but she stayed silent. Darlene smiled with approval. Seth had demonstrated how a proper Christian man chastised a disrespectful wife. Seth took a moment to enjoy his coffee and then spoke to Darlene in a tone he hoped came across as pained sincerity.

"Please forgive Maggie's improper words. We know God has a reason for not blessing us with a child yet. Satan tries to make us despondent and angry, but we do our best to fight his evil from entering our lives."

Darlene nodded sagely. "Just remember that there are three people in a marriage. The husband, the wife, and Jesus. When you have Jesus in the middle, he's the glue that holds the marriage together."

"Of course."

"Have you tried going to a fertility clinic?"

"Fertility clinic? Well, we've been meaning to go, but our schedules are so crazy, and we haven't found the right one yet."

Darlene poked around the many pockets of her satchel until she found one of the New Miracle Fertility Clinic business cards she kept for such an occasion. She handed it to Seth. He read it and then stuffed it into the pocket of his sweatpants.

"I personally know of at least five couples who have had great success with this clinic," Darlene said. "Next time I come by for a visit, I expect to see a receipt for treatment, or at the very least your appointment card."

"Okay," Seth said.

"Now that we got that taken care of, let's have a seat in the living room."

Darlene sat on the sofa, and Seth perched on the edge of a wingback chair. Darlene took a tape recorder out of her satchel and placed it on the coffee table between them. She pressed the Record button and held the device close to her mouth.

"Case worker Darlene Thomas on routine inspection of convert Seth Ginsberg, case file 6857. Preparing to receive affirmation statement."

She pointed the tape recorder at Seth. He stared at it as if it were a snake about to bite him.

"Tell me, Seth, how has Christ changed your life recently?"

Seth leaned toward the recorder.

"Well, I've been compelled to read the Bible more. I was angry that Josiah, the neighbors' boy, rode his tricycle around in circles so much that he killed the grass and now there's a dirt circle in my back yard, but then Jesus made me realize that Josiah is a gift from God more precious than my lawn. I think that's all for now."

Darlene shut off the recorder and put it back in her satchel.

"How did I do?" Seth said.

Darlene smiled and shook her head.

"This is not a test, Seth. We're trying to help you stay on the path of righteousness so that you'll go to Heaven. You don't want to burn forever in the lake of fire, do you?"

"No. I sure don't."

Darlene stood. "I'll begin my inspection now," she said, and began rambling around the townhouse, opening drawers and examining book titles. She checked the dates stamped in Seth's Church Attendance Book. While she made sure there weren't any secular influences in the house that might cause Seth to backslide, Seth called his office to let them know that he would be unavoidably late.

After Darlene climbed the narrow staircase to inspect the second floor, Seth and Maggie huddled in the kitchen and spoke softly.

"Wife, still thy tongue?" Maggie asked.

"Sorry, I panicked," Seth said. "I was trying to sound Protestant. Stiff and authoritative."

"It almost worked. I'm making myself breakfast. Do you want me to make you something?"

"I can't think about eating now."

Seth stared at the ceiling and tried to follow Darlene's creaking footsteps overhead. Drawers were pulled open and slammed shut. He prayed she wouldn't poke around his gun range bag. If Darlene found his tallis, he'd not only go to jail for a long time, Maggie would kill him.

Maggie took eggs, butter, and wheat bread from the refrigerator and lined them up on the counter.

"The condom," she said. "Are you sure it was your last one?"

"I'm sure," Seth said.

"You didn't have time to flush it. Where did you put it?"

"I was in such a hurry, I didn't have a chance to take it off."

Maggie's eyes widened.

"You're wearing it now?"

Seth grimaced.

"Yeah."

Maggie giggled as she cracked open eggs and slid the yolks into a bowl. Seth sat on a stool at the breakfast bar and sipped his coffee. Maggie heated butter in a frying pan and added the eggs. The sizzle and smell made Seth's stomach grumble, but he was still too nervous to eat. Not only was he on edge because there was a government representative inspecting his underwear drawer, but he and his wife had been forced to stop making love before they were finished. He was feeling blue all over.

"Darlene is annoying, but she's not out to get you," Maggie said. "Why are you so scared of her?"

"She has a direct line to the National Church," Seth said. "I have to go through channels."

Maggie was done with breakfast and had washed her dishes by the time Darlene lumbered downstairs. She declared the townhouse clean of secular influence, but suggested Seth add more crosses and maybe a reproduction of *The Last Supper*. As she was leaving, she instructed Seth to "Have a blessed day."

"Did you see the way Darlene whipped out that fertility clinic card?" Maggie asked. "Does she get a commission for every baby they help produce?"

Darlene had touched a nerve in Maggie by bringing up kids. Everybody at church, everybody at work, even the people at the grocery store were constantly asking why she wasn't pregnant yet. According to the Marriage Protection Amendment, marriage was for the sole purpose of procreation, but Maggie felt that shouldn't include telling her when to procreate.

Seth fished the business card out of his sweatpants pocket and put it on the counter.

"We could just have a baby," he said. "That would shut everybody up."

Maggie put her hand on his cheek. "Does it bother you that I don't want to have children right now?"

Seth moved away from her hand. "Not at all."

"You sure about that?"

"You wouldn't end up like your mother. I'll be there."

Maggie bit her lower lip. "That's not it at all. Why should I have to give up my career because people say I should?"

"You're right. Hey, I'm not ready for kids right now either, but what do we tell Darlene when she asks for proof that we went to this fertility clinic?"

Maggie got a box of matches out of the junk drawer, lit the card on fire, and dropped it into the sink. The flames reduced it to a curled piece of black ash, which she washed down the drain.

"Tell Darlene I lost the card," Maggie said. "And would she be kind enough to give us another."

AMERICAN JUDAS

CHAPTER 5

As Seth entered Senator Sam Owens's main office, staff members talked rapidly on their phones and interns hurried from desk to desk. He relaxed. It was a typical day. Seth waved hello to Tisha, the receptionist, on the way to his private office. As the senator's main speechwriter, Seth was allowed a few extra privileges. After dropping his briefcase and tote bag beside his cluttered desk, he loosened his tie and ignored his phone's blinking message light.

Reginald Cooke, Senator Owens's Chief of Staff, entered the office.

"Look who finally decided to come to work," he said, crossing his arms.

"At least this time I have a legitimate excuse."

"Did you hear about Deacon Wingard's claim that Chip Randall committed suicide?"

"Yeah. Any comment from the White House yet?"

Reggie slouched into a visitor's chair. "Nope."

Seth did not envy the White House Press Secretary today. Reporters were going to demand that he either confirm or deny that one of the architects of the Greatest Awakening was in Hell.

"Do you need to take the day off?" Reggie asked.

"Why would I need to do that?" Seth said.

"You worked in Randall's office."

"It was an honor working for Congressman Randall, but that was nine years ago. Besides, he didn't socialize with us worker bees. I doubt he even knew my name."

"Come on, you helped make history with Randall. Doesn't his death make you feel like the tectonic plates of your life just shifted?"

Reggie was ribbing Seth, but there was an element of truth to what he said. Seth had been a member of Randall's staff during the creation of the CHRIST Act, and though he had been just a cog in Randall's legislative machine, Seth was well aware that the law would change the course of the country forever. There had been many days when Seth was sure the bill would be killed as it struggled through the House, the Senate, received the President's signature, and passed legal challenges that went all the way to the Supreme Court.

"Randall threw a big party when the CHRIST Act finally became law," Seth said. "He gave a speech in which he said, 'Now the Devil can't hide anywhere in our country anymore.' That stuck with me."

Reggie picked a piece of lint off his shirt. "I guess he was wrong about that."

Seth's office phone buzzed. He pushed the intercom button. "What's up, Tisha?"

"Is Reggie still in there with you?"

"He is, indeed."

"Senator Owens wants to see both of you in his office."

Seth followed Reggie into the hallway. Tisha winked at them as they walked past her desk on their way into the senator's spacious office.

Before he became Senator Sam Owens, junior United States Senator from Tennessee, he was Pastor Samuel Owens of the Holy Trinity AME Church in Memphis. There was nothing unique about a former clergyman becoming a politician; however, after the Greatest Awakening, it was practically a requirement to prove one was fit for office. When he was a pastor, Owens was known for his diamond-encrusted cross-shaped cufflinks and for wearing too much cologne. Nothing changed when he became a senator.

Owens came around his desk and put his arm around Seth's shoulder. Seth knew from past experience that if he spent too much time in close proximity to Owens, the senator's cologne would stick to him all day.

"I heard you had an unexpected visit from your FFV agent," Owens said.

"It's no big deal," Seth said. "Just made me a little late, that's all."

"What's your agent's name?" Reggie asked.

"Darlene. Darlene Thomas."

"You think she knows that she's about to be out of a job?"

"What do you mean?"

"She's a woman. Working women keep good men from getting

good jobs."

"Women don't need to be working anyway," Owens added. "They have husbands to support them."

"If she knows she's going to get canned, then why go through the trouble of a surprise visit?" Seth asked

"Vain attempt to impress her boss?" Reggie said. "Not that it'll do her any good. A male agent will be taking her place any day now." Owens squeezed Seth's shoulder. "I can make this go away," he said, his voice deep and smooth. "I can make a phone call this afternoon and your file will be classified as FVWD, faith verified without doubt."

"Please don't make that call, sir," Seth said. "If it ever got out that you arranged my faith verification, the potential damage to your reputation would be problematic. I don't want to be responsible for anything that would derail the good work we're doing here."

Owens released his grip on Seth and slapped him on the back. Seth winced.

"My man," Owens said happily. "That's the kind of Christian Soldier I need in my army. Now, speaking of work, let's get some done. I made a couple of notes on Sunday's speech."

The senator went to his desk, located the speech, and handed it to Seth. Notes were scrawled on the pages.

"It's mighty fine," Owens said. "But I want it to be perfect."

Senator Owens had been chosen to be one of the speakers at the tenth-anniversary celebration of the CHRIST Act at National Church One, the main national church in Washington. This was the first time Owens had been invited to participate. It was a tremendous honor, and the event would be televised on all channels.

"I know what you're thinking," said Reggie, wagging his finger at Owens. "You think this speech might be your ticket to a seat on the SCBLA."

The SCBLA, Senate Committee on Biblical Law and Administration, was the most powerful committee in Congress and oversaw how Biblical Law was incorporated into everything from the military to schools to financial markets. The committee worked closely with the National Church, which made it even more prestigious.

"Don't be ridiculous," Owens said. "I am humbled to be a small part of this momentous occasion."

Reggie and Seth glanced at each other.

"You're absolutely correct, sir," Seth said. "There's nothing political about this at all."

"Just a small part for a humble man," Reggie said.

Owens held up his hands in surrender. "Okay, okay, it's a big deal. Of course, I want to be on the SCBLA. Who doesn't? But remember, when my profile goes up, so does yours. I'm the rising tide that lifts all boats."

Seth flipped through the pages of the speech. "Should I add something about Chip Randall?" He knew the senator wouldn't dare heap praise on a man who had taken his own life, but he had to ask anyway.

Owens worried his diamond cufflinks. "There'd be no CHRIST Act without him, but maybe we should leave Randall's eulogy to the pastor-in-chief."

Just as the President was the commander-in-chief of the armed forces, he was also the head pastor of the National Church.

"Do you think Randall hanged himself?" Reggie said. "Deacon Wingard claims he saw the body."

Owens leaned forward and glared at his Christian Soldiers. "I will believe whatever President Reed tells us. And so will you."

CHAPTER 6

The Judy Cross Show staff members scurried into the conference room. No one touched the coffee and donuts at the center of the table. Maggie Ginsberg arrived with Amy Bird. At nine a.m. on the dot, Judy Cross entered and locked the door behind her. A moment later, a production assistant's face appeared at the door's window. He knew better than to try and get in. Judy had told the staff on more than one occasion that if she could arrive on time then so could they.

Judy lowered her head and everyone did the same. After a brief silent prayer, she poured a cup of coffee and grabbed two donuts. As soon as she was done, staff members served themselves.

"All right," Judy said. "Let's not dilly-dally. I have a meeting with sales at eleven. Bill, get us started."

Bill Garmon, the show's executive producer, addressed the room. "On today's show we have parents who rescued children from the Devil's influence."

"Is it just the parents, or did they bring the kids?" Judy asked.

Bill checked his notes. "Parents and kids. The youngest is a six-month-old baby girl. Her birth parents were members of an underground cult. She was rescued by a couple in Silver Spring."

Judy placed her hand over her heart. "Lord Jesus is so powerful in His goodness."

"The rest of the kids range in age from three to fourteen. We could include the older kids in the cooking segment so that they get a treat on air. Talk about your extra blessings from the Lord."

"That's a lovely idea, Bill," Judy said as she licked glazed sugar off her fingers.

Bill peered at Amy and Maggie. Amy was the on-air chef for the cooking segment called, "What's Cookin' in Amy's Kitchen," which took a dish related to a non-Christian religion and re-interpreted it as a Christian Nation dish. Maggie was the segment producer.

"So, what's cooking in your kitchen today, Amy?" Bill said.

Amy turned to Maggie. "I don't know," she said. "What am I making today?"

Maggie gave Amy the stink eye. "Hamantashens," she said.

"Human what?" Judy said.

"Hamantashens. A triangle pastry served during the Jewish holiday Purim. We're calling them Patriot Tarts."

Judy dunked a section of her donut in her coffee and popped it into her mouth. She talked with her mouth full. "I had plenty of Jewish friends back when they ran the media, and not one of them ever mentioned a holiday called Purim. I think you made it up because you're too lazy to do the research."

"I can show you the research," Maggie said. "But you make a good point. If you're not familiar with the holidays of other religions, then there's little chance our audience is. We could start making them up and save me hours of work."

"Don't you dare. You just know there'd be one know-it-all viewer who'd catch us and create a big ruckus over nothing. People like that don't realize they're serving Satan when they cause unnecessary problems for God's warriors."

"Yes, ma'am."

"Okay, glad we got that settled," Bill said with more than a hint of exasperation. "Let's move on."

They reviewed the rundown, making notes of any last-minute details that still had to be taken care of.

"Well, if that's everything, I need to skedaddle," Judy said.

"There's just one more thing, Judy," Bill said. "Graphics needs to know the subject of your closing sermon so that they can whip up some over-the-shoulder art."

"I haven't a clue what the sermon is for today."

The staff stared at Judy. Every show on NCTV, National Christian Television, ended with a sermon. Judy was proud of the fact that she was one of the few hosts who wrote her own sermons. For her to admit that she didn't have a sermon was as unbelievable as hearing the president take the Lord's name in vain.

"Maybe the twins could sing an extra song," Judy said.

Conjoined twins Rosie and Renee Huffstetler were show regulars. They sang traditional gospel songs in perfect harmony and delivered sermons about the evils of abortion while heaping praise on their mother for refusing to terminate her pregnancy after her obstetrician informed her that her daughters would enter the world fused at the pelvis. Below the waist they were one person with two legs. Above the waist, they had one trunk with two heads and two arms.

"We can't do that, Judy," Bill said. "Shows have to end on a sermon. Let's throw it out to the staff. Give me some topics."

Staffers jumped on this rare opportunity by calling out sermon ideas.

"You could bless the troops again."

"You've only talked about the tenth anniversary of the CHRIST Act once. You could do an updated sermon."

"Revealing false messiahs always gets good ratings."

"End of days. It's been months since you talked about end of days."

"What about Chip Randall?" Maggie asked. "A major political figure just died. You could do a eulogy."

Judy started on her second donut while the subject of Chip Randall caught fire with the rest of the staff.

"Judy worked closely with Congressman Randall when he was in office. She has the personal angle."

"He spearheaded the CHRIST Act and then kills himself right before its tenth anniversary. Can't get more controversial than that. I don't know why the news hasn't done more with this story."

"Judy could be the first to talk about his death and how taking his life affects his legacy."

"We could speculate on what sort of eternal damnation he's suffering in Hell."

Judy slammed her palm on the table, the sound as sharp as a gunshot. Everyone stopped talking.

"*The Judy Cross Show* shall never ever mention the name of Chip Randall!" she shouted. "That's an order!"

"No problem, Judy," Bill said. "I'm sure there's plenty of other subjects you'd like to sermonize about instead."

Judy's lower lip quivered, and tears welled in her eyes. "That's just it, Bill. There really isn't. I love that America has become the greatest, most righteous nation in the world, in all of history, but I never guessed that being the best could be a little bit of a problem.

There's nothing to save Americans from anymore. Not when there's one religion, one party, and one church. We've cleansed the country of liberals, feminists, abortionists, Islamofascists, Satanists, and the homosexual agenda. Let's face it. We've won. There's nothing else to say."

The staff looked at one another in confusion. Except for Maggie. She bit the inside of her mouth to keep from laughing.

"What about Jesus Zombies?"

Bill scowled as he scanned the table to silence whoever had made that suggestion, but Judy had already grabbed onto it.

"That's an excellent idea," Judy said, "because there's no such thing as a Jesus Zombie. It's a myth created to discredit Savior Camps by old fuddy-duddies who can't deal with the fact that the National Church joined all the denominations under one roof. People like having only one denomination. You live in America. You go to the American church."

"My next-door neighbor is a Jesus Zombie," Maggie said. "He hasn't been able to hold a job since he got back from Savior Camp. He spends most of his time standing on his porch reciting Bible verses."

Judy gave Maggie a dismissive wave of her hand. "Hush, you're not helping."

"Jesus Zombies are a bad idea," Bill said. "At least for now. Let's wait until after the CHRIST Act anniversary, and then we can discuss it."

Judy crossed her arms and narrowed her eyes at Bill. "What's wrong with ending the disgusting myth of Jesus Zombies once and for all?"

Bill rubbed his forehead. "No matter how we do this story, it'll end up being about the Savior Camps and whether they actually rehabilitate sinners or destroy their minds. Congress is thinking about shutting them down. We don't want to risk ending up on the wrong side of this debate."

"That's what makes the subject so perfect. We can influence public opinion to save the camps and the good work they do."

"It didn't do Chip Randall much good," Maggie said.

"That's another thing," Bill said. "The White House hasn't

confirmed or denied the rumor that Randall killed himself."

"He did it," Judy said. "Chip was mentally unstable and spiritually compromised. That's why he was sent to a Savior Camp. Sadly, there are those few souls who are so tainted with evil, they can't be saved." She refilled her coffee cup. "Bill, tell the graphics department I want a picture of a camp with a glowing cross over it. Today's sermon will be about the true blessing of Savior Camps and the false myth of Jesus Zombies."

Bill held his hands out in a pleading gesture. "Judy don't do it. Not now."

Judy added sugar to her coffee. "We must be brave in the face of evil. We're done here, people. Let's put on a great show today."

She unlocked the door and left the room with her coffee in hand. The meeting was over.

CHAPTER 7

In her office, Judy found a man studying the wall photos of her posing with presidents, congressmen, national clergymen, entertainers, and an endless parade of conservative political pundits.

"There you are," she said, holding out her arms. "Give your mother a hug."

Julian Cross ignored her request.

"Look at you," he said, tapping a photo of Judy posing with a televangelist. "You were so thin back then."

Julian's comment was cruel but true. The photo had been taken when she was young and at the height of her career as an outspoken critic of the corrosive liberal secularists threatening to destroy America. Judy had possessed a cold beauty with cheekbones so sharp they could draw blood, a body that would make an anorexic jealous, long red hair, piercing blue eyes, and a permanent smirk.

Judy studied her reflection in the glass protecting the photograph. She was heavier now and wrinkled. She wore her hair in a matronly bob and dyed it food-coloring orange to hide the gray. She had committed a woman's worst sin. She had gotten old.

She eased herself into her leather desk chair and kicked off her high heels. Julian sat on the sofa across from her.

"When's your meeting with Freeman?" Judy asked.

"Thursday," Julian said.

Judy shook her fists in triumph. "Hallelujah! I have prayed for this for so long, and finally Lord Jesus has delivered."

Julian stretched out on the sofa. "What exactly is involved in becoming a member of the Brethren?" he asked. "Is it like joining a fraternity? Is there a hazing period that ends with a secret ceremony where a line of men spank my naked ass with paddles?"

"I wouldn't know. Women are not allowed to join."

Julian grinned, and Judy could see from the glint in his eye that he was building up to being really nasty. Her son was as ambitious as she was, but he enjoyed hurting her even more. There was a demon in Julian that he had inherited from his father. But once Freeman Wingard brought Julian into the Brethren, his close proximity to the awesome power of the Lord would certainly cast the evil out of him.

"Come on, Mother," Julian said. "Certainly, you got some member of the Brethren to tell you their secrets as the two of you snuggled up after a night of sweaty sex."

Judy gritted her teeth. Even after all these years, he still found new ways to inflict fresh wounds.

"I only had intimate relations with one member of the Brethren," she said. "And that was your father."

"That's not how I remember it."

Back when Judy was young and glamorous, she had made some stupid mistakes, the biggest being Julian's father. Another was not doing a better job of convincing Julian when he was at an impressionable age that the things he read about her in the decadent press were malicious lies created to feed an insatiable beast.

"I sent you to the finest schools," she said. "I've bailed you out of countless embarrassing situations. Why must you treat me so horribly?"

The bookshelf next to the sofa was filled exclusively with books written by Judy and illustrated her evolution from acid-tongued pundit to Born-Again Christian. Julian ran a finger across their spines, pulling out, *Gutless and Bloated: Why Liberals Hate Freedom.* He flipped open to the middle and read a random sentence. "We must sterilize the liberals before they breed any more of their ilk. As a service to humanity, we must cut out the disease before it spreads."

Judy tilted her head in confusion. "What's your point, dear?"

"This is my real mother," Julian said, slapping the book. "You think you buried your rage at this ridiculous world by pickling your brain in religion, but you just passed your anger on to me."

"You make it sound like I cursed you."

"It wasn't a curse. It was a blessing."

The tears welling in Judy's eyes threatened to ruin her makeup. "Jesus saved me when I was lost. He can save you, too, if you'd just open your heart."

"Keep telling yourself that, Mother. If you believe hard enough, maybe it'll come true."

MAGGIE CHECKED THE SET ONE MORE TIME. ALL THE INGREDIENTS FOR THE Patriot Tarts were lined up for easy access. She resisted the urge to dip her finger in the bowl of strawberry filling. Completed pastries were on baking sheets in the backstage refrigerator. They would be placed in the set's oven on low heat shortly before Judy and Amy acted out the cooking instructions. Judy always insisted on tasting the final result on camera so that she could proclaim it was "a gift from Heaven."

Amy sauntered onto the set and leaned against the counter. "Why do you keep pushing Judy's buttons?"

"Why can't you remember the production schedule?" Maggie said. "This is your show, too."

"Judy is a relic from the past, but she still has a lot of power. Don't mess this up for me."

To bolster the idea that the Patriot Tarts were indeed patriotic and not just an assimilated Jewish treat, the set had been decorated with small New Glory American flags and pictures of Saint George Washington wearing a tricorn hat. Maggie straightened a row of flags that had wilted.

"I thought we were equal partners," Maggie said. "But lately, I feel like I'm working for you, and you're a lousy boss."

Amy and Maggie had been close friends until "What's Cookin' in Amy's Kitchen" became popular and Amy blossomed into a minor celebrity. The audience fell in love with her sweet disposition and face full of freckles. As Amy's star rose, she saved her sweet disposition for when she was on camera. Off camera, she became a demanding diva, berating the staff and leaving Maggie solely responsible for getting the cooking segment on air.

When Amy bothered to show up for production meetings, instead of contributing ideas, she bragged about hanging out with famous singers and actors. Most popular entertainers were genuine God Squad and dedicated Christians, but Amy preferred the company of celebrities who claimed publicly that they were believers, but in private were secular hedonists.

Maggie was horrified by Amy's stories of house parties where everyone indulged in drugs, booze, and unmarried sex. In pre-Greatest Awakening days, a celebrity scandal meant embarrassing headlines and a short stint in rehab. Now when celebrities were caught raising hell, they were labeled as CINOs, Christians in Name Only, riding the Jesus Gravy Train. Not only were their careers destroyed, they were sent to prison or a Savior Camp. Amy brushed off Maggie's concerns and assured her that nothing bad was going to happen to her.

Amy made sure the ingredients for the Patriot Tarts were in the order she wanted. "It's true," she said. "I'm not your boss. But soon I will be."

Maggie stopped fussing with the flags and stared at Amy. "What's that supposed to mean?"

"NCTV offered me my own show. I told them I'd only do it if you were executive producer."

Maggie's scalp tingled. As Amy's executive producer, she'd make more money, have more creative control, and best of all she wouldn't have to deal with Judy Cross.

"When were you going to tell me?"

"I'm telling you now. So, what do you say? Are you with me? I'm the rising tide that floats all boats."

Maggie wondered if she wasn't trading one dysfunctional boss for another, but then Amy was still her friend, she hoped, and maybe being the star of her own show would keep her so busy that she wouldn't have time for sinning with celebrities. Maggie held out her arms.

"Give me a hug, you big boat."

CHAPTER 8

On their way to National Church 58's Wednesday evening service, Maggie made Seth stop in front of a boutique so that she could window shop. She had her arm hooked around Seth's, which always made him feel good. It had rained earlier in the day and the leftover humidity coated their skin with filmy dampness.

"Will you look at that swimsuit?" Maggie said. "It's absolutely scandalous."

Seth studied the four mannequins in the display window. They were all modeling knee-length swim dresses that ensured modesty, but then he got what Maggie meant. Three of the swim dresses were drab gray, while the fourth was a bright, cheerful yellow.

"If you wore something that vibrant, I don't think I'd be able to control myself," he said. "In fact, I know I wouldn't, so don't tempt me."

As they walked past the store, Maggie giggled like a shameless schoolgirl while Seth lamented the death of thongs.

"There's something I've been meaning to tell you," Seth said.

"Don't mention thongs," Maggie said. "I didn't wear them when they were allowed."

"I still have my tallis bag. I still have my prayer shawl and my yarmulke. I didn't throw them away."

Maggie's forehead creased. She pulled Seth closer to her. "Are they well hidden?"

"Yes," Seth said.

"As well hidden as the condoms and the other contraband we have in the house?"

"Yes."

Seth knew that he should also confess that he'd been lying about going to the shooting range after work. He wanted to tell her that he was secretly practicing Judaism. Again. But admitting to his wife that he was committing treason against his country wasn't easy, so he made no more confessions.

National Church 58 had been a bar and seafood restaurant before the Greatest Awakening. A fishy, stale-beer stench lingered in the worship hall even after it had been thoroughly scrubbed and consecrated. Strings of lights and plastic lobsters still contoured the walls, and a ship's wheel hung on the wall behind the stage which had formerly been a bar. The dining room now accommodated rows of pews. With so many churches in America, no one imagined there would be need for more, but once attending services became mandatory, the existing churches filled up quickly. Empty bars became the perfect surrogates.

Seth and Maggie welcomed the blast of cool air that hit them as they entered the building. Most of the members of their church were young professionals like them. A certain amount of schmoozing was required. New babies had to be admired. Gossip had to be passed along. Sports predictions had to be argued. Once this was accomplished, Seth and Maggie were able to settle into a pew for the service.

Reverend Mike, the F.C., was a former Air Force colonel. The majority of the National Church's federal clergymen were Air Force veterans, their sermons attacking sinners like jet fighters on a strafing run. He stood on the stage with a young, bald man wearing retro-style glasses, who, to Maggie, looked like every video graphic artist she'd ever worked with.

"Omar is an ex-Muslim," Reverend Mike said. "He's going to witness for Christ today. Omar, tell us how you converted to the God of the Bible."

The reverend stepped aside, and the young man faced the congregation.

"Actually, my name is Amir," he said. "I emigrated from Bosnia nine years ago. Six years and four months ago, I discovered the Gospel of the Kingdom."

Ten minutes later, Amir finished the tale of his journey from Islam to Christianity and returned gratefully to his seat. After the prayer service, Seth and Maggie congratulated him.

"I was terrible," Amir said. "Seth did much better."

Like all converts, Seth was required to witness. He'd given his speech the year before. "I had an unfair advantage," he said. "I write speeches as part of my job."

Reverend Mike joined them. He had the patina of a good-natured jock. He wrapped his arms around Seth and Amir and gave them a bear hug.

"It's good to see men rescued from the darkness to the light of Jesus," Reverend Mike said. "But I must say, Seth could take some lessons from Omar, here. His wife's pregnant. They had to go to a fertility clinic, but there's no shame in that. Omar, what's the name of that clinic? Something like Miracle Baby. Give Seth the name of that clinic."

Amir's cheeks flamed with embarrassment. "New Miracle Fertility Clinic," he stammered. "I can email you the information."

"That's okay, we already have it," Maggie said. "Reverend Mike, could you stamp Seth's attendance book?"

The reverend led them to the alcove where he kept his official National Church stamp. It had once been the server's station. Amir tagged along and took out his own book.

"I'm going to go ahead and stamp your books for this coming Sunday as well," Reverend Mike said. "I know most everybody has plans to celebrate CHRIST Act Day with family members, and that's the same as attending a church service."

Seth and Maggie didn't tell Reverend Mike that they had no intention of spending time with family on Sunday. Instead, they thanked him and said goodbye. They almost made it past the porthole front door when they ran into their next-door neighbors, the Bruner family. Seth liked the wife, Kelly, and their five-year-old son, Josiah, but Larry Bruner gave him the creeps.

"You guys headed home?" Kelly said. "We can walk together."

Maggie put on her sad face.

"I'm sorry," she said. "We have dinner plans."

"'I fast twice a week,'" Larry said. "I give tithes of everything I earn. Luke 18:12.'"

Kelly ignored her husband. "If you don't already have plans for Sunday's celebration, give us a call," she said. "You know where we live."

Josiah tugged on Seth's pants leg. He knelt next to the boy.

"I did a drawing of me and mommy and daddy and Jesus. We're

on a picnic," Josiah said. "Want to see it?"

He unrolled a sheet of construction paper. As he pointed out who each stick figure represented, Seth noticed that Kelly beamed, but Larry glared.

"He's so good with kids," Kelly said to Maggie. "You two will make great parents. Any plans for your own bundle of joy?"

Before Maggie could come up with her latest excuse, Larry scooped Josiah away from Seth.

"Woe to those who call evil good and good evil and who put darkness for light and light for darkness!" Larry said.

"What's that supposed to mean?" Seth said.

"It means it's time for us to go home." Kelly pushed Larry toward the door. "Josiah needs to take a nap."

The Bruner family hurried out, clanging the bell on their way.

"That was really weird, even for Larry," Seth said.

"Let's talk about it over dinner," Maggie said.

"That's right, we apparently have dinner plans."

"We do now."

CHAPTER 9

FIVE YEARS EARLIER

Exit polls suggested Owens would win by a comfortable margin. Seth didn't care if the senator won or not. Campaign experience looked good on a resume. He waited in the Peabody Memphis Hotel's Grand Ballroom for the final count, along with campaign staff, members of the media, Owens's former congregation, volunteers, well-wishers, and party crashers. The Rendezvous restaurant catered the event and provided an open bar. Prohibition laws wouldn't be passed until the following year, so booze was still legal.

A gospel group performed "Blessed and Highly Favored" on the main stage, as the audience clapped and swayed to the joyous proclamations. Seth huddled in a corner, nursing a bourbon and Coke. He would have preferred some lonesome Memphis Blues. He had enjoyed the months on the road, the long nights of strategy sessions, even the lousy food. The hectic pace had been exciting and kept him from missing Maggie. But now that the election was almost over, he couldn't stop thinking about her.

He would have called her, but she was busy with election-night coverage at CSPAN. Maggie hated working there and had recently applied for a position as a segment producer for a talk show at PBS, which had just been re-christened NCTV.

The local news stations announced the results from three more districts, widening Owens's lead by a few more percentage points. The ballroom crowd cheered. Seth left his corner, eyeing pork ribs on the buffet table that looked like dinosaur bones stacked in a shallow tar pit of vinegary sauce, but he had no appetite. What he needed was fresh air. As he jostled his way through the crowd, he saw Owens's campaign manager, Reggie Cooke, bearing down on him. Reggie said something, but Seth couldn't understand a word he said. He leaned forward and Reggie shouted in his ear,

"I've been trying to reach you," Reggie said. "Did you turn off your phone?"

Seth pulled his cellphone out of his sport coat pocket. Sure enough, there were three messages from Reggie. Seth pointed to his ear. "It's too loud in here. I didn't hear it ring."

"Senator Owens wants to see you."

Reggie led Seth to the elevator and used a passkey to access the Presidential Suite. In keeping with political tradition, Owens would wait in the suite with his family and key members of his staff until enough results were in to declare a winner. Only then could he enter the ballroom and officially claim victory.

Seth and Reggie didn't speak in the elevator. In all the months Seth worked on the senator's campaign, Reggie never spoke to him or any other member of the campaign staff unless it was about the campaign. His silence only fueled staff members' desire to dig up whatever they could about him. They learned that Reggie's entire career was tied to Samuel Owens from when Owens was Pastor of the Holy Trinity AME Church in Memphis to when Owens entered politics. Since Senator Owens's Chief of Staff announced that he was retiring whether the senator won or not, it was clear to everyone that Reggie would be Owens's next COS.

As for his personal life, Reggie was a member of a half dozen men's social groups, which might have explained why no one had ever seen him on a date. With all that group activity on top of his busy work schedule, where would he have found the time?

Reggie was buff, kept his hair in a short buzz cut, and wore Burberry suits. While he wasn't the toughest or the most condescending boss Seth had ever had, he was in the top five.

The elevator doors opened, and Seth followed Reggie to the Presidential Suite.

"Wait here," Reggie said, using his passkey to get inside.

Seth shoved his hands in his pockets and leaned against the wall. He speculated on why he had been summoned. Maybe Senator Owens wanted to thank each member of his staff individually for helping him get re-elected. He seemed like the type to do that. If that were the case, Seth would use the opportunity to ask Owens to write him a letter of recommendation at the senator's earliest convenience.

The door to the Presidential Suite opened, and a fellow staff member walked out.

"Hey, Rudy," Seth said to the rotund man. "How's the mood inside? Has the senator started his victory dance yet?"

"I didn't notice," Rudy groused. "I asked Owens for an office position and he said I wasn't the kind of Christian soldier he needs in his army."

"He actually used the words *Christian soldier* and *army*?"

"I shit you not. That's what happens when ex-clergymen get elected to the Senate. They care more about how much you love Jesus than actual political experience."

"If that's how Owens rolls, then I'm glad that I'm not looking for a job with him."

Rudy slapped Seth's shoulder. "It's been a blast," he said. "You got my number, stay in touch."

They shook hands. As he was leaving, Rudy let Seth know that he planned to drink as much of the free booze downstairs as his large frame could hold. Seth resumed slouching against the wall until Reggie appeared and led him into the suite.

The foyer was spacious enough to hold a church service. Senator Owens's wife and grown children were on a couch, their attention glued to the election coverage on the suite's massive flat screen TV, while Owens's grandchildren chased each other around the room. Near the couch, a group of distinguished-looking men and women knelt in prayer on the carpet.

A grandson crashed into one of the prayer warriors, a middle-aged woman wearing a flamboyant hat known in black churches as a crown. She picked the boy up and held him still.

"God wants grandpa to win," the boy chirped.

"Bless you, child," the woman said as she released the boy, who ran off.

Reggie knocked on the bedroom door and opened it without waiting for a reply. He ushered Seth inside. The bedroom TV was also tuned to the election results, but the sound was muted. Senator Owens sat at a desk covered with documents, a pair of reading glasses perched on his nose. When he saw that he had company, he stood to give Seth a strong-gripped handshake.

"Mr. Ginsberg! I cannot tell you how happy I am to have you share this joyous occasion with us. I would not be on the verge of victory if not for the efforts of my dedicated staff, of which you were a vital member. A very vital member. Please, sit down. Sit down."

The senator seated himself at the desk, while Reggie claimed the easy chair next to the window. Seth perched awkwardly on the edge of the bed; it was the only place left for him to sit.

"You know, people told me not to hire anyone who ever worked for Chip Randall," Owens said. "But I didn't listen. Tell Mr. Ginsberg why, Reggie."

"Senator Owens believes everyone deserves forgiveness and should be judged on their merits," Reggie said.

Seth could feel sweat pouring down his sides. He hadn't listed his time in Randall's office on his resume, but he should have known that he couldn't keep it a secret. Chip Randall's name used to open doors for ambitious young men like Seth, but then the former congressman began speaking out against the Greatest Awakening. Randall claimed that President Reed's war of choice against Muslim countries stretched the armed forces too thinly and wasn't a holy crusade but an imperial invasion. He complained about the creation of the National Church. He accused Congress of tipping the country from a democracy to a theocracy.

"Because you worked for Chip, I had Reggie show me your background check," Owens said.

"Oh, really?" Seth said. "Find anything interesting?"

"You're a former Jew."

Irritation replaced Seth's fear. It was like being reminded of having a mullet before realizing how lame they were. He had left that part of his life behind. "That's true," he said, "but I have accepted Jesus as my Lord and Savior."

Senator Owens leaned forward in his chair until his knees touched Seth's. Seth wanted to pull back but was afraid to look weak.

"Jesus has a special place in His heart for those who were lost but then found," Owens said. "It's especially wonderful when the descendants of those who rejected the Lord come to accept Him. What about your parents? Have they seen the light?"

"They moved to Israel after the Christian Citizen Law was passed."

"Did they make hallelujah?"

"It's called Aliyah, Israel's law of return," Seth said.

He relaxed. He was a curiosity to Senator Owens, nothing more. Exhausted, what he wanted most in the world at that moment was to sleep in his own bed next to his wife.

"What do you think about what became of Chip Randall?" Reggie asked.

Reggie had been so quiet that Seth had almost forgotten he was in the room. Seth hesitated. The government grew tired of Randall's bellyaching, but since he carried too much influence to ignore, they painted him as deranged and under the influence of Satan. To save Randall's eternal soul, they sent him to one of the newly built Savior Camps. President Reed went on TV and explained that Randall was there to help him find his way back to Jesus.

Maybe it was fatigue, or maybe it was indignance, but Seth decided to give a brutally honest answer even if it cost him a letter of recommendation from the senator. "Randall's right," he said. "We're becoming a theocracy. But hopefully we can find a way to balance theocracy and democracy."

"Hopefully?" Reggie said. "America is the greatest country God ever made. You don't think America can manage to mix freedom and Christianity in perfect harmony?"

Seth looked at the two men. Senator Owens had an easy smile on his face. Reggie had his arms crossed and showed no emotion.

"It can," Seth said. "If elected officials like Senator Owens make sure it does."

Senator Owens and Reggie looked at each other. Reggie smiled. "I told you he was our man," he said.

"What just happened?" Seth asked.

"I need honest men such as yourself on my staff," Owens said. "Will you join us?"

Seth hesitated. It was a huge step in his young career. He should consult Maggie first, but he was afraid the offer would expire once he left the room. He would be crazy to stick his nose up at the Senate.

"Yes, sir, I'd like that very much," he said.

Senator Owens stood. Seth and Reggie followed his cue and stood as well. The senator and Seth shook hands. Reggie was about to escort Seth out of the room when the phone rang. Owens answered. After a short conversation, he hung up and lowered his head in prayer. Seth looked at Reggie for a clue as to what was going on, but his face gave away nothing.

"It's time to go," Owens said.

He entered the foyer. The room fell silent as everyone turned their attention to Senator Owens. Even the grandchildren stopped playing.

"That was my opponent on the phone," Owens said. "He called to congratulate me. I've won the election."

Everyone cheered. There were lots of hugs and people hopping up and down, followed by a mass exodus for the elevator so that the senator could deliver his official victory speech in the ballroom. Seth stayed behind, forgotten in all the excitement.

Alone in the Presidential Suite, he phoned Maggie but got her voicemail. He left a message saying he had important news to share with her and to call him first chance she could. Nobody had thought to turn off the flat screen TV. A local news anchor announced that Senator Owens was ready to speak. Seth watched the senator deliver his acceptance speech. The content of the speech was boilerplate, but the senator's experience as a preacher delivering fire and brimstone from the pulpit gave it more power than it deserved. When he was done red, white, and blue balloons floated down from the ceiling.

Seth suddenly felt like an intruder in the suite. He was just a hired hand, not part of the inner circle. Maybe later that would change. He took the elevator down to the ballroom, where supporters celebrated by dancing, cheering, and stomping on balloons. The gospel singers had been replaced by an R&B group singing "Celebration." Local and national reporters lined up to interview Senator Owens. They all asked the same questions, and he gave the same answers. When the senator had done his part to feed the belly of the media beast, he proceeded to make the rounds, shaking hands with the men and hugging the women.

Seth was in the mood to get shit-faced drunk, but the open bar was swamped with thirsty revelers. The bar in the lobby was packed as well, but there was a bar in a side hallway that was nearly empty. Seth sat on a stool and charged bourbon and Cokes to his hotel room.

Three hours later, the bar closed, and Seth carefully got off his stool and wobbled over to the Grand Ballroom. The reporters and Senator Owens were long gone. The R&B band had been replaced by Christian rock on the ballroom's stereo system. A few diehards were still dancing and toasting the senator's victory. The wait staff looked at their watches, while the cleaning staff began stacking chairs and sweeping up dead balloons. It was two a.m.

Seth got on the elevator alone and, on impulse, punched the button for the roof. He would be leaving in the morning, a few hours away, and he wanted to see the Memphis skyline before he left. He had no special love for Memphis. It just felt like the thing to do, a nice memory to take home with him.

The roof was colder than expected and Seth pulled his sport coat tight around him. The only light came from the Peabody Hotel's neon sign and the twinkling lights of the city. As he walked toward the edge of the roof to get a better view of the skyline, he heard something. A voice? Or ducks, maybe? The Peabody ducks were a tradition at the hotel. They marched through the lobby twice a day to the lobby's ornate fountain. In between their performances, they lived in cages on the roof.

No, this was definitely a human voice. A man was moaning. Seth searched for the source of the voice and realized that he had walked right past two men. Seth didn't recognize the man leaning against the wall, but the man on his knees was Reggie Cooke. Reggie was sucking the man's penis, and apparently very well.

The men were too absorbed in the moment to notice Seth, and he wanted to keep it that way. He was retracing his steps as quietly as he could when his phone rang. On the quiet roof, the ring sounded like an emergency alarm. Seth frantically mashed buttons until he managed to turn the damned thing off. He looked back to the wall. Reggie was glaring at Seth. The other man was gone. Seth couldn't tell if Reggie was angry or scared. Or both. He wanted to tell Reggie not to be afraid, his secret was safe, but he couldn't find the words.

Finally, Reggie left. Seth waited huddled against the bracing wind until he felt sure he was gone. Thirty minutes later in his hotel room, Seth returned Maggie's call. They had a lot to talk about.

ONE YEAR AFTER THE RE-ELECTION

The package arrived on a Saturday, along with two bills and a mailer pleading for donations to help build a creationist museum in Rockville. Maggie and Amy were at the D.C. Farmers Market trying to coax culinary secrets from the jumble of ethnic groups who sold trinkets next to strange vegetables. Seth would have gone with them, but Senator Owens was presenting his Owens-Zurrett Mandatory School Prayer Bill on Monday, and he had to polish up the senator's speech.

The mailman's delivery was a welcome break. A line of Flag of Israel stamps covered the top edge of the package. Seth's name and address were written in English, but the return address was in Hebrew. The package didn't surprise Seth. Lately, everybody was getting mail from Israel with offers to visit the Holy Land to walk the path of historic Jesus. Seth used a kitchen knife to cut through the layers of packing tape. Inside were his father's tallis bag, and a letter from his mother.

Dear Seth,

Please don't throw this letter away without reading it first. I know you probably never wanted to hear from me again, but I'm your mother and the fifth commandment says you have to listen to me.

Your father died three months ago. I would have told you sooner, but I was too filled with grief to deal with anything for weeks. One of his dying wishes was that you have his tallis. Robert didn't want me to give it to you. He changed his name to Barak, so remember to call him that if you ever see him again.

Barak said he couldn't understand why your father would want an ex-Jew to have his prayer shawl. His behavior reminds me of the Bible story where Esau is cheated out of his birthright by Jacob, but maybe I'm only projecting because he's your older brother

When you left the faith, your father was very upset. I think in time Eli would have forgiven you and maybe even welcomed Maggie into our family, but then the U.S. passed that stupid Christian Citizenship Law and again we Jews were forced to leave our homes. Thank God Israel was here for us.

Eli and I had to adapt to a whole new way of life, which wasn't easy for people our age. Barak and Rachel and the girls took to it right away. Once we settled in, life was good. We had a nice apartment, we had friends in the same building that we knew from America, and we saw our grandchildren at least once a week. When Eli was diagnosed with prostate cancer, we didn't worry. The doctors would take care of it.

I wanted to tell you earlier, but Barak said it wasn't safe. He said that you had joined the enemy who drove us out of America, but I felt it was important for you to know that your father died peacefully with his family by his side.

I know you're not the enemy. You're my son.

Love,

Mom

P.S. Do you like how I wrote my address in Hebrew? Actually, Barak's oldest daughter, your niece Dvora, did it for me. You probably remember her as Debbie.

Seth crumpled the letter and tossed it across the room. He changed his mind, retrieved the letter, smoothed it out, folded it twice, and put it into his file of utility receipts. He paced from room to room, anxiously returning to the box on the kitchen counter to look inside at the tallis bag. Each time he looked, his stomach knotted.

He thought back to the night he told his parents that he'd found Jesus. He was certain they would have reacted better if he'd told them that he was gay. He expected them to be angry, but their blistering attack still shocked him.

"What are you trying to do, kill your mother?" his father shouted. "I won't have this. I disown you! My son is dead. Thank God I still have another son."

Seth left their house full of rage. His parents' love came with conditions. That wasn't real love. Neither was waiting three months to tell him that his father was dead. For that matter, Seth was never informed that his father had cancer to begin with. He felt the hand of his self-righteous brother behind that little omission. Barak, not Robert. An asshole by any other name was still an asshole.

He made the circuit back to the box in the kitchen, snatched it off the counter, and carried it to the fireplace in the living room. Most of the woodpile had been burned during the winter and was down to a few puny logs. Seth crammed the remaining logs into the firebox, and then hurried back to the kitchen for the church bulletins that had accumulated in the junk drawer. He lit some of the bulletins on fire, smoke curling lazily up the flue, and he wadded up other bulletins and stuffed them between the logs. He fed the fire until he had a steady blaze.

Seth took the tallis bag out of the box, feeling the soft, faded royal-blue velvet gently bristle at his touch. He traced his fingers over the silver embroidery of the Hebrew word "tallit." Even from the grave, his father was punishing him.

The folded prayer shawl was slightly larger than a human heart. Seth shook out the shawl and held it up. The fire reflected a dull orange on the white fabric, bisected by lines of blue stitching.

The tzitzit, knotted fringes of white strands on the four corners of the tallis, were blackened from decades of being twirled around fingers during services. The shawl's fabric had worn soft and thin from sitting on his father's shoulders. Manischewitz concord wine stains dotted the sides, historic markers of blessings-over-the-wine past. Seth could almost taste the too-sweet wine that would make you sick before it made you drunk.

Sweat dripped off the tip of Seth's nose. He was sitting too close to the fire. Absentmindedly, he used the tallis to wipe the sweat off his face, and he picked up the scent of his father's aftershave buried in the fabric.

How his father had loved going to synagogue. He never missed a Saturday morning service. Or a bar mitzvah. If the Ginsbergs got an invitation, they went. Eli Ginsberg would have crossed the country for a bar mitzvah reception, to gossip in the long line to the buffet table until it was his turn to fill his plate with fleshy chunks of pickled herring, scoops of egg salad that had been molded into the shape of a chicken, and bagels adorned with cream cheese and lox. Good bagels with poppy seed, sesame, and salt, not the *goyishe* bagels with cinnamon raisin or Asiago cheese. And then there was the dessert table overloaded with petit fours, brownies, almond cookies, and tart lemon squares.

Seth could almost smell the Sterno cans that kept the pans of potato kugel and poached salmon warm. He missed the food. He missed the voices singing in Hebrew. He missed the red marks on his left arm after taking off the leather straps of the tefillin. He missed the bellow of the shofar on the High Holy Days. He hadn't realized that he missed these things until he held father's tallis in his hands, and now he understood his father hadn't left it to him as a punishment. It was a gift to help Seth remember who he was.

Jesus had never been a good fit for Seth. He wanted to believe, he really did. For a while, he even convinced himself that he was a true believer. But still, a small voice in the back of his mind always disagreed. A voice that sounded a lot like his father's.

Seth put the tallis around his shoulders and said the words every Jew knew by heart. "*Shema yisrael adonai eloheinu adonai ehad.* Hear O Israel. The Lord is Our God. The Lord is One." He took a deep breath. He had just done something illegal, and it felt great.

"That's right," he said. "The Lord is one. Not two. Not three. Just one. That's all I need."

"SETH, I'M HOME." MAGGIE STRUGGLED TO GET HER OVERLOADED BAGS through the front door. "How is the speech coming along?" She carried the bags into the kitchen and put them on the counter. One fell over. Eggplants and squash rolled out. "You've got to see what I picked up at the market today. We got a ton of great ideas from the vendors. You don't know it yet, but you're our number-one guinea pig."

When Seth didn't respond, Maggie searched the house, which was unexpectedly warm. Eventually, she discovered the remnants of a fire in the living room fireplace. She called Seth's cellphone and heard it ring at his desk. Not only had he left his phone behind, his computer was open, and the senator's unfinished speech was on the screen. She called his office number and got his voicemail. Briefly, she entertained the bizarre possibility that the rapture had come and taken her husband away.

Maggie spent the rest of the afternoon trying to remain calm, while jumping at every sound that might be Seth coming home. She considered going out to look for him, but other than work, home, or church, she didn't know where to look. She resisted the urge to call the police. Seth might be doing something sinful. She would rather be his judge than the authorities.

The sun went down and there was still no sign of Seth. Maggie made dinner and ate alone. She put the leftovers in the refrigerator for Seth. She tried to watch TV, but she couldn't concentrate. She gave up and went to bed and just stared at the ceiling.

It was almost midnight when she heard the front door open. She leapt out of bed and hurried downstairs. Seth was in the living room, facing the fireplace.

"Where were you?" Maggie cried. "I was about to start calling the hospitals."

"We need to talk," Seth said.

This was it, Maggie thought. He was in love with another woman. She was probably some cute intern who wanted nothing more than to worship Seth's curly hair and give him fat babies. Maggie sat on the couch and waited. Seth sat in the wingback chair facing her.

Maggie noticed for the first time that Seth was clutching a blue bag.

"I want to be Jewish again," Seth said.

Maggie laughed. "Sorry. I shouldn't laugh. I thought you were going to say you're leaving me!"

"Are you sure you don't want to leave me?"

Maggie reached for Seth. He placed the bag in his lap and took her hand.

"I'm your wife," she said. "I could tell something wasn't right. I thought maybe it was your job, and that you weren't happy with what you were doing. There were times when I worried that you weren't happy with me anymore."

"That's never going to happen."

Seth released Maggie's hand and they gazed at each other.

"You want to be Jewish again?" Maggie said. "What does that mean?"

Seth kneaded the blue bag. Maggie saw there were Hebrew letters stitched into the side.

"I had a long talk with Reggie this afternoon," Seth said.

"I thought he hated you?"

"He hates that I know he's gay. Actually, hate isn't the right word. He's terrified that I'll turn him in. Well, now he knows I'm a Jew. So, we're even."

Maggie's eyes grew wide. "Why would you tell him that?"

"I couldn't wait. I had to find out if there were other people like me, Jews who want to be with other Jews. I figured that gay men must want to spend time with other gay men even if it's illegal. Especially if it's illegal. Reggie and I talked for a long time. He's in a lot of men's only social clubs. He admitted that those clubs are actually secret gay men's groups. I asked Reggie to see if any of the members know of any secret Jewish groups."

"Are you insane? You can't join a secret Jew club. It's too dangerous."

"I have to find my people, Maggie. It's important."

"What about me? Am I not important?"

"You're the most important thing in my life."

"Then don't put our lives in danger."

"You haven't said what you think about me being Jewish."

Maggie worried her wedding ring. The heat from the fire was gone, and the room was cool. "I think if you want to be Jewish, then you should be Jewish. Just don't tell anyone other than Reggie." She pointed at the blue bag. "Does that have something to do with all this?"

Seth told her about the package in the mail and his father's death. He unzipped the bag, took out his father's tallis, and showed her how to wear it. "I also found this in the bag," he said, handing Maggie a black skullcap. On the inside was printed: Bar Mitzvah of Seth Adam Ginsberg. Congregation B'nai Israel. March 13. The year was rubbed off from constant handling.

"They made these for your bar mitzvah?" Maggie asked. "How adorable is that?"

"It's kind of a tradition."

Other than the yarmulke and the tallis, Maggie wore only a T-shirt and panties. Seth wondered if this wasn't some Jewish boy's sexual fantasy.

"Do I look like a Jew?" Maggie asked.

"Absolutely."

They hugged each other tightly.

"When we have children," Seth said, "I want them to be Jewish. Or at least, half-Jewish."

Maggie stepped back and gave Seth a hard look. She wanted to say, "Don't you mean if we have children?" but she kept quiet. Seth misunderstood her intention and amended his statement.

"Well, they should at least be exposed to Judaism."

CHAPTER 10

The man behind Reggie grunted loudly and clutched Reggie's hips with his sweaty hands. No matter how quickly the man ejaculated, it was never quick enough. Every time the bloated belly pressed against Reggie's ass, revulsion rippled through him.

The man on the verge of releasing his seed inside Reggie was Roy Arnold. Roy was spiritual advisor to many powerful men, including the president. He was arguably the most influential man in the country, and yet he held no official office. He owned no property. Reggie had no idea who provided Roy with the steady flow of money required to maintain his Beaux-Arts mansion in Kalorama or paid for his Lincoln Town Car and chauffeur.

Roy froze mid-thrust and moaned, and Reggie mimicked the sound. He had learned that if he didn't convincingly express sexual satisfaction, there would be repercussions. Roy would pout for the rest of the day, and then later something bad would happen. If Reggie was gathering support for one of Senator Owens's bills, the senators who had signed on would suddenly have a change of heart. Funding for a pet project that had long ago been approved would disappear, as if by magic.

Roy pulled out and waddled into the bathroom. He returned shortly wearing a silk kimono over his fish-belly pale body. He offered Reggie an identical robe, but yanked it out of reach when he tried to take it. The remaining strands of Roy's graying hair clung to his sweaty head as he admired Reggie's muscular, dark brown body. Finally, with a satisfied smile, Roy let him have the kimono.

"Let us pray together," he said. It was not an invitation.

"Yes, Mr. Arnold."

"Now how many times have I told you? When it's just the two of us, call me Roy."

"Yes, Roy."

Reggie slipped on the robe and followed Roy to his prayer room.

There was no Bible there because Roy felt no need for one. His faith was above the Bible, above religion. His faith was pure. Jesus and only Jesus.

Reggie waited silently as Roy put on the traditional Jewish tefillin and tallis. Roy had told Reggie how they had been specially made for him.

The tefillin consisted of two black leather boxes with Torah verses inside, attached to leather straps. One strap was wrapped around the left arm with the box next to the wearer's left side, close to the heart. The other box was placed on the forehead, with two straps keeping it in place. The scrolls inside the black boxes of Roy's tefillin had the Sermon on the Mount written on them. "For God so loved the world, that he gave his only begotten Son, that whosoever believeth in him should not perish, but have everlasting life. John 3:16" was embroidered on the neck of the tallis.

The prayer room had a bronze statue of the crucifixion the size of a mini-fridge. Pale blue pillows were spread around the statue. Roy knelt and beckoned Reggie to do the same. The men clasped their hands in prayer and bowed to the statue.

"Oh Lord Jesus, we give thanks for your continued guidance," Roy said. "After the Jews broke their covenant with God by refusing to accept you as their savior, the mantle of the chosen fell upon us, your true disciples."

Roy rambled on for twenty minutes, veering from condemning non-believers to marveling at how God had chosen him and him alone to carry Christ's word to the world. Reggie's knees began to ache. Sperm trickled from his anus down his thigh, leaving a warm, slimy trail.

"And bless you, Jesus, for bringing brother Reginald to me, so that I might personally provide him the strength and guidance to defeat his homosexual affliction. Amen."

"Amen."

As they were about to leave the prayer room, Roy hooked his hand around Reggie's arm. Reggie hung his head and hoped Roy wasn't in the mood for more sex.

"I'm expecting a guest today," Roy said.

A guest meant an important person was coming to visit. Reggie was never allowed to know the identities of guests, and Roy never let them know about Reggie.

Roy kissed him, and then went into his personal bathroom to clean up. Reggie wiped his lips and went downstairs to the guest suite. In the shower, he vigorously scrubbed his skin but couldn't wash away the feeling of Roy's hands. After he toweled off, Reggie dressed in the tailored suit that he'd brought with him.

As he descended the back staircase to the kitchen, Reggie heard voices coming from the living room. Roy's guest had arrived. From the kitchen, Reggie had direct access to the garage. Roy wouldn't allow him to park on the street where someone might recognize his car. He should have left right away but he was curious about the visitor. Powerful people came to see Roy, including President Reed. Reggie couldn't resist taking a peek.

He entered Roy's study through the back door. The shades were drawn, keeping the morning sun out. Before Roy moved into the mansion, the room had been a library with built-in bookshelves and a soot-stained fireplace. Despite the absence of books or logs, it still smelled of old books and burnt wood. The study's front door led directly to the living room.

Reggie quietly worked his way around Roy's massive desk, which was covered with stacks of top-secret government files. Roy insisted on receiving the confidential documents even though he rarely opened them because he was too busy bringing the light of Jesus to the world. Reggie understood that possessing the files was a tangible sign of Roy's power. He didn't need to know what was in them.

The door to the living room was ajar, and Reggie peeked through the crack. Warm sunlight filled the room. Roy and his visitor sat on facing couches. The guest was Federal Deacon Freeman Wingard. Reggie's heart pounded in his chest. Freeman was like a cobra, able to strike quickly and with deadly force. He didn't flaunt his power, but he didn't hesitate to use it. Freeman opened the briefcase on his lap and took out a folder fat with documents.

"Here's the file you requested," Freeman said.

"Put it on my desk," Roy said.

As Freeman approached the study, Reggie tried to decide if he could reach the back door before Freeman entered, and do so without knocking something over in the dark room, but he wasted too many precious seconds deliberating. He put his back against the wall and prayed that the deacon didn't push the door into him.

Freeman stepped inside the study and was fumbling for the light switch when Roy called out to him. "Tell me the plan in broad strokes."

Freeman dropped the file on the desk and rejoined Roy in the living room. Reggie stopped holding his breath and he sucked air into his lungs as quietly as he could.

"We're raiding the underground church next week," Freeman said. "We would have done it sooner, but we have our hands full with the CHRIST Act celebration."

"These people are of the Jewish faith?" Roy said.

Reggie inched closer to the door and peered through the crack.

"They are," Freeman said.

"Which makes this raid so unfortunate," Roy said. "Our Lord is a Jewish carpenter."

Reggie could see Freeman drumming his fingers on the armrest.

"They're still guilty of illegal religious activity," the deacon said. "Besides, these Jews will not be among the 144,000 redeemed after the Rapture."

"Of course not," Roy said. "I'm concerned about the optics."

Roy got up and moved out of Reggie's line of sight. He didn't need to see Roy to know that he was gazing out the window at a bucolic yard dotted with cherry trees. The man loved his lawn.

"Do you ever wonder what sort of people join these groups?" Roy said.

"No, I do not," Freeman said.

"Doesn't a member of this church work in Senator Owens's office?"

Reggie shuddered at the mention of Senator Owens.

"People of the Jewish faith don't call their house of worship a church," Freeman said. "They call it a temple or a synagogue."

"That's right. A synagogue." Roy drew the word out as if he were tasting it.

"Stop beating around the bush, Roy. The file was just an excuse to have me come over."

Reggie was shocked by the harshness in Freeman's voice. He'd never heard anyone talk to Roy that way. Roy left the window and sat on the couch next to Freeman. He put his hand on Freeman's shoulder. Freeman faced away from Reggie, so he couldn't see the deacon's expression.

"The president is worried about you," Roy said.

"Because of what I said on *The Pauly Pilgrim Show*?"

"Reed didn't want to make a statement on how Chip Randall died until after Sunday's celebration. Now he has to deal with an unpleasant distraction when the nation should be rejoicing this momentous occasion."

Freeman slammed his fist on the armrest. "Reed didn't want the truth to ever come out. I serve at the president's pleasure, but I owed it to Chip. If Reed wishes to replace me, then he can go ahead and do it."

"You've always been the Brethren's most loyal servant," Roy said. "President Reed doesn't understand what's come over you."

"He could have asked me."

As much as Reggie feared Roy, he admired his ability to calmly diffuse tense situations with praise and redirection.

"I know you and Chip were close," Roy said.

"I loved him like a brother."

"There was a time when I was fond of him, too. But Chip Randall took the coward's way out. His suicide means we must reduce him to a mere footnote in the history of the Greatest Awakening."

Freeman rose and moved out of Reggie's line of sight.

"I can't explain what I'm feeling," the deacon said. "I've been praying mightily for Jesus' guidance. But this much I know: I failed Chip Randall."

Everyone in Washington viewed Deacon Wingard as a pillar of strength with unshakable faith. Hearing him voice his doubts made Reggie almost feel compassion for him.

"You did everything you could for him," Roy said.

"His death is proof that I didn't."

"You're right. If you loved him as much as you say you did, you would have done more to lead him back to the Lord."

"I'm not sure Chip was the one who went astray."

Roy sprang to his feet. "How can you say that? Have you lost your mind?"

Reggie had never seen Roy lose his temper. Never.

"Maybe," Freeman said. "Jesus was tested in the wilderness. I believe the Lord is testing me now."

"Are you saying that America, the greatest country ever created by God, is the wilderness?" Roy said.

"The wilderness is inside me."

"As it is inside all of us. Only our faith can lead us out. Let's go to the White House. I want you and the president to put this matter behind you."

"Now?"

"The sooner the better."

Reggie saw Freeman return to the couch and retrieve his briefcase.

"I want your blessing to bring Julian Cross into the Brethren," Freeman said.

Roy lowered his head for a moment, then lifted it and smiled.

"I think it's an excellent idea," he said. "This is the Lord at work. That young man was born and raised in the wilderness. Bringing him into the light will serve you as well and put you back on the righteous path."

The two men left the house.

This was Reggie's chance to leave undetected, but he couldn't move. He stared at the file Freeman had left on Roy's desk. It contained information on Hedge Protection's plan to raid Seth's secret synagogue. Seth was one of his few true allies.

Reggie had to know what was in it.

Roy was probably never going to read the file, would never notice it was missing. It was also possible that he would. He would know right away who had taken it. He could have Reggie sent to jail. Taking the file would be a bad decision. Bad decisions were what had led to Reggie becoming Roy's sex toy.

But Reggie had to know.

He snatched the file from Roy's desk, hurried out of the study, through the kitchen, and into the two-car garage where Roy had Reggie park his car so that it would be out of sight.

Reggie hid the file under the spare tire in the trunk. Once he was behind the steering wheel, he waited for his racing heart to slow down. Sweat had soaked his shirt and had seeped into the armpits of his tailored suit. As Reggie backed out of the garage, he turned the air conditioner on high to dry off. With a little luck, nobody in the senator's office would smell the fear on him.

Chapter 11

The limousine pulled up to the entrance to Camp David. The driver rolled down the window and spoke briefly to the marine on guard. The marine opened the gate, and the car entered the country retreat for the President of the United States.

"That was impressive," Julian said.

Freeman used to feel blessed to have access to places like Camp David, but he'd been in his position long enough now that it was commonplace. He envied the thrill that Julian Cross must be feeling as he experienced it for the first time.

The road sliced through lush forest. Through the trees, Freeman caught glimpses of the cabins' rustic exterior. The limo arrived at a parking lot filled with official government vehicles. The driver got out and held the door open for Freeman but not for Julian. The deacon took a moment to appreciate the cool morning air and the citrus smell of the pine trees.

Freeman and Julian followed a walkway through the woods that took them past a Ten Commandments monument carved into a block of granite. At Laurel Lodge, a marine stood guard at the red wooden door. He recognized Freeman immediately and opened the door for them. Inside, a blonde woman wearing a long skirt and lots of make-up greeted them.

"Deacon Wingard," she said. "So glad to see you again. Who's your friend?"

"This is Julian Cross," Freeman said. He gestured at the young woman. "I'm sorry. I forgot your name."

"Abigail," she said. "It's an honor to meet you, Mr. Cross. The menfolk are thataway."

Abigail pointed at a hallway. As Freeman and Julian moved through the lodge, they passed a dining room where more women with blonde hair in long, demure skirts and heavy make-up were arranging plates and silverware on long tables. The guests, all men, were in a large room with floor-to-ceiling windows. Blinds kept the early-morning sun out of their eyes. Men lounged on couches and easy chairs or stood in clusters as the women brought them coffee.

"When did the Brethren start having their prayer breakfasts at Camp David?" Julian asked.

"A couple of years now," Freeman said. "We have them once a month. We considered skipping today since it's so close to Sunday's celebration, but Roy felt it was important to maintain a spiritual consistency."

"Roy? As in Roy Arnold?"

"Do you know of another Roy of high position in the Brethren?" Julian chuckled.

"No, sir," he said. "I sure don't."

Freeman stood out in the crowd. He was over six-feet tall, with broad shoulders, and a military buzz cut that kept his white hair close to his head. Though the men greeted him warmly, Freeman could tell from their forced smiles and awkward body language that he made them uncomfortable.

He was certain that they were unhappy with him for revealing how Chip Randall had died, but their wariness toward him wasn't new. It had started shortly after he was sworn in as deacon of Hedge Protection. His department kept foreign enemies and their wickedness from getting into the country. But Hedge Protection also kept the personal secrets of the Brethren from getting out.

Freeman could point to almost any man in the room and recite his sin. That senator was an alcoholic. That ambassador beat his wife. Protecting the Brethren's secrets hadn't bothered him before now. He had believed that the good they brought to the world outweighed their sins. Chip's suicide had produced a seed of doubt inside him that was beginning to sprout.

Abigail brought Freeman a cup of coffee black with no cream or sugar. Even if he couldn't remember her name, she remembered his preferences. He took a sip and gazed at the ceiling. The lodge had wooden crossbeams that were similar to those in the Camp Glorious Rebirth's barracks. As Freeman stared at them he thought of the Bible verse that Chip Randall had written in blood.

If we say we have no sin, we deceive ourselves, and the truth is not in us. John 1:8.

The coffee churned in Freeman's stomach. For over thirty years, he thought that he had always done the right thing. Chip's death had forced Freeman to face the fact that he had committed a sin against his friend.

It was an open secret among the Brethren that Chip Randall and Judy Cross were having an affair. When Judy became pregnant, Chip confided in Freeman that he intended to divorce his wife Eleanor and marry Judy, a decision Freeman argued relentlessly against.

"You made a sacred vow to love, honor, and cherish Eleanor until death do you part," Freeman said.

"But I don't love her," Chip said. "I love Judy."

"Don't throw away all the good things you've worked on for this Jezebel."

During this time, Judy had been an attention-hungry firebrand. Certainly, she still was, but back then her desire for the spotlight was all-consuming. Freeman was certain that she was incapable of loving anyone but herself and saw Chip as a way into the Brethren, since her gender excluded her otherwise.

Chip ignored Freeman, until Freeman threatened him with expulsion from the Brethren.

"I will not stand idly by as you descend into a life of sin," Freeman said. "Nor can I in good conscience call you brother. You leave me no choice but to demand that the Brethren cast you out."

Chip ended his relationship with Judy and went on to do great things in the name of Jesus, most notably passing the CHRIST Act. Judy gave birth to Julian and continued to build her personal brand.

Looking back, Freeman realized that he had been wrong to intervene. After their breakup, Chip started drinking heavily and Judy's rhetoric toward non-believers became extremely bitter and cruel. Whenever Freeman and his wife Mary had dinner with Chip and Eleanor, Freeman could see that they were unhappy, trapped in a loveless and childless marriage.

Maybe Chip and Judy really did love each other. It wasn't Freeman's place to judge them, and his cheeks burned with shame. Not only had he denied his best friend his chance to be with the woman he loved, he had denied Chip the chance to be a father and raise his son.

Julian nudged Freeman.

"When do we eat?" Julian said. "I can smell bacon and it's making me hungry."

Freeman glanced at Julian and then back at the crossbeam. It was clean of imaginary bloody words.

"We won't start until Roy gets here," Freeman said. "He hates to be the center of attention, so he always makes sure he's the last one to arrive."

"Mom used to do the same thing when we went to church. She arrived late so that no one would miss her grand entrance."

Freeman was about to defend Roy when he heard a thumping sound overhead. Everyone stared at the ceiling for a moment before moving outside to watch the approaching helicopter. Freeman and Julian walked out together. A Night Hawk helicopter with a green body, white top, and New Glory flag decal descended toward the Camp David helipad.

"Is that Marine One?" Julian said. "I didn't know President Reed was attending."

"It's not Reed," Freeman said. "It's Roy."

The helicopter disappeared behind the trees. Everyone filed back into the lodge and went directly to the dining room. Freeman instructed Julian to sit next to him. Thirty minutes later, everyone rose as Roy entered the room.

"The donkey Jesus rode into Jerusalem had to have been more comfortable than the creaky old golf cart I just rode over here from the helipad," Roy said.

Everyone burst out laughing. Roy took his seat at the head of the table, and then everyone sat down with chairs scraping and napkins tucked into collars. The women entered and began pouring glasses of orange juice and carrying out platters of scrambled eggs, bacon, buttered toast, and pancakes. Once the food was in place, the room fell silent. Everyone joined hands and bowed their heads. Roy recited the prayer.

"Lord, we thank thee for good food, good friends, and for granting us your never-wavering vision for a better world. Our pledge to you our Lord Jesus is strong and true. Amen."

Everyone responded with an amen. Platters were passed around. Julian forked a stack of pancakes and five strips of bacon onto his plate. Freeman wasn't hungry but took some eggs and a slice of toast so that he wouldn't have an empty plate. The women stayed in the kitchen, coming out occasionally to replace empty platters and bring fresh carafes of coffee. The conversation was lively and good-natured but stopped abruptly whenever Roy spoke. Then the men leaned in his direction to catch every pearl of wisdom that fell from his lips.

After the meal, the women cleared the dishes, and guest speakers gave short speeches, most of which were about CHRIST Act Day and the significance of celebrating the law's tenth anniversary.

Roy was the last speaker.

"I didn't prepare a speech," he said. "I don't need to. I could speak from my heart for hours about how much I love America, the greatest, most righteous country in the world, in all of history. But I won't. I won't because we can't sit back on our laurels. We Americans owe our blessings to God, and He commands us to spread the word of Jesus. Some may view world domination as a wicked endeavor, but not when it's done in the service of God Almighty. Good day, gentlemen. I'll see you all in church on Sunday."

There was a moment of confusion as it sank in that Roy had no more to say. He left the table and stood by the red wooden door, creating a logjam. Everyone wanted a brief word with him before returning to their lives. Freeman and Julian waited in line for their turn.

"Roy," Freeman said. "This is Julian Cross. Judy's son."

Roy peered at Julian.

"Oh my," Roy said. "I haven't seen you since you were knee-high to a grasshopper. The Famous Rape Baby has grown up into a fine young man."

Freeman frowned. He'd hoped to make it through the prayer breakfast without anyone recalling that Julian had once been known as The Famous Rape Baby. But of course, Roy would remember since he was the one who created the myth.

The Brethren didn't want the general public to find out whose baby Judy was carrying. They also hadn't wanted Judy to abort the baby, since that would only have compounded the sin. Roy solved the potentially embarrassing situation by concocting a story that Judy had been raped by a stranger as she was walking to her car at night after a speaking engagement. It had been too dark for her to see her attacker. And though Judy had been viciously violated, she decided to keep the child and raise it to be a good Christian.

Freeman had to help Roy convince Judy to agree to the rape story. But once she was on board, Judy used Roy's fiction to propel herself to greater popularity. She wrote a book titled *My Precious Rape Baby: A Story of Survival and Faith* which was made into a TV movie, and did publicity appearances with baby Julian. The press nicknamed him The Famous Rape Baby as a snide comment on the way Judy used her child as a prop. But then, Julian grew up, was sent to boarding school, and the world forgot about him.

"That's me," Julian said. "The Famous Rape Baby. Nice of you to remember."

IN THE LIMO THE WAY BACK TO THE CITY, FREEMAN WORKED ON HIS LAPTOP while Julian stared out the window.

"Normally, I can read people pretty well," Julian said. "But you guys are a mystery to me. I can't tell how I did."

"You didn't do anything wrong today," Freeman said, without looking away from his computer.

"Does that mean I'm in?"

Freeman turned toward him, wondering why he'd never noticed before that Julian had his father's eyes and receding hairline.

"Do you even know what it means to be a member of the Brethren?" Freeman said. "Be honest. I can read people as well, so I'll know if you're lying."

Julian smirked. The expression made him look more like his mother.

"Power," Julian said. "The Brethren run America. If they don't already run the world, they will soon enough. I want to be part of that."

"It's not about power," Freeman said. "It's about obedience to God and to the Brethren's mission to spread His word to the world."

Julian shrugged.

"I can do that."

Freeman turned his laptop around so that Julian could see the screen.

"This video was taken by an undercover missioner," Freeman said.

The grainy hidden-camera footage began inside a warehouse. A line of people waited to enter a moving truck. Julian stood next to the loading ramp. People paid him before entering the truck. He added their money to an ever-growing roll of bills. Once the truck was filled with human cargo, Julian faced the camera.

"Close the door," Julian said. "It's time to go."

The scene changed to the undercover missioner driving the truck through the desert at night. The vehicle's headlights barely illuminated the bumpy road.

"We use this route every night," the missioner said. "Shouldn't we change it up to throw off the Hedge Clippers?"

The hidden camera swung over to Julian in the passenger seat.

"I pay the Hedge Clippers good money for this route," Julian said. "They're not going to bother us."

The video was interrupted by static. When it returned, the truck was parked in another warehouse. The door was open, and Julian stood next to the loading ramp.

"Welcome to Mexico," Julian said. "Now get the hell out of here."

Once the smuggled people had left the warehouse, Julian motioned for his men to load a stack of boxes. The missioner carried two of them into a back room. The camera swung back and forth as he checked to make sure no one was watching him. He opened the boxes. Inside one were plastic bags of white powder. In the other were pornographic DVDs. He quickly closed the boxes and carried them to the truck. The video ended.

Freeman slammed his laptop shut. Julian wiped sweat off his brow with the back of his hand.

"Are you sure you can obey God and the Brethren?" Freeman said.

Julian crossed his arms.

"I suppose if it weren't for Mother, you would have taken me to jail instead of a prayer breakfast," he said.

"This has nothing to do with Judy. I reached out to you because of the love and respect I have for your father," Freeman said. "I believe that there is enough of his goodness buried inside you that you can be redeemed."

"But nobody knows the identity of my father. It was too dark for Mother to see his face when he raped her."

Freeman drummed his fingers on the cover of his laptop. This man was as frustrating as his mother.

"Do you really believe that?" he said.

"My father used to call Mother and beg her to let him see me," Julian said. "But she always refused. Which was fine by me. I had absolutely no desire to meet him then, and I don't want to see him now."

"That's impossible. Any decent person would want to know the identity of his father."

Julian sneered and Freemen resisted the urge to slap him.

"Mother was very attractive back in the day. I can see why men wanted to screw her," Julian said. "But I can't understand why anyone would have wanted to sleep with that cold bitch more than once. I heard enough of her conversations with my father to see that they had a relationship. Any man stupid enough to fall in love with her is not worth knowing."

Freeman stared at Julian. No wonder he had been thrown out of every boarding school he'd attended. The lack of a strong male figure in his life had left him morally bankrupt. Without a father with a firm hand teaching him right from wrong, it had only been a matter of time before Julian fell in with a bad crowd.

Julian gazed out the window.

"I'm sorry your plan to redeem me fell through," he said. "Believe it or not, I appreciate the effort."

"I haven't given up yet," Freeman said. "I want you to work for me."

"As a missioner? We both know I wouldn't pass the background check."

"I need to save you as much as you need to be saved. Let me lead you to Christ."

Julian narrowed his eyes at Freeman, who could tell that the young man was weighing his options, trying to find the best angles to get what he wanted. But Freeman had spent decades dealing with members of Congress, the best con men in the world. There wasn't anything that Julian could pull on Freeman that he wouldn't see coming from a mile away.

"Okay," Julian said. "What do I have to do?"

Freeman opened his laptop and typed an email to Missioner Lim telling her that he had successfully recruited Julian Cross.

"Before you learn to obey Christ, you have to learn to obey me," Freeman said. "I want a complete list of all my Hedge Patrol missioners that are getting payoffs from you. From this moment on, you are a Hedge Protection informant. Use your present occupation to gather intel on illegal border activities."

"You want me to continue being a smuggler?" Julian said.

"Continue to smuggle people across the border. They hate Jesus, America, and everything we've done for them. I say good riddance to bad rubbish. But stop bringing drugs and illegal contraband into the country."

"Drugs are more than half my income."

"If you refuse, I'll have you sent to a Savior Camp."

Julian sighed.

"I didn't know that getting saved was going to be such hard work."

CHAPTER 12

Maggie dialed her mother's number. The line was busy and had been for over an hour. Honoring parents was a Big Ten law that was rarely enforced, because most of them refused to report their children. Then there were parents like Maggie's mom, who called the police if she didn't receive a minimum of one phone call a week. Seth once claimed that his mother would have never put him in the same position. Maggie had pointed out that Seth was lucky that his parents had moved to Israel because forcing children to call home was a Jewish mother's dream come true.

Another attempt failed. The line was still busy. Mom could be talking to a church friend. She was very active at the N.C. in her neighborhood. One of Maggie's three brothers or two sisters might have decided to call today, and it was entirely possible that all of them had. Her siblings were never good at working together, and thankfully there wasn't a law that said Maggie had to contact any of them.

She could call later. Maggie had until Saturday before the week was officially over, but she wanted to get it out of the way.

Growing up in a tiny overcrowded house in Midland, Michigan, Maggie had fought with her mom constantly, but she'd never hated her even when she was full of teenage rage. Mainly, Maggie was afraid that she would end up as miserable as her mother.

Mom had wanted to have adventures; instead she'd had babies. She and Dad were Catholics, and that meant no birth control and no abortion under any circumstances. Dad stayed at work and Mom stayed home, but they had still managed to have six children.

Maggie was their second child and first daughter. She'd felt trapped by her mother's overactive womb, helping with bottles and diapers by the time she was eight. Maggie had wanted adventures too, simple ones like going on dates and to parties. Instead, she had to stay home and be junior mother to her siblings.

Dad was a ghost to Maggie years before he died. He spent the little spare time he had with his sons. With him gone, Mom filled her days with church, stories about her grandchildren, and weekly phone calls.

Maggie was about to call her mother again when the phone rang. She glanced at the caller ID and was surprised to see Amy's number.

"Amy, I'm glad you called," Maggie said. "We need to talk about tomorrow's show."

Friday's special guest was Bobbi Sue Sunshine, and she had specifically requested to be in the "What's Cookin' in Amy's Kitchen" segment.

"Yeah, I love Bobbi Sue," Amy said, "but that's not why I called."

"Is this about NCTV's offer to give you your own show?"

"No. I mean, it's still going to happen, but the reason I called was to apologize for the way I've treated you these past months. I've been a bad Christian, and a bad friend."

Maggie considered asking Amy to repeat herself.

"You haven't been a bad friend," Maggie said.

"Yes, I have," Amy said. "I promise you those days are over. I'm letting God back into my life. Do you forgive me?"

Maggie couldn't believe what she was hearing. Amy had found Jesus. If that got her to clean up her life and be more serious about her job, then hallelujah.

"Of course, I forgive you," Maggie said. "It hurt to not be close like we used to be. I feel like you're more than a friend."

"More like a sister?" Amy said. "Yeah, I feel that way too."

"Amy, I'm so glad you called."

"I love you, Maggie. I'll see you tomorrow."

Amy hung up and Maggie realized they hadn't discussed tomorrow's show. No problem. She would talk to her in the morning. Amy's phone call had been like a miracle.

Maggie tried dialing Mom's number again and didn't get a busy signal this time. Her mother picked up on the third ring. Maggie was flabbergasted. Two miracles in one day.

SETH CAME HOME TO FIND MAGGIE STRETCHED OUT ON THE LIVINGROOM sofa with her eyes closed and a wet cloth on her forehead.

"So, how's your mother?" Seth asked.

"She talked for two solid hours," Maggie said.

Seth went into the kitchen to make himself a snack. The back door flew open and Josiah ran inside.

"I saw you were home!" the boy shouted. "Come watch me ride."

Seth broke off a banana from the bunch on the counter.

"Lead the way, little man," he said.

Seth followed Josiah to the fenced-in back yard. Kelly was waiting for them.

"Sorry about that, Seth," she said. "I know you just got in from work. You probably want to chill out."

"And miss Josiah break the sound barrier?" Seth said. "No way."

Seth stood next to Kelly. He peeled his banana and took a bite. Josiah got on his tricycle, and his little legs pumped as he traveled in circles.

"The Lord told Noah to build Him an arky, arky!" Josiah sang as he pedaled.

"Go, Josiah, go!" Seth said.

"You're going to be such a great dad," Kelly said. She lowered her voice and added, "I wish I could say the same about Larry."

Seth ate his banana to avoid talking. Before he'd gone to Savior Camp, Larry Bruner had been the kind of father Seth wanted to be. He had doted on Josiah and boasted about how, once his son was old enough, Larry was going to train him to master every sport in America.

The fence door creaked. Seth and Kelly turned to see Larry holding the door halfway open as if he couldn't decide whether to enter or make a quick getaway.

"Hey, Larry," Seth said.

Kelly crossed her arms.

"What do you want, Larry?" Kelly said.

Larry stepped back and let the door slam shut.

"How's he been lately," Seth asked. "Any luck finding work?"

"Nobody hires former campers. I was lucky to get a work voucher," Kelly said. "Otherwise, we'd be broke."

Seth tossed his banana peel into the trash can next to his back door. Josiah waved madly as he completed another circuit in the yard.

"Hang onto your job," Seth said. "A lot of companies have stopped hiring women."

"I'm not worried," Kelly said. "I'm a middle-school teacher. Teaching children is still considered women's work. That and cleaning houses."

As Seth watched Josiah, he kept glancing at the fence gate expecting Larry to make another appearance. Savior Camp was supposed to make Larry into a better Christian and a better father. Instead, he avoided people, was a stranger to his family, and wandered the neighborhood day and night mumbling to himself. The camp had hollowed out his personality and filled his head with scripture. No wonder the campers who returned home were referred to as Jesus Zombies.

Seth knew how he must look to Larry as he stood here next to his wife and watched his son showing off his tricycle-riding skills. He wasn't trying to take Larry's place. Everyone close to Larry wanted him to snap out of his stupor and be the dad he used to be. But until that happened, Josiah was desperate for attention, and Seth loved kids. They were drawn to each other.

Seth and Kelly cheered on Josiah in his one-man race. The sun reached that hazy point in the day when it can't decide if it really wants to dip under the horizon or stay where it is. The fence door creaked again, and a policeman entered the back yard. Josiah stopped pedaling to admire his crisp blue uniform and thick black belt loaded with police gear.

The policeman strolled over to Seth and Kelly like a cowboy approaching the bar in a saloon. When he reached them, he put his hands on his hips. Seth took a deep breath to calm his nerves. He was in his own back yard and he'd done nothing wrong.

"Is there anyone else here?" the policeman said. "Did anyone leave recently?"

"No, it's just been the three of us back here," Seth said. "Is there a problem, Officer?"

"I got a report that there was a man taking the Lord's name in vain in this yard," the policeman said. "I am going to assume that young man is not the perpetrator."

He pointed at Josiah. Josiah pointed back.

"Phew, phew," he said, as he shot two imaginary bullets at the policeman.

Seth expected the officer to play along and grab his chest as if he'd been shot, but he apparently wasn't in the mood for games. He glared at Seth and Kelly.

"Officer, I've been back here the entire time," Kelly said. "Seth hasn't uttered one inappropriate word."

"Ma'am, this man has been accused of a Big Ten offense," the policeman said as he pointed at Seth. "Don't interfere with an officer of the law."

"It's okay, Kelly," Seth said. "He's only going to give me a ticket and I'll pay a fine. It's no big deal."

"It is a big deal," Kelly said. "You're innocent." She turned to the officer. "What exactly did he supposedly say?"

"The person who reports the crime does not have to embarrass themselves by repeating the offensive words defiling our Lord Jesus," the policeman said.

"Who reported Seth? Was it Larry?"

Seth cringed. He could see that the policeman was getting angry. Kelly needed to back down before he charged Seth with something else. Seth worried how Darlene was going to react once she learned he'd been charged with a Big Ten offense. This could delay his faith verification, or even make Seth unverifiable altogether. That meant deportation or worse.

Maggie came outside and joined them, smiling at everyone as if she'd arrived just in time for a party.

"I heard strange voices in my back yard," she said. "Is this nice policeman here to arrest Josiah for speeding?"

The policeman looked down at Josiah.

"I like to go fast," Josiah said.

The policeman laughed, and his laughter was contagious. Everyone joined him, even Josiah, who had no idea what was so funny. Maggie had broken the tension, giving Seth yet another reason to be proud of her.

"Look," the policeman said, "maybe this lady's telling the truth. The guy who reported this wasn't in the yard. Maybe he only thought he heard something. But I still have to write you a ticket. Here's what I'll do. I'll put it down as an unconscious offense. You meant to say something else and a curse word accidentally slipped out. It's a fifteen-dollar fine, and it doesn't go on your record."

"That's very generous of you, Officer," Seth said.

"It's the Christian thing to do," he said as he wrote Seth's ticket.

CHAPTER 13

Taking the Lord's name in vain was a Big Ten offense, but no one could prove that Maggie had done it because she hadn't said it out loud. A dozen times. Or that she hadn't said out loud the words for bowel movement and sexual intercourse over a dozen times each.

She was internally screaming obscenities because Amy Bird was missing.

The Judy Cross Show went live in thirty minutes. Everything and everyone were in their place and ready to go, except for Amy. Maggie had dealt with her showing up to work hungover, high, and bitchy, but until today Amy had never been late or not shown up at all.

Yesterday's phone call from Amy had meant nothing. Her promise to be a better Christian and a better friend had been a lie. She was the same selfish, inconsiderate egomaniac she'd always been. If Maggie survived this day, she was going to tell Amy exactly what she thought of her.

A production assistant informed Maggie that Bill Garmon wanted to see her in master control "right now if not sooner." Maggie silently took the Lord's name in vain again. She walked across the studio with her head down. Her deodorant couldn't keep up with the buckets of sweat pouring out of her, and she was sure everyone could smell her.

Maggie entered master control, feeling like she was walking into the principal's office after being caught smoking cigarettes in the girl's bathroom. She answered Bill's question before he asked.

"I don't know where Amy is, but I'm sure she'll be here soon."

Bill had worked in live television for twenty-five years. Not much fazed him.

"The cooking segment is after the midway point," Bill said as he flipped through the script. "That buys us some time, but not much. What do we do if she doesn't show up?"

"I don't know," Maggie said. "You're the executive producer.

What do you think we should do?"

Bill shuffled through the script again and shook his head. "Find Amy."

Bill put his headset on and barked directions to the crew. It was his way of letting Maggie know that their conversation had ended. Now it was up to her to produce a miracle. She left the control room and hurried to make-up.

"I will not panic," she said. "I will remain calm. I will not set the studio on fire."

Maggie flew into the make-up room. Her mouth dropped open. Amy Bird was sitting in front of the mirror as Wanda, the make-up artist, applied blush to her face. Maggie almost fainted with relief.

"There you are!" she shouted. "I'd hug you, but I don't want to muss you up."

Amy gave Maggie an apologetic smile. "Sorry," she said. "I would have called, but my phone died. I forgot to recharge it."

"Where were you?"

"I had a doctor's appointment this morning. It took longer than I thought."

"Why would you make an appointment before a live show?"

"It was the only time the doctor was available."

That didn't make sense. On-air talent had better access to health care than worker bees like Maggie. Amy could see a doctor any time she wanted. But this wasn't the time or place to discuss it.

"It doesn't matter now," Maggie said. "You're here. I thought I was going to die. Why is Wanda putting so much blush on your cheeks? You hardly ever wear blush. Wanda, why all the blush? Can you tell I'm totally freaked out and that's why I'm talking a mile a minute?"

"She's very pale today," Wanda said. "I'm trying to put some life back in her."

Maggie peered closely at Amy. Her face was pale. She had probably been partying all night, and that was why she had the complexion of a zombie. Maggie wanted to remind Amy that her bad behavior was putting both of their jobs in jeopardy, but she held her tongue. She needed Amy in good spirits.

Wanda finished Amy's make-up and Amy went to her dressing

room. Wanda shook her head sadly.

"There's something not right with that girl."

"Yeah, she's hanging around the wrong people," Maggie said.

"I mean physically. You didn't see her when she first came in. I felt like I was preparing a cadaver for a funeral-home viewing."

MAGGIE WATCHED *THE JUDY CROSS SHOW* FROM BACKSTAGE. DESPITE the headaches and pressure, Maggie loved live television. It was like walking on a tightrope high above the ground. If something went wrong, there was nothing anyone could do to change it. The difference was that when someone slipped and fell during a live TV program, they didn't plummet to their death.

Judy was in an especially good mood today. She was probably looking forward to giving the first of her series of sermons about the benefits of Savior Camps for our society, but that wouldn't come until the end of the program.

She started the show by reading a Bible verse and then introduced the Huffstetler Twins. Conjoined siblings Rosie and Renee sang two hymns and then delivered a sermon that equated motherhood with sainthood. They spoke in a seesaw rhythm, with Rosie saying a sentence, followed by Renee saying the next, and then back again. Their sermon was extremely moving, and the cameras made sure to get close-ups of audience members weeping.

After a commercial break, Judy brought out pop star Bobbi Sue Sunshine. The audience sprang to their feet and cheered. Bobbi Sue took the stage and sang her latest hit, "Jesus Jesus Jesus (Jesus Jesus)."

While Bobbi Sue performed, Maggie made the final preparations for the cooking segment, which came after the next commercial break. Everything was ready. The only thing missing was Amy. Maggie found her sitting in her dressing room, hunched over and clutching her stomach. She put her hand on Amy's face.

"You're burning hot," Maggie said.

Amy pushed her hand away. Make-up barely concealed the dark rings under her eyes.

"I'm fine," she rasped. "I'm just really thirsty."

"I'll get you a bottle of water," Maggie said.

As she hurried out of the dressing room, Maggie heard Bobbi Sue finish her song, followed by thunderous applause. Maggie had two minutes to get Amy's water. She grabbed a bottle from the craft services table and returned to the dressing room with a minute to spare.

"Here, drink this," Maggie said to the empty room. Amy had left. Maggie glanced at the dressing room's studio monitor. Amy was standing on the cooking set with Judy and Bobbi Sue. Maggie stayed in her dressing room and watched the show from there.

"Welcome back," Judy said. "It's time for a visit to 'What's Cookin' in Amy's Kitchen'."

"This is my favorite part of the show," Bobbi Sue said. "In fact, I have my assistant videotape just this part of the program for me."

Watching Judy squirm while Bobbi Sue gushed over Amy made Maggie happy for the first time that day.

"Amy, tell us what we'll be cooking today?" Judy said.

"Patriot Tarts," Amy said. "We've brightened up an old Jewish recipe with good ole American ingenuity."

"Whatever it is, it smells divine!" Bobbi Sue said.

The segment was going smoothly. Maggie relaxed, twisted the cap off the water bottle, and took a sip. She was about to sit down in Amy's chair when she noticed a red mark on the seat. Maggie touched the stain, which stuck to her fingers. It was blood.

Bobbi Sue shrieked.

Maggie looked at the monitor in time to see Amy collapse.

Judy, ever the professional, calmly said, "We'll be right back after these commercials."

Maggie dropped the bottle of water and ran to the set. She arrived as Bobbi Sue's publicist hurried the singer offstage, and Judy ordered the Huffstetler Twins to perform another song after the commercial break. Audience members jostled for the best view of the woman on the floor. A crew member quickly pulled a curtain around the cooking set to shut them out.

"Somebody call 911!" Maggie shouted, but everyone was so busy keeping the show going that no one paid attention. She pulled her cellphone out of her pocket and made the call.

Amy was on her back, clutching her stomach. Her apron had a large wet spot where it covered her crotch. A pool of blood spread beneath her. Maggie kneeled down and gently placed Amy's head in her lap.

"Everything's going to be all right," Maggie said. "An ambulance is on its way."

Tears ran down Amy's face. "It's not going to be all right. I did a terrible thing and now I'm being punished for it."

"You're not being punished. There's something wrong with you, and the doctors are going to fix it."

Amy grabbed Maggie's hand and squeezed tightly. Maggie winced from the pain.

"I had an abortion," Amy said. "This morning. I went to this doctor to take care of it, and I don't think he did it right. The room was so dirty."

Amy covered her eyes with her other hand and sobbed. Maggie stroked her hair. The studio lights were blazing hot, but Amy's skin was cold. The dark red pool had reached Maggie's knees. A sharp iron smell mixed with the tart strawberry filling of the pastries, still warm in the set's oven.

No one from the crew joined Maggie at Amy's side. The show continued as if nothing had happened. Maggie could hear the Huffstetler Twins singing on the other side of the curtain. They sounded like angels, and angels were the last thing she wanted to hear at that moment.

Finally, two paramedics arrived.

"Thank God you're here," Maggie said. "She suddenly fell down in the middle of the show."

One paramedic did all the talking. While the silent one checked Amy's vital signs, he lifted Amy's bloody apron and examined her soaked crotch.

"Ma'am" he said. "Did you have an abortion?"

"Yes," Amy said. "And now God is punishing me."

The paramedics looked at each other gravely. The silent one jerked his head to the side. They repacked their gear and started to leave.

"Where are you going?" Maggie said.

"The law states that I can refuse to aid a sinner beyond salvation," the paramedic said.

"Are you kidding me? She's dying. Aren't you bound by the Hippocratic Oath to save her?"

"Not in a case like this. She's a Jezebel and a child murderer. It's against our beliefs to give her comfort."

"At least take her to a hospital."

"Waste of time. No hospital is going to admit a baby killer."

Amy's grip on Maggie's hand became limp. Maggie pulled Amy into her lap and gently rocked her. This was her best friend and her life was leaking out while these jerks refused to save her.

"Don't worry, Amy," Maggie said. "I'll get you to a hospital if I have to carry you myself."

"I'm so sorry," Amy said. "I hope I don't get you in trouble."

A uniformed policeman arrived. Maggie was relieved. He would fix it. He'd force them to save Amy.

"I just got the call," he said. "What's the situation?"

"My friend is dying, and these idiots have refused to save her life," Maggie said.

The paramedic pointed at Amy like she was a rabid dog that needed to be put down.

"She's a Jezebel," he said. "She had an abortion, and now she's paying the price for her sin."

Amy closed her eyes. Maggie leaned close to make sure she was still breathing.

The policeman grabbed the paramedic's shirt and pulled him close. Spit flew into the man's face as the cop yelled at him.

"You morons! You have to save this woman so that she can tell us the identity of the doctor who performed the abortion."

The paramedics blinked in confusion as the policeman's words sunk in. Then they dove down next to Amy, pushing Maggie aside. They placed an oxygen mask on Amy and cut off her pants. Maggie hovered over them as they struggled to stop the bleeding. The talking paramedic ordered her to step back. As Maggie obeyed, she noticed that her shoes were leaving red prints on the studio floor. She'd been standing in Amy's blood and her jeans were soaked from the knees down. On the other side of the curtain, she heard laughter and applause.

Minutes that felt like hours passed until finally, the silent paramedic shook his head. They couldn't stop the bleeding. He checked his watch to determine the time of death. They lifted Amy's body onto a gurney and covered it with a white sheet.

"No!" Maggie said, grabbing her head. "She can't be dead. You were supposed to save her. Why didn't you save her?"

"We did our best," the paramedic said to the policeman. "But we were too late."

Maggie held herself to keep from falling apart. She followed the policeman and the paramedics as they wheeled Amy to the ambulance. Outside, the sun shone like it did almost every day. Maggie tried to get into the ambulance, but was told that unless she was a blood relative, she couldn't come. Amy and Maggie hadn't really been sisters. It had only felt that way. Maggie stood on the sidewalk and watched the ambulance take her friend away.

CHAPTER 14

A conference-room light flickered and died as Rabbi Leah led the congregation through the Maariv, the Jewish evening service. Since the building was officially closed, there would be no requests for maintenance to replace the bulbs. Leah led the service barefoot. She had mentioned at an earlier service that she liked the feel of the sand on her feet, and there was nothing in the Torah that said the rabbi had to wear shoes.

Seth kept his shoes on. He stood in the second row and swayed back and forth as he prayed. He had only been taught to recite Hebrew, so he had no idea what he was saying. He didn't care. The rise and fall of his voice, joined with the voices of the congregation, calmed his jangled nerves.

As he was zigzagging through the Bethesda office park on his way to services that evening, Seth heard a noise that sounded like metal hitting the ground. Instead of walking calmly out of the office park as if he were just passing through, Seth had panicked, bolting like a frightened rabbit. He dove behind a bush, his heart pounding, while sweat trickled down his neck.

Seth was supposed to always be on alert, but he'd been thinking about how he wanted to revise the speech Senator Owens would deliver at the tenth-anniversary celebration of the CHRIST Act and had let his guard down. Owens had asked him to include statistics about how much safer Americans felt a decade later. Seth was all too aware that a sense of safety was a matter of perspective.

He had stayed behind the bush long enough to feel foolish. There were no more metallic sounds. Only birds and wind. His thighs had become sore from crouching. He stretched his legs and wiped the sweat off his face. He didn't mention the sound to Howard when he let Seth into the building or to Rabbi Leah when he arrived at the seventh-floor conference room. Nobody had noticed his hands shaking as he put on his tallis and yarmulke.

Now that Seth's paranoia had subsided, guilt took its place. He still hadn't told Maggie about attending services. He hated lying to her, but in a way, it was her own fault. Maggie knew Judaism was a vital part of Seth's life. She had forced him to lie to her. In a way, he was protecting her. If Seth got caught, Maggie could honestly say that she had no idea he was practicing an illegal religion.

He did a head count of his fellow worshippers. There were thirty Jews here tonight, including Seth. They were all adults, no children. Certainly, some of them were parents. There were the type of people who never attended church until after they had children because they wanted their kids to have religion. These parents didn't dare expose their offspring to this danger. Seth wondered where they told the babysitter they were going before they came here.

After the service, Seth took a long time to put away his things. He knew Maggie was expecting him, but he didn't want to leave just yet. He stood near the Torah as if he were absorbing its energy.

When Seth finally took the elevator downstairs, Howard waited in the shadows of the warehouse for him to leave. Instead, Seth stayed rooted inside. He thought about the metallic noise he'd heard earlier, and his paranoia returned.

"How do we know that Hedge Protection missioners aren't out there right now?" Seth said.

"We don't," Howard said. "We'll never be completely safe. There's no such thing."

"Maybe we should look for a new place."

"We're lucky to have this one. I seriously doubt we can do any better."

MGGIE STOOD AT AMY'S CUBICLE AND WATCHED THE BIRDS.

Rather than avoid her avian last name, Amy Bird had embraced it. Her cubicle was covered in a flock of bird photos, bird paper holders, stuffed-animal birds, wind-up toy birds, ceramic birds, wooden birds, angry birds, and happy birds. Amy easily had the most colorful workplace, beating out co-workers who had decorated their cubicles with a heaven's worth of angels.

By contrast, Maggie's cubicle was an avalanche of recipe books, scripts, and production schedules. The only personal item she allowed herself was a photo of her and Seth thumb-tacked to a bulletin board.

Amy was teased about her bird collection, but Maggie loved the whimsy and bright colors. She helped Amy name them. Maggie's favorite was a hand-carved wooden bluebird they called Sidney. Maggie didn't know how they came up with that name. They just thought the carving, painted neon blue with a tomato red belly, looked like a Sidney.

Maggie took Sidney off his perch on the bookshelf and held him in her hands. She ran her fingers over his smooth head and along the ridges carved to create his feathers. Still kneading the wooden bird, she sat at her desk and reached for her phone. She called Seth, but was connected directly to his voicemail.

"Seth," Maggie said. "It's me. Where are you? Call me the second you get this message. This is super important."

Maggie needed to call Amy's parents in South Carolina, but kept putting it off. Surely, the police had informed them of their daughter's death, but they deserved to hear from a friend.

Almost as soon as the ambulance had gone, two missioners had arrived at the station. One was a tall white man, and the other was a petite Asian woman. They escorted Maggie into the conference room and questioned her for two hours. She explained over and over again that she didn't know the identity of the doctor who had performed Amy's abortion.

"I didn't even know Amy was pregnant until she collapsed on the floor," Maggie said. "If I knew who butchered her, I'd tell you. I want him behind bars as much as you do."

When the missioners finally told Maggie that she was free to go, she fled the conference room with a pounding headache, sick with grief. The blood stains on her pant legs had dried, making them brown and stiff. She had no other clothes to change into.

The show was over, and audience had left. Most of the crew had gone home. Maggie avoided reporters lurking in the lobby and went to her cubicle to get her purse. That was when she had become mesmerized by Amy's aviary.

Maggie didn't notice the Huffstetler Twins standing at her cubicle until she felt them staring at her. She'd been around them for years, but they still managed to freak her out. Rosie's face was puffy, and her eyes were red from crying, while Renee scowled angrily.

"I feel so terrible for poor Amy," Rosie said, her voice catching. "She died without asking for Christ's forgiveness. She's going straight to hell. She's probably there right now in a burning lake filled with dismembered fetuses. Just thinking about it makes me want to cry again. Renee, hand me a tissue. They're in the pocket on your side."

Renee fished a tissue out of their pants pocket and handed it to Rosie, who wiped her eyes and blew her nose.

"I'm glad Amy's in hell," Renee growled. "She could have had a baby and she threw it away. I would love to get pregnant, but our pelvis is too compressed."

Maggie ran her fingers over the wooden bird, marveling at how one body could have two arms, two legs, two heads, and not contain an ounce of compassion.

"Excuse me," Maggie said. "I have to make an important phone call."

She didn't wait for the twins to leave. She picked up the receiver and dialed Amy's parents' home number. Amy's mother answered on the fifth ring.

"Hello," she said, her voice quavering.

"Edna. It's Maggie Ginsberg."

"Oh, hello Maggie. I thought it was the hospital calling with more information. Hold on, I'll have Leo pick up the extension. Leo! Leo! Pick up the other phone."

Maggie could hear Leo's voice far away. Their accents reminded Maggie of Amy's Southern roots. Amy had worked hard to lose her accent because she felt it would hinder her career.

"Is it the hospital?" Leo called.

"No, it's Maggie," Edna called back. "You remember Maggie."

"Of course, I remember Maggie," Leo shot back.

Maggie had gone with Amy to her parents' home in Gaffney, South Carolina many times. Seth always managed to find something important to do those weekends and never came with them. Maggie could picture the Birds's tidy home in a quiet suburban neighborhood with modest houses and neatly trimmed yards. Amy had inherited her mother's love of cooking. The kitchen was always full of wonderful smells, like the nutty freshness of baked cornbread and the tang of fried chicken sizzling in a skillet.

Leo picked up the extension.

"How are you holding up, Maggie?" he asked.

"I was going to ask you that," Maggie said.

Edna sighed. "We're doing the best we can. The hospital is not being near as helpful as I think they should considering the circumstances."

"Have you told Henry and Silas?" Maggie asked. They were Amy's brothers.

"They're on their way over," Leo said. "You know, neither of the boys left Gaffney. Just our Amy. She always did have stars in her eyes."

Maggie gripped the wooden bird tightly, and the beak dug into her palm.

"I'm so sorry about Amy. If only I had known maybe I could have helped her."

"She didn't tell you about her condition?" Leo asked.

Even now, Leo couldn't bring himself to say out loud that his unwed daughter was pregnant.

"Not until today," Maggie said. "When she fell down."

"She was a headstrong girl," Edna said. "I don't imagine there was anything any of us could have done."

"I'd like to come to the funeral," Maggie said.

As soon as Maggie made the request, she knew it was a mistake. People in Gaffney were going to say terrible things about Edna and Leo's only girl. Amy's funeral would be a family-only affair. It was the only way.

There was a long silence. The line crackled.

"I don't think that's a good idea," Leo said.

"We appreciate the offer," Edna said.

"I understand," Maggie said.

A call-waiting alert beeped on the line.

"That must be the hospital," Edna said. "Thank you for calling, Maggie."

The phone went dead before Maggie could say goodbye. She

dialed Seth's number, and the call went to his voicemail again. She didn't bother leaving a message. Maggie knew that she should go home, but she couldn't get her body to move. Her phone rang.

"Seth?" she said.

"Nope, it's Bill," Bill Garmon said. "I'm in Judy's office. We need to talk."

"Now?"

"Yes. Now."

Maggie shut her eyes for a moment. "I'm on my way."

She hung up and put Sidney on top of a stack of cookbooks. Judy's door was open. She was at her desk while Bill was seated in one of the guest chairs. Judy told Maggie to shut the door behind her. Maggie did and sat in a chair next to Bill. The TV on Judy's desk, which was usually locked on NCTV, was on NNN instead. The sound was turned off. Occasionally, Judy glanced at the TV.

"If you'd like, I can send flowers on behalf of the show to Amy's family in Gaffney," Maggie said.

Judy gave Maggie one of her best fake-sad smiles.

"I wish we could, Maggie dear," she said, "but we can't. We just came out of a lengthy meeting with NCTV's legal team and Hedge Protection. Amy has been accused of abortion and suicide. For the sake of *The Judy Cross Show*, we must distance ourselves from her crimes."

"Amy didn't commit suicide," Maggie said. "She had a bad abortion. The doctor butchered her."

"Do you know that for a fact?" Bill asked.

Maggie was confused. She thought Bill liked Amy.

"No, I don't," she admitted.

"I am all about loving the sinner and hating the sin," Judy said, "but I'm responsible for my entire staff. I can't risk their jobs because of Amy's selfish behavior."

Bill swiveled his chair toward Maggie and narrowed his eyes at her.

"Why didn't you tell us Amy was pregnant?" he said.

Maggie stared back at him.

"I'll tell you exactly what I told the missioners three-hundred times. I didn't know until she was dying in my arms."

"Leave her alone, Bill," Judy said. "Maggie's a good girl. She would have come to me the minute Amy told her."

Normally, Maggie would have gotten a good laugh out of Judy's fantasy, but she was too worn out. Judy glanced at the TV and pointed frantically. Shaky video of Amy, Judy, and Bobbi Sue was on the screen. Judy grabbed the remote and turned the sound on.

"NNN has obtained exclusive video recorded on a cellphone by an audience member of *The Judy Cross Show*," the anchor reported. "It shows Amy Bird collapsing during the live broadcast."

In the video, Amy appeared ill at first and then dropped out of sight. Maggie saw herself rushing to Amy's side just as the video ended and the screen cut back to the anchor at his desk.

"We should consider banning audience members from bringing their cellphones to the shows," Judy said.

"Coroner's reports have listed her death as the result of blood loss from her illegal abortion," the anchor said. "Hedge Protection has joined the Metropolitan Police Department in the investigation into the identity of the abortion doctor. They released a statement saying it's only a matter of time before he's caught. Rest assured that the doctor will face the Almighty and the United States Legal System for his crime. As for Amy Bird's crime, the Lord has already rendered His verdict. We go now to our reporter, Myste Bright, with more on this rapidly developing story."

An attractive blonde with too much lipstick came on the screen with a publicity photo of Amy over her shoulder.

"'What's Cookin' in Amy's Kitchen' was a popular part of *The Judy Cross Show*," Myste said. "Sources tell NNN that NCTV was about to give Amy Bird her own show. She was often described as wholesome and perky. Her fans are shocked to discover that Amy was not a true Christian. In reality, she was a harlot who had impure sex with men out of wedlock. In a recent NNN poll, we asked viewers, do you think Amy Bird is in Hell?"

A chart appeared on the screen. Myste Bright read the results.

"Eighty-five percent believe Amy is in Hell right now paying for her sins. Ten percent believe she will spend an eternity in Purgatory before moving on to Hell and five percent are undecided."

Judy turned the set off. She glared at Bill.

"NCTV was going to give Amy her own show?" Judy said. "When were they going to tell me?"

Bill rubbed his temples.

"As you might have guessed," Bill said, "'What's Cookin' in Amy's Kitchen' has been cancelled as of today. We'll assess whether we want to have a cooking segment with a new chef at a later date."

"There is a silver lining to this awful tragedy," Judy said. "Now the show can devote more time to supporting Savior Camps."

Maggie looked from Bill to Judy. They had already moved on from Amy, and the day wasn't over yet.

"If there's no cooking segment," Maggie said, "does that mean you're letting me go?"

Bill shook his head.

"You'll be an assistant producer until we decide where you fit in best," he said.

Judy grinned at Maggie. She knew that grin. It never meant good news.

"You put so much time and effort into the cooking show," Judy said. "Use this opportunity to think about the best way to serve Christ. Haven't you put off starting a family long enough? Think of it as a way to correct Amy's sin."

Maggie felt an icy chill race down her spine.

"Yeah, Maggie," Bill said. "Have a child to replace a child. What a wonderful way to honor Jesus."

"After the baby's born," Judy said, "we'll have you come back for a special segment."

"I'm not gone yet," Maggie said. "I still work here."

Judy grinned at Maggie again.

WHEN MAGGIE GOT BACK TO HER DESK, SHE WAS STUNNED TO FIND THAT Amy's cubicle had been cleaned out. Her flock of birds was gone. Maggie had been in Judy's office for less than an hour, and already the station had erased her friend. She shouldn't be surprised. Judy and Bill had just told her that they would gladly erase her, too.

Maggie balled her fists and pressed them against her forehead. She sat down heavily into her chair, picked up the phone, and dialed Seth's number. The call immediately went to his voicemail. "Where the hell are you?" she shouted before slamming down the receiver.

Maggie's eye caught a gleam of neon blue. Sidney was where she'd left him on a stack of cookbooks. He stared at her with his indifferent black eyes. He wasn't on Amy's desk, so whoever had cleaned out her cubicle must have assumed that he belonged to Maggie. She cradled Sidney in her hands.

Chapter 15

The Metro station was nearly deserted. The arrival board read that, due to a technical delay, the next train wouldn't arrive for another thirty minutes. Seth considered calling Maggie to let her know that he'd be late getting home, but he decided it was best to wait to reinsert his phone's battery until he was on the train. He felt something annoying in his shoe. Taking it off, he saw that he had gotten sand in it from the conference-room floor. He shook out the sand and brushed his sock before putting his shoe back on.

A man in a rumpled suit who smelled like old gym socks ambled over to Seth's bench.

"Spare some Christian Charity?" he mumbled.

He stared at Seth with sad eyes and held his hands at his side, ready to snatch anything that was offered. Seth wondered how these guys could afford to get into the Metro station, and then he remembered reading a report that for many of them, their jobs ran out before the stored value on their fare cards did.

They reminded Seth of the Japanese businessmen who pretended to go to work every day rather than face the embarrassment of telling their families that they had lost their jobs. Like them, these secretly unemployed men dressed for work every morning and then spent the day visiting museums and hanging out in parks.

Seth had read the government's unemployment studies that were never shared with the public. Many of these panhandlers in expensive suits had been pillars of their communities. Before their careers had crashed and burned, they had spearheaded charity drives to help the unfortunate. They couldn't tell their wives that they were the needy, especially when the government was telling them that the economy was booming, blessed beyond all expectations. These once-proud men believed that they must have done something wicked and that Jesus was punishing them for their sins.

Seth dug into his pocket and came out with a handful of loose change. The man in the rumpled suit said a quick "Bless you" before he set off in search of another handout.

"Blessed greetings, Metro passengers," boomed a recorded voice from the station's intercom system. "I'm Federal Deacon Freeman Wingard of the Department of Hedge Protection. Please join me in our nation's efforts to keep this anointed country safe from the Devil's influence. Report any suspicious non-Christian behavior to the nearest law-enforcement agent. Or call 911. Let's work together to keep America strong in Christ's glory. Thank you."

Seth glanced about to see if anyone was exhibiting non-Christian behavior.

He missed the euphoria he had felt when he accepted Christ. He didn't even mind taking his U.S. Christian Citizenship Test. Seth had always been good at taking tests and had no problem answering questions like name two born-again presidents (Jimmy Carter and George W. Bush), or what is the role of the National Church (The National Church provides all citizens with free access to the salvation of Jesus Christ). The swearing-in ceremony had been a bizarre experience, since he was pledging allegiance to the country he'd been born in.

But Seth didn't mind. He had joined the club. He wasn't an outsider anymore. The American image of mom, apple pie, and baseball always had a Christian vibe to it.

As the National Church gained prominence and laws were passed to ensure America really was a Christian nation, Seth had been proud to be part of the transition. The country felt cleaner. It was worth giving up craft beer, violent movies, and teenage girls in string bikinis. America's streets were safer, kids were taught morals, and people trusted their government again. All everyone had to do was accept Christ and obey Him. And His government.

Seth had been staring at the ground when he noticed feet standing in front of him. He felt a wave of annoyance.

"Sorry, I'm all out of Christian Charity," Seth said without looking up.

"Each of you should give what you have decided in your heart to give, not reluctantly or under compulsion, for God loves a cheerful giver, 2 Corinthians 9:7."

The man standing in front of Seth was not a panhandler. It was Larry Bruner, his friendly next-door neighbor Jesus Zombie. Anger swelled up inside Seth. He wanted to confront Larry about what had happened in his back yard and make Larry admit that he was the one who had lied to the police about Seth taking the Lord's name in vain. He swallowed his anger. Larry could easily deny that he had called the police. The law protected the identities of people who turned in sinners. Larry could claim Seth falsely accused him. Bearing false witness was a worse Big Ten offense than taking the Lord's name in vain. Seth had no choice but to be cordial.

"Hey, Larry," Seth said. "How's life treating you?"

"Though I don't have a job, I know that I'm highly blessed," Larry said as he sat on the bench next to him.

Seth studied the arrival board. It was still estimating thirty minutes before his train was expected to arrive. He stifled a groan. There was no chance they could sit together for that long without starting a conversation. Seth had to beat him to the punch and come up with something to talk about that was safe and completely unrelated to religion.

There was a large ad on the wall facing them for the National Gallery of Art, announcing an upcoming exhibition of Impressionist paintings. After the Greatest Awakening, there were calls to destroy all art with any sort of objectionable political or sexual imagery. Cooler heads prevailed. The offending images had been locked away instead. That included most Renaissance art, despite the abundance of biblical subject matter. There was just too much nudity.

Impressionists were safe. They painted flowers and landscapes and people fully clothed. The poster for the National Gallery show featured a reproduction of Monet's "Woman with a Parasol."

"That's a lovely painting," Seth said, nodding toward the ad. "If I didn't know the painting was done in the nineteenth century, I'd swear it was a portrait of Kelly and Josiah. It looks just like them."

Seth congratulated himself on his cleverness. He'd compared Larry's wife and son to a beautiful painting. That should get Larry talking about his family.

"Yes, it's lovely," Larry said. "But let me tell you about the most beautiful painting I've ever seen. It was a close-up of a man's open hand on a wooden board. Another man's hands hold a spike and a hammer and he's about to drive the spike into the man's wrist. Can you guess what it's a painting of?"

"A Roman soldier about to nail Jesus to the cross?" Seth said.

"So that he may die for our sins."

Seth couldn't believe it. Larry had managed to turn the conversation to Jesus after all. The arrival board updated Seth's train to twenty-five minutes away. It would have been easier to walk home at this point.

A man in a cashmere overcoat that was too heavy for the warm weather walked over to them.

"Spare a little Christian Charity?" he asked.

"Forgive me, brother," Larry said. "My pockets are empty. All I can offer you are my prayers of love. Blessed are the poor in spirit, for theirs is the kingdom of Heaven, Matthew 5:3."

The man in the overcoat made a sour face before beating a hasty retreat. Seth was impressed. He was going to have to remember that one.

"What brought you to this part of town?" Larry asked.

Normally, Seth wouldn't have answered because it was none of Larry's business. But Seth remembered the fine he paid for curse words he never said.

"My favorite shooting range is just down the street," Seth said, as he patted his range bag.

"Really, which one?" Larry said.

"The Second Amendment Shooting Range. I love to unwind after a hard day with a little target practice," Seth said, hoping he sounded like a true red-blooded American.

"What kind of gun do you have?"

"A Springfield XD 9mm."

"Mind if I see it?"

Seth opened his bag and took out his gun. He popped out the empty clip and checked the chamber before handing it to Larry, who held it carefully as he turned it from side to side. Seth had gotten the gun as a Christmas gift from Senator Owens. He gave the same gun to everybody in the office.

As Larry quizzed him about which ammo he used and his shooting

preferences, Seth was surprised at how easily he answered Larry's questions. He knew a lot more about guns than he'd realized, a result of all the times he'd gone to the range because he didn't feel safe going to services.

Seth had a stack of shooting targets that proved his many nights of target practice had made him a good marksman. He only purchased the simple bullseye targets, and avoided the ones with images of Muslim Terrorists, Lesbian Feminists, and Illuminati Jewish Bankers. He only kept the targets so that he could show them to Maggie if and when she asked him how he was doing at the range.

Larry handed Seth's gun back to him. As Seth returned the weapon to his range bag, he pretended he didn't notice Rabbi Leah as she sat down on a nearby bench. She always waited until the other congregants had enough time to catch their trains before leaving herself, but she had no way of knowing that Seth's train had been delayed. She made a point of not looking in his direction.

"Nice gun," Larry said.

"Thank you," Seth replied.

"Why did you lie to me?"

Seth's cheeks grew hot.

"I didn't lie," he said.

"You didn't go to the range tonight."

"Of course, I did."

Larry reached under his dirty sweatshirt, pulled out a handgun, and held it in his palm for Seth to see. Seth recognized it as a Glock 33, also known as a pocket rocket. A small, powerful handgun that was easy to conceal.

"This is my gun," Larry said. "I was at the Second Amendment Shooting Range tonight, and I know you weren't, because the manager complained that I was the only customer who'd been in the entire evening."

Seth struggled to come up with a believable excuse, but only managed to make confused guttural sounds. Rabbi Leah instinctively stood to come help him. Seth saw what she was about to do and frantically shook his head. She sat back down and awkwardly ignored him, but it was too late. Larry had noticed their silent exchange.

"Oh Seth," Larry said as he slipped his gun back into the shoulder holster under his sweatshirt. "Adultery is one of the worst Big Ten crimes. You could go to jail."

"It's not what you think it is," Seth said.

"How could you cheat on Maggie? And if you're going to cheat, can't you do better than her?"

"I don't even know that woman."

Leah's train arrived. Seth silently prayed that she would get on her train without looking back, but she glanced over her shoulder and stared right at him as she boarded. Seth groaned. Leah was a wonderful rabbi and a brave woman, but she was a lousy actress and would've made a terrible spy.

"The face is okay, but her ass is huge," Larry said. "She looks like she has two volleyballs stuffed down her pants. Kelly used to have a great little ass. But since Josiah was born, it's been getting bigger every year."

The fear clouding Seth's thoughts cleared enough for him to realize that Larry wasn't talking about Jesus. In fact, he was starting to sound like someone who'd never been to a Savior Camp. Seth saw this as a ray of hope.

"Kelly has a big ass?" Seth said. "I hadn't noticed."

Their train finally pulled into the station. As they stood, Seth was painfully stiff from clenching his muscles. Larry put his arm around him in a brotherly fashion.

"Listen, if you're going to step out," Larry said. "Go to a whorehouse. In fact, I insist you come with me. The whorehouse I go to is the best in town. Delight yourself in the Lord, and he will give you the desires of your heart, Psalm 37:4."

CHAPTER 16

Seth knew something was wrong the moment he came home. The lights were off. Normally at this time of night, Maggie was in the kitchen writing scripts or experimenting with recipes. He checked the kitchen and found two cleaning bottles in the sink, both filled with soapy water. Black-market alcoholic beverages came in cleaning-product bottles complete with factory safety seals. The containers had to be washed afterwards to erase any trace of booze.

"What the heck has been going on around here?" Seth asked the kitchen, but it refused to answer.

Seth hurried upstairs. He found Maggie in the bedroom, sitting on the bed and sipping from a coffee cup. She glared at him with red-rimmed eyes.

"About time you got home," Maggie said.

"Did you drink two bottles of wine by yourself?" Seth said.

"Maybe. Probably. Didn't you get my messages?"

"I was at the firing range. I can't hear the phone when I'm wearing earmuffs, and then later I saw that the battery died. You'll never guess who I ran into at the Metro."

"Didn't you hear the news?"

"I've been completely cut off for hours. Why? What happened?"

Maggie drained her wine and put the cup on the nightstand. She sniffed and rubbed her nose.

"Amy's dead."

Seth sat on the bed and grabbed Maggie's hands.

"Oh my God. How?"

The whole terrible story poured out of Maggie. The illegal abortion, the paramedics' delay that cost Amy her life, and the NNN poll about Amy's possible location in the afterlife. By the end, Seth had Maggie in his arms and was stroking her hair.

"I never would have thought Amy was capable of killing her own child," Seth said.

Maggie pushed Seth away and jumped off the bed. She crossed her arms.

"How can you say that?" Maggie said.

"If she hadn't chosen to kill the baby, they'd both be alive," Seth said.

"If Amy had access to a safe and reliable medical facility, she wouldn't have died."

"But what about the baby?"

Maggie slammed her fist against the wall.

"Why is the baby's life more important than Amy's?" she said.

Seth got out of bed and stood on the other side of the room.

"That's not what I meant. I hate abortions."

"Then don't get one!"

Seth and Maggie stared at each other from opposite sides of the bed.

"Amy was pregnant and single," Maggie said. "If she had kept the baby, she would have been fired, become an outcast, and would probably have been sent to a Savior Camp."

Seth's shoulders slumped. Maggie was right. She was always right. He sat on the bed and patted the mattress. Maggie sighed and sat next to him. Seth took Maggie's hand and kissed her knuckles.

"I get it," he said. "Amy should have had a choice, but she didn't."

Maggie squeezed Seth's hand.

"Now there's the man I married. I just wish he wasn't such a liar."

Seth's mouth went dry.

"What's that supposed to mean?"

"You think I don't know? You weren't at the firing range. You were attending services again. That's why your phone was off. When I caught you last time, you promised me you'd never go back."

Seth let go of Maggie's hand.

"How did you know?" he said.

"I wasn't sure until now," she said.

"I'm a Jew. I need to be around other Jews. Why can't you understand that?"

"I wish you had a choice, but you don't. Going to services is too dangerous."

Seth sat on the edge of the bed with his back to Maggie. There was a bird carved out of wood on Maggie's dresser that he'd never seen before.

"I'll stop going," he said.

Maggie put her hand on Seth's back.

"I lost Amy," she said. "I don't know what I would do if I lost you."

Seth and Maggie stretched out on the bed, and he put his arms around her.

"Don't squeeze me," Maggie said. "I'm full of wine and if you squeeze me too tightly it might come out."

Seth quickly eased his grip on her.

"We have to leave," Maggie said.

"This house?" Seth said.

"Not just the house. This country."

Seth lay on his back and stared at the ceiling as if God would help him out. All he saw was a water stain that he hadn't noticed before.

"We can't leave," he said. "The borders are closed. If we tried to cross, Hedge Patrol would shoot us on sight."

"We have to find a way," Maggie said.

"You're talking about leaving our entire lives and starting over with nothing."

Maggie curled up next to Seth and put her hand on his chest.

"What kind of life is this?" she said. "You're not allowed to be Jewish. I'm not allowed to be childless."

"You never want to have children?"

"Maybe. Do I have a choice?"

Wives were expected to provide children for their husbands. Refusing to do so was grounds for divorce.

"I fell in love with you," Seth said. "Not your uterus. As for leaving the country, let's think about it for a couple of days before we make a final decision."

"Sure," Maggie said. "Think about it. Meanwhile, I'm not having intercourse with you until we're out of America."

Seth bolted upright as if he'd been hit with a cattle prod. He stared wide-eyed at Maggie.

"No sex?" he said.

"I didn't say no sex," Maggie said. "I said no intercourse. I don't want to get pregnant and be forced to have a baby. Not in this country.

There are plenty of things we can do that don't cause pregnancy."

Seth put his hand on his chest.

"Thank God. I can feel my heart beating again."

Maggie punched Seth in the arm.

"Who did you run into at the Metro?" she asked.

"Larry Bruner."

"That must have been weird."

"Yes, weird is a good way to describe it. Larry caught me lying about going to the firing range. Then he got the idea that I'm having an affair with my rabbi."

Maggie cocked her head like a confused dog, so Seth filled in the details for her.

"He calls the cops when he thinks you're taking the Lord's name in vain," Maggie said, "but he doesn't report you for adultery?"

"It turns out Larry is not a total Jesus Zombie," Seth said. "He insists that I go with him to his favorite brothel so that I can have sex with a prostitute instead of Rabbi Leah."

Maggie grabbed her coffee cup and pouted when she saw that it was empty.

"This day just keeps getting better," she said.

CHAPTER 17

ANNOUNCER: You're listening to NCR, National Christian Radio. The time is 10:00 a.m. *The Pauly Pilgrim Show* will continue right after a word from our sponsors.

COMMERCIAL VOICE TALENT: Don't miss Buy City's End of Days Sale. With our nation in the hands of our Lord, it's only a matter of time before the Rapture comes! Enjoy the material things of life before Jesus takes us all to heaven.

This week's special is stereo systems. We have speakers with fidelity so clear, we'd swear that you can hear the angels singing through them, that is if we swore, which we don't, because taking the Lord's name in vain is a Big Ten crime.

Worried about overextending your credit card or going into debt? Just remember, there are no overdue bills in heaven. Hurry on down to your local Buy City for the End of Days Sale or everything will be gone before you're gone from this earth.

ANNOUNCER: And now back to *The Pauly Pilgrim Show*.

PAULY PILGRIM: Welcome back true believers, Pauly Pilgrim here, continuing to spread the good news about Jesus and the greatest nation God ever created. An old friend has stopped by to share the next hour with me. She's the host of her own daytime talk show and the author of many fine books about the importance of Christian sacrifice. Welcome back to the show, Judy Cross.

JUDY CROSS: Great to be back, Pauly.

PILGRIM: I have to tell you that my wife never misses your show.

CROSS: Thank you, Pauly. Give my love to Sally.

PILGRIM: Actually, Sally is my second wife. My current wife's name is Luisa. You had a catastrophically terrible thing happen to you. Your chef, Amy Bird, died right next to you during a live broadcast.

CROSS: I still can't believe she's gone. Amy seemed to be a delightful girl full of promise. I honestly thought she was good and pure.

PILGRIM: But we have since discovered that Amy Bird led a double life. On "What's Cookin' in Amy's Kitchen," she ex-emplified Christian values and wholesome cooking, but behind the scenes, she walked a dark path under Satan's influence. She engaged in dangerous pre-marital sex. When confronted with her unexpected pregnancy, she chose to sadistically maim and destroy the child. When the coroner's report comes out, I wouldn't be surprised to find out that Amy was also addicted to black-market drugs.

CROSS: (sobs) I loved her as if she were my own child. I think of all my staff as my children.

PILGRIM: Amy betrayed you, Judy. How do you keep from hating her for all the pain she's caused you?

CROSS: Jesus died for our sins so that we might learn to forgive each other. When I think of Amy, and these days, I think of her often, I pray just a little bit harder.

PILGRIM: I know I should forgive this wanton woman as well, but when I think of the life she snuffed out, I get so angry.

CROSS: Do you mean Amy or the baby?

PILGRIM: The baby, of course.

CROSS: The most tragic aspect of this story is that it was entirely preventable. If Amy had come to me when she found out she was pregnant, I could have given her guidance. I too was with child outside of wedlock. I too had to face the prospect of single motherhood. I could have helped Amy find the strength to make the right choice.

PILGRIM: I know you would have, Judy.

CROSS: The first thing I would have done for her is have her sent directly to a Savior Camp. They would have broken Satan's bonds on her heart, and through their tough love, she would have found her way back to Christ's glory.

PILGRIM: Amen, sister.

CROSS: Can you believe there are people in this country who doubt the sacred mission of the Savior Camps?

PILGRIM: I know, Judy. It's shameful.

CROSS: I will not let Amy's death and the death of her unborn child mean nothing. I will dedicate myself to educating the public on how the Savior Camps fit into Jesus' plan for our great nation.

PILGRIM: That's very brave of you, Judy.

CROSS: Thank you, Pauly. If just one unwed mother finds the guidance she needs at a Savior Camp because of my efforts, then I know it was all worthwhile.

PILGRIM: And on that note, it's time to go to a break. Any last comment before we go, Judy?

CROSS: Oh yes, before I forget, my guests today on *The Judy Cross Show* will be Desember Evans from the popular sitcom, *Jesus Loves Me, Don'tcha Know* and all the way from Denver, Colorado, the gospel group, The Rocky Mountain Disciples.

Chapter 18

Seth wasn't sure what he had expected a post–Greatest Awakening brothel to look like, but he definitely hadn't expected it to look like the Family Bible Store. He could have passed by the Mount Pleasant business a hundred times without noticing it. If and when he did notice, he would have wondered how the store stayed in business since every home in America had a state-issued Bible that was delivered to their door like the phone book.

Seth didn't want to be here. Only two days had passed since Amy Bird died. She hadn't just been Maggie's friend. Amy had been Seth's friend too. She had laughed at his jokes, and his jokes were terrible.

He should have been in services tonight so that he could recite the Mourner's Kaddish for Amy. Instead, he let Larry Bruner drag him here because Larry was under the false impression that Seth was having an affair with his rabbi. Though both the synagogue and the brothel were illegal, Seth believed that he was safer here.

Inside the store, praise music played from the stereo system. They had wedding Bibles, children's Bibles, large print Bibles, various languages Bibles, student Bibles, audio Bibles, illustrated Bibles, electronic Bibles, Bible covers, Bible tabs, and Bible marking kits. Seth's favorite items were the Bible bookmarks with biblical-character finger puppets glued on the tip. Larry went directly to the front desk. A middle-aged woman in a mustard-yellow polyester pantsuit and helmet hair stood behind the cash register.

"I want to get my wife something special for the tenth anniversary of the CHRIST Act," Larry said.

"That's tomorrow," the woman said. "Just like a husband to wait until the last second."

Larry grinned and shrugged, pretending to be the helpless husband who can never get his act together to go shopping before it's almost too late.

"My friend Raphael said you carried some excellent antique Bibles," Larry said.

"We do indeed. Because of their delicate nature, we don't keep them out on display. I'll let the manager know you'd like to see them."

She left the room and returned shortly with the manager, a gray-haired man wearing an argyle sweater vest and a congenial smile.

"I understand you're interested in seeing our selection of antique Bibles," the manager said. "Who did you say recommended our store?"

"My good friend Raphael," Larry said.

"Ah yes, Raphael. How charitable of him to send you here. Please follow me."

The manager led them through a door marked "Employees Only." They entered a storeroom and walked past metal shelves filled with more Bibles. The manager stopped outside another door and turned to face them.

"Turn your cellphones off," he said.

Seth and Larry obeyed. The manager unlocked the door. It led to a basement stairway. As they descended the steps, the Praise music from the Bible store receded, and Seth could faintly make out a steady thumping sound that reminded him of the large clothes dryer he used to use at the laundromat before he and Maggie bought their own laundry machines.

The basement was filled with stacks of boxes. At the far end of the room was a set of metal double doors. The manager opened one of them and held it for Larry and Seth to enter. Larry handed the manager a five-dollar bill.

"Have a good evening, gentlemen," the manager said.

Loud forbidden music, flashing red lights, and exposed skin hit Seth in a rush of sensations. The space was huge and seemed to go on forever. The thumping Seth had heard earlier was dance music. Barely dressed women wandered among men seated at tables. The place smelled of perfume and testosterone.

Though most of the women wore traditional stripper outfits of

skimpy bras and panties, a good number had red devil's horns, devil's tails, and plastic pitchforks, as if they were going to a Halloween party. A stage dominated the center of the room on which a woman wearing only a nun's wimple and veil performed acrobatic moves on a stripper pole.

"This is the fanciest titty bar I've ever seen," Seth shouted into Larry's ear.

"This is the main room," Larry shouted back. "There are smaller rooms in the back that aren't as loud."

As they made their way through the crowd, many of the strippers said hello to Larry by name. He knew their names as well. Seth wouldn't have minded that Larry was a regular, except that this place couldn't be cheap. He hadn't had a steady job since returning from Savior Camp, which meant he must be spending Kelly's money.

A man who knew Seth's name stopped him, offering to buy him a drink. Seth didn't recognize him at first, but then realized that he was the communications director for the Minority Whip of the House of Representatives.

"Can I get a raincheck on that drink?" Seth said. "I'm here with a friend."

Seth scanned the room to see if he recognized anyone else. Indeed, it seemed half the customers were politicians, which Seth realized should not have surprised him at all.

Larry led him to a room that was smaller and much quieter. While the main room was set up as a rocking strip club, this one was an elegant bar. There were less than a dozen customers and only a few dancers. Its main function seemed to be for drinking. Larry and Seth perched themselves on stools at the bar. Larry ordered a boilermaker. Seth ordered a gin and tonic.

Larry dropped the shot of whiskey into his glass of beer and held it up for a toast. "Give strong drink to the one who is perishing, and wine to those in bitter distress. Let them drink and forget their poverty and remember their misery no more. Proverbs something something."

"Amen to that," Seth said.

They clinked their glasses. Larry downed his drink in long, sloppy gulps while Seth took a healthy sip and savored the way it stung his throat. Larry slammed his empty glass on the bar and ordered another.

"Man, I am in the mood for some pussy tonight," Larry said.

Despite being surrounded by gorgeous women, Seth was not in the mood for pussy. Not here. He only wanted Maggie, even if she swore she wouldn't have intercourse with him until after they escaped America.

Seth hadn't taken her ultimatum seriously. She was upset when she made it. Ordinary citizens were not allowed to leave the country. The borders were closely guarded by Hedge Patrol agents. Once Maggie got over the shock and grief of Amy's death, she would realize that they were trapped here and the only thing they could do was make the best of it. Then she would drop her ban on intercourse.

The bartender brought Larry a fresh drink. He dropped the shot in his beer and downed half the glass. Seth narrowed his eyes at Larry.

"You got the full Savior Camp experience," Seth said. "How is it that you're here getting drunk, and screwing prostitutes?"

Larry belched.

"Josiah," he said. "During my darkest moments in the camp, I focused on him. For his sake, I refused to let them destroy me. Josiah needs me to make sure the government doesn't do the same thing to him."

Larry got ready to take another gulp of his drink but put the glass down. He grabbed Seth's shoulder, making him wince. It was like talking to a wild bear; Seth never knew when Larry was going to take a playful swipe at him.

"I'm sorry for getting you fined," Larry said. "We both know you didn't curse. When I saw you playing with Josiah, the way I wish I was still able to play with him, but I can't because my head is so fucked up, I lost my mind."

Larry let go and Seth rubbed his shoulder.

"Forget about it," Seth said. "Water under the bridge."

Larry leaned in close. His beer-and-whiskey breath washed over Seth.

"You'd make a good father," Larry said. "When are you going to knock up Maggie? Behold, children are a heritage from the Lord, the fruit of the womb a reward. Psalm 127:3."

"Is this appropriate conversation to have in a whorehouse?" Seth said.

Larry guffawed and slapped him on the back. The bear took a swipe at him after all.

A statuesque woman with large balloon breasts and narrow hips slunk over to the two men. She draped her slender arm around Larry's shoulder. She smelled of lavender and vanilla.

"Hey, Larry," she said.

"Hey, Angel," Larry said.

Her name was appropriate. She wore a silvery-white corset, a white wig, white panties, and white stockings held up with white garters. Strapped to her back were fur-lined angel wings.

"Am I the lucky girl who gets to take you to heaven tonight?" Angel said.

"Love each other deeply, because love covers over a multitude of sins. Peter 4:8," Larry said.

"I'll take that as a yes."

Larry downed his drink and tossed money on the bar. He put his arm around Angel's waist, winking at Seth.

"Find yourself a girl," Larry said, "and meet me back here in two hours."

Larry and Angel left Seth alone at the bar. He had wondered how he was going to get out of actually having sex with a prostitute, and Larry had solved his problem. Larry would never know if Seth found a girl or not. He just had to chill out on this barstool for two hours. Plenty of time to make up a story about getting laid. Meanwhile, there was a TV over the bar tuned to a football game. The Baltimore Apostles were playing the New England Blessed. He couldn't stand the Blessed, so he prayed that they would lose.

Seth had just ordered another gin and tonic when two men sat on stools next to him. One was tall, flabby, and wore an ill-fitting suit. The other was short and sinewy, with slicked-back red hair and cold blue eyes.

Flabby Guy seemed nervous and out of place. He probably felt out of place everywhere he went. Short Guy wore expensive clothes that clung to his body to show that he worked out and had money. His posture was rigid to make him appear taller. They ordered drinks and were soon engaged in conversation. Seth turned his attention to the television and forgot about them. He tried to concentrate on the game but kept checking his watch for when Larry was supposed to return. The two men spoke softly, and their voices became background noise, until Short Guy started shouting.

"Damn it!" he said. "Stop dicking me around. Do you want to cross the border or not?"

Flabby Guy looked around the room nervously.

"Keep it down," he said. "People will hear you."

Short Guy slapped Flabby Guy. The sudden aggression got everyone's attention.

"We're in a fucking illegal whorehouse," Short Guy said. "Nobody is going to turn us in."

Flabby Guy rubbed his cheek and stared at the floor. The bartender hurried over to them.

"Hey," the bartender said. "If you can't behave yourself, then you'll have to leave."

Short Guy held up his hands.

"It's okay," he said. "I'm a salesman and sometimes I get too assertive trying to make a sale."

Flabby Guy took out his wallet and placed money on the bar.

"I have to go," he said.

"What about our deal?" Short Guy said.

"I have to think about it."

Flabby Guy rushed out of the room. Short Guy sighed and

hunched over his drink. He downed it and ordered another.

"Can you believe that jerk?" Short Guy said.

Seth looked around to make sure he was talking to him. They were alone at the bar and the bartender had his back to them.

"I don't know," Seth said. "I have no idea what you two were talking about."

The Short Guy laughed.

"I didn't make it obvious enough?" he said.

Seth debated whether or not to continue this conversation. His first impression of this man was that he was an asshole. Then again, Seth worked in politics. He talked to assholes all day.

"Can I ask you a question without you slapping me?" Seth said.

Short Guy chuckled.

"Depends on the question," he said.

"Are you a coyote?"

"That depends. Are you a road runner? Beep. Beep."

"You know what I mean."

The bartender brought Short Guy a fresh drink. He took a gulp before placing it on the bar.

"Do I smuggle people across the Mexican border for a fee?" he said as he puffed out his chest. "Yes, I do."

Seth wondered if Short Guy was telling the truth. He agreed that it was safe for a smuggler to talk freely about his business in an illegal brothel, but he didn't think a true smuggler would brag about it, especially not to strangers.

"Julian Cross," he said, reaching his hand over the stools between them.

"Seth." They shook hands.

Julian moved over so that they were sitting side by side. Seth took a sip of his gin and tonic. He could feel the alcohol buzzing in his brain. Since New Prohibition, he only drank contraband booze on special occasions. His body wasn't used to this much alcohol in one sitting, and his tongue was getting ahead of him.

"Just out of curiosity," Seth said. "If somebody did want to cross the border, how would they go about doing that?"

"I'm pretty good at reading people," Julian said. "I had a feeling you wanted to go south."

Seth recognized the term "go south" as slang for crossing the border into Mexico.

"I'm just asking for a friend," Seth said. Which was technically true. Maggie wanted to leave America more than he did.

Julian slid a business card out of his wallet and handed it to Seth. It was for a towing service in Canaan, Indiana.

"Call the number on the card," Julian said. "Tell whomever answers that you need help getting home and they'll bring you to me. I'll take care of the rest."

"How much?" Seth said as he studied the card.

Julian mentioned a number and Seth's eyes widened. Julian laughed.

"I'm expensive because I guarantee safe passage," Julian said. "Nobody else can do that."

"Really? How can you guarantee that Hedge Patrol won't catch you?"

"That's none of your damn business. I don't take checks. Cash only."

Seth put Julian's business card in his pocket. He'd show the card to Maggie when he got home. That would prove to her that he was taking her seriously about going south, without having to actually call the number.

One of the strippers wearing devil's horns, tail, and red lingerie slinked into the room. She leaned against the bar next to Julian.

"Hi, I'm Lucy," she said. "Am I the lucky girl who gets to drag you to hell tonight?"

Julian looked her over and nudged Seth.

"What do you think?" he said.

"She's a hot little devil," Seth said.

Lucy grinned and ran her finger from her neck to her belly button.

"You know what they say," she said. "You can't be saved until you sin."

"What the hell," Julian said as he fished his wallet out of his back pocket. He handed her two twenties. "Can we do it here?"

"Sure," Lucy said.

Seth's stomach lurched. He'd never heard of any brothel where the prostitutes had sex with the johns out in the open. Weren't they supposed to go to a room somewhere? He didn't want to watch Lucy and Julian have sex, but he was too shocked to move.

Lucy stripped off her bra and panties but kept her horns and heels on. She asked the bartender to play "Pour Some Sugar on Me." The song blasted from the room's dedicated sound system. Julian leaned on the bar and watched Lucy's nude body sway.

Seth motioned for the bartender.

"Need a refill?" the bartender said.

"She asked if she could take him to hell," Seth said. "I thought that was some kind of code for soliciting sex."

The bartender watched Lucy as she bounced her ass at Julian.

"Nope," he said. "She was just offering him a table dance."

Seth blushed.

"You could see why I assumed that," he said.

"This part of the Family Bible Store is strictly a strip club," the bartender said. "The brothel is in the back. The girls here only dance. The girls back there only fuck. Would you like directions to the brothel?"

"No, thank you."

Seth got off his stool and tested his legs which weren't as woozy as he feared. He left Julian and Lucy in the middle of her table dance. He searched the main room until he found Larry. He was at a table near the back, slumped in a chair with his legs spread wide. A woman danced naked in front of him, but it wasn't Angel. She wasn't an angel or a devil. She had short brown hair, small breasts, and wide hips. For one crazy moment, Seth thought the woman was Larry's wife. Not that Seth would know what Kelly looked like naked.

Seth sat in the chair next to Larry, who didn't acknowledge his presence. His full attention was focused on the dancer's butt.

"Larry, we need to go," Seth yelled.

Larry didn't respond, so Seth waved his hand in front of his face. He looked at Seth and blushed like a man who'd been caught paying for a table dance from a stripper who looked just like his wife.

"I made a covenant with my eyes not to look lustfully at a young woman. Job 31:1," Larry said.

"Are you sure about that?" Seth said.

"Has it been two hours already?"

"Come on. It's time to go home."

They left the Family Bible Store. Outside, the cool air brought welcome relief from the stifling heat of the club, yet it couldn't remove the smell of perfume and alcohol that clung to their clothes.

"Are you sober enough to drive?" Seth said.

"I only had two drinks," Larry said.

They climbed into the car, and Seth watched Larry as he drove.

"I'm guessing that you never drink enough to get drunk," Seth said.

"Can't afford to drink that much," Larry said.

"Do you ever go to the brothel or do you just get table dances?"

"Can't afford the brothel either."

Despite Larry's time at the Savior Camp, he was still a decent liar. He almost sounded convincing.

"That girl who was dancing for you," Seth said. "The one with short brown hair. She was very pretty."

Larry nodded slowly.

"For where your treasure is, there your heart will be also. Matthew 6:21," he said.

"You know," Seth said. "You could try talking to Kelly."

"I tried. But the Bible verses kept getting in the way."

CHAPTER 19

Freeman and Mary Wingard's limo arrived at National Church One at the same time as Roy Arnold's. They climbed out of their respective cars and stood together on the sidewalk.

"Look at those clouds," Roy said. "God is about to cry tears of joy because the CHRIST Act has returned the rule and reign of the cross to America."

Freeman and Mary gazed at the darkening sky. The rain would be here soon, and if the strong winds were any indicator, it was going to be a heavy downpour.

"Sometimes a storm is just a storm," Mary said.

Roy, Freeman, and Mary ducked inside, happy to escape the bone-chilling gusts blowing off the Potomac River. National Church One was the country's main house of worship. Formerly the John F. Kennedy Center for Performing Arts, the site was chosen because of its ample space and proximity to the nation's seat of government. Better to serve as a place where the spirit of God dwells than an elitist entertainment club.

They entered the Grand Foyer. The John F. Kennedy bust had been replaced with a white marble statue of Jesus from Michelangelo's Pieta reclining in the lap of Abraham from the Lincoln Memorial. The figures were life-sized, giving the impression that they might rise and join the congregation.

"Where are your two sons?" Roy asked.

"Knowing how busy their father was going to be today," Mary said, nudging Freeman in the ribs, "they decided to celebrate with their in-laws."

As if to prove Mary's point, Missioner Lim approached Freeman and requested a moment in private.

"Go on without me," Freeman said. "I won't be long."

While Roy and Mary climbed the stairs to their reserved box seats,

Missioner Lim led Freeman to the box office.

"We have a gate crasher, sir," Lim said.

Freeman was about to reprimand her for bothering him with such a trivial matter, before realizing that Lim wouldn't have brought it to his attention unless it was absolutely necessary.

"Who is it?" Freeman said.

"Eleanor Randall," Lim said. "She doesn't have an invitation, but she insists that we let her in."

Freeman dug his hands into his pockets and studied the carpet pattern on the floor. National Church One was open to the general public during regular weekly services, but on holidays like Easter or the CHRIST Act anniversary, an invitation was required to get in. Otherwise, congressmen wouldn't be guaranteed a seat.

"Where is she?" Freeman said.

"We've detained her in the gift shop," Lim said. "It's closed today."

"I'll talk to her."

Freeman followed Lim. She took a route that avoided the crowd gathering outside the entrances to the three theaters which had been renamed Pilgrim's Hall, Patriot's Sanctuary, and the Billy Graham Auditorium. There were services being held in all three today, but the most prestigious was taking place in Patriot's Sanctuary.

There were many people who would rather not see Chip Randall's widow on this day in particular. No one minded that Chip had been in a Savior Camp; it was as if he'd gone into rehab, and he was sure to return fully blessed. Once Freeman had revealed the truth about how Chip died, however, pundits and politicians quickly rewrote history so that his role in the creation of the CHRIST Act was diminished to the point where he was hardly involved at all. It wasn't fair to make Eleanor Randall pay the price of her husband's dishonor. She had as much right to be here as anyone.

Eleanor sat in a folding chair in the middle of the gift shop. Two missioners stood behind her. They were surrounded by racks filled with souvenir T-shirts and shelves loaded with baseball caps, Bibles, laminated copies of the CHRIST Act, and miniatures of the statue of Jesus in the lap of Lincoln. Eleanor clutched her purse over her chest like a shield. When Freeman entered the store, she sprang to her feet.

"Freeman!" she said. "Thank Jesus. Tell your people that there's been some sort of mistake."

Freeman glanced at Missioner Lim. She nodded and motioned for the other missioners to follow her out of the shop, leaving Freeman alone with Eleanor.

"I'm sorry about this," Freeman said. "You should have called me."

"They upset me so much," she said. "I must look atrocious."

Eleanor adjusted her glasses and patted her gray hair. She had never been an attractive woman, and the years of dutiful suffering hadn't been kind to her.

"You look wonderful," Freeman said. "But I'll make sure you have a chance to freshen up."

Eleanor snapped open her purse and took out a wadded tissue. She dabbed her dry eyes.

"I don't mean to make a fuss," she said. "My invitation must have gotten lost in the mail. Certainly, I'm on a list somewhere that proves I was invited."

"We both know you weren't invited," Freeman said.

Eleanor glared at Freeman over her glasses.

"Don't you dare kick me out," she said. "I never lost faith in God or country. Haven't I been punished enough for his actions?"

"Come sit with me," Freeman said. "I know Mary will be thrilled to see you."

Eleanor used her tissue to dry real tears.

"Bless you, Freeman," she said.

Freeman and Eleanor arrived at the deacon's reserved box seats just as a group of teenagers in matching red-and-gold robes with their school insignia on their chests were walking out onto the stage. Mary leaped to her feet and hugged Eleanor. She pointed at the stage, explaining to Eleanor that the teenagers were the winners of a national high-school gospel-choir competition.

"How delightful," Eleanor said.

Roy stood and took her hand.

"What a pleasant surprise," he said. "Thank you for joining us."

Roy gave Freeman a sideways glance. Freeman understood this to mean that Roy was indeed surprised, but not in a pleasant way, and wasn't at all thankful that Eleanor was joining them.

The church was packed with members of Congress, all nine Supreme Court justices, high-ranking military officers, foreign dignitaries, CEOs of major corporations, and special guests. Mary and Eleanor sat together by the railing, while Freeman and Roy sat behind them. The service was presided over by the chaplain of the Joint Chiefs of Staff. Television cameras beamed the service live on every channel.

After the high-school choir group finished their performance with a rousing rendition of "Onward, Christian Soldiers," disabled veterans of Operation Ultimate Crusade were honored with special prayers. Servicemen in dress uniform lined the stage as the chaplain blessed the vets for their sacrifice and perseverance. The tribute ended with everyone standing for the pledge of allegiance to the New Glory flag.

The veterans hobbled off or were wheeled away. Next on the program were the honored speakers. Roy had chosen them and decided in what order they would appear. Political careers hung on how well their speeches were received.

As Judy Cross stepped onto the pulpit, many men rose from their seats and exited the sanctuary. Eleanor also left her seat. She spun around and scowled at Roy.

"You don't invite me," Eleanor said. "Yet you let that woman give a speech?" She thrust her hand toward the stage.

Roy formed a church steeple with his fingers.

"Judy has something to offer the Brethren," he said. "Do you?"

Eleanor struggled to respond but only managed to make a few strangled noises before she stormed out. Mary rushed after her. Freeman wondered if perhaps he should go as well, but Roy put his hand on Freeman's arm.

"Are you still planning on raiding the Jewish church tomorrow?" Roy said.

Freeman glanced at the door. Mary would know how to console Eleanor better than he could. He was better at running Hedge Protection.

"We take them down tomorrow," Freeman said. "I know you were worried about how it would look to arrest Jews. The synagogue is in an isolated location. The raid will be a covert operation. The public will never know."

Roy leaned close to Freeman as if they were on a date.

"I want the raid to be public," Roy said. "I've already notified NNN that Hedge Protection will contact them with details about the time and location of the raid."

Freeman's fingers drummed the armrest.

"You're not concerned that they're Jewish?" he said.

"It's more important that the American people know that they're safe," Roy said.

CHAPTER 20

The storm the city had been waiting for finally arrived, and unleashed a heavy downpour. Seth ignored the steady patter on his windows. It was time for Senator Sam Owens to deliver the speech that Seth had written for him. Owens firmly believed that the success of the speech would determine whether or not he would be assigned to the committee on Biblical Law and Administration, and he had assured Seth that both of their fortunes would rise as a result.

Seth turned up the sound on his television.

Senator Owens showed no apprehension as he strutted to the podium in Patriot's Sanctuary. As a former minister, preaching the gospel was where he was most at home. His diamond cufflinks sparkled in the spotlight.

"As a Christian Nation, we are under attack from numerous enemies," Owens said. "But I am not afraid. Are you afraid? Of course, you aren't. Because of the CHRIST Act, America has returned to praising the Lord instead of hiding from Him. Now, it's our enemies who hide. They hide because they know that under God's protection, America has become an indestructible fortress."

Seth glanced at the ceiling. Maggie was upstairs asleep in bed. She had told him to wake her when Owens came on, but Seth decided to let her keep resting.

Maggie had been sleeping a lot since Amy Bird died. No matter how much Maggie slept, she never seemed rested. Seth understood why. Not only had Maggie lost her best friend, she'd lost the career she'd worked so hard to build.

Owens reached the part of the speech where he listed the enemies of America that every citizen must be on the lookout for. Along with the usual suspects like sexual deviants and vegetarians, Owens listed those who deny the authority of Christ, those who depart from the faith, and those who deny the scriptures. He promised that America would cast them out like vermin.

Seth's stomach lurched.

Though he'd written and rewritten the speech and had read it aloud for pacing, he had needed Owens to deliver it as a fire-and-brimstone sermon to hear it clearly.

Seth had departed from the faith, and by doing so he was denying the authority of Christ. He had put himself on the list of enemies that must be cast out. Seth didn't believe he was America's enemy, and he certainly didn't think of himself as vermin, but from the way the audience was shouting amen, the American people were convinced that he was.

Seth muted the television and went into the kitchen. He took the orange juice out of the refrigerator and got a plastic bottle with a label that read "white vinegar" from the cabinet under the sink. The bottle contained contraband vodka, and Seth mixed the two together into a screwdriver that was more alcohol than orange juice.

He took a generous sip of the drink to drown his colossal stupidity. He still felt incredibly dense, so he took another sip. Drink in hand, he stood at the kitchen window and stared at his back yard.

Josiah had left his red tricycle in the yard. It sat on a dirt patch that the driving rain had turned to mud. Sweet rambunctious Josiah. As he grew older, he would learn in school that people like Seth were his enemy. Seth shivered.

He carried his screwdriver into the living room and started a fire in the fireplace. He fetched his copy of Owens's speech, along with all the early drafts from his briefcase, and fed them into the flames page by page. He paused when he heard Maggie coming down the stairs.

She entered the living room wearing a T-shirt and yoga pants. Maggie's hair was a mess and her eyes hadn't fully opened yet. She came over to Seth and leaned into him. He put his arms around her. She smelled of sleep and Maggie.

"When does Sam give his speech?" Maggie said.

Seth frowned at the television. A gospel group was singing.

"You missed it," Seth said.

Maggie placed her hand on Seth's chest.

"You were supposed to wake me up," she said.

"You needed your sleep."

Maggie smiled at the fireplace.

"Nice fire," she said. "What are you burning?"

"The speech I wrote for Senator Owens. You were right. We have to go south."

Maggie's eyes opened wide. She picked up his drink and tasted it.

"I think I'm going to need one of these," she said.

While Seth fixed Maggie a screwdriver in the kitchen, he told her about how he'd finally gotten his head out of his ass and realized that they needed to find a way to get across the border into Mexico. As she sipped her drink and nodded her approval, he told her about meeting Julian Cross at the Family Bible Store.

"Julian Cross?" Maggie said. "That's Judy Cross's son."

"No way," Seth said. "It couldn't possibly be the same guy."

They stared out the window at their yard, which the rain had turned into one big mud puddle.

"When do we go?" Maggie said.

"We'll need supplies," Seth said. "Food, money, clothes."

"I can get that on my lunch break tomorrow."

Seth panicked. Though he had just said they should go, he didn't feel ready to actually do it.

"We can't move too fast," Seth said. "Someone will notice. We'll take small amounts of money out separately once a week and put it aside. Get non-perishable food when you go to the grocery store, but not too much."

"Why not just grab everything we need and go before anyone knows what's happening?"

"Nothing alerts the police faster than someone leaving in a hurry."

Maggie pouted. Seth had been married long enough to know the pout meant she didn't agree with him, but she wasn't going to argue about it. For now. Maggie rubbed her arms.

"It's cold," Maggie said. "Let's turn on the heat."

"I have a better idea," Seth said. "Let's burn the rest of the speech."

CHAPTER 21

The African American boy couldn't have been older than sixteen. He wore his baseball cap sideways and a large gold cross on a thick chain around his neck. He was out of breath from running after Maggie. He thrust his hand toward her.

"You forgot this, ma'am," he said.

He handed Maggie a credit card. Her card. She didn't normally forget things like this, but today wasn't a normal day.

"Do you work for the store?" Maggie asked.

"No ma'am. I was in line behind you. The cashier noticed you forgot your card, and I said I'd take it to you."

Maggie took out her wallet and reached for a ten-dollar bill. The boy waved his hands.

"No need for that," he said. "Have a blessed day."

"I will. Thank you."

The boy smiled. Maggie smiled back. He headed back toward the store.

Maggie took her large shopping bag, which contained two hiking packs and assorted trail snacks, to her car. She put it in the trunk, next to shopping bags filled with supplies that she'd purchased at other malls that day. Though Seth had insisted that they gather their supplies for going south over a careful period of months, Maggie decided to do most of it today, shopping for each item at a different location.

She hadn't planned on shopping today. It was her first day in her new position as Bill Garmon's production assistant. Bill had two PAs already, and didn't need another one. After some deliberation, he'd sent Maggie out to get donuts. When Maggie got back with a box of assorted pastries, she lied and told Bill she had an appointment at a fertility clinic that afternoon. Bill told her to take the rest of the day off. Maggie was certain that he was going to give her all kinds of mindless busy work, but she had conjured up the magic word. Baby.

After stowing away her shopping bag, Maggie realized that she hadn't eaten since breakfast and it was already past two. She went to a café and bought a grilled-chicken sandwich and a small salad. Yesterday's rainstorm had moved on, and the sun had returned, so she sat at an outdoor table.

Of all the shopping centers Maggie had visited that day, this place, Downtown Silver Spring, was the most affluent. As Maggie ate, she watched people go by. Everybody looked happy and relaxed. Children in swimsuits played in an interactive fountain.

Four teens, two boys and two girls, and their chaperone stood in front of the movie theater and debated which movie to see. The boys carried AK-47s that were almost as tall as they were, struggling to look cool under the weight of their weapons. The girls had pink pistols in matching holster belts of fluorescent orange with a sparkly cross on the buckle.

The boys wanted to see *Seven Years*, an action thriller full of special effects about life after the Rapture, during the chaotic years of Tribulation, but the chaperone overruled the boys and chose a romantic comedy called *When Jerry Met Terri in Heaven*. Maggie guessed that the chaperone was the mother of one of the girls. They both had light-blonde hair and athletic bodies. "Mom. Remember you said I could get bullets for my gun today," the girl whined, proving Maggie right. "I said, I'd think about it," the mother replied.

The boy who returned Maggie's credit card sat at a nearby table with an older woman that Maggie guessed was his mother. An elderly white couple sat at the table next to them.

The man leaned toward the boy's mother. "Excuse me," he said. "What's your denomination?"

"I was Baptist," the mother replied, "but now I'm American."

"We were Presbyterian," the man said, pointing at his wife and himself, "but now we're American too."

"I heard there was going to be a performance today," the man's wife said. "I can't remember if it's a snake handler or a laying on of hands."

The boy took out his smartphone and his thumbs ran over the surface.

"It's a snake handler," the boy said. "3:30 on the Christian Heritage Stage."

Maggie made a mental note to avoid that area. She didn't like snakes. Gazing at the shops, she noticed a familiar name, New Miracle Fertility Clinic. Bill might ask Maggie for proof she actually went to a clinic. She finished her lunch and went inside.

The lobby was painted in pink and light blue. Large photo prints of smiling babies hung on the walls. The receptionist was a young woman wearing fancy eyeglasses.

"Do you have an appointment?" she asked.

Maggie shuffled to the receptionist desk.

"Sorry, I don't," she said. "I was hoping to pick up a brochure or maybe just a business card."

"It's okay if you don't have an appointment. I'm sure we can fit you in."

"No really, I'm not ready. I still need to talk this over with my husband. Do you have something with the name of the clinic on it that I could take with me?"

The receptionist leaned over the desk.

"Don't worry," she said. "We understand. Fertility treatments are expensive, and you're not sure you can afford them."

"Yes," Maggie said. "That's it. I can't afford them. Do you have a price sheet that I could show my husband?"

The receptionist picked up her phone and pushed a button.

"Christie? There's a young lady out here who'd like to discuss payment options. That's right. Thank you, Christie." The receptionist hung up the phone. "Have a seat, ma'am. Christie will be right out."

Maggie considered leaving without some kind of proof to show Bill that she'd been here, but now she was curious to know how much infertility treatments cost. She didn't have to tell them that she wasn't infertile. Maggie barely had time to sit down and flip through a *Christian People* magazine before an athletic brunette in a dark-blue business suit entered the lobby.

"Hi, I'm Christie," she said, firmly shaking Maggie's hand. "I'm a sales representative for New Miracle. Let's go to my office."

Christie's office was neat, modern, and smelled like freshly installed carpet. She didn't waste time laying out Maggie's payment options.

"You're looking at a minimum of twelve thousand. I know that seems like a lot of money, but I can show you our success rate and testimonials from former clients. Insurance will not cover the treatments. We offer installment plans, and there are some low-cost options, but we'd have to determine if you're eligible."

"How do most people pay?" Maggie asked.

"Various methods. They borrow money from their parents. I know one woman did a fundraiser at her church. Many of our clients take out loans."

"You can get a loan for fertility treatments?"

"There's a bank around the corner that we do a lot of business with. If you have time, I could call them and get you set up with a loan today."

"Today? Even without my husband?"

Christie laughed.

"Like he's going to say no when he finds out it's for a baby?"

An hour and a half later, Maggie walked out of the bank with a fifteen-thousand-dollar loan and a checking account to write checks from it. Maggie felt like a bank robber, but when she told them that it was for a baby they practically forced her to take the money.

Poor Christie. She was so sure Maggie was another woman desperate to become pregnant that she never bothered to get Maggie's name. Christie was waiting for her to come back to the clinic to fill out the paperwork for her fertility treatments, but instead Maggie got in her car and drove until she spotted another branch of the same bank. She went into the bank and cashed a check for eight-thousand dollars.

At first, the teller eyed the check suspiciously, until she saw that Maggie had written "for fertility treatment" on the memo line.

"I love babies," the teller said, "don't you?"

"I do now," Maggie said.

CHAPTER 22

A s the sun set and the sky turned a dark blue interlaced with streaks of pink, Seth began gathering his things. He'd have to get going if he planned to make it to services by sundown. Seth was full of nervous energy. He dreaded telling Rabbi Leah that tonight would be the last time he attended services.

Seth explained to Maggie that he wanted to go one more time so that he could tell Rabbi Leah that he was leaving the congregation. Otherwise, she would worry that something had happened to him.

He turned off his computer, swung the strap of his range bag over his shoulder, and his phone rang.

"Cheese and rice. I almost made it."

Seth recognized the number on the Caller ID. He picked up the receiver.

"Hey, Reggie. I was just about to walk out the door."

"I need to see you in my office. Now."

Seth was about to ask why, but Reggie had already hung up. Hopefully, whatever he wanted wouldn't take long. Seth thought that maybe he could still be on time, and took his range bag with him.

The moment he entered the room, Seth could feel something was wrong. Reggie sat hunched over his desk. He lifted his head. His eyes were puffy.

"Have you been crying?" Seth said.

Reggie pulled a tissue from a box on the desk and wiped his face. He motioned for Seth to sit in the visitor's chair. Seth placed his bag on the floor.

"Who died?" Seth said.

"Don't go to your secret Jewish church."

Seth gripped the armrests.

"Why?" he said. "What do you know?"

Reggie opened his desk's top drawer and took out a file folder stamped with the word "Confidential." He extracted a stack of photographs from the file and spread them out across the desk.

At first, Seth wasn't sure what he was looking at. The photos were of people walking toward a building. Then, Seth recognized himself, Rabbi Leah, and other members of the congregation. They were surveillance photos of his congregation entering their secret location.

"Where did you get these?" Seth said.

"Hedge Protection has been watching the church for weeks. They're going to raid it tonight."

Seth stood up abruptly and almost tripped over his chair. "I have to warn them," he said. Reggie hurried around his desk and got to the door before he could and wrapped his arms tightly around Seth.

"It's too late," Reggie said. "Agents have already surrounded the building. They'd grab you before you got in the door."

"How do you know all this?"

"You have to leave town immediately. At the most, you have a couple hours' head start."

"How long have you known?"

"About the raid? Just a few days."

"Why did you wait until now to tell me?"

Reggie released Seth's arms and motioned for him to sit down. Seth reluctantly complied, and Reggie returned to his chair.

"Does the senator know?" Seth asked.

"No," Reggie said. He bit his lower lip. "I had to do it. They caught me."

"Again?"

Tears ran down Reggie's face. He pulled another tissue from the box and wiped his nose.

"I got caught cruising in Montrose Park," Reggie said. "I knew I shouldn't be there. I tried to be strong, but I was weak."

Seth almost felt sorry for Reggie. This would be his third offense. After his first two times, Reggie received gay conversion therapy. The third time meant they were going to castrate him. The government no longer used chemical castration. Reggie had known that if he got caught they would surgically remove his testicles.

"I thought they were going to take me directly to a hospital for the operation," Reggie said. "Instead, Deacon Wingard himself met with me."

Seth glared at him. He balled his fist, but instead of hitting Reggie he shook his head. Seth couldn't believe that he had considered this man to be one of his closest friends. Reggie glanced at him, then quickly looked away.

"You told Deacon Wingard about me to save your balls?" Seth said.

"Catching a secret Jew gave him a bigger hard-on than castrating a faggot."

"How long has Hedge Protection been watching me?"

"Since I made the deal."

Seth pounded his forehead with his fists.

"That still doesn't explain how you got the file."

"It doesn't matter how I got the file. The point is, I got it, and it says the raid is tonight."

Seth looked out Reggie's window. The sun had set. Seth pictured Rabbi Leah standing in front of the tiny ark and opening her siddur, letting the group know that the evening service was about to begin. Those good people wouldn't just be arrested and sent to a Savior Camp. Practicing a non-Christian religion was treason, punishable by death.

"I led Hedge Protection right to them," Seth said. "Their blood is on my hands."

Seth stood and picked up his range bag. His mind raced at double speed, trying to decide the best way to escape.

"I'm sorry," Reggie said.

"I really want to punch you in the face," Seth said.

"If you had time, I'd let you. But you have to go. Now."

MAGGIE HAD JUST PARKED THE CAR IN THE GARAGE WHEN HER CELL-phone rang. Seth's name was on the caller ID. He was calling sooner than she expected. Maggie had hoped she would have time to hide the things she'd bought today. Seth would freak out if he knew what she'd done.

"Hey, when are you coming home?" Maggie said.

"They've been watching me," Seth said. "They know everything."

Maggie leaned against the car and slumped down until her butt was on the ground.

"Oh my God!" she said.

"I almost didn't call," Seth said. "They might be listening."

"Take a cab home," Maggie said. "I'm already here."

Seth began to cry. Maggie yearned to hold him.

"I'm so sorry for getting you into this," he said. "Get in the car and drive away."

"I'm not going anywhere without you. Please, Seth. Come home to me."

CHAPTER 23

Maggie took the stairs too quickly and tripped. Her knee banged into the step, but she managed to hold on to the two hiking packs in her hands. Ignoring the pain, she hurried up the last steps and into the bedroom, where she opened drawers, pulled out clothes, and stuffed them into the packs. Once they were full, she split the eight-thousand dollars she'd gotten that day into two stacks and put one in each pack, just in case she and Seth were separated. The idea of not being with Seth made her want to cry.

She peeked out the window. There was no sign of Seth. There was also no sign of Hedge Protection. That didn't mean they weren't out there waiting for him to get home.

Maggie carried the backpacks downstairs and into the kitchen. She was shoving bags of trail mix into the packs when she heard the front door open.

"Seth?" she said.

"Yeah," he said.

Maggie rushed into Seth's arms and hugged him tightly.

"Let's grab some food, a few clothes, jump in the car, and go," he said.

"Way ahead of you."

She grabbed his wrist and dragged him into the kitchen, beaming as he inspected the hiking packs.

"This is everything we need," Seth said. "When did you do this?"

"I went shopping today," Maggie said. "I know you said to wait, but I couldn't."

"Thank God you never listen to me."

"I do sometimes."

They were about to leave by the kitchen door when the doorbell rang. They froze.

"Can't be Hedge Protection," Seth said. "They wouldn't bother to ring the bell."

"Whoever it is, we can't get out of the driveway without them seeing us."

The doorbell rang again.

"I have to answer the door," Seth said. "Put everything in the car."

WHILE MAGGIE SLIPPED OUT THE BACK DOOR, SETH HEADED TOWARD THE front of the house. He took deep breaths to calm himself. Whoever was out there leaned on the doorbell, showing their impatience. Seth opened the front door and shook his head. He should have guessed.

"Hello, Darlene," he said.

CHAPTER 24

The tension inside the Hedge Protection Mobile Command Center was unmistakable. The SWAT team wasn't accustomed to having a deacon personally direct a tactical operation. Normally, Freeman Wingard oversaw raids from the command center at Hedge Protection headquarters. The last thing anybody wanted to do was screw up in front of the big boss.

"Missioner Stevens, status report," Freeman said into his headset.

"Alpha Team is in position," Missioner Stevens said. "All exits are covered. We are ready to move on your word, sir."

Freeman preferred to let his people do the jobs they were trained to do without him micromanaging, and would have stayed at headquarters if it hadn't been for Roy Arnold's insistence that the raid receive maximum news coverage. When the operation was over, Freeman would have to appear before the cameras, and that forced him to get personally involved.

Missioner Lim sat next to Freeman in the command center. She was usually in charge of these raids, and the deacon was glad to have her at his side.

"How am I doing, Missioner Lim?" Freeman said.

"Excellent, sir," she said.

Freeman studied the monitors. He counted nineteen thermal images of people sitting in rows. Nineteen people who had rejected Christ's blessing. Freeman turned his attention to the audio-surveillance monitor. They were singing in Hebrew. Their evening service had begun.

"Alpha Team stand by," Freeman said. "Commence attack in sixty seconds."

Missioner Lim started the digital countdown.

Another row of monitors had the green-tinted night vision of Alpha Team's helmet-cam video feeds. The missioners created white trails of light as they checked their weapons one last time.

The digital clock counted down to zero.

"Alpha Team go," Freeman said.

A missioner used a heavy-duty cable cutter to snip the line connected to the building's alarm system. With Missioner Stevens in the lead, Alpha Team hurried up the loading dock stairs and busted open the back door with a battering ram. Moving quickly through the dark, they stationed two men at the service elevator, while the rest of the team headed for the stairs.

"Deacon Wingard," Missioner Lim said. "They stopped singing."

Freeman's attention had been on Alpha Team as they approached their target. He turned to the thermal images of the congregation. Missioner Lim was right. They weren't singing, and they weren't sitting in rows. The heat signatures were huddled together into one large, glowing orange blob, and they were whispering to each other.

"Turn up the volume," Freeman said. "I want to hear what they're saying."

The audio-surveillance monitor was turned up until the whispers filled the interior of the mobile command center and echoed off the steel walls. Too many voices spoke at once. Freeman yanked his headset off and strained to pick out words. He couldn't tell if they were speaking English or Hebrew.

The whispering stopped, and each person repeated the same word. "Masada."

Freeman jammed his headset back on. "Stevens," he yelled, "the target has been alerted. I repeat, the target has been alerted. Get up there fast."

"I don't understand, sir," Missioner Stevens said.

"Am I the only one here with knowledge of ancient Israel besides the time of Jesus?" Freeman said.

The missioners stared at him in confusion.

If he'd had time, Freeman would have explained that Masada was a mountain fortress in Israel during the first Jewish-Roman War where a group of Jewish fighters were surrounded by the Roman army with no chance for escape. Rather than surrender, the Jews killed themselves and their families. Masada became a symbol of defiance against overwhelming odds.

"They know they can't escape," Freeman said. "They're going to kill themselves."

Every light in the twelve-story building came on at once. Alpha Team's night vision bloomed a bright white. A yellow cloud swallowed the thermal images of the nineteen Jews. Freeman shielded his eyes from the monitors as if he were blocking the sun. In his headset, he heard the confused shouts of Alpha Team as they struggled to regroup. Their shouts of frustration were suddenly drowned out by staccato bursts of gunfire. The audio was still turned up, and Freeman instinctively ducked from the barrage of sound.

"Man down!" Missioner Stevens shouted. "Multiple gun shots! Alpha Team fire at will!"

Freeman watched helplessly as chaos erupted outside his state-of-the-art mobile mission control center.

"Lower the volume," Missioner Lim said.

The monitors were quickly readjusted as the sound of gunfire continued. The chatter from Missioner Stevens and his team informed Freeman that they were under attack but couldn't determine the number of combatants.

Freeman looked about the control room. Lim had taken temporary control of operations. The missioners inside the mobile unit did what they'd been trained to do, calmly communicating with Alpha Team as they struggled to regain control of the situation in the office building. Freeman wished desperately that he was back at the command center.

Finally, the shooting ended, but the echo of gunshots rang in Freeman's ears. He watched Alpha Team's helmet-cam feeds as they moved cautiously across a brightly lit storeroom. Behind a fortress of copiers, they found a dead man clutching an Uzi sub-machine gun. Empty shell casings were scattered around him like confetti.

"I think he was a lone gunman," Missioner Stevens said.

"What are our casualties?" Freeman asked.

"Two confirmed deceased, three wounded."

Freeman glanced at Missioner Lim. She was coordinating the medical team.

"Medics are on their way," Freeman said. "Proceed with caution. He may not be the only armed resistance."

As Alpha Team methodically made their way up the stairs to the seventh floor, Freeman impatiently drummed his fingers on the armrests. He glanced at the monitor. There were no longer nineteen heat signatures. There was only one. Freeman could hear a female voice chanting in a rolling drone.

"*Yis'ga'dal v'yis'kadash sh'may ra'bbo.*"

Freeman guessed that it was some kind of Jewish prayer.

"*B'olmo dee'vro chir'usay v'yamlich malchu'say.*"

Alpha Team had reached the seventh floor and was preparing to break open the meeting-room door with their battering ram.

"*Ba'agolo u'viz'man koriv; v'imru Omein.*"

"Missioner Stevens," Freeman said, "see if the door's locked before you destroy it."

Stevens did as he was ordered. The door was unlocked. He pushed it open with his rifle barrel and led his men into the meeting room.

"Are you seeing this, sir?" Missioner Stevens said.

People were scattered about on the floor. Most of them were couples embracing, with eyes closed as if they had decided to take a nap. Alpha Team checked for vital signs and found none. On the table at the front of the room was a line of empty pill bottles.

"There's something on the floor," Stevens said.

"Besides dead people?" Freeman said.

"I believe it's sand."

One member of the congregation was still breathing. The lone survivor was a woman kneeling in front of a small open cabinet that contained what Freeman recognized was a Torah.

"Show me your hands!" Missioner Stevens ordered.

The woman didn't acknowledge his presence. She continued reciting her prayer. A white prayer shawl covered her head, shoulders, and arms. Her hands clutched a prayer book, and rocked back and forth as she chanted.

"*Yisborach v'yishtabach v'yispoar v'yisromam v'yismasay.*"

Freeman pointed at the monitor for Missioner Stevens's helmet cam.

"Missioner Lim," Freeman said. "Can you identify that woman?"

"Yes sir," she said. "That's Leah Gordon. She's the rabbi."

Missioner Stevens aimed his weapon at Rabbi Leah.

"Show me your hands now!" he said.

Rabbi Leah kept her eyes on her prayer book.

"I need to finish the prayer first," she said.

There was such authority to her voice that Missioner Stevens hesitated.

"What do I do, sir?" he said.

"She's not going anywhere," Freeman said. "Let her finish."

"*Oseh sholom bimromov, hu ya'aseh sholom olaynu, v'al kol yisroel; vimru Omein,*" Rabbi Leah said.

"Ask her what that prayer was," Freeman said.

"What were you singing?" Missioner Stevens said.

Rabbi Leah held her prayer book to her chest.

"It's the Mourner's Kaddish," she said

"As in mourning the dead?" Stevens said. "You prayed for these people here?"

"I recited the Kaddish for my people before you arrived. Then I recited it again for me."

Rabbi Leah dropped the prayer book, reached inside her shawl, and pulled out a handgun. She fired once. The view from Missioner Stevens's helmet-cam swayed and wobbled before it landed on the floor. Freeman saw the helmet-cams of the other missioners veer toward the woman. He saw the flash of their weapons as they shot her. Rabbi Leah's body slumped next to Missioner Stevens.

CHAPTER 25

As Darlene waited for Seth to invite her in, he noticed details about her that he'd never noticed before. For instance, she always wore the same maroon business suit with the FFV patch stitched to the jacket's shoulder, but now he saw that the suit didn't fit her well and the patch was faded.

Seth couldn't believe that he used to be scared of Darlene. Of course, he'd had good reason to fear her. With one bad report, she could have sent him to a Savior Camp. But that was before he'd found out that Hedge Protection was after him. Savior Camp would seem like summer camp compared to where they would send him.

"Can we do this some other time?" Seth said. "I was just about to leave."

Darlene pushed past Seth into the house.

"I called New Miracle, and they informed me that you didn't make an appointment," Darlene said.

"New miracle?"

"New Miracle Fertility Clinic. Remember?"

"You're right. We didn't."

Darlene's eyes grew wide and then narrowed into angry slits.

"Looks like I'll have to do an extra-careful inspection today," Darlene said.

Sweat trickled down Seth's back. He had to get rid of Darlene. Now. He could kill her, but he wasn't a murderer and it was way too messy. He remembered something Reggie had said the last time Darlene had made him late. Seth wasn't sure if he was more angry or hurt that Reggie had betrayed him, but he didn't have time to think about that now. Darlene was beginning to do her usual march through the house.

"Is this you as a boy?" Darlene said as she pointed at a photograph. "How old were you in this picture? You were so cute."

"We both know this is a waste of time," Seth said.

Darlene glared at him.

"I provide an important service for Hedge Protection," she said.

"Nothing you do will save your job. Has your supervisor discussed your severance pay? What about insurance?" Seth said.

Darlene fumbled with her briefcase, took out Seth's file, and scribbled on a page.

"You really did it this time, mister," she said. "You can't disrespect a Federal Faith Verification case worker."

"You know what I do for a living," Seth said. "I have access to information before it becomes public. Hedge Protection is about to terminate all female employees on FFV's staff."

Darlene's hand stopped with her pen suspended over the report. Seth could see doubt creeping into her.

"The Devil must have taken over your mind," she said. "Why else would you make up something so vile?"

"I'm sorry, Darlene," Seth said. "You deserve to know the truth."

"They can't fire me. I have seniority."

"Your supervisor was probably waiting until after the CHRIST Act celebration to tell you. Hard to enjoy the festivities if you've lost your job."

Darlene's eyes widened.

"But I'm one of their top case workers," she said.

"Doesn't matter. You're a woman. They figure your husband will provide for you."

The pen and the report fell from Darlene's hands.

"My husband is out of work. Hasn't been able to find anything for months. My kids are grown, but we look after my grandchild because my daughter and her husband can't find enough work to support their little boy. I can't lose this job. My family depends on me."

Seth felt terrible. As much as he hated Darlene's inspections, he knew that she thought she was doing God's work.

"I don't believe you," Darlene said. "I'm calling my supervisor right now, and he's going to tell me you're nothing but a liar."

Seth swallowed hard. He hadn't planned on what to do if Darlene called his bluff. He wanted to run out the door, jump in the car with Maggie, and drive away as fast as their car could go, but he was too scared to move. Seth stood helplessly as Darlene took out her cellphone and dialed her supervisor's number.

She walked out on the porch so that Seth couldn't hear her. Again, he told himself to run, but his legs still wouldn't budge. Two minutes later, Darlene came back into the house.

"They were going to tell me next week," she said. "They've already hired a man to replace me." Darlene handed Seth his personal file. "Here's a souvenir. Just so you know, I should have verified your conversion months ago, but I was told to prolong my inspections for three years. Had something to do with government funding and quotas. Now if you will excuse me, I have to go home and tell my husband that we can't afford to take our grandchild to the doctor next week."

After Darlene left, Seth opened his range bag, and took out his handgun and belt holster. He'd never worn a gun before, but he felt now was an appropriate time to start. Seth went to the garage, but Maggie wasn't in the car. Neither were the hiking packs. This seemed like the perfect time to drop dead from a heart attack.

Larry's car backed out of his tiny garage. Seth turned away to avoid talking to him. He heard the car window roll down, but pretended to be looking for something in his garage. Seth was in no mood to listen to Larry recite scripture or suggest another trip to the Family Bible Store.

"Seth," Maggie hissed. "Get in."

Seth spun around. Maggie was in Larry's car, and Larry was driving. She motioned for Seth to get in the back.

"Hurry up," she ordered.

Seth got into the back seat. Larry pulled out of his driveway and onto the street.

"Maybe you should lie on the seat," Larry said. "Just to be on the safe side."

"Yeah," Maggie said. "Get down, Seth."

He did as he was told. With his head on the seat, all Seth could see were trees and street signs flash by, which added to his confusion.

"Will somebody please explain what's going on?" Seth asked.

"I saw Maggie putting two backpacks in the trunk of your car," Larry said. "I used to keep three in my garage, for me, Kelly, and Josiah. I wanted to be ready in case we had to go south. I was waiting for things to get bad enough, but I waited too long."

Without turning around, Maggie stretched her arm over the seat. Seth grabbed her searching hand and squeezed it gently.

"When Larry showed up, I thought we were dead," Maggie said. "But then Kelly came out and said not to worry."

"Kelly knows about this too?" Seth said.

"I told her I saw Maggie packing your car," Larry said. "I could tell she was in a big hurry. Kelly figured that meant you two were in trouble. She suggested I give you our car because the police would track yours down in no time flat."

Seth stared at the back of Larry's head.

"You and Kelly are talking?" Seth said.

"I took your advice," Larry said. "We talked. We had sex for the first time in months."

"That's great."

Maggie leaned over the seat and narrowed her eyes at Seth.

"You went to a whorehouse and instead of getting laid, you gave marriage advice?" she said.

"Yeah, I guess I did," Seth said.

Maggie kissed her finger and placed it on Seth's lips. He could tell by the car's acceleration and the sound of cars zipping by that they were on the highway.

"We should listen to the radio for any Scarlet Alerts," Seth said.

The car radio clicked on and Gospel music blared. The volume was quickly lowered, and the radio was tuned to NCR.

"Preserve the memory of Sunday's tenth anniversary of the CHRIST Act with a set of special commemorative plates," an announcer's voice said. "What better way to remember this historic occasion than with a keepsake that can be passed down from generation to generation? If you order now, you get a set of commemorative cups and saucers at half price."

"There's nothing on the electronic billboards," Maggie said.

"Larry, why are you doing this?" Seth said.

"Give to the one who begs from you, and do not refuse the one who would borrow from you. Matthew 5:42," Larry said.

"No, I mean why are you driving? Kelly told you to give us the car."

"Maggie told me the whole story. The police are going to be looking for you in your car. They might be looking for Maggie too, but not with me. You have a better chance of getting out of D.C. with me driving."

Seth felt like a jerk for the second time that day. He regretted having avoided Larry in the driveway.

"You know what you are, Larry? You're a mensch."

"Is that good?"

"The best."

Chapter 26

Freeman slipped on the standard-issue Hedge Protection blue windbreaker before stepping in front of the gang of reporters and cameramen. The reporters thrust their microphones at him and shouted questions. Freeman figured this was what a mother bird felt like when she was about to feed worms to her babies. He held up his hands and they stopped yelling.

"I'll make a statement," Freeman said, "and then I'll answer a few questions. Earlier this evening, Hedge Protection missioners conducted a raid on an illegal religious group. Their center of operations was located on the seventh floor of a vacant office building. Missioners were met with armed resistance. At this time, we have confirmation that two missioners paid the ultimate sacrifice to keep our country safe. The enemy was defeated, and the threat has been neutralized. We'll provide more details later. Now I'll take questions."

The shouting began again. Freeman pointed to an NNN reporter.

"Why did you choose to supervise the raid?" he asked.

"I felt this group posed a large enough threat that I had to handle it myself," Freeman said.

"Other than the two deceased missioners, were there any other casualties?"

"Yes."

"How many?"

"We'll provide details later."

"Is Seth Ginsberg among the casualties?"

Freeman glared at the reporter. The camera lights felt like they were burning his skin.

"We'll provide details later," Freeman said. "That's all the questions I'll be taking at this time."

Freeman hurried into Hedge Protection Mobile Command

Center and slammed the door. He slumped into his chair at the console. The row of monitors before him were off now. Most of the missioners were busy inside the office building. Missioner Lim entered and sat in the chair next to him.

"I assure you, sir," she said. "No one in our department leaked the identities of the church members to the press."

Freeman wasn't worried about his missioners leaking information. He was certain Roy Arnold had supplied Seth Ginsberg's name to the press at the same time he told them about the raid. Freeman had no idea why Roy had felt it was necessary to single out Ginsberg. His job was difficult enough without Roy revealing identities to the press and then neglecting to warn Freeman about it.

"What's done is done," Freeman said.

Freeman and Missioner Grace Lim had worked closely for years now. Mary jokingly referred to Lim as Freeman's work wife. Although they were both very good at hiding their emotions, each always knew how the other one felt. Right now, Freeman could tell that Lim was upset.

"Federal clergymen have been sent to the homes of our three fallen missioners," she said.

"Three?" Freeman said. "I thought there were only two."

"Missioner Stevens died on the way to the hospital. Leah Gordon fired a single bullet that barely grazed him, but it was enough to kill him. It sliced the side of his neck, severing his carotid artery."

Freeman drummed his fingers on the console. Stevens's death was his fault. By allowing the rabbi to finish her prayer, she was able to distract them long enough to kill one of the finest missioners Freeman had ever had the honor to command.

"Our intel on the office building was incomplete," Missioner Lim said. "The owner, Howard Greenblatt, had backup generators installed during initial construction in case of a black out. He had also installed an impressive redundant security system. When our missioners cut the line to his alarm system, it activated a secondary system. Greenblatt has been identified as the lone gunman who fired on our men."

"Do you think the Weinsteins purposely didn't tell us about the security system, or do you think they just didn't know?" Freeman said.

"My guess is that Greenblatt didn't tell anyone."

Missioner Lim had had church members Sam and Esther Weinstein arrested weeks earlier. Lim told the Weinsteins that they would never see their six-month-old baby again unless they cooperated. They cooperated. Lim let them see the baby one last time before they were sent to a Savior Camp. The baby was taken to family services.

"Thank God Greenblatt was the only one. We could have lost more men," Freeman said.

"We've searched the entire area," Lim said. "All religious paraphernalia have been gathered and stored as evidence."

"Have we determined the cause of death of the people in the conference room?"

"One of the church members owned a pharmacy. The final toxicology report won't be ready for days, but speculation is that the pharmacist supplied a combination of pills both lethal and narcotic to insure a quick and painless death."

Freeman thought about those poor misguided fools who had condemned themselves to eternal damnation. He had studied their files. Howard Greenblatt was divorced with three grown children. He owned four office parks and three shopping malls. Leah Gordon had two sons, ages twelve and ten. They had lived in Montreal with their father. Freeman couldn't begin to fathom what kind of mother left her children to engage in subversive activity.

"The public must never find out about the mass suicide," Freeman said. "We don't want to create any martyrs."

"Yes sir."

A missioner entered the command center.

"Sir," he said. "We just found out that reporters are set up outside Senator Owens's house. We believe it's related to tonight's raid."

Missioner Lim switched one of the monitors to their broadcast feeds. She switched channels until she got to NNN. A graphic with the words "Breaking News" filled the TV screen, and the program cut to a reporter standing outside a mansion with a well-kept lawn.

"We have new details on Hedge Protection's raid on an illegal religious group earlier this evening," he said. "One of the members of the church has been identified as Seth Ginsberg. And here's the chilling part, this alleged secret non-Christian is a legislative assistant to Senator Sam Owens, the junior senator from Tennessee. I am outside Owens's home, where I recently asked him for his reaction."

The scene changed to a confused Senator Owens, wearing a robe over his pajamas. In the glare of a portable spotlight, Owens looked like a teenager who'd been caught trying to sneak into the house after curfew.

"Senator, do you have a Seth Ginsberg working in your office?" the reporter asked as he pushed his microphone toward the senator.

"Seth Ginsberg?" Owens said. "Yes, I know Seth. Has something happened to him?"

"Ginsberg has been accused of engaging in unlawful religious activity. Were you aware of his involvement with an underground Jewish church?"

Owens's mouth dropped open, and he wobbled like a broken toy before regaining his composure.

"I have no idea what you're talking about."

"Do you care to comment?"

"Definitely not."

The senator went inside his house and slammed the door with the reporter still asking questions. Missioner Lim turned off the monitor. Freeman's fingers beat the armrest.

"Have you identified the bodies of the church members?" Freeman said.

"No, sir," Lim said. "Nineteen people. Takes time."

"I understand. Can you at least determine if Seth Ginsberg is one of them?"

"I'll go talk to the forensics team personally and will report back here as soon as possible."

"Thank you, Grace."

There was another thing Freeman knew about his work wife. She always blushed when he called her by her first name. Once she was gone, Freeman turned the monitor back on. NNN was focusing on a possible Owens connection to the raid, and pundits were filling air time by playing the *What did he know, and when did he know it?* game.

Freeman now understood that this was why Roy Arnold had given Seth Ginsberg's name to the press. Roy was punishing Senator Owens for having a gay man and a Jew on staff. The sad part was that Owens might have known about Reginald Cooke, but it was highly unlikely that he knew that Seth Ginsberg had gone back to his old religion. Owens didn't strike Freeman as brave enough to keep a secret Jew on his payroll.

The constant drone of talking heads, combined with coming down from the adrenaline rush of the raid, caused Freeman to nod off to sleep. He jerked awake when he felt a hand touch his shoulder. Missioner Lim stood next to his chair. He could tell she wasn't happy.

"How long was I asleep?" Freeman said.

"Two hours, sir."

She sat down next to him. Freeman muted the sound on the monitor. He realized that he'd been drooling in his sleep. He took a handkerchief from his back pocket and wiped his mouth.

"Did you find Ginsberg?" he said.

"No, sir. He's not among the bodies we found on the seventh floor. We searched the entire building. He's not here."

Freeman drummed his fingers.

"How is that possible?" he said.

"He didn't attend services tonight. Our surveillance records show that he sometimes changed his mind at the last moment and went to the local shooting range instead. He wasn't at the office building tonight. I dispatched missioners to the range, Senator Owens's office, and his home. He wasn't at any of those locations. Best-case scenario is that instead of attending services he decided to take his wife out to dinner and we'll arrest him when he returns home."

"Worst-case scenario?"

"Ginsberg found out about the raid and is on the run."

Freeman looked up at the muted TV screen. Below footage of the office building was the banner "Illegal Religious Group Discovery."

"If he's anywhere near a TV or radio, then he knows he's in trouble," Freeman said. "Issue a Scarlet Alert for Seth Ginsberg."

CHAPTER 27

ANNOUNCER: It's twelve noon and you're listening to NCR, National Christian Radio. Thank you for joining us at the start of this glorious afternoon.

A nationwide Scarlet Alert has been issued for suspected terrorist, Seth Ginsberg. He is approximately five-feet-ten-inches tall and weighs around one-hundred-and-eighty-five pounds. He has brown hair and blue eyes. Ginsberg may not be alone. His wife, Margaret Ginsberg, is missing. Authorities are concentrating their search on the Washington, D.C., area; however, Scarlet Alert messages are already appearing on electronic highway signs nationwide. Ginsberg is believed to be armed and dangerous. If you see Ginsberg, do not approach him. Call 911 immediately.

Ginsberg was a member of the underground church that was raided yesterday by Hedge Protection. Three missioners were shot and killed by church members during the raid.

The White House released this statement from President Reed.

PRESIDENT REED: We have seen once again why America must be ever watchful for enemies not just outside but inside our borders as well. The men and women who disobey our Lord have the mark of Cain on them. They wish nothing less than the destruction of Christianity and the murder of all Christians.

ANNOUNCER: In international news, Cyclone Gabriel ripped the coast of Australia on Friday, leaving hundreds without power and causing fifty known deaths. The death toll is expected to rise once the Australian government has a chance to assess the damage. The White House released a statement that the cyclone was the wrath of God punishing Australia for pulling its troops from the U.S.-led coalition for Operation Ultimate Crusade. No comment yet from Australian officials.

Coming up, a special edition of *The Pauly Pilgrim Show* featuring an exclusive interview with Senator Sam Owens.

But first, this message.

COMMERCIAL VOICE TALENT: Tonight, on *Discover Jesus*, don't miss the latest installment in the ongoing series, "The Apostles." Tune in at eight when this award-winning program examines the life of Peter. Don't miss "Peter: The Other Simon" tonight at eight o'clock on *Discover Jesus*, all Jesus all the time.

ANNOUNCER: And now the show hosted by the man who stands for Truth, Justice, and the Christian Way: Pauly Pilgrim.

PAULY PILGRIM: A blessed good afternoon. Thank you for joining us today. My special guest is the junior senator from the great state of Tennessee, Senator Sam Owens. For years, terrorist-at-large Seth Ginsberg worked in Owens's office without raising suspicions about his true nature. Senator, I've known you for a long time. You are an intelligent, observant man, but were you really duped, swindled, hoodwinked, and bamboozled by this Ginsberg character?

SENATOR OWENS: First let me thank you for calling me intelligent, Pauly. I've been called a number of things today that would be the exact opposite of intelligent. I'm not here to make any excuses for my poor judgment. When I hired Seth Ginsberg

five years ago, I was aware that he was of Jewish blood, but I did not judge him based on that knowledge. He convinced me that he had accepted Jesus in his heart.

PILGRIM: But Senator, we now know that Ginsberg not only rejected Jesus, he joined a group of radicals who hated and despised Christianity. Wouldn't you agree that by embracing religious intolerance, Seth Ginsberg is a Judas to the Judeo-Christian beliefs of America?

OWENS: Absolutely, Pauly. Seth Ginsberg is the ultimate American Judas. And just as Judas gained Jesus' trust only to betray him, so Seth gained mine and betrayed me. Now again, I am not trying to make excuses for myself. I am guilty of turning a blind eye to the wickedness in my house. I have sinned against my country, and I beg her forgiveness. I have sinned against my Lord Jesus, and I ask that his precious blood wash and cleanse the stain until it is in the ocean of God's mercy.

PILGRIM: Wow. Just wow. I hope you people listening felt that because I definitely felt the spirit of the Lord here in the studio. You can't see what I'm seeing, but the guys in the control room are giving the senator a standing ovation. Senator Owens, we need more men like you in Congress, men with your humility and pureness of heart.

OWENS: Coming from a man of God like you, that means a lot to me, Pauly. But I feel I need to do more to make amends for my sins. Did you know that if there had been a security camera on Seth's street, he'd be in custody right now?

PILGRIM: Do you feel we need to spend more on national security?

OWENS: We must if we are going to win the holy war against radical anti-Christian hate groups. You might have a religious terrorist living right next to you and not even know it. We need more police on the street. We must have more programs that encourage people to report suspicious behavior. And we definitely need more security cameras. In every neighborhood, every playground, and any place that's got people, there should be a camera watching to keep our families safe.

PILGRIM: Senator, you know some softhearted fool is going to complain about their loss of civil rights and claim this is an invasion of privacy.

OWENS: Softhearted? Don't you mean softheaded? Christians don't worry about being watched. They know God is already watching them day and night. If you have faith in Jesus and do as the Bible tells you, then you have nothing to hide.

PILGRIM: Are you sure this is enough, Senator? Ginsberg worked for you. How can we trust our elected officials if there are people like him among us?

OWENS: We should have every citizen sign an oath of loyalty to Christ and America, starting with everyone who works for our government. I want Congress to conduct hearings on those accused of disloyalty. The time has come for a great cleansing. The future of our nation depends on it.

PILGRIM: Amen, brother Sam, amen. For those of you just joining us, my guest today was Senator Sam Owens. Sadly, the senator has other engagements and has to go. We're going to break away for a word from our sponsors, and when we come back, I'll talk to an expert on Islam who will reveal how Muslims are taught at an early age to hate Christians.

CHAPTER 28

The early-morning sun cast long shadows as Maggie climbed out of the driver-side door and stretched. Though the rest-area parking lot was nearly deserted, Seth stayed in the car. The back seat was littered with fast-food wrappers and coffee-stained Styrofoam cups. Seth rolled down his window.

"Are we sure about this?" Seth asked. "I don't mind going into the woods with a roll of toilet paper."

Maggie responded with a jaw-cracking yawn.

"There's hardly anybody here," she said. "We've been driving for fourteen hours. I have got to use a real toilet and wash my face. Stay here if you want to. Me, I'm going in."

Maggie reached into the back seat for her purse, closed the door, and walked toward the bathrooms. Seth needed to make a decision soon or his sphincter was going to make it for him. He put on the baseball cap and sunglasses he'd had Maggie buy for him the last time they refueled. It was a frigid morning, made even colder by the wind created by the eighteen-wheelers hauling ass down I-40. Most rest stops Seth had been to weren't built directly next to the highway. Maybe it was an Arkansas thing.

Seth felt exposed outside the car. He'd seen his face on so many electronic billboards that he felt like it belonged to someone else, someone dangerous that he should avoid. He pressed his wrist against the gun in his belt holster. The gun made him feel safer not because it provided protection, but because it helped him blend in with everyone else.

There was a utilitarian simplicity to the bathroom. It was clean and warm and had just what you needed and nothing more. Seth had the place to himself. He entered the last stall and slid the lock.

Seth was disappointed by the absence of traditional graffiti on the walls. Gone were the sex jokes and scatological rhymes. There wasn't even a crude drawing of a penis. Instead, there were Bible verses, with John 3:16 the most popular.

The verses made Seth think of Larry. Shortly after crossing the Virginia border, Larry had pulled into a restaurant parking lot in Johnson City, Tennessee. He said a prayer for Seth and Maggie's safety, left his keys in the ignition, and then got out of the car. The last time they saw him, he was walking toward the city's transit center a few blocks away with the intention of catching a Greyhound bus back to Washington, D.C.

Larry's car was a comfortable mid-size sedan, but after fourteen hours, Seth felt like he was still moving, and he and Maggie were only half-way to Mexico. Canada was closer to D.C., but crossing the Canadian border was more dangerous. Canada aggressively extradited illegal Americans because the country felt it needed to maintain the strong trade relationship with its neighbor.

After relieving his bowels, Seth began to feel less like a ball of twisted nerves. Washing his hands, he'd wished that he had remembered to bring his toothbrush from the car. Seth put his cap and sunglasses on the edge of the sink so that he could wash his face. A beer-barrel of a man, sporting a walrus mustache and an NRA baseball cap, emptied his bladder and washed his hands in the sink beside him. He turned to Seth and opened his mouth to speak, but then changed his mind. He hurriedly wiped his hands on his jeans and left the bathroom.

Seth was sure the man had recognized him. He was too afraid to leave. He dried his hands under the air dryer, and then twisted the nozzle around to point upward. As hot air blasted Seth's face, he imagined Beer-barrel Man calling the police to tell them that Hedge Protection's most-wanted man was in a rest stop outside West Memphis, Arkansas.

He had to leave. Maggie was waiting. Seth put his sunglasses and cap back on and did his best impression of a calm person. As he opened the door he saw a State Trooper walking toward him.

Seth fled back to the stall he'd just left and, with shaking hands, locked the door. He sat down on the toilet and waited. He put his hand on his gun. The trooper's shoes clacked across the tiled floor until they were outside Seth's stall. He tried to push the door open, but the lock kept him out.

"Occupied," Seth said.

"Sorry," the trooper said.

Seth looked through the slit between the door and the side of the stall as the trooper moved out of sight. Seth heard a stall door slam shut and the lock slide across, but it was too far away to be the stall next door. While Seth was waiting for the trooper to get good and occupied, someone entered the stall between them. Seth had been concentrating on the trooper and hadn't noticed him enter the bathroom. The bathroom's warm air began to feel stiflingly hot.

A hand holding a folded brochure appeared at the bottom of Seth's stall. His next-door neighbor had reached under the wall between them. Seth debated on whether to take the brochure or not and decided not taking it was potentially more dangerous.

Seth took the offering and the hand immediately retreated. The brochure was for the Daisy Airgun Museum. Along the margins his neighbor had written, "Meet me at the last picnic table on the north side. A friend."

Seth's mystery friend exited his stall and then the bathroom. He waited five minutes before leaving.

The cool outside air chilled him instantly. Seth spotted Maggie standing by the vending machines doing a bad imitation of someone who can't make up their mind about which snack they want. She hurried over to him and slipped her arm around his.

"I was beginning to think you fell in," she said.

"I ran into a situation," Seth said.

"I saw the trooper go in. I'm guessing he didn't see you."

"He's still inside. But then somebody slipped this to me."

Seth handed Maggie the brochure. She read the handwritten message quickly and then she scanned the picnic tables.

"Which way is north?" Maggie said.

"That way," Seth said, nodding to their left.

Beer-barrel Man sat at the picnic table farthest away from the rest center, and a comfortable distance away from the trooper's patrol car.

"It's too dangerous," Maggie said. "Let's get in the car and go."

"If this guy recognized me, then why didn't he tell the trooper?"

"He probably wants to blackmail you."

"I'd rather pay him off than have him report us."

Seth and Maggie stayed arm in arm as they approached Beer-barrel Man at the picnic table. They looked like a young couple in love out strolling on a brisk morning.

"He's wearing an NRA baseball cap," Maggie said.

"Who doesn't wear an NRA baseball cap these days?" Seth said.

The man nodded at them.

"Morning," he said. "Please have a seat."

Seth and Maggie reluctantly sat down on the bench opposite him. He leaned forward and rested his hairy arms on the table.

"My name is Jerry Hays," he said. "I know who you are, but don't worry. I'm a big fan. The American Judas overthrowing the government from within. I just knew there was an underground resistance."

"Please don't take offense," Seth said. "But you don't exactly look like the type who would support overthrowing this particular government."

Jerry scratched the stubble on the side of his face.

"I wasn't," he said, "until my momma caught me drinking home brew. I told her that I was being like Jesus, only instead of turning water into wine, I was turning it into beer. She didn't buy it. She called Hedge Protection to come take me to a Savior Camp."

Maggie pointed at Jerry's cap.

"Why didn't you just shoot the missioners when they came to get you?" she said.

Seth could tell that Maggie was being sarcastic, but Jerry didn't seem to notice.

"I thought of that," Jerry said. "Momma swore I'd have to shoot her first. I couldn't do that so I'm going south."

"Sorry to bust your bubble, Jerry," Seth said, "but I wasn't trying to overthrow the government. I was caught attending synagogue."

Jerry's mustache drooped with disappointment.

"Certainly, somebody is planning a coup of this damn Christian Taliban," he said.

"Not that I know of," Seth said.

Jerry shook his head as he squinted at the sky, and then leaned forward.

"Listen," he said. "You'll never make it to the border on the highway. There are too many cameras out there."

Seth noticed the State Trooper leaving the bathroom and getting in his patrol car.

"What do you suggest?" Seth said.

"If you're going to drive, then take the back roads," Jerry said. "Takes longer, but at least you eventually get there."

"Makes sense. Any other advice?"

"Are you sure there's nobody plotting to take back our country?"

"Sorry, Jerry. It's not happening."

Jerry stood and glared at Seth.

"You should've done something when you had the chance," Jerry said. "What's the point of being the damn American Judas if you don't make it so that a man can drink his beer in peace."

Jerry stalked away.

"We should go," Maggie said.

They stood and headed toward their car.

"It's my turn to drive," Seth said.

Maggie reached into her purse and handed Seth the car keys. They got into the car, buckled up, and Seth started the engine. As they pulled out of the parking lot, they passed a church van pulling in.

"He's right, you know," Maggie said.

"About taking back roads?" Seth said.

"No. That'll take too long. He was right that we should have overthrown the government when we had the chance."

CHAPTER 29

Freeman hated the name. American Judas. As if there were only one. And if there were only one, it certainly wouldn't be Seth Ginsberg. He was too insignificant. And yet, Ginsberg's face was on the television in Freeman's office over the shoulder of a pundit warning everyone that the American Judas was roaming free and hell-bent on spilling innocent Christian blood. Hedge Protection had been flooded with calls from frightened citizens and concerned congressmen demanding to know when missioners would put an end to this one-man menace to society.

There was a knock at his office door and Missioner Lim entered. She had a file folder in one hand and a plastic bag in the other. Freeman turned off the television.

"I know you have an update for me in that folder," Freeman said. "But what's in the bag?"

"Lunch," Lim said. "When you get busy you forget about meals. I can brief you while we eat."

Freeman knew it was useless to argue, and, besides, the smell of cooked meat had already caused his stomach to grumble. He stacked files on his desk to make room for their food. Lim had gotten Freeman a steak sandwich and Coleslaw, and a salad topped with grilled chicken for herself. Lim laid out the food, and they said a short prayer.

"We haven't done this in a while," Freeman said, as he bit into his sandwich.

"No, we haven't," Lim said as she opened her file. "Shall I begin?"

"By all means."

"We believe we know what car Ginsberg is driving. His personal vehicle is still in his garage, but his neighbor left in his car last night and returned home by city bus late this morning." She peered at her notes. "The neighbor is a Laurence Bruner. He lives with his wife and son in the house directly adjacent to the suspect's residence."

"There are a number of plausible reasons why Bruner would have returned without his car."

"I agree, sir. However, it was the timing that caused us to investigate further. Bruner left his home about the time Ginsberg would have needed to escape."

"Have Bruner brought in for questioning."

Missioner Lim ate a forkful of salad before continuing.

"We've already done that, sir," she said. "The problem is that Bruner spent time in a Savior Camp. All we've been able to get out of him are Bible verses. So far, he's recited the entire book of Matthew."

"When he gets to Corinthians let me know," Freeman said. "I have a special fondness for those chapters."

Lim took out a pen and made a note. Freeman thought about explaining that it was just a joke, but continued eating instead. He sometimes forgot that most of his missioners, including Lim, lacked a sense of humor.

"Stay on Bruner for a few more hours," Freeman said. "If he doesn't provide any useful intel, cut him loose, but keep an eye on him. What have you done about the car?"

"We put out an APB," Lim said. "We were tracking the car's GPS, but then it stopped transmitting. The last coordinates we have on the vehicle are on I-40 in Arkansas."

Freeman got ready to take another bite of his sandwich and then put it down.

"I-40 in Arkansas?" he said. "Could Ginsberg really be foolish enough to take the direct route across the country to the border?"

"He might have assumed that we wouldn't find out that he's driving Bruner's car," Lim said. "He'd want to take the quickest route possible."

Freeman wiped his mouth with a paper napkin.

"If we don't pick him up before he reaches the border," he said. "Then Hedge Patrol will catch him."

For the rest of the meal, they chatted about other things. Freeman

was expecting his first grandchild, and Lim's younger sister was getting married. When they were done, Lim insisted on cleaning up. After she was gone, Freeman turned the television back on. A reporter announced that Senator Owens had called for Congressional hearings to determine the Christian loyalty of government employees. Somewhere up in heaven, Saint Joe McCarthy was smiling.

Freeman thought of the Bible verse that Chip Randall had written in blood. "If we say we have no sin, we deceive ourselves, and the truth is not in us. John 1:8." He thought of the verse a lot lately, but especially when dealing with those who claim to be the most righteous.

As a former congressman, Freeman understood exactly what Owens was doing. He had turned a problem into an opportunity. But that didn't mean Freeman had to like it. The longer Seth Ginsberg, American Judas, was a free man, the worse it would look for Hedge Protection. People would claim that Freeman's department wasn't able to protect the American people from domestic terrorists. Freeman was forced to dedicate a huge amount of resources to a low-level fugitive. In fact, if Ginsberg hadn't been elevated to a one-man plague on America's decency, Hedge Protection would have let him run.

Freeman's personal phone rang. Only a handful of people had the number.

"Wingard," he said.

"Freeman," Roy Arnold replied. "How did you manage to lose that dirty little Jew?"

Roy didn't often lose his temper. Most people quaked with fear when he did, but Freeman had known Roy for too long.

"Ginsberg didn't go to services," Freeman said. "That's how he got away. But we'll catch him soon enough."

"Is it possible that someone warned him about the raid?" Roy said.

"I don't see how that's possible. Only my top missioners had access to the names of the congregants, and I know they wouldn't have contacted anyone on that list."

"I had the list of names. Are you certain that I didn't contact Ginsberg?"

Freeman laughed.

"I'm sorry, Roy," he said. "I shouldn't laugh, but Hedge Protection has been under a lot of stress lately, and the idea is so absurd."

Roy chuckled. His tone softened. The temper tantrum had ended.

"I shouldn't have snapped at you," Roy said. "I just hate seeing good Christians citizens worry about this American Judas. I really hate that name."

"I hate it too," Freeman said. "As if Ginsberg were the only one."

"When you do catch him, and I have complete faith that you will, make sure the country knows that it was your men who arrested him. We need to show the American people that sinners cannot escape Hedge Protection."

Freeman wished Roy wouldn't tell him how to do his job. Having Hedge Patrol make a big show out of arresting Ginsberg was yet another waste of valuable resources, but if Freeman didn't do what Roy wanted, he would have President Reed tell him to do it.

"Don't worry," Freeman said. "When we catch Ginsberg, the whole world will know it."

CHAPTER 30

Seth twisted the dial on the car radio, hoping to catch a news report. He kept the volume low so as not to wake up Maggie, who was curled up on the back seat. She'd been asleep for four hours, ever since they refueled outside of Little Rock.

Seth scanned past a Christian soft-rock station, a Christian hard-rock station, and a Christian country-music station. He was about to dial past a Gospel music station when a commercial for Ho-Jo's Auto Mart in Hot Springs ended and the monotonous tone that signaled a Scarlet Alert came on.

"We have an update in the search for Seth Ginsberg," the announcer said. "The suspect is driving a dark-green Chevrolet Malibu, license-plate number KYH 7478."

Seth drifted into the next lane and a truck blared its horn. He jerked back into his lane, worked his way over to the shoulder, and turned off the engine. Seth stared at the long ribbon of road ahead. He couldn't just sit there waiting to be caught. Seth reached over the seat and shook Maggie harder than he meant to. She looked at him through squinted eyes.

"Is it my turn to drive?" she said in a small, sleepy voice.

"They know we're driving Larry's car."

"Cheese and rice, you're kidding me," Maggie said, fully awake.

Seth repeated the terrible news as she climbed into the front seat. He started the car and eased back onto the highway. Traffic was light, but they watched each vehicle that passed them for signs that they'd been recognized.

"We have to get rid of this car," Seth said.

"And then what?" Maggie asked. "Hike the rest of the way?"

"We could steal a car."

"You know how to steal a car?"

"I still have that business card Julian Cross gave me."

"How do we know we can trust the person who answers the phone?"

"It's not like we have a lot of options here."

Maggie placed her hand on Seth's leg. He glanced over at her and she gave him a sad smile. The decision had been made.

Seth took the next exit. There were a couple of gas stations and a smattering of fast-food restaurants before endless nothing stretched out in either direction. He drove past the gas stations and the fast-food joints on a winding two-lane road. When all they could see was woods on either side of them, Seth pulled onto a dirt road that led into the forest. The sedan rocked from side to side as it rolled deeper into the shade of pine trees. He guided the car into a field of tall grass, the tips licking the windows, and turned off the engine. All they could hear were birds chirping and their own hearts pounding.

Seth got out and left the keys in the ignition. A light breeze brushed the blades of grass, carrying the scent of rotting vegetation. They pulled their backpacks out of the trunk and searched the interior for anything useful to bring along. They had bought a six-pack of bottled water during one of their fuel stops. There were two bottles left. Maggie stuffed them both into her backpack.

They took a moment to say a last farewell to the car that had carried them this far, and then they hiked back to the highway exit. They held hands as they walked. The sun was starting to dip behind the trees when they reached a dusty four-pump gas station. The smell of gasoline stung Seth's nostrils. They were about to go into the station to see if it sold prepaid mobile phones, but it turned out that one of the country's last remaining pay phones was at the edge of the parking lot. Seth picked up the receiver and put it to his ear. There was a dial tone. This made him cautiously optimistic that he and Maggie were going to be okay.

With the sun going down, the temperature dropped. Seth considered pausing to get his coat out of his pack while he searched his wallet for the business card but decided to get this call done first. When Julian had given the card to him, Seth had only glanced at it briefly before stuffing it into his wallet. Now that he read it more closely, he had to laugh at the obvious joke. It was for Moses and Aaron's Towing Service in Canaan, Indiana. In Exodus, Moses and Aaron led the Jews out of Egypt to the land of milk and honey. They were the original Exodus Express.

Seth dialed the number and after four rings got an answering machine.

"Hey, Aaron here," the recording said. "I'm not available at the moment. Leave me a number and I'll get right back to you as soon as I can."

At the sound of the beep, Seth said, "Hey, Aaron. My buddy Julian told me if I ever needed your services to give you a call. Here's the number where you can reach me." Seth squinted at the phone for its number and read it out loud. Both his and Maggie's cellphones were in a gas-station trashcan in Knoxville, Tennessee.

"What do we do now?" Maggie asked.

"We wait."

"For how long?"

"I don't know. How long do you think we should wait?"

"I don't know."

Seth sat by the phone with their backpacks while Maggie walked to a McDonald's. She came back with a paper sack. Seth's cheese-burger tasted like it had been seasoned with axle grease. As they ate, a pickup truck pulled into the parking lot, and a man wearing a trucker cap and a flannel work shirt with the sleeves torn off got out. Trucker-Cap Man walked over to the phone and started to reach into his pocket for change.

"Do you mind?" Maggie said. "We're waiting for a friend to call us back on this phone."

"Yeah, I do mind," Trucker-Cap Man said.

"Please, can't you use a different phone?"

Trucker-Cap Man narrowed his eyes at them. He shirt wasn't tucked in, and he pulled the tail around the handle of the handgun in his belt holster. Seth had a gun too, but this wasn't the time or place for a showdown. Seth took Maggie's hand and led her a few steps away.

"Best we let him make his call," Seth said.

He was too nervous to finish eating. The first stars were visible in the sky when Trucker-Cap Man finally hung up the phone. He walked past his pickup truck and into the gas station. They could see him talking to the attendant and pointing at them.

"Do you think he recognized me?" Seth said.

"I think if he had, he would have shot you instead of reporting you," Maggie said.

"I think we've waited long enough."

"You're right. We should go."

As they were reaching for their backpacks, the pay phone rang. Seth and Maggie rushed over to it and Seth picked up the receiver.

"Hello? Hello?" he said.

"Hey, this is Aaron's wife," said a woman's voice. "Where you at? I'll have somebody come fetch you."

"Oh God, where am I?"

"We're in Arkansas just off I-30," Maggie said. "We took the Sticky Road exit."

Seth repeated the location. He could hear Aaron's wife tapping on a keyboard. Sweat rolled down the side of Seth's face as he watched Trucker-Cap Man leave the station and head toward them. Seth breathed a sigh of relief when Trucker-Cap Man got into his truck and drove away; but then he noticed that the gas-station attendant was standing at the glass door with his hands on his hips, staring at them.

"How big a hurry are you in?" asked Aaron's wife.

"We're in the open by a pay phone outside of a gas station," Seth said.

"Sounds like you're in an emergency situation."

"That's putting it mildly."

The gas station attendant took out his cellphone and made a call. As he talked, he pointed at Seth and Maggie.

"I can have somebody pick you up in about an hour," Aaron's wife said.

"We might not have an hour," Seth said.

"That's the best I can do."

"There's a Wendy's here. My wife and I will wait inside."

"If anybody asks, tell them you're waiting on the church van to take you to the retreat."

Aaron's wife hung up before Seth could ask for more details. He and Maggie hoisted their backpacks and walked past the McDonald's to the Wendy's. It felt stiflingly warm inside after standing outside in the cool night air. The smell of sizzling meat normally caused Seth to salivate, but his stomach was too busy doing somersaults.

"Why did you tell them to meet us here? We just ate," Maggie said.

"We have an hour to kill," Seth said. "Order something you can eat slowly."

Maggie ordered a salad and a cup of coffee. Seth ordered fries and a large soda. The dining room was crowded with families. Exhausted parents watched dully as their offspring squealed and chased each other between the tables. Some customers seemed mildly curious about Seth and Maggie's backpacks. They found an empty table in the far corner.

Maggie picked at her salad as Seth ate his fries. Even though they had only walked a short distance, Seth's back ached from carrying the backpack. He put his hand on his forehead.

"I didn't tell them who I was," he said. "They don't know what we look like. I can't call them back. Not after the way the gas station attendant stared at us."

As if an imaginary alarm had sounded, the parents gathered their children and headed for the exits. Under their tables, they left behind mashed French fries, pieces of hamburger, and soiled napkins. Other than three elderly couples, Seth and Maggie had the place to themselves.

Seth checked his watch obsessively. The hour was almost up, but there was no sign of anything resembling the Exodus Express.

An Arkansas State Trooper arrived and got out of his car. Seth and Maggie ducked their heads and took a newfound interest in their food. The officer entered, scanned the dining room, and then approached them. Seth broke out into a cold sweat. There was no way that the officer wouldn't know that he was the American Judas. It was too late to run. They weren't going to make it to Mexico.

"Are those your backpacks?" the trooper asked.

"Yes sir, they are," Seth said.

"Been camping?"

"Not yet. We're going on a retreat with our church. We're waiting on them to pick us up."

"Is there a problem, Officer?" Maggie asked.

Curious Wendy's employees gathered by the cash register. The elderly couples watched openly.

"Have I seen you before?" the trooper asked.

"I don't think so," Maggie said.

"I meant him."

The trooper jerked his thumb at Seth. He felt the blood drain from his face. This was it. He was going to get arrested. But he wasn't going to make it easy for the officer.

"Do I remind you of somebody famous?"

"That's probably it," the trooper said. "Got a report of suspicious behavior. A couple was hanging around the gas station and wouldn't let anyone use the phone."

Seth couldn't believe it. He didn't make the connection.

"We were waiting on a phone call," Maggie said.

"From your church?" the trooper said.

"Yeah. We wanted to let them know where they could pick us up."

"Nobody answered the first time we called, so we left a message and were waiting for them to call back," Seth added.

The trooper put his hands on his hips. His blue shirt and black pants were neatly pressed. His wide-brimmed hat was as stiff as his back.

"I know most of the churches in this area," he said. "What's the name of the church you're waiting for?"

Maggie stammered but couldn't get any coherent words to come out of her mouth. Seth took her hand and looked into her eyes before he turned to face the policeman.

"We aren't going on a church retreat," Seth said. "We don't even know the person who's coming to pick us up. We aren't from here. I lost my job and when we could no longer make the payments the bank took our home. We hitchhiked here from Knoxville, and we spent the last of our money on this food."

The trooper looked at their unfinished meal, and then at their backpacks. Seth glanced at the packs and his stomach lurched. They were shiny and in perfect condition. Having brand-new backpacks wasn't going to help convince the trooper that Seth and Maggie were penniless. The trooper rubbed his chin.

"You say you don't know who you're waiting for," he said.

"All I know is this man is related to a friend of mine and he said he had some work for me. Officer, I'm not even sure which town this man lives in, but I don't care. I don't want charity. I just want to work."

"Can you prove anything you just told me?"

Seth stared at the table. He had conned the trooper this long, he might as well go all the way.

"No sir, I can't," he said. "Go ahead and arrest us, Officer. At least then I know my wife will get three squares a day."

Maggie gave the trooper the saddest face she could muster. He wrinkled his nose. Seth glanced out the window. A black van pulled into the parking lot. On the side, it read, "Holy Comforter Lutheran Church." There was no address. A middle-aged couple climbed out and entered the restaurant. They glanced at the officer, at Seth and Maggie's table, and then studied the menu on the wall.

"Wendy's," the woman said. "Albert, I hate Wendy's. I told you I wanted McDonald's."

They went back to their van and drove away. Seth's heart sank as he watched them leave.

"You look like good Christians," the trooper said as he tipped his hat back on his head. "Stay away from the gas station and don't impede anyone's access to a public phone."

"Yes Officer," Seth said. "Thank you."

Seth and Maggie waited until the trooper had driven away before they dared speak.

"I can't believe he didn't recognize you," Maggie said. "Your face is everywhere."

"Maybe God is watching over us," Seth said.

"I'm serious. Why didn't he know you?"

"We were extremely lucky. Let's get out of here before he figures it out."

"But the van left without us."

"Maybe our luck hasn't run out. Maybe they'll come back."

They got their backpacks and headed for the door. A woman in a Wendy's uniform blocked the exit. She shoved a bag into Maggie's hands.

"If we'd known you were hurting, we wouldn't have taken your money," she said with tears in her eyes. "Take this food and may the Lord be with you."

She scurried away. Maggie peeked into the bag. It was full of steaming hot hamburgers.

Once they were outside, the church van pulled up next to Seth and Maggie. The driver rolled down the window.

"You must be the folks who called for a pick up," he said.

"Yes, we are," Seth said.

"Hop in and let's get out of here."

Seth slid open the door and they lunged into the vehicle. They slung their backpacks into the seat behind them. The woman in the passenger seat turned around to face Seth and Maggie.

"Hi, I'm Barbara and this is my husband, Albert," she said. "Are those hamburgers I smell?"

"Yes," Maggie said. "This nice lady gave me a whole bag of them."

"Can I have one? I love Wendy's hamburgers."

CHAPTER 31

Seth didn't realize how quickly American Judas's infamy had grown until he saw the church signs. Traveling through what felt like every small town in Arkansas and Texas, they passed endless houses of worship. Every church presented a sign. A majority of them hadn't been updated from the past Sunday's big tenth anniversary of the CHRIST Act. The signs said things like "The CHRIST Act is Christ in ACTion." But plenty of them were about Seth, some even mentioning him by name: "History's three biggest traitors. Judas Iscariot. Benedict Arnold. Seth Ginsberg." Others were less specific: "Beware the Judas in your house." "God hates traitors." One sign made Maggie laugh out loud: "Forgive the Jew. He knows not what he do."

"At least the illiterate forgive you," she said.

Seth offered to help with the driving, but Albert refused. Albert was the pastor of the Holy Comforter Lutheran Church in Texarkana.

"We took Texarkana off the side of the van," he said, "so that the police wouldn't wonder why we were so far from home. They assume that we're a local church and let us be."

"There aren't many churches left that aren't a member of the National Church," Seth said.

"Every year there are fewer independents. It doesn't help that Congress constantly threatens to take away our tax-exempt status. But I'm not worried. The ICC has our back."

Seth had dealt with the Independent Christian Council's lobbying group. They were an underfunded laughingstock in Washington, but he didn't dare tell Albert.

Seth had to keep reminding himself that the windows of the van were tinted and resisted the urge to duck under the seat whenever they stopped at an intersection. He didn't need to tell Albert and Barbara that they had America's most-wanted man in their van. His photo was everywhere. He felt like his identity was a live grenade held in his hand. The pin had been pulled, and if he ever relaxed his fingers, his identity would explode and destroy anyone close to him.

In Odessa, Texas, Seth and Maggie said goodbye to Albert and Barbara and climbed into another church van. The side of the van read Friendship Church, and the driver was a pudgy man with a bushy mustache named Carlos. Two middle-aged women named Megan and Mindy moved aside to make room for Seth and Maggie in the back of the van. Other than providing their names, Megan and Mindy didn't speak until the van passed yet another house of worship, a little white country church with a black steeple.

"We wanted to have a church wedding," Megan said, "but there weren't any in our area that would marry gay people. We ended up going to the courthouse."

"We both wore tuxes," Mindy said. "Even then, I had a feeling it wouldn't last. I mean, I knew Megan and me would be together forever. There are just too many people who can't accept us."

Megan put her arm around Mindy's shoulder.

"We were legal for seven years," Megan said.

"What was your wedding like?" Mindy asked.

Maggie shrugged her shoulders.

"We also got married at the courthouse. Seth's parents wouldn't come because he converted to Christianity and my mother wouldn't come because Seth wasn't Catholic."

THE VAN STOPPED AND WOKE SETH FROM AN UNCOMFORTABLE SLEEP. HIS muscles ached from sleeping sitting up and he needed to pee.

"Are we at the safe house?" Seth asked.

Maggie squeezed Seth's arm.

"I don't know where we are," she said.

"This is crazy," Carlos said. "Who are these people?"

Seth's grogginess dissolved when he saw that the two-lane road was covered with people. They were the overflow of a crowd that was gathered in the desert. Cars and pickup trucks were parked along the side of the road. There was a light coming from the middle of the crowd, but Seth couldn't make out its source.

"How do we get through?" Maggie asked.

A policeman rapped on the driver-side window, causing everyone inside to jump. Carlos rolled down the window.

"The road's closed for at least an hour," the policeman said. "You're welcome to join us. You'll be glad you did."

"Okay," Carlos said. "Let me park."

Carlos carefully backed up and eased the van next to a mammoth SUV.

"We can't go out there," Maggie said.

"Lady, we can't stay in here," Carlos said. He nodded at Seth. "Put your cap on and keep the lid down over your face."

Seth put his baseball cap on and lowered the bill. He held Maggie's hand.

"Out there, I'm like a drop in the ocean," Seth said. "No one notices anybody in a crowd."

"Stay close to me," Maggie said.

Carlos got out and came around to open the sliding door. A wave of heat rolled over them. They joined the mass of humanity. Carlos led the way through the crowd. Maggie held onto Seth's arm while Mindy and Megan avoided touching each other.

"Is this the whole town?" Mindy asked.

"This crowd is as diverse as a soda commercial," Megan said.

They finally saw the source of the light, a large bonfire in a man-made pit. Women handed out candles with drip protectors. A pickup truck was parked in front of the fire, and two men stood in the truck bed. With their backs to the fire, they were in shadow. One of the men spoke into a bullhorn. His amplified voice bounced off the crowd and ricocheted into the desert. The second man said nothing.

Once he got used to the echo, Seth was able to understand the man with the bullhorn. He explained that the city was having a prayer vigil because they needed to protect the most vulnerable in their community. They couldn't depend on the government. They needed prayer warriors to fight against the evil that infested their country. The American Judas had betrayed everything decent about our great nation.

A spotlight flared on and revealed the two men. The man with the bullhorn kept talking but Seth didn't hear him. His hearing became muted, as if he were submerged under water. The silent man was an effigy made from a male mannequin dressed in a gray suit, a curly brown wig on its head, and a large rubber nose taped to its face. A sign hung around its neck that read SETH GINSBERG. AMERICAN JUDAS.

Maggie dug her fingers into Seth's arm, but he didn't feel it.

Behind the truck was a wooden pole with a pulley on top. The man with the bullhorn slipped a noose around the American Judas effigy's neck and tightened the noose. Seth felt his throat close up. The man pulled the rope, and it rose like a flag. He tied the rope off, and the effigy dangled in the air. Seth had trouble catching his breath.

The crowd was a sea of candles. They sang a solemn hymn. The man in the back of the pickup truck took a grill lighter and held the wand against the effigy's leg. The pants caught fire, and within seconds the entire mannequin was blazing. Black oily clouds carried the chemical stench of burning plastic. Flaming globs dripped into the bonfire as tears rolled down Seth's face. The head was the last part to burn. It stuck to the noose until the fire burned through the rope and it fell.

There were no cheers when it dropped into the burning pit, but Seth could feel a collective sigh of relief ripple through the crowd. They had rid themselves of a terrible thing. The candles were snuffed out and the people meandered to their cars. Seth realized that it was a weeknight. There were kids to get to school and jobs waiting in the morning.

"Let's get out of here," Carlos said.

The group followed him back to the van. Seth felt as if he was walking waist deep through mud. He hoisted himself into the seat and hung his head. Maggie held his hand and leaned against him. He felt a hand on his shoulder. Mindy was in the seat behind him and had leaned forward.

"Didn't look a thing like you," she said.

CHAPTER 32

It was almost midnight when the church van arrived at a quiet Tucson suburb. It turned into the driveway of an adobe-style ranch house with a wooden fence at the end of a cul-de-sac. The van's headlights revealed a brown-dirt yard with scattered clumps of cactus and stubborn bushes. Most of the other homes on the street were boarded up, making the house a lonely survivor.

The back yard sloped dramatically into a ravine. A train track ran through it, and a chain-link fence along the edge of the yard kept anyone from falling down the slope and into the path of an oncoming locomotive. Strings of colored lights led from the house to a barn. The van parked behind a pickup truck in the driveway.

"Wait here," Carlos said.

He got out of the van and knocked on the house's back door. Immediately, there was the sound of dogs barking. A woman answered the door. Carlos went inside, and after two minutes he returned to the van holding a box filled with paper bags. He poked his head inside.

"You'll stay here tonight," Carlos said.

Seth didn't move. He hadn't spoken since the prayer vigil or taken off his baseball cap. He had spent the hours staring out the window. Maggie took his hand.

"Come on, Seth," Maggie said.

Everyone climbed out of the van. Mindy yawned without covering her mouth, and Megan smacked her arm. Maggie took Seth's cap off and lightly touched his hair. He gave her a crooked smile. A train whistle blew in the distance. Shortly, a train rushed through the ravine. The ground shook as a line of railcars rolled past the house.

Carlos waited until the train was gone before having them each take a paper bag from the box. He explained that it was their dinner and that it was actually quite good. He then led the two couples across the yard to the barn. Inside, Maggie was hit by the smell of wet fur and dog shit. Carlos flicked on the overhead lights, revealing rows of cages filled with Scottish Terriers. A few dogs began barking, but most of them, trembling with excitement, stood with their noses pressed against the bars.

"The lady who lives here breeds Scottish Terriers," Carlos said. "All the dogs are registered. You'd be surprised what people are willing to pay for a purebred Scottie."

The group filed past the dogs to the south end of the barn. Carlos unlocked a door to a stairway that led to the loft. They walked down a narrow hallway with a door on either side, both of which Carlos opened. Inside each room were two single beds, a straight-backed chair, and a stool with a lamp on it.

"Choose any room," Carlos said. "They're all the same. It's okay to push the beds together. The bathroom is around the corner. It's only a half bath. No tub or shower. You can do what my momma called a lick and a promise."

"We'll take this one," Megan said.

She and Mindy entered the room to the left.

"This is wonderful," Maggie said.

"Thank you," Seth said, speaking for the first time since they'd arrived.

Seth and Maggie entered the other room.

"See you in the morning," Carlos said.

Maggie closed the door. She could still smell the fur but thankfully not the shit.

Seth and Maggie sat on the bed and examined the contents of their bags. There were green corn tamales, beef and spinach casserole, and lime Jell-O with mayonnaise, cottage cheese, and walnuts inside. Maggie worried that Seth wouldn't eat, but he tore into the bag. They had to try hard not to gobble the food. This was their first meal in three days that didn't come with packets of ketchup and mustard.

Seth and Maggie changed out of the clothes they'd been wearing since they left Washington and took turns in the bathroom. They pushed the two single beds together and climbed in under the sheets. The mattresses sagged but the sheets were clean, and Maggie was thrilled to sleep on something that wasn't moving.

A train whistle blew in the distance and the dogs below them responded by howling. Soon another train rumbled by, causing the bed to shake and the chair to dance a few steps across the floor. The vibration set Maggie's teeth on edge. Seth turned onto his side and curled into a fetal position. Maggie put her arms around him.

"Talk to me, Seth," she said.

He sat up.

"Rabbi Leah. Howard. The entire congregation is dead because of me."

"They knew the risks."

"I led Hedge Protection right to them. I'm a Judas all right. I'm a Judas to them. And a Judas to you. You're on the run because of me."

"You can't think about it that way."

"But it's true."

Seth got out of bed and sat in the chair. The overhead light was off, but the lamp on the stool surrounded them with an oval of light.

"I should never have joined the synagogue," he said.

Maggie hugged a pillow. "Don't do this to yourself."

"It was one thing to risk my life, but I had no right to put your life in danger. What I did was inexcusably selfish."

Maggie thought about the burning effigy of her husband and hugged the pillow tighter. "That thing those people were burning. It was terrible."

"When we get to Mexico, are you going to leave me?" Seth said.

"Why would I do that?"

"Because of this." He gestured at the room.

Maggie swung the pillow against Seth's knees.

"I'm not leaving you," she said.

"Thank you."

Maggie rubbed her nose. There had been moments since they'd

gone on the run that she had been furious with Seth. She had imagined beating his head with her fists for doing this to them. But then, she saw how people had turned Seth into this monster called the American Judas. She saw how they dumped their hate and fear on him. Seth could be a complete and utter idiot, but he was never a monster. Maggie's anger at Seth had been replaced with a desire to protect him, and so maybe she had a motherly instinct after all.

"Why didn't you ask me to come to services with you?" she said.

"It wasn't your religion," Seth said.

"I should have supported your decision. It was a brave thing to do. As of now, no more talk of feeling guilty. Okay?"

"Okay."

Seth got back under the covers next to Maggie. She snuggled up close to him.

"Make love to me," she said.

Maggie felt Seth's body go rigid. She felt terrible. He'd just been through a terrible experience. She was sure that the last thing on his mind was sex.

"I understand if you don't feel like it," Maggie said.

Seth turned to face her.

"I want to," he said. "But I don't have a condom."

"Who cares? We'll be in Mexico tomorrow."

"Maybe we should wait until then, just to be safe."

"Seth, we have gone beyond safe. After all we've been through, I need to feel something other than fear."

They stripped off their clothes. Seth's kisses were minty fresh from his recently brushed teeth. His hands roamed her body, teasing her in familiar ways. She stroked him and was rewarded with a contented sigh. When he entered her, he said, "I'm home." He said this every time they made love, and she loved hearing it every time because it was always true. The way they made love that night, Maggie felt like another train had gone by.

CHAPTER 33

As the church van drove into the cavernous warehouse, Seth felt like a modern-day Jonah entering the mouth of a whale. People clustered around vans that had already arrived. In the center of the warehouse was a moving truck with mud-caked tires.

"I see our rest-stop buddy made it," Maggie said.

She pointed at Jerry Hays, who stood by the truck.

"See the guy Jerry is talking to?" Seth said. "That's the guy I met at the Family Bible Store. I can't remember his name."

"That's Julian Cross," Maggie said. "He's Judy Cross's son. Do we care that the man smuggling us into Mexico is the son of my ex-boss?"

"Less than a week ago she was still your boss. I feel like it's been years since we left Washington."

Jerry was flailing his arms about, while Julian's arms were crossed. Seth could tell that they were not having a friendly conversation.

Seth and Maggie got out of the van, retrieved their backpacks, and joined the crowd of men, women, and children migrating toward the moving truck. Seth picked up a faint scent of piss and vomit inside the vehicle. Since this was Julian's smuggling operation, the crowd was forced to wait for him and Jerry to finish their argument.

"I still don't see why I have to give you my gun. You have a gun," Jerry said, pointing at Julian's belt holster. "How can I be sure you won't rob me?"

Julian sighed wearily. "My truck, my rules."

"I say we put it to a vote. Everybody who thinks we should be allowed to keep our guns, raise your hands."

Hands went up. Julian rolled his eyes.

"We don't have time for this," he said. "We're on a very tight schedule."

Megan and Mindy joined Seth and Maggie.

"Look at the other smuggler," Megan said. "He's getting nervous."

The man in question stood behind Julian. His head pivoted from side to side as he glared at the crowd. He held a rifle tightly against his chest.

"I would suggest we leave and find another way across the border," Megan said. "But Carlos and the van are gone."

Seth twisted around. All the church vans were either gone or driving away. Unless they planned to walk across the border, they had no choice but to stick with Julian. Seth pushed his way to the front of the crowd.

"Will you give us your word that you'll return our guns when we get to Mexico?" Seth said.

Jerry and Julian stopped talking, and Julian stared at Seth.

"You look familiar," Julian said. "Have we met before?"

Seth was going to remind him that they had met at the Family Bible Store, but Jerry cut him off.

"This is the American Judas," Jerry said as he clamped his hand on Seth's shoulder. "He's a genuine celebrity."

Julian smiled as if he'd just won the lottery.

"Since we have a celebrity on this trip," Julian said. "I will make an exception to the rules. Everyone can keep their guns."

"All right!" Jerry said. "That's what I'm talking about."

"But you have to give me your bullets."

Jerry yanked his hand away from Seth's shoulder.

"My gun is no good without bullets," Jerry said. "You know that."

"This isn't a democracy," Julian said. "Take it or leave it. Give your ammo to my partner, Dewey."

Dewey stopped cradling his rifle and held out a burlap bag. Jerry mumbled under his breath as he slid the magazine out of his handgun and tossed it into the bag. Seth expected only a handful of people to have weapons on them, but it seemed that everyone was armed. Handguns and rifles appeared as if out of nowhere. Even Megan and Mindy were carrying.

By the time Seth took his Springfield XD out of the holster and removed the magazine, a line had grown in front of Dewey that snaked around the warehouse. Seth got into the line and waited his turn. While Dewey gathered ammo, another lined formed to pay Julian for the border crossing. Seth watched as Maggie handed Julian a roll of bills. She pointed at Seth to let him know that the money was for both of them.

The line to pay Julian moved more quickly than the ammo line because a number of people held onto the security of their weapon for as long as they possibly could, waiting until they were standing at the burlap bag before unloading their magazines.

Seth watched Julian wander over to a corner of the warehouse. He didn't like the way Julian had looked at him after Jerry blurted out that he was the American Judas. Julian took out his phone and made a call. It seemed like an odd time to be calling a friend since he was about to smuggle people illegally across the border. As Julian talked, he scanned the crowd, zeroing in on Seth. When he realized Seth was looking at him, he smiled and waved. Seth didn't wave back.

Maybe this was a bad idea after all, Seth thought. Maybe walking to Mexico was safer than trusting Julian. He felt a surge of panic, but then he reached the head of the line.

"Give me your bullets," Dewey said. He held the burlap bag open. "You're holding up the line."

Seth looked over at Maggie. She was waiting by the truck. They had come this far. He had to have faith that they would make it the rest of the way. He tossed his magazine into the bag.

CHAPTER 34

The truck hit another bump, and Maggie grabbed Seth's arm to keep from pitching onto her side. The engine rumbled like an upset stomach. Only a few slivers of light leaked in. Fuel exhaust filled her nose and stuck to her skin. Fear was the other smell that filled the cramped, dark box. Children whimpered, and parents whispered words of assurance.

Maggie tried to imagine what life would be like in Mexico. After paying Julian, they didn't have a lot of money left over. She had no idea what kind of work was available or where they would live. Her train of thought was interrupted by Seth's hand on her knee.

"We're stopping," he said.

The truck slowed down and jerked to a halt. The panic that had been held in check broke loose among the passengers. They hadn't been traveling long enough to reach Mexico. Had the truck broken down? Would they have to walk the rest of the way?

Maggie could hear the lock slide and the ramp being pulled out. The door swung open and Dewey stepped inside.

"All right, potty break," he said. "Make it quick."

With a collective sigh of relief, people began filing out of the truck. Maggie stood up and slung her backpack over her shoulder.

"Why are you taking your backpack?" Seth asked.

"We might not get the same spot when we get back in. I don't want to lose track of our stuff."

"Good point." He grabbed his backpack.

The cool night air was a welcome change from the sweaty press of humanity inside the truck. Maggie needed to pee, but there was no way she was going to squat in the dark where there might be scorpions or God knows what waiting. Seth left his backpack with Maggie while he went to find a private rock. Maggie watched parents coax their reluctant children to relieve themselves with warnings that they wouldn't get another chance. Mothers and fathers took turns holding their frightened children as they dashed behind rocks for a quick pee.

Maggie decided to stretch her legs while she had the chance. She reasoned that the backpacks would be safe by the truck's rear tire while she walked toward the front of the vehicle. In that direction was freedom. As Maggie got closer to the truck's cab, she could see an unsteady light in the desert, blue and flashing. She squinted to get a better look.

"Oh my God," Maggie said. "They found us."

SETH FELT MUCH BETTER AFTER EMPTYING HIS BLADDER AND STRETCHING his legs, but now he was really thirsty. He didn't have any water bottles in his backpack but he knew Maggie had a couple left in hers. Seth found their backpacks, but Maggie wasn't there with them. She must have gone off to pee after all. He patted the sides of her backpack to find the bottles and thought he felt the right shape in a side pocket. Seth unzipped the pocket and snaked his hand inside. He pulled out the first solid thing he touched. Instead of a water bottle, he had a red-and-blue wooden bird in his hand. Seth stuck the bird in his pants pocket and reached back into the backpack.

He felt around until his fingers touched a smooth shape. It was slightly damp. It had to be a water bottle sweating condensation. As he was about to pull the water bottle out, Jerry Hays appeared next to him.

"Please tell me you hid extra ammo in your pack," Jerry said.

"Sorry," Seth said. "I'm getting a bottle of water out."

"I don't trust these coyotes. I want bullets for my gun."

"Right now, all I want is a drink of water."

Seth almost had the bottle out when he heard Maggie's voice.

"Run, Seth, run! Hedge Patrol is coming! Hedge Patrol! Hedge Patrol!"

Her warning spread through the crowd and people began to

shout and run in different directions.

"I knew it!" Jerry yelled. "Let's go!"

He grabbed Seth's shoulder and yanked him away from the backpack. The water bottle slipped out of his fingers and fell to the ground.

"Let me go!" Seth said. "I'm not going anywhere without Maggie."

"Worry about her later."

Sirens wailed and flashing blue lights brightened the night sky. Seth held his ground as people flew past him. He saw Maggie running toward him. Their eyes met.

"Run!" she shouted.

Seth turned and sprinted. Jerry ran next to him. He had no idea where they were going. Gunshots rang out, causing more panic. Seth ran faster.

"Don't stop!" Jerry yelled. "Whatever you do, don't stop!"

Seth heard a gunshot directly behind him and glanced over at Jerry. There was a black hole under his right eye. Jerry stumbled a few steps before tumbling to the ground. Seth hesitated and looked back. He didn't see Maggie, but a Hedge Patrol missioner was gaining on him. The missioner aimed his gun at Seth and fired. The bullet whizzed past Seth's head, and he started running again.

MAGGIE HAD BEEN BEHIND SETH UNTIL A MAN COLLIDED WITH HER, THE two of them falling hard on the ground. He got up and ran, leaving her behind. Maggie stood and found herself facing the barrel of Julian Cross's gun.

"Where the hell do you think you're going?" Julian said.

He grabbed Maggie's arm and dragged her to the moving truck. The desert's chilly night air and the feeling of hopeless dread left her shivering. Maggie's teeth chattered. She thought of her coat rolled up inside her backpack but doubted she would ever see the pack again.

Maggie flinched at every gunshot and scream as somewhere in the dark Hedge Patrol missioners chased her fellow passengers. They returned to the truck leading freshly caught prisoners. Megan and Mindy had been apprehended. They didn't take their eyes off the ground as they were led into the truck. Maggie watched in horror as missioners dragged dead bodies back from the desert and tossed them in with the living. She examined each passing person to make sure it wasn't Seth. When they lugged Jerry's body by, she saw that he had lost his NRA cap.

"See what you did," Julian said. "They died because of you."

A Hedge Patrol missioner with a big, white cowboy hat and a bigger stomach ambled over to Maggie and Julian. His attitude more than the insignia on his uniform told Maggie that he was in charge. He ejected an empty magazine from his gun and inserted a fresh one.

"Chief Anderson," Julian said.

"Julian," Anderson said. "Thanks for the call. I've got the press standing by in Tucson. This haul is going to look great on TV."

"Where's Ginsberg?"

"Out there somewhere." Anderson waved his gun toward the desert.

"You let him get away?"

"I didn't let him do anything. A few always escape on these late night raids. He won't get far. We'll find his body in a couple of days."

"We can't wait that long. You have to find him tonight."

Anderson spat in the sand.

"Ginsberg could be anywhere out there," he said. "I'm not risking the lives of my men looking for him when he's as good as dead. No way he can survive out there."

"That's not good enough," Julian said. "The only reason Deacon Wingard had me call you was so that you could arrest Ginsberg."

Maggie glared at Julian.

"You work for Hedge Patrol?"

Julian raised his hand to slap Maggie. She flinched, and he smirked instead of striking her.

"Hell no," he said. "I pay them to look the other way when I cross the border."

"Come on, lady," Anderson said. "Get in the truck."

He pushed Maggie into the vehicle.

"Seth's death is your fault as well," Julian said.

The door slammed shut, leaving Maggie in the dark.

CHAPTER 35

Maggie couldn't help but notice her. Passengers on the train were not allowed to leave their seats without asking permission and, even then, they had to wait for an escort, but this girl did as she pleased without a chaperone. The armed guards made no attempt to stop her.

Sayings like "cute as a bug's ear" were invented for girls like her. Her light-blonde hair shone like a halo, and her smile was as big and wholesome as the heartland of America. She was smiling now as she plopped down in the seat next to Maggie. She smelled like strawberries and vanilla.

"Mind if I sit here a spell?" the girl said.

"Sure, knock yourself out," Maggie said before turning her attention back to watching the land of the free rush by in a blur.

"My name's Tiffany. Tiffany Unklesby. What's yours?"

"Maggie Ginsberg."

They rode in silence. Maggie ignored Tiffany. Maggie used to like trains. She enjoyed the sound of the chugging engine and the way the cars rocked as they hugged the rails. But she didn't like this train. She knew where it was taking her, and she knew it was going to be bad. Very bad. Maggie tried not to cry again, but she couldn't stop the tears. She sniffed and sniffed. She really needed to blow her nose, and looked around for something to blow into. The only possible prospect, other than her sleeve, was the box in her hands.

A guard had thrust the box into Maggie's lap a short time after she'd been put in her seat. She clutched it tightly in an effort to keep from completely freaking out, and hadn't bothered to look at it until now. On top of the box, it read TRAVEL MEAL along with logos for a popular fast-food chain and the National Church. Maggie opened the lid. Inside was a ham sandwich wrapped in cellophane, a bag of potato chips, a box of grape-flavored juice, and a white napkin encased in plastic. Maggie was about to tear it open to get to the napkin when Tiffany grabbed her wrist.

"You're going to want to keep that napkin," Tiffany said.

Maggie gave Tiffany the stink eye.

"I was going to use it to blow my nose," she said.

"You might want to use your sleeve instead. I know that sounds gross, but you're going to want to keep that napkin."

"Why would I want to do that?"

Tiffany sat up straight and folded her hands in her lap.

"It's a long train ride," she said. "You're going to get hungry. You can try to get by on just the juice and the chips, but eventually, you'll eat the sandwich. After you do, you're going to need to go to the bathroom. Those sandwiches have a way of going right through you. You're going to want that napkin, because they stopped putting TP in the bathrooms months ago. That's another thing. When you do go to the bathroom, remember to hold your nose before you go in and don't breathe until you leave. They aren't cleaned as regular as they should be."

Maggie closed the box and stared at Tiffany.

"How do you know all this?" Maggie said.

"My brother Kenny works on the train. He's my little brother, though you'd never know it when he's standing next to me. He's tall and got big shoulders."

"Your brother is a guard?" Maggie said, looking at the armed guard slouching at the head of the car, his hand resting on his semi-automatic rifle.

"Yeah, but not on this train. I know all the guards through Kenny. That sounded awfully boastful, didn't it?"

"Did your brother turn you in?"

"Gosh, no," Tiffany said. She giggled. "I volunteered. The Savior Camps have a quota to fill if they're going to stay in business. There's been a shortage of new campers, and I didn't want Kenny to lose his job. Mom and Dad said that it was one of the most Christian sacrifices I've ever made, but honestly, it's going to be fun. And I get to skip school."

Maggie had been in a daze since she left the desert. She lost track of Megan and Mindy when the missioners formally arrested her and processed her in Tucson. Maggie had hoped to find them when the missioners herded her onto the train, but they were nowhere in sight.

And then, God decided that Maggie wasn't confused and lonely enough and dropped this strange girl into the seat next to her. She felt her head swimming.

"I think I'm going to be sick," Maggie said.

"Looks like you might need that napkin sooner than I thought you would," Tiffany said.

Chapter 36

Judy Cross struggled to get comfortable. Sitting on the set, waiting for the countdown to the show's return from a commercial break, she could feel her Spanx rolling down. Judy thought cancelling "What's Cookin' in Amy's Kitchen" would help her lose weight. Instead, her in-between-meal snacking was out of control. Amy's cooking was a special treat worth waiting for. Now that there was nothing special to look forward to, Judy treated herself constantly to cookies, chips, and soft drinks.

"Thirty seconds," the floor director announced.

Judy peered down at her notes once more before setting them aside. She turned to the audience and gave them a friendly wave. She was rewarded with a smatter of women giggling.

"Ten seconds."

Judy sat up straight and gave her orange blazer a quick tug. She looked straight at the camera. The floor director used his fingers to count down the last five seconds. The applause sign lit up, and the audience obeyed its command.

"Welcome back to *The Judy Cross Show*, I'm your host, Judy Cross. Becoming a Christian Nation has not always been an easy road. Some Americans suffered culture shock. It was like eating too much candy on Easter Sunday. Too much sugar can make you a little cuckoo."

That got a good laugh from the audience. Judy waited for the laughter to subside.

"To help those people who couldn't find their way in our new Christian Nation, President Reed ordered the construction of the Savior Camps. It was the government's tough love that gave these people the environment they desperately needed to develop spiritually in the service of Jesus."

The applause sign lit up again. The audience not only obeyed, they got to their feet and cheered. Judy closed her eyes and lifted her chin to better soak in the love. Then she motioned for them to bring it down so that she could continue.

"Despite the fact that the camps have been a proven success, there are those who still oppose their existence. They claim that former campers have been brainwashed. They even have an ugly name for them. Jesus Zombies."

The audience booed. Judy stuck out her chest to show that she was ready to face this problem bravely.

"The most vocal critic of the Savior Camps is the Independent Christian Council, a once-respectable organization. I worked alongside them in the past, but on this subject, I strongly disagree with their position. Here to present the ICC's side of this controversial subject is Beatrice Portillo Shanahan."

The applause sign came on, but the audience clapped with little enthusiasm. Beatrice was short and stocky, with a kind face and quick, intelligent eyes. She walked confidently, as if she were entering a boxing ring. Judy stood to shake Beatrice's hand before she sat down. Beatrice perched on the edge of the couch facing Judy.

She didn't wait to be prompted. "I don't know where you're getting your facts, Judy, but we have numerous affidavits from family members of Savior Camp victims testifying that their loved ones were psychologically damaged as a result of their time inside the camps."

The bitter look Judy gave Beatrice made it seem she was ready to bite the poor woman's head off, but in reality, Judy's stomach was growling. She wanted to bite into something, but not Beatrice. There was a half-eaten box of cookies in the top drawer of her desk calling her name.

"Victims?" Judy said. "Come on, Beatrice, don't be so melodramatic. Graduates of Savior Camp are indeed changed, but for the better. Savior Camp breaks down their cultural shackles and remolds them in the image of Christ. It's understandable that family members might be overwhelmed by the change. Hopefully, they're challenged by the graduate's purity to become more Christ-like themselves."

"Family members weren't the only ones concerned. We spoke to employers of Savior Camp victims who were forced to fire them. They couldn't complete the simplest duties, were unable to communicate, and in some cases physically attacked their fellow employees."

"All hearsay from outside observers. Did you bother to actually talk to a former camper?"

"We talked to over fifty victims. They all showed signs of extreme mental trauma most commonly associated with torture and brainwashing. These are American citizens who committed no crime."

Judy smiled. She could see the doubt in Beatrice's eyes.

"I don't have fifty graduates, but I do have one man who spent a year at Camp Cleansing Sin in North Dakota," Judy said. "Welcome to the show, Shane Waters."

A tall, handsome man with blond hair, a mouthful of white teeth, and a well-toned body came bounding out onto the stage. He hugged Judy and shook hands with Beatrice before sitting beside her on the couch.

Shane's real name was Matthew Eichelberger. Other than a few commercials and a small part on a cancelled sitcom, his acting career had been all but dead until a single call to his agent resurrected it. *The Judy Cross Show* wanted an actor who was equal parts handsome and obscure. After proving that he could improvise his character convincingly, Judy assured Matthew that if he nailed today's performance, Shane Waters, the former camper, might become a recurring role.

"Thank you for taking the time to join us today, Mr. Waters," Judy said. "Tell our viewers what it is you do for a living?"

"I'm the assistant manager at the Loaves and Fishes restaurant in Capitol Hill," he said, flashing a big smile. "You can call the general manager if you don't believe me. Just ask for Antoine."

Judy and the audience laughed. Beatrice didn't.

"I'm sure that won't be necessary," Judy said. "How long have you worked for Loaves and Fishes? By the way, I love the name."

"It's one of the reasons why I applied there. I was thrilled to discover that it wasn't just a biblical reference to attract customers.

Everyone at the restaurant is like me, a person of deep faith and commitment to Jesus Christ."

"That's not what she asked you," Beatrice said.

Shane put his hand on Beatrice's shoulder in a friendly manner. She glanced at his hand but didn't move away.

"You're right," Shane said. "Let me see. I've worked there for a year and a half."

"Had you been an assistant manager anywhere else before Loaves and Fishes?" Judy said.

"No. This is my first time. I was hired as a waiter. After three months, I was promoted to my present position."

Shane beamed another bright-white smile at the audience. Women in the front row tittered with delight.

"And how would you describe your experience at Savior Camp?" Judy said.

"Gee," Shane said. "Let me think. Every day I thank God for allowing me to receive the life-changing message of Jesus Christ in such a nurturing environment."

"Were you ever physically abused?"

"If getting plenty of fresh air, eating lots of healthy food, and going on nature hikes is considered physical abuse, then sign me up for more. I had such an amazing experience, I didn't want to leave."

"They didn't brainwash you? Didn't make you memorize Bible verses?"

"We did study the Bible every day. I learned so much about Jesus that I never knew before. And I'm here to tell you that I am no Jesus Zombie. I do occasionally quote scripture, but only because the words carry so much truth and beauty."

There was no need to turn on the applause sign. The audience stood and applauded on their own.

"Shane, you were at Camp Cleansing Sin for a year. Is that right?" Beatrice said.

"Correct," Shane said. "I was a little worried about being up there in the winter, but the camp quarters were well-insulated and heated.

One day we had this great snowball fight, campers versus counselors. Campers won."

"You're probably not aware that there was some argument about building the camp in the Lostwood National Wildlife Refuge. Former campers have complained about the local wildlife that the refuge was created to protect. Did they bother you at all?"

Shane smiled and looked at Judy. Beatrice looked at Judy too, but Judy only smiled back at Shane.

"Nope," Shane said. "I love all of God's creatures."

Judy stepped in. "Tell me, Beatrice, why did the ICC waste so much time and money studying Savior Camps? Does the ICC want to close them down?"

"The sooner the better," Beatrice said. "People shouldn't be forced into believing in Jesus."

"Do you believe that sinners will only repent if they're swaddled in a warm blankie with bunny slippers and a cup of hot cocoa? Sinners need tough love, not bleeding hearts."

"How can you claim to be a follower of Christ while condoning brainwashing and torture? Especially you, Judy, considering your close friend Congressman Randall was driven to his death in a Savior Camp."

Judy drew back her hand as if she were about to slap Beatrice. To her credit, Beatrice didn't flinch. Judy's hand hung in the air for seven seconds, her eyes wide with anger, before she slowly lowered her hand.

"I'm afraid we've run out of time," Judy said. "I want to thank my guests, Beatrice Portillo Shanahan and Shane Waters, for joining us today. When we come back, I'll talk to a woman who is an expert at crocheting Bible covers. She has some secret techniques that you'll only see here on *The Judy Cross Show.*"

The applause sign came on and again the audience obeyed. Once the floor director let them know that they weren't on the air, Bill Garmon walked onto the set and hustled Shane away.

"How dare you bring up Chip," Judy said. "For the record, he committed suicide because his faith was weak."

"I stayed in touch with Chip until they took him away," Beatrice said. "He regretted how things ended between you two. He really cared about you."

Judy grabbed Beatrice's wrist.

"Never mention his name in front of me again," she said.

"You're hurting me," Beatrice said.

Judy let go. She looked away and when she turned back to Beatrice, her sunny smile had returned.

"What was that wildlife thing about?"

"The Lostwood National Wildlife Refuge has more ducks than any other region in the United States. Campers at Camp Cleansing Sin are constantly barraged by ducks quacking and crapping on them as they fly over the camp."

"Why didn't you bring up the ducks when you had the chance?"

"And embarrass your pretty boy? Besides, why bring it up today when I can release the information to the press tomorrow and it'll last more news cycles?"

Judy made a mental note to inform Bill of Beatrice's impending attack in the press and to prepare a defense.

"Why did you bring in a ringer?" Beatrice asked. "I would expect that kind of trick from the old Judy Cross, but not someone as dedicated to the teachings of the New Testament as you."

Judy shrugged.

"We ran out of time," she said. "Eventually, we would have found the right person."

"In other words, everyone you interviewed was a Jesus Zombie."

The floor director came over to Judy.

"Two minutes to air, Judy," he said. "We need you on the other set."

"I'm coming," she said.

"You claim Jesus Zombies don't exist," Beatrice said. "Even though you proved that they do."

The old Judy would have responded with something extremely

nasty. But the reborn Judy had the truth of the Lord in her bosom.

"America is the greatest, most blessed nation ever put on this earth by God," she said. "With Jesus in charge, America can do no wrong, which means the camps are good. Now if you will excuse me, I have to see a woman about crocheted Bible covers."

THE SNOWFALL WAS EARLY EVEN FOR MONTANA. WHITE FLAKES COVERED the ground in patches. Maggie shuddered more from the sight of Camp Glorious Rebirth than from the weather. The *Saved Through Faith* sign over the entrance may have looked like it had been taken from a Vacation Bible School, but it didn't fit in with the concrete guard towers and the barbed wire.

"I love snow," said Tiffany Unklesby. "It always makes me think of Christmas and hot chocolate with little marshmallows."

Other than the train track that ran parallel to the camp there was no sign of civilization. The flat land stretched for miles before sloping upward toward the snowcapped Rocky Mountains. Maggie and the rest of the prisoners were led off the train and onto an asphalt parking lot. Snowflakes stuck to their hair and clothes.

Armed camp guards marched the prisoners through the front gates. From loudspeakers nailed to every barrack blared Bobbi Sue Sunshine singing the hymn "All to Jesus I Surrender." The campers already living here were nowhere in sight, but then Maggie caught a few faces peeking out of barrack windows. She was moving too quickly to discern any details about them. To Maggie, they looked like ghosts.

The prisoners' march ended at a red-brick building with a tall chimney and a wraparound porch with rocking chairs. Standing on the porch was a large and sturdy man who gave Maggie the impression of an oak tree. Despite the winter weather, the sleeves of his flannel shirt were rolled up to his elbows, exposing his muscular forearms. A black chin curtain beard framed his ruddy face, and below the bangs of his bowl haircut, his hazel eyes twinkled.

"Welcome to Camp Glorious Rebirth," the man said. "I am Pastor Buck Graves, and I am the pastor in charge here."

"Howdy!" Tiffany shouted as she waved.

Pastor Graves ignored her.

"The camp is surrounded by electric fences, so try not to touch them. You might reckon that you're prisoners here. Nothing could be further from the truth. The guards and fences are here to keep evil out and Jesus' healing love locked inside."

The snow began to fall harder. White flakes caught in Pastor Graves's beard and made him look as if he were aging before their eyes. Maggie hugged herself. She was wearing the clothes she had on when she was captured in the Arizona desert. She had asked for a blanket on the train and had been ignored. Some of her fellow prisoners were wearing shorts and T-shirts. Their teeth chattered as they tried to rub a little warmth into their arms.

"I envy you," Pastor Graves said. "There is no greater moment in a person's life than when he surrenders to God's glory and gives himself completely to Jesus Christ. In that moment, he is born again. I have accepted Jesus Christ into my heart. You will too. It will be a hard journey. You will suffer as you've never suffered before. Removing Satan's hold on your soul is no walk in the park, but when we are done with you, you will experience the greatest joy your heart has ever known."

Pastor Graves's eyes were wide open, and Maggie wondered how he kept from blinking. His energy was like blinding headlights speeding toward her on a rainy night. She tensed as if he were about to crash into her.

"Counselors Stu and Bunny will take over now," Graves said. "Have a blessed day."

Pastor Graves sauntered into the house. A man and a woman in heavy coats stepped in front of the prisoners. They were like Jack Sprat and his wife. He was lean, and she was fat.

"Listen carefully as we explain the rules," Counselor Stu said. "They will not be repeated."

The male and female counselors alternated reciting the rules line by line.

"When you earn permission to speak to us, you will address us as Counselor Stu and Counselor Bunny. We will address you as campers."

"Remove all clothing before your medical examination. The camp provides your garments during your stay here. This includes undergarments. For the sake of modesty, you will be thoroughly clothed."

"You will begin with black clothes. As you prove worthy, you will receive clothing in lighter shades of grey until you earn the right to wear pure white."

"The lighter the shade, the more privileges you will have."

"You earn privileges by how well you memorize your Bible verses."

"And how obediently and efficiently you do your chores."

"You must ask permission before taking any action."

"Men and women will be separated and not allowed to speak to each other."

"Anyone who disobeys the rules will be punished."

"A loss of privileges for first offense."

"An increase of chores for second offense."

"Isolation for third offense."

"When do I get to see my children?" a woman called out. Maggie recognized her from their capture in Arizona.

Counselor Stu and Counselor Bunny exchanged glances.

"This is your first day, so I won't punish you," Counselor Stu said. "You must earn the privilege to speak to us, and when you do, address me as Counselor Stu."

"Counselor Stu," the woman said, "when may I see my children?"

Counselor Stu walked over to the woman.

"That is your first offense," he said. "It will take you twice as long to earn the right to do anything without asking a counselor for permission."

"I'm sorry," the woman said, "but I've never been away from my children. I need to know what happened to them."

"That is your second offense. You will do twice as many chores as the others. If you say one more word, I will be forced to put you in isolation. You are doing this to yourself. Do you want me to put you in isolation?"

The woman clasped her hands together.

"Please, just tell me if they're okay."

Counselor Stu motioned at the guards.

"I wish I could bend the rules just this once for you considering this is your first day, but that would only delay your salvation," he said.

Two of the guards grabbed the woman's arms and led her away.

"Anyone else have anything to say?" Counselor Stu said. The prisoners hung their heads and stayed silent. "Okay. Let's go. Men follow me, women follow Counselor Bunny."

The men shuffled behind Counselor Stu while the women lined up behind Counselor Bunny. Guards flanked the campers. The counselors marched the men and women in opposite directions. At the women's barracks, Counselor Bunny stood at the door while the women filed inside. When Maggie reached the door, Counselor Bunny thrust her arm out and blocked Maggie from entering.

"The camper we took to isolation," Counselor Bunny said. "Will you join me in praying for her soul tonight?"

Maggie said nothing.

"Well?"

"Forgive me," Maggie said. "I haven't earned the privilege to speak, Counselor Bunny."

Counselor Bunny leaned close to Maggie. She could tell that the counselor had eaten onions recently. Normally, this would have grossed Maggie out, but she had eaten so little lately that the smell made her stomach grumble.

"I give you permission to speak," Counselor Bunny said.

"I will join you in praying for the woman taken into isolation," Maggie said.

"Well done. But don't go thinking you can be saved too quickly."

Counselor Bunny put her arm down and Maggie went inside. Despite getting shelter from the cold wind, Maggie couldn't stop shaking.

CHAPTER 37

Using the toe of his tennis shoe, Seth nudged the headless man's plastic water jug. Instead of life-preserving water, a gopher snake, yellow with brown splotches, poured out and slithered away. The headless man wore a Baltimore Apostles football jersey with large holes in the faded purple-and-gold fabric. Seth missed the pre-Christianized names of NFL teams. The Ravens sounded much cooler than the Apostles.

The body was as shriveled as beef jerky. Seth wondered why predators only carried off the head. Maybe it was tastier than the rest of the body, or maybe it was just easier to remove.

"Sure wish you hadn't lost your head," Seth said. "I bet you were wearing a hat. I could sure use a hat."

The desert was no place for the fair-skinned and blue-eyed. Seth's arms and neck were an angry sun-burned red. Using his shirt as a head wrap deflected some of the sun's intensity, but he still ended up squinting until his eyelids ached. He wondered if the reason he smelled so terrible was because he was being cooked alive.

He shielded his eyes with his hand and studied his surroundings. A battalion of saguaro cacti dotted the hills, their prickly arms held up in surrender. They didn't know which direction he should go either. Beyond the hills, jagged mountains stretched toward a cloudless sky.

Seth had grown up in a suburb. The only thing he knew about surviving in the wilderness was that the sun rose in the east and set in the west. But the sun never seemed to move. It was always there, beating down on him all day and then suddenly, it was gone, and he was shivering in the night, trying to catch some sleep among the thorny shrubs.

He was fairly certain that two days had passed since the night Hedge Patrol had tried to kill him. Every so often he'd hear the bullet whizzing by that had almost split his head open. Occasionally, he took his gun out of the holster and checked to see if it was loaded, even though he knew damn well that he'd taken the magazine out in Tucson. He didn't need bullets now. He just needed something to do while he was walking.

Seth headed toward the mountains.

Two more days passed. Temperatures during the day rose to 110 degrees. The ground temperature was closer to 150. Seth's body temperature was rising too. He was too dehydrated to sweat out the heat building inside him. His tongue was thick, and he struggled to swallow because he had stopped producing saliva. Somewhere in his clouded mind, he thought about how he should have drunk his own urine, but he had pissed his pants while he slept, and the sun had baked it dry.

Seth bent down to sit and rest a moment, but his knees wobbled, and he fell over on his side with his face against the hot sand. He tried to push himself into a sitting position, but his arms were boiled noodles. He felt like the ground was magnetized and he was stuck to it, unable to budge. As Seth edged toward sleep, the pain and the scorching heat eased out of him.

"Hey sleepy head, you just going to lie there?"

He was surprised to see Maggie standing over him. She wore the white, thin cotton shirt and pants that she'd looked so good in during their trip to St. Simons. She was tanned a deep brown, which made her teeth bright white when she smiled. She was smiling now.

"Maggie?"

"Come on," she said, gesturing for him to follow. "Let's go."

Seth didn't know how he managed to get back on his feet, but he did. He stumbled after Maggie. She waited for him at the top of the hill. The closer he got to her, the stronger he felt. Once he reached her, they walked side by side. Maggie swung her arms in an easy rhythm.

"That shirt is practically transparent," Seth said. "You should wear it more often."

Maggie laughed. "Can you imagine if I wore this at work?"

They smiled at each other shyly like new lovers.

"I'm sorry I ran away," Seth said.

"I told you to run," Maggie said. "What were you supposed to do? Stay and get shot?"

"I still feel terrible. When I finally stopped running I didn't know where I was. It's pitch black at night."

"You're lucky you didn't trip and break your head open."

"I did get scratched up." He showed her the scabs on his arms. "And I got these sticky things on my ankles that hurt like hell. I couldn't pull them off. I had to throw away my socks."

Seth reached for Maggie's hand, but she moved out of reach.

"Do you remember the first time we met?" Seth said.

"Corey Klein's birthday party," Maggie said.

"I saw you at the other side of the room and you took my breath away. The feeling was so strong it scared me. I almost avoided you."

"I saw you and thought you were cute. You came over and introduced yourself. You asked me questions about myself. You were confident without being a dick."

"Inside I was freaking out. I knew you weren't just some gorgeous girl that I was hitting on at a party. Even then, I knew you were the one."

Maggie pulled a stray strand of hair behind her ear. The sun didn't seem to bother her blue eyes.

"Are you ever sorry we got together?" she asked.

"You're the best thing that's ever happened to me," Seth said.

"If it weren't for me, you'd probably be in Israel right now with your family, married to a sexy Israeli woman, raising lots of strong Jewish babies."

Seth wiped the grit off his forehead. He hated seeing Maggie sad.

"I know we don't talk about God and fate much, but I believe we were meant to be together," Seth said.

"Do you hear that?" Maggie said.

"Hear what?"

"Children."

Seth heard the sound of children shouting. They followed the noise over a hill topped with palo verde trees full of yellow blossoms. The hill dropped down into a valley with huts made from spare boards. Next to the huts were clotheslines filled with faded shirts and simple dresses drying in the hot sun.

A group of boys of various ages played a spirited game of soccer on a dirt field. The dusty boys yelled at each other in Spanish.

"Look Maggie," Seth said. "It's a village. We made it."

He turned around, but she wasn't there.

"Maggie, where are you?"

He hurried to the other side of the trees and then back again, panic rising in him, but there was no sign of her.

"Maggie!" he shouted. "Maggie! Come back!"

THE CHILDREN STOPPED PLAYING THEIR GAME TO STARE AT THE STRANGE man on top of the hill. One of the older boys was certain that the man had gone insane from wandering in the desert. He warned the other boys not to go near the crazy man, he might be dangerous, and then the boy ran to get his father.

CHAPTER 38

The days passed as fleeting images. Hands washing his body. Sips of water followed by sips of soup. Cool rags pressed against his forehead and chest. Voices softly speaking words Seth couldn't understand. His dreams were filled with repeating images: Maggie shouting, guns firing, the black hole in Jerry's head, and running in the darkness. In his jumbled dreams, he tried repeatedly to change the events so that he didn't end up lost in the desert, but each attempt failed. Every dream ended with him wandering endlessly under the hot sun.

Seth woke up one morning with a clear mind. He was in a single-room house with cinder-block walls. The windows had tattered curtains and no glass. A group of brown-skinned boys stared at him through the window. He was on a bed of straw covered with stained sheets. He was naked under a cheap blanket. On the other side of the room, an old woman with gnarled hands chopped vegetables at a wooden table. Behind her, steam rose from a kettle on a wood stove.

Seth propped himself up on his elbows. His movement caught the old woman's attention.

"Hello," he said.

The old woman wiped her hands on a scrap of fabric and left the house. The boys in the window continued to stare. Seth looked around the room. There were four more straw beds in an opposite corner. There were no sinks or a bathroom. The house didn't have running water. There was a layer of grit on everything, but it was tidy. A brightly colored painting of the Virgin Mary hung on the wall. Whatever the old woman was cooking on the wood stove smelled inviting.

A thin man with skin the color of dark chocolate entered the house. He wore overalls, a baseball cap, and no shirt. He took off the cap, revealing a thicket of black hair. He shooed away the boys at the window with a wave of his hand. He pulled a chair over from the table and sat next to Seth. He grinned, showing the few yellow teeth he had left.

"You are a very lucky man, Seth Ginsberg," he said.

"How do you know my name?"

"I looked in your wallet and found your driver's license. I didn't take any money. I am an honest man."

Seth rubbed peeling skin off his forehead.

"Do you have a phone I could use?"

"There are no phones here. Who would we call?"

"You saved my life. You know my name, but I don't know yours."

"I am Enrique," he said, putting his hand on his chest. "The woman you saw earlier is *mi madre*. She is the one who rescued you. I just carried you inside. She was the one who nursed you back from the dead."

"I'll thank her personally when she comes back."

"Do you speak Spanish?"

"No, I'm afraid I don't."

"Then I will thank her for you. She speaks very little English."

"But you do."

Enrique tilted back in his chair.

"I lived in the states for eight years," he said. "I was undocumented. I mainly did landscaping and construction, but I also picked fruit and worked for a chicken factory. I had to learn English to survive."

"When did you come back?"

"Shortly after your country went *loco*. I'm a good Catholic, but even I know not to let the church run the government."

"After all those years of Mexicans illegally crossing the border into the United States, how does it feel to see us crossing illegally into Mexico?"

"Well," Enrique said, scratching his head. "I wish the *gabachos*, *perdóname*, gringos had left some of their gringo ways back home. Also, they should learn to speak Spanish."

Seth told Enrique how he was crossing the border when his group was attacked by Hedge Patrol. How they shot and killed the man running beside him. How Seth had wandered in the desert. Enrique's mother returned, and Enrique introduced her to Seth. He told her *muchas gracias*. She patted his head and went back to her cooking.

"You walked across the desert in four days," Enrique said. "*Sin agua*. We are close to the border, but not for a man on foot. It is a miracle that you are alive."

Seth rubbed the stubble on his chin.

"I don't know about miracles. I wasn't trying to get to Mexico. I wanted to go back to Tucson and I went the wrong way."

Enrique cocked his head to the side. "Go back? Didn't you want to escape?"

"I don't know if Hedge Patrol captured or killed my wife. If she's alive, I need to find her."

CHAPTER 39

Maggie could smell the coffee. On the mornings Seth managed to get up on time, he would leave the house shortly before Maggie's alarm rang. Before he left, he always placed a cup of coffee on her nightstand so that she would wake up to a fresh cup. He never forgot to add skim milk and honey, just the way she liked it. Breathing in the earthy aroma of the coffee, she waited for Seth to kiss her forehead before he left.

The 4:00 a.m. siren wailed, and the barrack's lights came on. There was no coffee and no kiss. Maggie had been dreaming. After two months at Camp Glorious Rebirth, she still hadn't gotten used to the siren. She reluctantly opened her eyes and saw a woman ransacking Tiffany's cabinet. She and Maggie had adjacent beds.

"What you doing?" Maggie slurred. It was too early in the morning to make words properly.

"I need whites," the woman said, pulling out clothes and holding them up to her chest. "They won't let me see him without whites."

The woman wore black. Maggie had graduated to light gray.

The woman was as nervous as a bird about to be eaten by a cat. Her rank body odor made Maggie's eyes tear up. Lately, Maggie had been hypersensitive to smells, especially bad smells, and this place was full of them. The woman was about to bolt with Tiffany's clothes when she realized Tiffany was standing behind her.

Maggie wondered how Tiffany managed to look good in the modest undergarments they all wore. The knee-length bloomers and loose camisoles made Maggie feel like they were living in an episode of *Little House on The Prairie*.

"I don't think Jesus would approve if you attained your reward by cheating," Tiffany said. She had her hands on her hips, and her head tilted to a degree indicating disappointment.

The woman held the clothes tightly in her arms.

"You must let me have them," she said. "I can't get my boy back unless I have whites."

"If you had loved and submitted to the Lord, you wouldn't have lost your boy in the first place," Tiffany said. "You have no one to blame but your own wicked ways."

Maggie woke up enough to see past the woman's untamed hair and the dark circles under her eyes. She recognized her as one of the expectant mothers in Maternity Barracks.

"Weren't you wearing white last week?" Maggie asked.

The woman turned to Maggie, sensing a sympathetic ear. "After I gave birth, they took the whites away. They only let me hold him for a minute." She held out her arms as if cradling a child. "They took him away when I was asleep. I didn't even get a chance to count his toes."

"Don't take the clothes," Maggie said. "They'll see you take them on the security cameras and put you in isolation."

"But I have to get him back. If you were a mother, you'd understand."

Maggie remembered when *The Judy Cross Show* interviewed parents who had rescued children from the Devil's influence. A couple from Bethesda had a six-month-old baby girl who had been confiscated from a religious cult. Maggie remembered the baby because she wouldn't stop crying no matter what the adopted mother did to comfort her.

Tiffany put her arm around the woman's shoulder and urged the woman to sit with her on her cot. She had replaced her scolding tone with a kinder, gentler attitude.

"Don't be sad," Tiffany said. "My brother told me what happens to babies born in the camps. Your boy will be raised in a good Christian home where he'll be treated with love and kindness. He'll never know that he was born to a sinner."

The despair on the woman's face was so great that Maggie had to look away. The woman dropped the white clothes and shambled off.

Maggie and Tiffany grabbed their towels and toiletries and got in line for the latrine. Since they weren't allowed to have hot water, showers were brief or skipped completely. With the arrival of harsh winter weather, Maggie normally got by with a quick wash of individual body parts at the sink. But with her sense of smell so acute, she forced herself to strip out of her modest undergarments and shower. The icy water stung, but at least it woke her up. Afterwards, she brushed her teeth at the sink and looked at herself in the mirror. Maggie hadn't had acne since her early twenties, but now her forehead was covered with zits.

She was fumbling with her clothes when the guards entered to escort the campers to the fellowship hall. Her heavy woolen gray dress meant she didn't have to ask a guard or a counselor for permission to sit before eating in the mess hall, but she still had to ask to go to the bathroom and couldn't go without an escort.

Tiffany had graduated to the coveted white clothes during her second week at camp. She already knew most of the Bible verses by heart. Despite the lack of sleep, privacy, decent food, and heat, she was never unhappy. She seemed to thrive in the camp's tough conditions. The counselors couldn't figure why Tiffany was sent to camp in the first place, but then they discovered that she had volunteered to come to the camp to help out her brother the train guard. Such Christian sacrifice had to be honored.

The counselors decided to use Tiffany. With her blonde hair and white clothes, she looked like an angel. Whenever a camper struggled with their Bible verses or collapsed from exhaustion, a counselor would suggest the camper look at Tiffany Unklesby for inspiration, since she was living evidence of the power of Jesus' love. While Tiffany always blushed when this happened, she never noticed that the other campers feared and avoided her.

Maggie's stomach growled, but Pastor Graves believed that the spirit needed to be fed before the stomach. He gave a sermon in the fellowship hall every morning before breakfast. To get there, campers had to shovel a path through the three feet of snow that had accumulated during the night.

Maggie was thrusting her shovel into the heavy, wet snow and hating the way it kept slithering down inside her rubber boots when she felt a ball of nausea race up her throat. She retched what little she had in her stomach. Maggie leaned on her shovel until she felt better, then quickly covered the vomit with snow. She put a handful of clean snow in her mouth to wash away the foul taste.

Inside the fellowship hall, campers sat on hard pews while Pastor Graves stalked from one side of a raised stage to the next holding a Bible and wearing a headset microphone.

"Straying from God's path is easy," Pastor Graves said. "Especially for the weak-minded. You let go of the hand of the Holy Spirit. You reject the love of Jesus. You no longer take pride in this nation chosen by God to be the only country where Christians are free to be true Christians."

This wasn't the first morning Maggie had vomited. The cause could have been any number of things: bad food, illness, lack of sleep, stress from constant physical activity, but she felt certain that none of them were responsible for her queasy stomach.

"Sinners must repent," Pastor Graves continued. "Maybe you think you can outfox Jesus. Maybe you think you can avoid God's wrath. But there is no escape."

Maggie had missed her last period. The only blood she'd passed was spotty. She was having headaches, morning sickness, and her breasts ached. She'd counted the weeks from the last time she'd had unprotected sex with Seth, and it all added up.

Maggie was pregnant.

"You have danced with Satan. Now you must pay the price for your wickedness. There is only one way to avoid the fiery pits of Hell that await you."

Pregnant. She had been scared of getting knocked up before because of how it would affect her life and career. But she always told herself that if it did happen, she'd accept it and be happy. She would try to be a good mother, and she knew Seth would be a great father. He had always wanted children.

"You must submit completely to Jesus. It's the only way to avoid eternal damnation. You can only be freed from your sins by his blood."

Seth. She didn't know if he was alive or dead. This baby might be her last link to him.

"You must submit completely to Camp Glorious Rebirth and be born again in the eyes of the Lord. Stop following your brain and follow my heart. I am your shepherd and you are my flock."

But the baby wouldn't be Seth's any more than hers. Maggie thought of the woman who tried to steal Tiffany's clothes. The look of despair on her face. She knew she'd never see her child again. She would have been better off if her baby had never been born.

If Maggie had this baby, it would be raised in what Tiffany called a good Christian home. Her child would never know that Seth was its father. Instead, it would be taught that Seth was an evil man known as the American Judas. A wave of nauseating fever engulfed Maggie and she could hear her blood pounding in her ears. She covered her mouth and held her stomach until she cooled back down.

And even if her child grew up in a good Christian home, if he or she made one stupid mistake, unintentionally broke one unbreakable law, aroused the suspicion of one overzealous neighbor, they would be sent to a Savior Camp. She couldn't allow her child to end up here. She had to find a way to get rid of the baby.

CHAPTER 40

Seth was working in the garden with Enrique's wife and two sons when Enrique squatted down next to him.

"I am going to Caborca tomorrow," Enrique said.

"Are there phones in Caborca?" Seth asked.

"Si. Caborca also has gringos and buses that go to the larger cities."

"Are you trying to get rid of me?"

Enrique put his hand on Seth's shoulder.

"*Si*. You don't belong here."

The next morning, Seth looked in the mirror. He had changed during his stay in Enrique's home. His face was thinner, with a patchy beard, and his skin was ruddy from the wind and sun. His own clothes had been destroyed by the journey through the desert and had been torn into rags. Enrique's mother used them to wash the floor.

Seth wore a flannel shirt and a trucker's cap. The worn cowboy boots hid the fact that his faded jeans originally belonged to a shorter man. The sunglasses hid his blue eyes. At first glance, he appeared to be another poor Mexican, which was exactly what he hoped others would think. He was a wanted man. He didn't know if Hedge Protection's long arms reached into Mexico.

Enrique looked Seth over and shook his head. He pointed at the belt holster around Seth's waist.

"Only gringos show off their guns," Enrique said. "Come."

He took Seth to a neighbor's hut. The man had a collection of guns and holsters. Enrique worked out a trade where Seth gave the man his belt holster in exchange for an ankle holster. Seth asked the man if he happened to have a magazine that would fit his gun. The man examined Seth's weapon.

"Springfield XD 9mm," the man said.

He brought out a cardboard box filled with gun magazines. He rifled through the box until he found one for Seth. It was fully loaded.

"I have no way to pay for this," Seth said.

The man frowned and waved his hand.

"He's giving it to you as part of the trade," Enrique said.

Seth loaded his gun as he and Enrique walked back to the hut. He was surprised at how satisfying it felt to hear the click of the magazine as it locked into the gun.

"Where did that guy get all those weapons?" Seth said.

"Many gringos die in the desert," Enrique said. "Most of them were armed. That man goes out into the desert once a month, buries the dead, and collects their guns, which he sells at the market."

Seth helped load baskets of produce into the back of an ancient truck, and then said his goodbyes to Enrique's family. One of Enrique's sons, Seth couldn't remember if he was Victor or Francisco, handed Seth a bright-blue object. The boy spoke in English, something he hadn't done before.

"This was in your pocket," he said.

It was the wooden bird Seth had pulled out of Maggie's backpack. The boy traced circles in the dirt with his toe.

"I was going to keep it, but I don't steal."

Seth was impressed by the boy's honesty and was tempted to give him the bird as a gift, but it belonged to Maggie. He wanted to see her face light up when he gave it back to her.

THE POLLEROS, CHICKEN BUS, WAS BOARDING FOR NOGALES. ENRIQUE AND Seth sat in Enrique's truck, deciding how to say goodbye. In his lap was a small bag that Enrique's wife had given him that contained a change of clothes, a toothbrush, a bottle of water, and tamales in a paper bag. Seth took three twenty-dollar bills from his wallet and offered them to Enrique, who took the money without comment.

"Thank you for saving my life," Seth said.

Enrique nodded. "I hope you find your wife."

The two men shook hands. Seth got out, and Enrique drove

toward the open market to sell his vegetables. Seth climbed aboard the converted school bus painted in the green, white, and red colors of the Mexican flag and found a seat toward the back. There were transportation services that offered newer buses with comfortable seats and no passengers holding boxes of fruit or livestock in their laps, but they were more expensive. Seth wasn't sure how long his money would last, especially in Nogales.

The bus filled beyond capacity and Seth ended up giving his seat to an old woman who reminded him of Enrique's mother. Four bumpy hours later, he caught his first sight of Nogales. Tall, gleaming buildings stood in stark contrast to the barren desert. What he had heard was true. The skyline looked like Las Vegas.

As soon as it had become apparent that the United States really was going to become a Christian Nation, gambling industry leaders decided to relocate. They chose Nogales as their new home; it was on the border, had a decent airport, and already had plenty of cheap thrills. The casino owners bought up the land, tore down most of the local bars and hotels, and built a new strip of high-end gambling palaces.

Seth's legs were stiff as he descended the steps of the bus. Across the street was a gleaming replica of the Chichen Itza pyramid, with a row of glass doors that led to the casino inside. Farther down the strip, he spotted the Chapultepec Castle. Seth was oddly pleased to see these tributes to the gambling industry's adopted country.

It was late afternoon, and a cool breeze warned of a cold night ahead. Seth needed a place to stay, but couldn't afford the casino hotels. He headed away from the strip, hoping to find a cheaper alternative.

"Welcome to Gomorrah" was spray-painted onto the side of a building, which made Seth chuckle. In Washington, he'd often heard politicians liken Nogales to the cursed city in Genesis. Apparently, the locals used the name here as well.

Seth couldn't shake the feeling that he was back in the states. All the signs were in English. Hamburger joints outnumbered taco stands. What had the gringos done with all the Mexicans? Many stores prominently displayed the American flag, and had signs that read "True Patriots" and "English Spoken Here."

He passed a number of shabby hotels that were probably in his price range, but he couldn't bring himself to go in. Nothing felt safe. It would be dark soon, and he hadn't eaten since he'd shared his tamales with his fellow passengers on the *polleros*. Seth glanced at one building's neon-blue light and almost ignored it because the place obviously wasn't a hotel, before realizing that it was a Star of David. Seth was standing outside of a synagogue.

RABBI SCOTT WORE TIGHT CLOTHES THAT SHOWED OFF THE HOURS HE SPENT working out. The rabbi's stylish hair was cut short, and his yarmulke was rainbow colored. His desk was neat and orderly, featuring a photo of a smiling Scott hugging a handsome man.

"Welcome to Bnai Ma'abarot," Rabbi Scott said. "Do you know anything about us?"

"I'm sorry," Seth said. "I don't."

"Bnai Ma'abarot means 'sons of the refugees.' We were in Austin, Texas before we moved down here. The synagogue's original mission was to provide a place of refuge for Jews who felt disenfranchised by traditional synagogues because of their sexual orientation. Here in Mexico, we've expanded that mission to include all Jewish-American refugees."

"Well, that would be me."

"The majority of our residents are homosexual. Will that bother you?"

"No."

Rabbi Scott crossed his arms and smiled pleasantly. Seth had deliberately not told the Rabbi his name, and still hadn't decided if he was going to reveal his true identity. He didn't want to lie, but he didn't want to put Bnai Ma'abarot in danger either. It might be safer if they didn't know who he was.

"Can you prove you're Jewish?" Rabbi Scott said. "There are plenty of places in town that will help non-Jews, which is why we don't feel guilty about only taking in mishpocha."

"I'm not sure how I can prove it," Seth said.

"Don't show me a circumcised penis. Most men your age are circumcised whether they're Jewish or not."

"I know. *Shema yisrael adonay elohenu adonay ehad.*"

"The Shema. That's a good one, but anybody could look that up on the Internet. What was your haftorah?"

Seth pressed his fist against his forehead. He knew this one but had to coax the memory out from the deep recesses of his mind.

"My bar mitzvah was on March thirteenth. My haftorah was Ezekiel something."

"Well done. Okay, one more question. This is for the bonus round. What was your worst bar mitzvah gift?"

"That's easy. Tallit clips. They looked like earrings my Bubbe would wear. I never used them. My mom gave the same clips to a guy who was in my older brother's Hebrew school class. To this day, I am convinced that his mother re-gifted them back to me."

Rabbi Scott reached across the desk and they shook hands.

"Welcome to Bnai Ma'abarot, Seth Ginsberg."

Seth let go of the rabbi's hand. "How did you know?"

"You think we don't keep up with what's going on *el Norte*? For weeks, your face was all over the news. I must say you look damn good for a dead man."

"They think I'm dead?"

"The U.S. government hasn't officially declared you dead, but they believe that it's just a matter of time before the Hedge Clippers find your bones in the desert."

Seth scratched his beard. "They're still looking for me. Maybe coming here wasn't such a good idea."

Rabbi Scott laughed.

"Everybody here is a fugitive. You just got more press than most of us. But to be on the safe side, I suggest you stay inside during the day and don't wander too far away from the synagogue."

"I don't want to be a burden."

"Then don't be."

Seth scratched his beard again. He wanted to shave it off but didn't feel it was safe to do so.

"I can wash dishes," Seth said. "I know how to cook kosher food."

Rabbi Scott's face lit up. "Can you cook traditional kosher food? The cooks we have now wouldn't know a kugel from a kreplach."

"Yes. My mother taught me. Nothing fancy. You know, matzo ball soup, chopped liver, that kind of thing."

The rabbi pointed at his mouth. "Can't you see I'm already drooling?"

CHAPTER 41

As Maggie squatted on her hands and knees along with a group of women campers, ammonia burned her nose, and the liquid irritated her hands as she scrubbed the dining-hall floor. A recording of the Huffstetler Twins singing the hymn "Does Jesus Care?" boomed from the loudspeakers.

Maggie fought the urge to vomit. She wasn't worried that the guard slouching at the front of the room would suspect that she was suffering from morning sickness. Lack of sleep and bad food had turned many campers into habitual pukers. She didn't want to have to mop up her regurgitated breakfast.

Maggie could tell her stomach was winning the battle and would soon empty its contents. She stood up too fast and the room spun for a moment.

"Get back to work!" the guard yelled, grabbing the butt of his rifle for emphasis.

"I'm about to throw up," Maggie said as she covered her mouth.

The guard rolled his eyes. "Can you make it to the kitchen?"

"I think so."

"Then do it in the sink. And then scrub the sink."

She was about to head for the kitchen when the nausea passed.

"It's okay. I'm fine."

"Then get back to work."

Maggie knelt and resumed scrubbing. She looked forward to the hours spent doing mindless labor. During this time, there were no counselors telling her that until she memorized her assigned Bible verses she was a sinner bound for hell. Still, Maggie worried about her pregnancy at every moment of every day.

By her estimation, she was three months along, and she couldn't hide her condition for much longer. Until now, the loose, modest clothes campers were required to wear had hidden her swollen breasts and slight stomach bulge. Maggie couldn't count on hard labor and malnutrition to cause a miscarriage. She had to find a way to abort the baby.

Maggie emptied the last drops from her bottle of cleaner into the bucket. It wasn't enough to cover the section of floor she was responsible for cleaning. She stood and held up the empty bottle. A few of the women glanced at her, and then looked back down at the floor. Maggie knew they were hoping she would break a rule so that they could report her later. Reporting rule breakers earned almost as many privileges as memorizing Bible verses.

"Now what?" the guard asked.

"I'm out of cleaner."

The guard sighed as if Maggie was really putting him out.

"There's more in the pantry. Hurry up and get another bottle."

Maggie walked past her fellow campers and through the kitchen to the supply room. She scanned the shelves, but saw no bottles of cleaner. In the back of the room, she came across a small metal storage closet. Inside, the shelves were filled with stuff that should have been thrown away. Brushes worn to the nub gathered dust next to cans of floor wax that were empty except for a hardened ring full of cracks. On the bottom shelf was a half-empty bottle of cleaner, enough to get her through today's chores. Maggie wondered how much ammonia she would have to drink to kill the baby without killing or crippling herself.

She unscrewed the bottle. If Camp Glorious Rebirth turned her into a mindless Jesus Zombie, wasn't that the same as dying? Why not get it over with now? She brought the bottle to her lips and stopped. No, she couldn't do it. Not yet.

As Maggie held the open bottle, she noticed that the ammonia didn't burn the inside of her nose. In fact, she didn't smell ammonia at all. She tilted the bottle, dipped her finger in the liquid, and tested it on her tongue the same way she'd done with unmarked bottles of clear liquid back at home in Alexandria. Then, she took a long swig of the liquid, feeling it burn her throat the way only good vodka could.

The kitchen door flew open and the guard stormed in.

"You're taking too long," he said. He grabbed Maggie's hair and forced her to the ground. "What are you up to in here?"

"This was all I could find," she said, holding the bottle up for him to see.

The guard glared at the bottle and then looked around the kitchen. He let go of her hair and gave her a rough push, which caused her to spill some of the liquid.

"Okay, I'll let it slide this time, but only this one time," he said. "Now get back with the others."

Maggie climbed to her feet and walked toward the door that led from the kitchen to the dining hall. The guard followed close behind her. When she stopped at the door, he almost ran into her. Maggie turned and faced him, holding the bottle in one hand and the cap in the other.

"My husband used to get this kind of cleaner," Maggie said. She quickly swallowed a mouthful before the guard could react. He stared at her in shock. "I didn't think you could get it in a place like this."

She handed the guard the bottle. He sniffed the liquid.

"Where did you find this?" he asked.

"In the supply room. In a closet."

"You're lying. That closet is locked."

"Check it yourself."

The guard took a step back. Maggie could smell his sweat. The illegal vodka belonged to him, or he was part owner along with other guards. He put the bottle to his mouth and took a drink.

"You can get just about anything for the right price," he said. "Even in here."

Maggie trembled slightly. She was taking a big step here, and she didn't know how much she could trust him.

"I don't have money," she said. "But I can barter."

"Yeah? With what?"

"My silence about the vodka. I could get my whites for this."

The guard took another drink. "You couldn't prove it. What

else have you got?"

Maggie held out her arms. He walked around her, taking sips of vodka and running his hands over parts of her body. She fought the urge to pull away from his probing.

"You still have some meat on you. They haven't starved you into a skeleton yet. I hate skinny chicks. Nothing to hang on to."

"So, you're ready to make a deal?"

"What do you want? More of this?" He held up the bottle.

"I need an abortion," Maggie said with a desperation that she couldn't conceal.

The guard took another drink. He was getting tipsy and it wasn't even lunch time. "Was it Kevin? I bet Kevin knocked you up. The idiot refuses to wear a condom."

"No, it wasn't Kevin."

"That's a big-ticket item. It's going to cost you a lot."

"I'm willing to pay any price."

"You don't just have to pay me. You'll have to pay the doctor too."

Maggie hung her head. She wasn't worried about cheating on Seth. This wasn't cheating. This was survival.

The guard went to the door and peeked into the dining room. The women were still scrubbing the floor. He leaned against the wall and unzipped his fly.

"My name is Gary. I want you to thank me after I come."

"Whatever."

Maggie got down on her knees in front of him. Compared to all the violations and indignities that she had suffered since arriving at Camp Glorious Rebirth this one hardly made the top ten.

THE JUDY CROSS SHOW STAFF MEMBERS SCURRIED INTO THE CONFERENCE room. They wanted to get in before Judy arrived at 9:00 a.m. and locked the door, but she was already at her place at the head of the table. They checked their watches to make sure they had the time right. Bill Garmon sat next to Judy.

"You're early," he said.

"Lock the door," Judy said. "I have something important to tell you."

"Can we wait until nine?"

"No. You can tell the other staff members later."

Bill locked the door. Judy ignored the coffee and donuts on the table, not to mention the staff members knocking on the door and calling out that it wasn't nine yet.

"As you all know," she said, "I've been very upset that we never found a suitable ex-camper to verify the good work of the Savior Camps."

"We interviewed dozens of them," Bill said. "They just didn't work out. Look at the bright side. Shane Waters has become a popular addition to the show."

"I love Shane. But we created him. I want a real camper. I prayed to Jesus for an answer, and last night he spoke to me in a dream."

Bill glanced at the other staff members as he poured himself a cup of coffee. Judy was so filled with the Spirit that she didn't mind that he touched the food before she did.

"What did Jesus tell you?" Bill said.

Judy closed her eyes and smiled.

"He said I was looking in the wrong place," she said. "He said I should go to a camp and show the world how it saves the wicked and puts them on the path to righteousness."

Bill took a sip of his coffee.

"Did Jesus tell you how you were supposed to do this?" he said.

Judy opened her eyes. She opened a notebook filled with handwritten notes and showed it to Bill. She had sketched out a rough proposal for a special live media event that included interviews with campers and counselors. The climax of the event would be a concert at the camp. Bill was skeptical at first, but by the time he finished reading Judy's plan, he was on board.

"We'll need to run it by the NCTV board and Hedge Protection," Bill said. "But I think this is going to be our biggest show ever."

"I'll talk to the board," Judy said. "Contact Bobbi Sue Sunshine's people. I'm sure she'll agree to be our headliner at the live concert."

"It'll be great for her image. And yours."

Judy grabbed a donut and took a bite.

"I'm not concerned about my image," she said as she chewed. "I am merely a vessel for Jesus."

Chapter 42

Techno Praise music blared from the gym's loud speakers. The DuPont Circle Health Club was crowded with sweaty bodies straining on exercise machines. Reggie had just reached his maximum speed on the treadmill when his phone rang. He lowered the machine's pace and checked the caller ID. It was a local area code, but he didn't recognize the number. Reggie wasn't surprised. He was deeply involved in the creation of the Committee on Immoral Activities, of which Senator Owens was chairman. Reggie had been dealing with many new people. He slipped the Bluetooth headset over his ear and accepted the call.

"Reginald Cooke speaking."

"Hello, Reggie."

Reggie stumbled and grabbed the handrail to keep from falling.

"Seth," he said. "I thought you were dead."

"I can barely hear you," Seth said. "Are you at a party?"

Reggie looked around the club. Everyone's attention was focused on their exercise routine.

"Are you insane?" Reggie said. "You can't call me. Hedge Protection listens to everybody's calls."

"Not inside the beltway. Congressmen don't like getting spied on."

"You're calling from a local number. Are you in town?"

"No, but you'd be amazed what you can buy in Gomorrah."

"I'm happy you're alive, and I want you to stay that way. Hang up and never call me again."

"I have to find out if Maggie is alive."

Reggie mopped his face with a towel.

"I can't help you," he said.

"Reggie, please."

"I'm hanging up now."

"You're the only person I can turn to."

"Leave me alone!" Reggie shouted.

Heads turned to see what the fuss was all about. Reggie stopped his treadmill. He put his towel around his neck, grabbed his phone and water bottle, and hurried outside to sit on a bench. The cold air was a sharp contrast to the steamy interior.

"When was the last time you saw her?" Reggie said.

"Three months ago, we tried to cross the border. Hedge Patrol found us. I got away. I don't know what happened to Maggie. I hope she was caught. They killed the guy next to me."

Seth sounded like he was about to cry.

"I'm sure she's alive," Reggie said.

"I have to know for sure," Seth said.

Reggie shivered. He wasn't dressed for the outdoors.

"If I find her in a Savior Camp," he said, "what are you going to do? A jail break?"

"If she's alive," Seth said, "I'll make a deal with Hedge Protection. I'll turn myself in if they promise to send me to Maggie's camp."

Reggie's breath came out in puffs of fog.

"Hedge Protection is not going to make a deal with you," he said.

"Deacon Wingard wants to get his hands on the dreaded American Judas," Seth said. "America will get to see me and Maggie reprogrammed into good little Mr. and Mrs. Jesus Zombie. Trust me, Wingard will make the deal."

"Maggie might already be a Jesus Zombie."

"Doesn't matter. I can't live without her."

Reggie took a drink from his water bottle. He watched a couple walk by. A gust of wind whipped around them. The woman hooked her arm through the man's and pulled him toward her.

"Give me a few days," Reggie said. "How do I get in touch with you?"

"I'll call you. It won't be this number."

CHAPTER 43

Evening services ended at midnight, which was early for Pastor Graves. Campers lined up outside the fellowship hall, men in the front of the building, women in the back. The campers' thin coats did little to keep out the freezing wind. Maggie blew into her hands to create a bit of warmth.

Not since the days when she was growing up in Michigan and her family camped in Twin Lakes State Park had Maggie seen so many stars in the sky. Her father always took them on the cheapest family vacations, but they still had a blast. After he died, there were no more vacations.

She was thankful that for once Tiffany wasn't standing next to her, jabbering about how much she loved the service. Perhaps Tiffany had found someone new to latch onto.

Gary the guard came out of the fellowship hall and spoke briefly with the women's guard. "Margaret Ginsberg," he said. "Come forward."

Maggie's heart raced. It had been three weeks since she'd made her deal with Gary. She'd had to service him two more times since then, and she was beginning to think he'd lied about arranging her abortion. She stepped out of line and hurried to the front.

"Follow me," Gary said. "Don't say a word."

He led Maggie toward the infirmary. She wished she was allowed to speak to Gary. There were many things she wanted to ask him, but one question in particular.

Was the abortion safe?

Maggie didn't want to die like Amy Bird did after she'd been forced to go to a back-alley butcher.

The flat-roofed infirmary was deserted and dark inside. Gary used his flashlight to lead them to an exam-room door.

"Go in," he said. "They're waiting for you."

She entered. The lights came on and she was momentarily blinded. When her eyes adjusted, she saw Pastor Graves, Counselor Bunny, Counselor Stu, Dr. Conger, and Tiffany Unklesby crowded in the exam room with her.

"Tiffany, tell us what you told Counselor Bunny earlier today," Pastor Graves said.

Maggie glared at Tiffany, who looked everywhere but at her.

"My bed is next to Maggie's," Tiffany said. "She hasn't had her lady time since we got here, and I've already had mine twice." She blushed from mentioning her period out loud. "She's starting to show that Jesus has kissed her belly."

"Praise Jesus," Pastor Graves said. "As much as I trust Tiffany's ability to recognize when a woman is pregnant, I think we should make sure."

Dr. Conger unwrapped a pregnancy test. Maggie had encountered Dr. Conger only once before, for her physical when she first arrived at the camp. He was a bald middle-aged man with a piggish face. He had smelled of menthol cough drops, and she'd known car mechanics with more compassion for the objects they worked on. Maggie could smell Dr. Conger's menthol cough drops from the other side of the room, and she wrinkled her nose in disgust.

"I suppose we can start with this," Dr. Conger said handing the test to Counselor Bunny. "Escort the woman to the bathroom down the hall."

"There's no need for the test," Maggie said. "Tiffany is imagining things. All campers puke. If you ate the same crap we did, you'd puke too."

"Then you won't mind taking the test," Pastor Graves said.

"This is America. I have rights. You can't force me to do this."

Pastor Graves moved close to Maggie.

"You gave up your rights when you sinned against your country. If you truly loved and submitted to me, our Heavenly Father, and the United States of America, then I wouldn't have to force you to get on the exam table."

Dr. Conger pulled out the stirrups on the exam table. Maggie saw the restraining straps and her face turned white.

"I agree with Pastor Graves," Dr. Conger said. "The exam is more conclusive. Counselors, if you please."

Stu and Bunny each grabbed one of Maggie's arms and pulled her over to the table. Panic rose in Maggie as she struggled against them. She almost broke free, but Dr. Conger joined them, and soon she was on the exam table with her wrists strapped down. Fear and frustration coursed through her as she writhed helplessly.

"You don't need to hurt her," Tiffany said.

Pastor Graves opened the door and called Gary in.

"Take Tiffany back to her barracks," Pastor Graves said. "It's way past her bedtime."

Tiffany looked crestfallen as Gary ushered her out of the room.

Maggie tried to kick Stu and Bunny as they removed her boots and bloomers. Her face flushed with embarrassment at having her lower half naked in front of these horrible people. The counselors strapped her ankles to the stirrups. The restraining straps bit into Maggie's wrists as she strained to break free.

"Okay, okay, you win!" she cried. "I'll pee on the stick. Just let me go."

"But, Maggie dearest," said Pastor Graves, "we want to share the miracle with you. When you witness the precious life that Jesus has placed inside your womb, you'll feel indescribable joy."

Dr. Conger greased the vaginal probe and frowned at Maggie's locked knees. He nodded at the counselors. "Hold her legs open," he instructed. "If you haven't the strength to keep this box un-wrapped, I'll administer a sedative."

"Doctor please," Pastor Graves said. "Don't be vulgar."

Each counselor grabbed a leg and exposed Maggie's vagina to the doctor's waiting probe. She rocked back and forth but went nowhere.

"This is rape, you bastards," she shouted. "Help! I'm being raped!"

Dr. Conger inserted the probe. Maggie reacted as if she'd been violated by a cattle prod that was shooting an electric current through her body. She lifted her ass off the table and screamed.

"Pastor, I need your assistance," said the doctor. "Hold her down. Counselors, don't waver in your resolve."

Pastor Graves placed his large hands on Maggie's chest and pressed her down on the table. Dr. Conger turned his attention to the video screen. Maggie gave up. She was trapped. Her face was red from exertion. She closed her eyes and sobbed.

"Why you got your eyes closed, silly girl?" said Pastor Graves. "Don't you want to see your beautiful baby?"

"There's no doubt about it," said Dr. Conger. "This girl is blessed with child."

Maggie forced herself to look at the video screen. In the middle of the grainy black-and-white cavern that was her womb was a small, dark shape. Yep, there it was.

Her baby.

CHAPTER 44

A huge man in a dark suit held the door open for Seth to enter the spacious office of Irby Belsky. Irby owned three Gomorrah casinos: The Zocalo, The True Patriot, and Irby's Vegas Vegas. Before the Greatest Awakening, he owned gambling establishments in Las Vegas and vast amounts of Nevada real estate. Irby was a billionaire, an Orthodox Jew, and a staunch supporter of Israel. He had donated massive amounts of money to American politicians who did the same. Seth wondered why rich men like Irby had given so much since all American politicians had always supported Israel. It was like paying them to breathe air.

After the Greatest Awakening, Irby found out that all his money and influence couldn't change the fact that he was a Jew in a Christian Nation. When the government outlawed gambling completely, he was forced to go south with the rest of the sinners.

Seth entered, but Irby didn't bother to get out of his chair.

"Sit down, you," he said. "Let's get this over with."

Seth put a paper sack on the edge of Irby's desk and sat in an overstuffed leather chair. He felt terribly underdressed in Irby's expensively decorated office. Though it dripped with wealth, the place stank of old cigars and body odor.

"The kitchen workers' demands are simple," Seth said. "They're asking for a modest pay raise. What they mainly want is healthcare benefits. I think we can negotiate a fair split on how much the employees pay and how much management covers. I've gotten all the casinos and restaurants to agree to our terms. You're the last holdout, Mr. Belsky."

"Unions in Gomorrah," Irby said, as if he were uttering a vile curse. "What the fuck is this world coming to?"

Seth laughed.

"You can't have it both ways, Mr. Belsky. You don't pay taxes, and you don't pay your workers a living wage. Most of your workers are refugees, so what are they going to say? But now many of those workers are having children and putting down permanent roots. Mexico's public healthcare system in this area isn't adequate to cover their needs."

"You're screwing me over for the kids?"

"Yeah, I guess I am."

Irby took a fat cigar out of a wood box and lit it. Soon the room stank even more.

"You're representing the kitchen workers," he said. "If I give in to them, how soon before the rest of my employees start reaching into my pocket?"

"We should go ahead and get them on board now so that you only have to make one deal."

Irby put his cigar in an ashtray, struggled out of his chair, and came around to the front of his desk. He had a lumpy body and pasty skin, but his clothes were tailor made, and he wore a pinky ring with a diamond-encrusted horseshoe. He opened Seth's paper sack and removed a plastic container filled with a reddish-purple soup. Irby pried off the lid and stuck a finger inside. He sucked on his finger and smiled contently.

"I can't remember the last time I had decent borscht." He held up the container, spilling some of the liquid on the plush carpet. "Is this supposed to be a bribe?"

"I am shocked by your insinuation, sir," Seth said. "I just thought this might make it easier for you to swallow the deal you know you have to make."

Irby put the lid back on. He studied Seth, his bushy beard and second-hand clothes. He moved over to Seth's chair, put his hands on the armrests, and leaned in close. Seth grimaced at the smell of Irby's rank cigar breath.

"You got a lot of fucking nerve coming into my office and trying to screw me over," he said. "Mr. American Judas, number one on Hedge Protection's most-wanted list. I should call them right now and collect the reward for your skinny ass."

Seth shrugged.

"If you were going to turn me in," he said. "You would have done it by now."

Irby went back to his desk. His cigar had gone out. He stuck it in the corner of his mouth and chewed on the end.

"You organized all the kitchen workers in the whole damn city, but you always work behind the scenes," he said. "You're like a fucking ghost."

"We're getting off subject, Mr. Belsky," Seth said. "Do we have a deal?"

"I don't know, do we?"

Seth had felt very positive when he first came into the office. He'd dealt with dozens of men like Belsky when he worked for Senator Owens. He'd only organized the kitchen workers because he felt sorry for them and he needed something to occupy his mind while he waited for Reggie to find out about Maggie. But Belsky's response just now threw him off balance.

"I'm sorry, you've lost me, Mr. Belsky," he said.

"I already decided to give the kitchen staff what they wanted before you came in," Irby said. "I just wanted an excuse to talk to you. You're supposed to be in hiding, but you couldn't resist playing politics. It's in your fucking blood."

He relit his cigar and puffed on it until he got it going again. He leaned back in his chair and blew smoke rings. Seth waited for him to continue, but he said nothing.

"I'll have the contract sent over for your signature," Seth said.

He stood, but Irby motioned for him to sit back down.

"I didn't appreciate getting kicked out of my own country," Irby said. "Especially considering how much I gave to it. But I'm not looking for revenge."

"No, you're a True Patriot looking to restore America to the great freedom-loving nation it once was before it went Christ crazy," Seth said.

The True Patriots were a self-described political party in exile. They had their headquarters in Nogales. Seth wasn't surprised that Irby was a member, considering he named one of his casinos in their honor.

"All the True Patriots do is sit around bitching and moaning," Irby said. "I need somebody who understands how politics really work. We don't get many political types here. They're too good at changing their stripes to fit in with whoever's in power."

"You're offering me a job?" Seth asked.

"No shit, Sherlock."

Seth entertained the idea. With Irby's deep pockets, he could build an influential organization. He could possibly make a difference.

"I'm sorry, Mr. Belsky," he said. "I can't."

"It's your wife, right?"

Seth felt the temperature in the air-conditioned room drop a few more degrees.

"Did Rabbi Scott tell you? I haven't mentioned her to anyone else."

"My Doris died of cancer ten years ago and I still miss her," Irby said. After all his bluster and menace, Seth was surprised to hear the emotion in Irby's voice. "I spent a few years wandering around the house, then I had to accept that she was never coming back. You need to move on with your life. Take the job. Work for me."

Seth dug his fingers into the armrests of the leather chair.

"Maggie isn't dead."

"You know that for a fact?"

"No, I don't. But I believe that she's alive and I'll find her."

Seth got to his feet quickly and almost lost his balance. He took a deep breath and waited for his head to stop spinning. *Don't do it,* he thought. *It won't make you feel any better.*

Seth slapped the container of borscht. The red soup splattered over the carpet. It looked like blood from a crime scene. He was right. He didn't feel any better. Seth left the office.

CHAPTER 45

The apples were a special treat. Campers rarely saw fresh fruit and vegetables at Camp Glorious Rebirth. The women in Maternity Barracks were fed a steady diet of thick gruel that stuck to their spoons. It contained more calories and nutrients than anything the rest of the campers received, but that was small consolation when trying to force down something that looked and tasted like pre-school paste. When the box of dark-red apples was split among the expecting mothers, a collective sigh of joy rippled across their dining hall.

Most of the women devoured their apple immediately, but Maggie slipped her apple into the pocket of her white maternity smock to save it for later. All the pregnant women were dressed in white, which didn't represent the purity of the mothers-to-be, but rather the purity of the fetuses inside them. Pastor Graves liked seeing the women's bulging bellies draped in white like a troop of angels carrying God's precious gifts.

After receiving their apples, the women were taken to the front of the camp. This was also a treat since Maternity Barracks was located in the back and isolated from the rest of the camp. Winter had finally receded back into the mountains, and with the warmer weather lush green grass had returned to the fields outside the electric fence. Maggie inhaled the fresh scent of pine trees and savored the feeling of the sun on her face.

The women of Maternity Barracks were excused from doing physical labor. The time they would have spent on chores was replaced with extra Bible study. Maggie found it hard to focus on anything but the sacred contents of the Good Book.

Maggie was aware that she was losing the battle against the camp's brainwashing. Six-months pregnant and barely able to see her swollen feet, she felt hopeless and lost. She would never escape.

They would take her baby. She would never see Seth again. She might as well drown in the scriptures and forget Maggie Ginsberg. Verse by verse, she was fading away.

"Have you ever seen such a glorious day?"

She didn't notice Tiffany come stand next to her. The other campers weren't allowed to talk to the pregnant women, but as usual the rules didn't apply to Tiffany.

"God is such an awesome God to have given us such beauty," she said.

Maggie was glad that Tiffany had joined her. She used her hatred of Tiffany Unklesby to stave off becoming a complete Jesus Zombie. Having the little snitch around helped her keep that fire inside her alive.

"Go away," Maggie said, knowing full well that Tiffany wouldn't listen.

She walked away from Tiffany. Undaunted, she followed. Maggie stopped a few feet from the fence. She could hear the hum of its electricity while the sun glinted off the barbed wire.

"See that barracks over there?" Tiffany said, pointing at the men's barracks closest to the front gate. "That's where Congressman Chip Randall hanged himself."

"What do you want from me?" Maggie said.

"Nothing. I just thought you might like to know."

"You already screwed me over. Wasn't that enough?"

"I had to tell them. Something might have happened to Zipporah. She could have died."

Dr. Conger announced the sex of the pregnant women's babies as soon as the ultrasound revealed it. Pastor Graves then chose names for the women's unborn children from a list of biblical characters. Zipporah, wife of Moses, was the name he gave to Maggie's fetus.

"Maybe I wanted the baby to die," Maggie said.

"You don't mean that," Tiffany said, grabbing Maggie's wrist. "You would never do anything to hurt precious Zipporah. Deep down, I know you're a good Christian."

Maggie pulled away from her.

"If you know I'm a good Christian, then why didn't you trust me to make my own decision?" she said. "Are you so perfect that you get to decide for other people?"

Tiffany's eyes grew wide.

"I'm not perfect," she said. "Just forgiven."

She reached out to touch Maggie's stomach, but Maggie slapped her hand away.

"That hurt," Tiffany said, shaking her hand.

"You have no idea what pain feels like," Maggie said.

"I'll pray for you."

Tiffany pouted and walked away. Maggie considered throwing her apple at Tiffany's head, but didn't want to waste it on the blabbermouth.

A chugging noise caught Maggie's attention. The filthiest minivan she had ever seen drove toward the camp, black smoke farting from its tailpipe. It sputtered to a stop in the parking lot. A woman and a girl climbed out and walked up to the gate. They wore layers of wrinkled clothes on their emaciated bodies.

A guard in the front gate tower called down to them. "This is a restricted area. Get back in your vehicle and leave immediately."

The woman held out her dirty hands. "Can you please help us?" she said. "My husband died two years ago. He was diabetic."

"I repeat, this is a restricted area," said the guard. "You must leave immediately."

The woman continued as if the guard hadn't said anything.

"My husband lost his job, and we couldn't afford insurance. We spent our life savings on doctor bills. And then he died anyway, and the bank took our house."

"Move away from the fence. We are authorized to shoot trespassers."

Pastor Graves arrived, whistling "Just A Little Talk with Jesus." He stood near Maggie on the other side of the fence from the woman and her child.

"No need to shoot anybody just yet," Pastor Graves said to the guard. "Let's hear what this unfortunate lady has to say."

The woman turned to Pastor Graves. "Please sir," she said. "For me, begging for a handout is worse than an airplane ride, but I'm doing whatever I can to feed my baby girl."

Pastor Graves shook his head.

"You ask and do not receive because you ask wrongly," he said. "God opposes the proud, but he gives grace to the humble."

"We're not asking for much. Something to eat, maybe a few dollars for gas, and then I promise we won't trouble you no more."

Pastor Graves stuck his hands in his pockets.

"Camp Glorious Rebirth may be a holy place, but it's not a church. You need to get your little girl to a National Church. They'll help you."

The girl let out a harsh, hacking cough that shook her thin frame. Her mother rubbed her back until the fit subsided.

"Every church we been to turned us away," the woman said. "They said they can't feed the people in their own community, much less a drifter like me. You're my last hope."

"I'm already responsible for a camp full of hungry mouths. Giving to you would mean taking away from them."

The woman's pleading hands curled into angry fists. Maggie realized that you didn't have to be inside the camp to get fed up with Pastor Graves.

"I fought to bring Jesus back to America," the woman said, "but now in my hour of need, America has turned its back on me. My little girl is starving to death. How can you stand there and watch her suffer and still call yourself a Christian?"

Maggie noticed the girl watching her and smiled. The girl smiled back shyly. Maggie wanted to do something for her. She reached in her pocket and took out the apple she was saving for later. The look of hunger in the girl's eyes broke Maggie's heart. Many years had passed since she had played softball, but she still had a good throwing arm. The apple sailed in a lovely arc over the barbed wire. The girl took two steps back, caught the apple, and took a bite.

Pastor Graves quickly stepped between Maggie and the fence. He held up his hands with his palms out.

"Stop!" he shouted. "Nobody move."

Maggie thought Graves was talking to her, but then realized he was talking to the guards in the tower who had their weapons aimed at her and the girl.

"Lower your guns," he said. "I'm allowing this transgression."

The guards slowly put their weapons down. The mother grabbed her daughter and held her close. Pastor Graves took off his hat and ran his fingers through his coarse hair.

"Eve gave Adam an apple," he said. "That's why childbirth is so painful. I suppose we can make room for one more. Open the gates boys and let this woman and her child enter."

Maggie glanced down at her pregnant belly and realized what would happen once the starving pair stepped inside.

"Don't do it!" she shouted. "You'll never see your daughter again."

Pastor Graves spun around and slapped Maggie hard across her cheek. She fell to her knees and stayed down, too dizzy to stand.

"Take her to the shed," Pastor Graves said. "Have counselors Stu and Bunny meet me there."

The guards climbed down from the tower and hauled Maggie to her feet. As they led her away, she looked over her shoulder. The woman and her girl had escaped, the minivan's engine backfiring as they drove away. Pastor Graves stood inside the gate and watched the vehicle disappear.

THE SHED WAS AS BIG AS A BARN. MAGGIE SMELLED OIL AND CUT GRASS AS the guards led her past gardening tools and lawn-care equipment. A sliding metal door led to a back room with harsh overhead lights and four restraining chairs. There were brown stains in the seats of the chairs and tools hanging on the wall, but Maggie couldn't tell what they were for. The guards forced her into one of the chairs and strapped her wrists, shoulders, and ankles.

"Why are you doing this to me?" Maggie said, tears running down her face. "I didn't do anything wrong."

Counselors Stu and Bunny entered the room.

"I see she's ready," Counselor Stu said.

"Return to your post," Counselor Bunny said to the guards, who left the room.

Maggie could hear Pastor Graves whistling "Are You Washed in the Blood?" He entered the room, slid the metal door shut with a loud clang, and locked it. He took off his hat and hung it on a peg in the wall. The counselors took positions behind Maggie's chair, while Pastor Graves bent over to eye-level with her and put his hands on his knees.

"Maggie," he said. "Why did you give your apple to that child?"

"She was hungry."

"But you almost got the poor child killed. You almost got yourself killed."

"I didn't know."

"You know you're not supposed to do anything without asking permission. Nobody told you that you could throw the apple."

Maggie felt something on the side of her mouth. She licked it and tasted iron. Pastor Graves's slap had given her a bloody lip.

"It was the Christian thing to do?" Maggie said.

Pastor Graves straightened and turned his back on Maggie. He put his hands on his hips and stared at the ceiling.

"The lesson we teach here is simple," he said. "To receive Christ's bounty, you only need to serve Christ."

"I'm sorry," Maggie said. "I'll never do it again."

The room was cold and smelled like vomit. Maggie peed a little in her pants.

"Prepare her," Pastor Graves said.

Counselor Bunny cut open the front of Maggie's shirt with a pair of pruning shears, exposing her swollen breasts. Counselor Stu was behind Maggie so that she couldn't see what he was doing. She heard hissing followed by metal clicking and then a steady whoosh. She thought she smelled garlic cooking.

"Tell me what you want me to say and I'll say it," Maggie said.

Pastor Graves put his palm against Maggie's cheek.

"It's okay. I forgive you. God forgives her," he said. He trailed his hand down her face to her collarbone and he jabbed his forefinger into her left breast. "But you need a reminder, a permanent sign so that you never forget that you belong to Jesus."

Counselor Stu came into view. He wore thick gloves and held a branding iron and an acetylene torch. The torch's blue flame turned the tip of the brand a glowing red. Maggie screamed and tried to rock, but the straps held her securely. Her screams were cut short when Counselor Bunny forced a leather strap between her teeth.

Pastor Graves took a Bible from the drawer of a metal table. Maggie thrashed her head from side to side.

"Having purified your souls by your obedience to the truth for a sincere love of the brethren, love one another earnestly from the heart," Pastor Graves said. "All flesh is like grass and all its glory like the flower of grass. The grass withers and the flower falls, but the word of the Lord abides forever. Peter 1:22."

The glowing brand was an iron cross roughly the size of Pastor Graves's fist. Counselor Stu pressed it against Maggie's chest. Her skin sizzled and smelled like burnt pork roast. She bit into the leather strap as the pain traveled through her body, squeezing her eyes shut as she banged her head against the back of the chair. Counselor Stu removed the iron and Counselor Bunny sprayed the bleeding brand with water from a squirt bottle. Smoke rose from Maggie's chest. Counselor Bunny placed an adhesive patch over the wound.

"Now you will never forget that your Lord and Savior owns your heart," Pastor Graves said.

He closed the Bible and put it away. Maggie could hear them speaking, but it was as if they were in another room.

"At least she didn't soil the chair," Counselor Stu said.

"See if there are any apples left," Pastor Graves said. "I'd say Maggie earned another one."

And then Maggie passed out.

CHAPTER 46

Steam filled the bathroom. Standing under the hot water, Reggie felt his tense muscles loosen. This was the only time he felt safe inside Roy Arnold's house. Shower time meant Roy was done violating him for that day. Reggie stayed in the shower until the hot water ran out and the cold water chilled his skin. If he lingered long enough, Roy would become involved with work in his study and shoo Reggie away, too busy to pray with him or dispense further spiritual guidance. "We'll pray together next time," Roy would say, because there was always a next time.

Reggie wiped a circle in the fogged bathroom mirror. He wasn't as handsome as he used to be. Despair was etched into his face. Maybe if he became ugly enough, Roy would lose interest in him and find a new man who needed to be cured of the affliction of homosexuality. He dried himself off and wrapped the towel around his waist. Entering the guest bedroom, he found Roy reclining on the bed. Roy wore his favorite white kimono bathrobe loosely enough to show that he had on nothing underneath.

"Did I scare you?" Roy said.

"A little," Reggie said. "I wasn't expecting you."

"I have exciting news and just couldn't wait."

Reggie leaned against the wall. "I'm all ears."

Roy sat up. His short legs dangled off the side of the bed.

"Come closer," he said, motioning with his hand. "I can't talk to you way over there."

Reggie's legs felt rubbery as he obeyed Roy's command. Roy grabbed the towel wrapped around Reggie's waist and pulled him closer until he stood between Roy's legs.

"I'm going away soon," Roy said. "I won't be back for a long time."

An involuntary shudder of relief rippled through Reggie's body. "Where are you going?"

With his index finger, Roy made lazy circles around Reggie's nipples.

"A better question is where am I not going?" he said. "I'm not going to Canada or Mexico." He ran his palms over Reggie's pectoral muscles.

Reggie looked down at the top of Roy's head and his pathetic comb over. He clenched his fists and fought to keep his stomach calm.

"Jesus wants Christians to rule the world," Roy said. "As God's new chosen people, the United States of America has no choice but to accept this awesome responsibility."

Roy massaged Reggie's abdominal muscles. He poked a finger inside Reggie's bellybutton.

"We have placed Christian brothers all over the world. I must tell them personally what God has told me. Now is the time to overthrow every non-Christian government and make Jesus king of His world again."

Roy yanked Reggie's towel off and smirked as he gazed at Reggie's penis. He reached out and stroked it gently. Reggie stayed flaccid, but he could see Roy's erection emerging from the folds of his kimono.

"That's wonderful," Reggie said. "When do you leave?"

"A better question is when do we leave?" Roy said. "You're coming with me as my personal assistant."

Reggie started to step back, but Roy gripped his penis tightly. Pain shot through his groin. He gritted his teeth and stood still. Roy eased his hold on Reggie.

"I would love to join you," Reggie said. "But I'm deeply involved with Senator Owens's Christian loyalty hearings. We must keep America safe from internal enemies."

Roy held onto Reggie's penis with one hand and fondled his ass with the other.

"Since I took you under my wing, your spiritual growth has been stupendous," Roy said. "You're destined for great things, but only if you come with me."

He dug his nails into the tender flesh of Reggie's ass. Reggie flinched.

"I am a Christian soldier in Senator Owens's army," he said.

"I know you took the file about the underground Jewish church from my desk," Roy said. "That's why I had your phone tapped."

Fear raced down Reggie's spine. Roy wrapped his fingers around Reggie's testicles.

"You warned your little Jew boyfriend about the raid," Roy said. "And you've stayed in touch with him."

"Seth is not my boyfriend," Reggie said.

Roy squeezed Reggie's testicles. Pain exploded inside him. He gasped and doubled over.

"You love him more than me," Roy said.

"Seth is just a friend," Reggie said. "We kept each other's secrets. At least, he kept mine. That's all."

Roy squeezed harder, and Reggie saw spots in front of his eyes.

"Reject the Christ killer," Roy said. "Obey me and love me with the same passion that I have for our Lord Jesus."

Beads of sweat gathered on Reggie's upper lip.

"Why are you doing this to me?" he said.

Roy released his grip and Reggie whimpered in relief.

"Isn't it obvious?" Roy said. "I love you. I refuse to let Satan take you away from me."

CHAPTER 47

Judy Cross sat in the front row of the fellowship hall at Camp Glorious Rebirth and watched the production crew transform the stage into the set of her show. After weeks of planning, building, bribing, and cajoling, her special live event was finally about to happen. In just a few days, she would show not just America, but the entire world, that Savior Camps saved lives with tough love and the glory of Christ.

The easy part had been convincing the board at NCTV to do the special. Savior Camps were controversial. NCTV execs immediately recognized the ratings potential and provided Judy with a generous budget.

Hedge Protection had been a harder nut to crack. Polls showed that the majority of Americans were uncomfortable with the camps and fewer people were willing to report sinful family members who would benefit from a visit to a Savior Camp. Judy thought Hedge Protection would have jumped at the chance for some positive publicity, but they turned her down.

Undaunted, she called prominent members of the Brethren and pitched the show to them. Soon afterwards, she received a call from Deacon Wingard, giving her the go-ahead to do the show, but only under his department's supervision. They chose Camp Glorious Rebirth, which included that mountain of a man Pastor Graves, his hands as big as catcher's mitts and an Amish beard. Judy's audience was going to love his deep, booming voice and flannel shirt.

Judy should have been thrilled. But she wasn't. She'd been binge eating more than usual. She had expected to find here in the majestic Rocky Mountains what she hadn't been able to find in Washington, D.C. Happy, well-adjusted campers filled with the healing power of Christ.

Instead, the inhabitants of Camp Glorious Rebirth were

traumatized and malnourished. If they weren't complete Jesus Zombies, they were well on their way. Judy was beginning to think that Beatrice Portillo Shanahan was right. The Savior Camps didn't save lives.

But Judy had put too much of her time and reputation into this special event to back out. She had been forced to hire actors to play the campers, while the real campers would be locked in their barracks during the show. She had wanted to keep the real counselors but ended up hiring actors to play them as well; the real ones upset the actors and couldn't remember their lines.

Bill Garmon hurried toward her. "I need your approval on some inserts," he said.

For the past week, Judy's crew had been videotaping segments of the actors doing camp activities to air during the program.

"Do I really need to see them?" Judy said. "I'm sure they're fine."

"You'll want to see these," Bill said.

Judy rolled her eyes and pushed herself out of her seat. As she and Bill walked through the camp, they passed Hedge Protection missioners in riot gear and workers cleaning and repairing barracks and spreading gravel over muddy paths. Professional artists had painted over the awkward camper-created murals on the side of the barracks with beautifully rendered Bible scenes. In the parking lot, an NCTV remote truck was parked next to a Hedge Protection Mobile Command Center.

Judy and Bill entered a barracks with a mural on the side of Jesus riding a donkey into Jerusalem. The barracks had housed male campers. They were relocated, and their beds were removed so that Judy's crew could use the barracks as an edit room and production office. Bill led Judy to where a young man sat at a console busily editing a video segment.

"Frank," Bill said. "Show Judy the women's Bible class we worked on today."

"Sure thing," Frank said.

He typed on his keyboard. The image on the video monitors

changed from an interview with Pastor Graves to a group of women, in better-fitting white uniforms than those issued by the camp, seated in a classroom.

"Frank," Judy said. "Why aren't you wearing your ID?"

Everyone who wasn't an actual camper had to wear an ID badge. Hedge Protection made it very clear that anyone not wearing their badge at all times could end up staying behind after the show was over.

"Sorry, Ms. Cross," Frank said.

He hurried away and came back wearing his laminated ID around his neck.

"Okay," Bill said. "Now that we've gotten that taken care of, show Judy the Bible class."

Frank played the video. A counselor with girl next door beauty stood in front of rows of clean and healthy female campers.

"To whom is the wrath of God going to be revealed?" the counselor said.

The women eagerly raised their hands. The counselor chose a girl with light-blonde hair that shone like a halo, and a smile as big and wholesome as the heartland of America.

"All men of ungodliness and unrighteousness who suppress the truth will receive the wrath of God," she said.

"Excellent!" The counselor hurried over to the camper and they high-fived. "Now, what was the sin in the church of the Corinthians?"

Hands shot up again and the counselor picked the same girl.

"Sexual immorality," she said.

The counselor continued to ask a wide variety of Bible questions, covering both the New and Old Testament. The blonde sat up straight and was the very definition of perky as she answered every question. At the end of the video, the women applauded her. She blushed and cast her eyes to the floor.

"That's no good," Judy said. "You had the same girl answer every question."

"I let her answer every question," Bill said. "Because she knew the answers without us telling her."

"Who is she? A Bible expert?"

"She's a camper here at Camp Glorious Rebirth."

Bill smiled mischievously as he watched Judy's reaction.

"A real camper?" she said.

"Judy Cross," Bill said as he gestured at the video monitor. "Meet Tiffany Unklesby."

Judy felt heat rush through her body. This delightful girl was no Jesus Zombie.

"She's the proof I was praying for," Judy said. "Savior Camps really do save lives."

"I don't know about that," Bill said. "There's hundreds of campers here, and she's the only one we found who isn't screwed up."

"He's right, Ms. Cross," Frank said. "This place is creepy. There are parts of the camp we're not allowed to see. What does that tell you?"

Judy smacked the back of Frank's head.

"That those areas are none of our business," she said. "I'm sure there are dozens of campers like Tiffany. She's just the first one we found."

Judy didn't want to admit that she had been disturbed by the lack of access at the camp. When she confronted Pastor Graves about it, he gave her a condescending smile and told her not to worry her little head about it. The old Judy would have been offended. She might have even kicked him in his man parts, but not this Judy. She smiled and accepted his decision.

"Now that we've found Tiffany, I know we're going to have a great show," Judy said. "We have a real camper filled with the Holy Spirit, and we're surrounded by the great Rocky Mountains. That must be why Hedge Protection chose this location."

Bill chuckled.

"The Rockies had nothing to do with it," he said. "This is the camp where Chip Randall hung himself. Hedge Protection is probably hoping our show will clean up the camp's image."

Judy swayed and put her hand on the table.

"You okay, Ms. Cross?" Frank said.

"I never paid attention to the name of the camp," Judy said. "I made a point not to pay attention. Is this really it?"

"Pastor Graves told me that this was where they kept Chip," Bill said. He pointed at the rafter above them. "See that crossbeam? That's where they found him swinging from a noose he made out of his bedsheet."

Judy looked up and stared at the rafter. Her cheeks flushed, and her eyes became unfocused. And when she fainted, she landed on top of Frank.

CHAPTER 48

Reggie Cooke's going-away party was a reminder of how few friends he had left in Washington. Senator Sam Owens insisted on having the party at his mansion in McLean, and the majority of the guests were there to schmooze with him. Since becoming chairman of the Committee on Immoral Activities, Owens's political dance card had been full. He was a frequent guest on the Sunday after-church talk shows.

In keeping with his new position of power, Reggie adjusted Sam's image from flashy preacher to somber judge. Sam hadn't minded wearing darker suits and less cologne, but he refused to stop wearing his diamond-encrusted cross-shaped cufflinks until Reggie pointed out that television studio lights made them sparkle in a way that was most unbecoming for such a serious man of God.

Reggie was standing in a corner holding a glass of ginger ale when Sam pulled himself away from two congressmen and draped his arm around his soon-to-be ex-Chief of Staff.

"Can I have a moment alone with you?" Sam said.

"Certainly," Reggie replied, placing his glass on a table.

The two men moved through the crowd. Sam's receptionist Tisha stopped them and threw her arms around Reggie's neck.

"I'm going to miss you so much," she said. "Won't be the same without you."

"I'll miss you too, Tisha," Reggie said.

Sam and Reggie continued on their way to the senator's study. It had dark wood paneling, a majestic oak desk, and crushed-velvet rugs. Sam gestured for Reggie to take a seat in one of the two Chesterfield leather chairs in the middle of the room.

Sam fished a key out of his pocket and unlocked a cabinet. He lifted up a false bottom and took out a bottle of single-malt scotch.

"Been saving this for a special occasion," Sam said.

He poured the whiskey into two glasses, handed one to Reggie, and sat in the chair beside him. They clinked their glasses before sipping.

Warmth spread through Reggie. He was exhausted. In less than two weeks, he was leaving the country with no idea when he would return. He still had to pack, sublet his apartment, and interview candidates to replace him. As it turned out, the most difficult matter to resolve had ended up being the easiest. Since closing the borders, it practically took an act of Congress for anyone to obtain permission to travel abroad. However, as Roy Arnold's new personal assistant, a passport and travel vouchers were hand-delivered to him by a Hedge Protection missioner. Reggie didn't even have to apply for them.

"I knew this day would come," Sam said. "I was lucky to have you as long as I did. I'm proud of you."

Reggie Cooke rubbed his tired eyes.

"I want you to know that I wasn't planning on leaving you," he said. "But this was an offer I couldn't refuse."

"Of course, you couldn't," Sam said. "Every ambitious young man in Washington would give his left testicle to be Roy Arnold's personal assistant."

"Senator," Reggie said with mock surprise. "Such language is unbecoming for such a distinguished personage."

Sam laughed, drained his glass, and went to his desk. He returned with the bottle of scotch and a small wrapped package. He filled their glasses and handed the gift to Reggie.

"A little going-away present," Sam said. "Go on. Open it."

Reggie tore off the wrapping paper. It was a small jewelry box. Inside were the senator's diamond-encrusted cross-shaped cufflinks.

"Sam," Reggie said. "I can't accept this. You love these cufflinks."

"I can't wear them," Sam said. "Might as well give them to someone who can."

Reggie closed the box and held it in his hand. Of all the things he wanted to do before he left the country, there was one thing that had been hanging over him. This might be his last chance.

"I want you to do something for me," he said.

"Anything," Sam said. "Just ask."

Reggie looked directly at Sam.

"Help me find out if Maggie Ginsberg is alive. If she is, I need to know where Hedge Protection sent her."

"Maggie Ginsberg? Seth Ginsberg's wife?"

"I have connections in Washington, but not with Hedge Protection. You could make an informal request and I'm certain that they'd tell you what became of her."

Sam jumped to his feet and dropped his glass. Whiskey stained the rug.

"Have you been talking to Seth Ginsberg?" he said.

"About twice a month," Reggie said.

"Do you have any idea the trouble you'd be in if word got out that you been conversing with a traitor? Not to mention the danger you put me in with your reckless actions."

Reggie ignored Sam's outburst.

"Seth wants to find out if his wife is alive. I'm sure if you didn't know where Mrs. Owens was, you'd be desperate to find her."

Sam shook his finger at Reggie. "Don't you dare compare me to that Judas! He lied to us. He broke the law. Such evil does not deserve our compassion."

Reggie stood up and glared at Sam. His exhaustion was gone. He picked up his glass and threw it against the wall, smashing it to pieces. Sam flinched.

"Cut the shit, Sam," Reggie said. "This is me you're talking to. I don't want our last words to each other to be bitter, but Seth was a good soldier in your army. He served you well as your assistant, and he served you even better when you turned him into the American Judas."

Sam leaned against his desk.

"Okay," he said. "Let's cut the shit. I admit that Seth was a good soldier, but why are you willing to risk both of our asses to help him?"

Reggie dug his hands into his pockets. Having Sam help him find

Maggie Ginsberg was dangerous, but it was nothing compared to the danger Sam would be in if he knew what Reggie's true relationship was with Roy Arnold.

"I owe Seth," Reggie said. "So do you."

Sam gazed at the broken glass on the floor. He fetched two new glasses and filled them with scotch. He handed one to Reggie.

"I'll call Deacon Wingard's office in the morning," Sam said. "I always liked Maggie Ginsberg."

CHAPTER 49

Seth was watching the night sky from the roof of Bnai Ma'abarot when Rabbi Scott joined him.

"I knew I'd find you here," Rabbi Scott said.

For the past six months, Seth had lived in a small room next to the synagogue's kitchen. During that time, he and Rabbi Scott had become close friends.

"You're always on the roof at night," Rabbi Scott said. "Is this the only place you feel safe outside?"

"I come up here to see the stars," Seth said. "I like to think that Maggie's watching the same stars."

They listened to the traffic. The heat of the day had worn off and the air was crisp. Rabbi Scott noticed the cellphone in Seth's lap.

"Were you about to call your secret friend?" he asked.

Rabbi Scott knew Seth had a contact in Washington, but Seth wouldn't reveal the person's name.

"We just finished talking," Seth said.

He scratched his beard, which had become a bushy cloud on his jaw. Put Seth in a black suit and a wide-brim black hat and he could easily be mistaken for an Orthodox Jew.

"I got a call from your friend, Irby Belsky," Rabbi Scott said.

"He's not my friend," Seth said.

"Irby feels bad about your last meeting. He wants to see you."

"He wants me to run the Belsky Foundation. The idiots he has running it now demanded that the U.N. impose economic sanctions against America for violating international treaties. The U.N. politely told the foundation to go fuck itself. Irby should have known better than to send thugs to play politics."

Rabbi Scott laughed and playfully smacked Seth's shoulder.

"You rarely leave this building, and yet you know everything going on in this city," Rabbi Scott said. "What's your secret?"

"I'm friends with all the waiters and kitchen staff," Seth said. "Most people don't even notice they're there, so they hear everything."

Rabbi Scott stared at the stars.

"It's been months and your contact in Washington still hasn't found Maggie," he said. "Even if you find her, she's no longer the same woman. The Savior Camps change people. It's time to get on with your life. Accept Irby's offer."

Seth crossed his arms.

"If you had asked me on any other day, I might have said yes," he said. "I almost gave up hope. Then I got a phone call. My friend in Washington found out that Maggie is in a Savior Camp in Montana, and he made a deal with Deacon Wingard. In exchange for turning myself in, Wingard has agreed to let me join her."

WASHINGTON WAS IN THE GRIP OF A HEAT WAVE. A HEAVY RAIN HAD FALLEN that morning, but instead of relief, it had brought a sauna-like stickiness to the air. Despite the office's air conditioning, Freeman's clothes stuck to his sweaty body. And yet, Missioner Lim looked cool and calm.

"I prayed to Jesus and asked him how I should bring in Seth Ginsberg," Freeman said.

"What did he tell you?" Missioner Lim said.

"Don't take any chances this time. Enough with Hedge Patrol dramatically arresting him in the desert. Ginsberg is right on the border in Nogales. I want you to pick him up there and take him to the Tucson Hedge Patrol Station."

"Praise Jesus. A simple and wise plan of action."

"Have we located Ginsberg's wife?"

"She's at Camp Glorious Rebirth."

Freeman drummed his fingers on the armrest of his chair.

"That's the camp where Chip Randall died," he said.

"And where *The Judy Cross Show* is doing their live broadcast," Lim said.

Freeman had spent most of his time recently testifying before the Committee on Immoral Activities. He found this frustrating, not only because he thought it was a waste of his time and taxpayers' money, but also because the committee was constantly creating reasons for his department to investigate other members of Congress.

While Freeman was tied up with the committee, he had trusted his missioners to make the arrangements for Judy's Savior Camp program and hadn't paid attention to what they decided. If he had known, he wouldn't have let them use Camp Glorious Rebirth.

"Can we move Judy's show to another camp?" he said.

Missioner Lim almost cracked a smile.

"The program begins in a few hours," she said.

"I'll work around it. Let the pastor in charge know that I'm coming to get Mrs. Ginsberg, and then we'll meet you in Tucson."

"Sir, may I speak freely?"

"You know you don't have to ask. What's on your mind?"

"Ginsberg agreed to turn himself in on the condition that you send him to the same Savior Camp as his wife. Why bring his wife to Tucson? Why not just send Ginsberg to Montana?"

Freeman closed the blinds. The sun had been in his eyes.

"The United States of America doesn't negotiate with traitors," he said. "I can't allow Ginsberg to dictate the terms of his surrender. He's not going to any Savior Camp. He'll spend the rest of his life in a maximum-security prison. But before I send Ginsberg away I'll let him see his wife. It's the Christian thing to do."

MISSIONER LIM LEFT TO ARRANGE THE FLIGHTS ON HEDGE PROTECTION JETS to transport Freeman to Montana and herself to Tucson. Freeman took out his personal phone to call Julian Cross. The call was long overdue. He hadn't talked to Julian in weeks, partly because of his busy schedule and partly because he kept putting it off.

His missioners had recently discovered that Julian was still smuggling drugs across the border. Freeman had requested that Julian send him a list of his fellow smugglers. The information he provided didn't include his own men, but was only a list of other smuggling operations. Obviously, Julian had hoped that Hedge Protection would eliminate his competition for him.

Julian picked up on the fourth ring.

"It's Freeman Wingard. How are you, Julian?"

"I'm busy at the moment. I'll call you back later."

"No. We'll talk now."

"Give me a minute."

Freeman could hear car engines running and people talking in the background. He assumed Julian was preparing a run across the border, smuggling people or illegal contraband, or both. Thirty seconds later, Julian was back in a quieter room.

"What's on your mind?" he said.

"This is very difficult for me to say, but I can't save you," Freeman said. "You made no effort to do what I told you to do."

"What are you talking about? Of course, I did."

"Don't lie to me, Julian. My missioners are watching you all the time."

Freeman drummed his fingers on his desk. Saving Julian was supposed to make up for losing Chip Randall, but he had failed both of them.

"What do I need to do to get back on track?" Julian said.

"There's nothing you can do," Freeman said. "I should send you to a Savior Camp, but out of respect to your father, I'm not going to. When you cross the border tonight, stay on the other side. If you ever come back to America, I'll have you arrested."

"Give me another chance. I admit, I didn't do what you told me to do, but it's partly your fault. I haven't heard from you in months."

"Yes, Julian. I bear some responsibility for your failure. I should have realized that a troubled soul like yours required constant mentoring if you were to ever learn that serving Christ is more rewarding that serving your wicked ego."

"The only decent thing I inherited from my mother was a desire to be a member of the Brethren. She was locked out because she's a woman. Don't lock me out because I screwed up."

Freeman stopped drumming his fingers.

"Perhaps there is a way," he said. "You could move to Washington. Live with your mother. I could mentor you on a regular basis. It might work."

"I'm desperate enough that I'm willing to live with Judy," Julian said. "But let me do something for you now that will prove I'm worthy of your trust."

"There is something you can do. You'll have to drop whatever it is you're doing."

"Consider it dropped."

Julian was probably expecting Freeman to ask for a list of smugglers, or to direct Hedge Patrol to one of his drug suppliers. But instead, Freeman gave Julian a mission to do that night that would prove he was a good Christian soldier in God's army.

When Freeman hung up, the weight on his heart was lifted. He wouldn't fail Chip after all. He called Missioner Lim and asked her to come to his office. When she arrived, she handed Freeman a printout with his flight information.

"There's been a slight change of plans," Freeman said. "Julian Cross is going to pick up Ginsberg and bring him to you at the Tucson Hedge Patrol Station."

Missioner Lim stared at him.

"Permission to speak freely, sir," she said.

"Again," Freeman said. "You don't have to ask."

"I think you should pray to Jesus and ask him about this so he can tell you that it's a bad idea."

Freeman glared at Lim, and then burst out laughing. "Have trust in the Lord," he said. "He is going to lead this wayward lamb back to the flock. Go to Tucson and wait for Julian to deliver Ginsberg."

CHAPTER 50

NCTV's decision to devote four hours of primetime to a special live episode of *The Judy Cross Show* paid off before the broadcast even began. Advertisers bought up every minute of the commercial breaks at premium rates. The corporation that purchased the most ad time was the same company that had been awarded the no-bid government contract to build the Savior Camps.

The program started with a short documentary about Camp Glorious Rebirth, narrated by Judy. It followed camper Tiffany Unklesby during a typical day, which began with Tiffany and her fellow campers singing hymns while a counselor led them in middle-school level calisthenics. Inspiring music played over scenes of campers enjoying hearty meals in the dining hall, studying the Bible, confessing their sins during group discussions, and staring in awe while listening to a rousing Pastor Graves sermon. In the center of each scene was beautiful Tiffany and her cheerful smile.

Tiffany watched the documentary on a large screen set up above the stage of the fellowship hall. She sat next to Judy. Pastor Graves and Shane Waters sat across from them. Tiffany wore a white flowing dress. Judy wore a royal-purple pantsuit. Pastor Graves and Shane Waters wore tailored suits. The audience was filled with the actors hired to play campers, while Hedge Protection missioners stood guard outside the fellowship hall and throughout the camp.

"Now, don't be nervous when the live show begins," Judy said to Tiffany. "Just be yourself."

"Okey dokey," Tiffany said.

"Did you get a chance to meet Bobbi Sue Sunshine?"

"Yes, ma'am. Mr. Garmon introduced us. She was super nice. I thought Kenny was going to faint. He has all her albums."

Judy furrowed her brow.

"Who's Kenny?"

"He's my brother. That's him right there. I took him with me to meet Bobbi Sue."

Tiffany waved at a guard with short blond hair standing backstage. He gave her a short wave back.

"Your brother's a guard here?" Judy asked.

"Usually he works on the trains," she said. "But they needed extra guards for the show."

"How does he feel about you being here?"

Tiffany looked down at her hands and blushed.

"I have to leave with him tonight after the concert. Momma told Kenny to tell me that I've done enough for him and it's time for me to come home because I've already missed enough school."

Judy blinked a few times before she could respond.

"You can't just leave a Savior Camp when you feel like it. The pastor in charge has to declare that you've done your penance and are ready to re-enter society."

"I was never charged with anything," Tiffany said. "I volunteered."

Judy turned to Pastor Graves.

"Tiffany says that she's leaving tonight. Did you know about this?"

Pastor Graves reluctantly tore his attention away from the big screen. The documentary was still at the part where he was giving his sermon to the rapt camper actors.

"We're going to miss Tiffany," he said. "I wish more people like her would volunteer. Makes a good example for the other campers."

The documentary ended with Judy standing in the camp's courtyard with the New Glory flag flying on the flagpole behind her.

"As you can see, the people here are not in some bizarre labor camp," she said. "Camp Glorious Rebirth is a nurturing environment that allows Christ's glory to envelop souls and change lives."

The documentary faded to black, the opening graphics for *The Judy Cross Show* came on the screen, and her theme music filled the fellowship hall. The floor director counted Judy in, but when the camera went live on her and the audience stood to applaud, Judy stared at the camera with her mouth open in disbelief. In the NCTV remote truck sitting in the parking lot, Bill Garmon jumped to his feet.

"What's wrong with her?" he shouted into his headsets. A cameraman suggested that she had been hit by a sudden case of stage fright. "Stage fright? Her chef dropped dead next to her and she didn't bat an eye. Stand by to go to a commercial."

Before Bill could do so, Judy snapped out of her stupor.

"Welcome to a special edition of *The Judy Cross Show*. I'm your host, Judy Cross. We're coming to you live from Camp Glorious Rebirth. We're going to show America what really goes on in a Savior Camp."

The rest of the show went smoothly. Judy asked her guests probing questions, and they gave their rehearsed answers. Pastor Graves had trouble memorizing his answers, so they had cue cards made for him to read. After Judy talked to Tiffany, Shane, and Pastor Graves, she carried a microphone off the stage and down to the campers seated in the hall.

"Are you forced to memorize Bible verses?" she asked.

The camper actor selected for this speaking part stood and Judy thrust the microphone at him.

"No ma'am," he said.

"Does Pastor Graves punish you with physical labor if you fail to memorize Bible verses?"

He sat down, and another camper actor stood to read her line into the microphone.

"Never!" she said.

"How do you feel about Pastor Graves?" Judy said.

The audience cheered. Pastor Graves smiled benevolently at his hired fans.

During commercial breaks, Judy brooded and didn't speak to anyone. At the end of two hours, she stood center stage.

"When we come back after the commercial break, Bobbi Sue Sunshine will appear on this stage for her special live concert," Judy said. "Before I turn this glorious day over to her, I want to express my overwhelming joy that we were able to bear witness to the truth about Savior Camps. They're not guilty of the heinous allegations made against them. They are part of Christ's plan to ensure America continues on its path as the greatest, most blessed, most Christian of all nations on this wonderful earth."

The floor director counted Judy out. Her shoulders slumped. She felt as if she'd aged twenty years in the past two hours. Tiffany bounced over to her.

"Thank you for having me on your show," Tiffany said.

Judy grabbed Tiffany's arm.

"Are you the only one?" she asked.

"You're kind of hurting me, Ms. Cross."

Judy released her grip.

"You came here already saved. Does anyone get saved after they come to the camp?"

"Sure. Everybody gets saved."

"Yes, I know," Judy said, trying not to let her frustration take over. "But, they act like zombies. Not you. You're perfect, a precious and obedient child of Jesus. Has the camp helped anyone become like you?"

Tiffany tilted her head and stuck out her lower lip, and then she smiled.

"The women in Maternity Barracks are like me," Tiffany said. "Well, almost like me. Someday I'll have my own little bundle of God's joy. We could visit them so that you can see for yourself."

"Maternity Barracks? As in pregnant women?"

"Yes, ma'am."

Since Judy hadn't heard of or seen a barracks dedicated to pregnant women, she had to assume it was in the part of the camp that she and her crew weren't allowed to enter.

"Can you get me in there?" Judy said.

"They let me go there any time I want. I can't see why they wouldn't let you go, Ms. Cross."

Judy looked around for Pastor Graves to officially demand that he allow her to go into the restricted area, but the pastor had already left the hall. Tiffany headed for the exit and Judy followed her.

"I know all the shortcuts," Tiffany said. "And I know how to avoid the guards."

"Yes," Judy said. "Let's avoid the guards."

"Tell me about it. They always stop me to tell me how pretty they think I am and ask me if I've ever been kissed. Gross stuff like that."

"I agree. That's gross."

Tiffany led the way on a winding path between and behind barracks. A watchtower's searchlight spun overhead. The two women were alternately exposed by the light and engulfed by the barracks' shadow. They walked past the men's barracks that was being used as *The Judy Cross Show*'s production office.

"That's where Congressman Chip Randall died," Tiffany said.

Judy felt a knot in her stomach.

"I would rather you didn't mention that man's name again."

Judy followed Tiffany into the restricted area. They didn't encounter a single guard along the way. They walked past dark barracks. Judy caught glimpses of hollow-eyed faces peering out of windows like lost souls on a doomed ship. As they walked, Tiffany jabbered non-stop about Jesus, birth, family, and anything else that popped into her head. Finally, they arrived at Maternity Barracks in its lonely corner of the camp.

"Come on in," Tiffany said, holding the door open.

Judy hesitated. Something didn't feel right.

"I don't know, Tiffany. I don't want to bother them."

"They're just pregnant. They won't bite you."

Inside, women at various stages of pregnancy were either in hospital beds or wandering about. A nurse sat beside a bed and ignored Tiffany and Judy. The room smelled of pine cleaner and overripe fruit. Judy felt the hairs on her arms stand up as she walked down aisles of beds. The women behaved as if she wasn't there. Most were silent, but a few murmured to themselves.

Judy leaned in close to one woman to hear what she was saying.

"Let us walk properly as in the daytime, not in orgies and drunkenness, not in sexual immorality and sensuality, not in quarreling and jealousy. Romans 13:13."

She repeated the Bible verse like a holy mantra.

Tiffany tugged on Judy's arm. "Come say hello to my best friend," she said.

She led Judy to a bed in the corner. The woman in soiled sheets looked as if she were due any minute. Her hair was a tangled mess. Her face was pale, and her eyes stared without seeing. She constantly scratched the left side of her chest. Tiffany pulled the woman's hand to her side.

"If you don't stop scratching," Tiffany said, "it's going to get infected again. Remember how nasty it was? All green and pus coming out. It's finally gotten a nice brown shade and the ruts in your skin aren't too deep."

The hair on Judy's arm rose and her eyes grew wide.

"Oh my God," she said.

"My gosh, where are my manners?" Tiffany said. "Judy, this is Maggie. Maggie, say hello to Judy. She has her own show on TV."

"Is that really you, Maggie?"

"You know her?"

"She used to work for me."

Tiffany put her head against Maggie's stomach. She didn't react.

"Baby Zipporah can't wait to be born," Tiffany said.

Maggie blinked at Judy.

"Judy?" she said.

"It's me, Maggie. Judy Cross."

Judy pulled a chair next to the bed. She held Maggie's limp hand. The horror of finding her here had passed.

"Oh Maggie," Judy said. "If only you had lived a righteous life. Such a waste. And that husband of yours. Did you know he was a traitor? Were you helping him?"

Maggie narrowed her eyes at Judy.

"Seth?" she said. "Do you know where Seth is?"

"You should have asked me for help. I could have guided you. And Amy. Both of you rejected Christ. But there's still time for you. You're not already in Hell like Amy."

Maggie pulled her hand away and scratched her chest again. Judy wasn't certain, but Maggie's eyes didn't seem as lifeless as they had been a moment ago. Maybe the foolish girl was waking up from her self-delusional dreams and was finally ready to beg for Christ's mercy. Not that it would help much now. At least her baby would end up in a good Christian home.

"Amy's not in Hell," Maggie said.

"Of course, she is," Judy said. She looked around the room. "This place is depressing. Tiffany said the women here were like her, but only God could have created Tiffany Unklesby. I don't think the Devil ever had a chance with her."

Judy couldn't believe it, but Maggie actually sneered at her.

"My baby," Maggie said. "My husband isn't the father."

"Oh really?" Judy said. "Did you have intercourse with someone here? Tell me. Who was it? Was it Pastor Graves?"

Maggie crossed her hands over her chest and gazed at the ceiling.

"I was raped," she said. "It happened when I was trying to cross the border into Mexico. A smuggler forced me at gunpoint to have sex with him."

Judy turned to Tiffany, who shrugged her shoulders.

"I always assumed it was her husband who got her pregnant," Tiffany said.

"I too am a victim of rape," Judy said. "Like Maggie here, I kept the baby. Best decision I ever made. My son, Julian, is the single greatest joy in my life."

Maggie grabbed her hand.

"Julian!" Maggie said. "He's the father. Julian was taking us to Mexico."

Judy yanked her hand free from Maggie's grasp. She wasn't enjoying berating her any more. She wanted to be free of this harlot.

"Not again," Judy said. "How many times, Julian? How many of your messes do I have to clean up?"

Pastor Graves entered the barracks with Counselor Stu and two guards.

"Ms. Cross," Pastor Graves said. "What are you doing here? This is a restricted area."

Judy didn't look at Pastor Graves. She and Maggie had locked eyes. A righteous anger rose inside Judy that reminded her of her old self. Instead of trying to tame the familiar fire, she let it consume her.

"I believe I earned the right to go anywhere I please," Judy said. "I insisted that Tiffany bring me here, but I have kept her long enough. Please see that she gets to enjoy Bobbi Sue's concert."

Pastor Graves nodded.

"Counselor Stu," he said. "Escort Tiffany to the fellowship hall. I'll take care of things here."

"I'd like to stay here a little longer with my friend, Maggie, if that's okay," Tiffany said.

Counselor Stu grabbed Tiffany's arm and pulled her to her feet.

"Come on," he said. "Let's go."

He dragged Tiffany out of the barracks.

"We need to talk," Judy said to Pastor Graves.

They stood outside the barracks. The night air didn't cool Judy's anger.

"Tell me about Maggie," Judy said.

"She had a few minor bumps," Pastor Graves said, "but she's come along just fine."

"Did you know that her husband is the American Judas?"

Pastor Graves took off his hat and scratched his head.

"Why no, I didn't know that. Doesn't really matter. Everyone here has a wicked past or else they wouldn't be here."

"The American Judas fooled the good and honorable Senator Sam Owens. He taught Maggie to be just as deceptive. Right before you arrived, she told me hurtful and wicked lies. She's still under the Devil's influence."

Pastor Graves put on his hat and rubbed the back of his neck.

"That may be true," he said. "But it doesn't much matter. I came here to fetch Maggie. Deacon Wingard sent word that he's coming for her."

Panic surged through Judy.

"How soon will he be here?" she said.

"A couple of hours, I suppose," Pastor Graves said.

That didn't give Judy much time. She didn't want to anger Freeman, because Julian's future depended on him. But she couldn't let Maggie walk out of here with Julian's baby in her belly. Judy moved close to Pastor Graves. He nervously took a step back.

"Freeman understands that campers receive discipline when necessary," Judy said. "He won't know whether the discipline was administered before or after he called."

Pastor Graves stared at the barracks.

"I suppose," he said, "that as long as Maggie is still breathing and doesn't show any obvious signs of discipline, Deacon Wingard can't complain."

Judy sneered.

"I feel responsible for Maggie," she said. "She used to work for me. I want to personally make sure that she receives the salvation that she deserves."

Pastor Graves spat into the grass.

"Curing demonic possession requires a strong hand and a stern heart," he said. "You have both in spades, Ms. Cross. But I can only give you an hour at most."

"That will have to be enough."

CHAPTER 51

Seth sat on an Adirondack chair on the roof of Bnai Ma'abarot. Hopefully by tomorrow, he would watch the stars with Maggie. He wore the flannel shirt, faded jeans, cowboy boots, and trucker's cap that Enrique had given him. The clothes he'd collected while living in Nogales were in a cardboard box in the bedroom next to the synagogue's kitchen. In his lap was his Springfield XD 9mm handgun, snugly packed in its ankle holster. Since he couldn't take it with him, he planned to give it to Rabbi Scott as a gift.

The rabbi joined Seth on the roof. Seth put the gun in the chair and stood. The men hugged.

"It's good that you're leaving now," Rabbi Scott said. "I've put on ten pounds since you started cooking for us."

"You were too skinny," Seth said. "I made mandel bread this afternoon. It's in the fridge."

"Your ride is here."

Seth nodded and picked up the gun.

"A petite Asian woman, last name Lim?" Seth said.

"No," said Rabbi Scott. "It's a guy. Didn't give his name."

Seth froze. Deacon Wingard was very specific about the missioner he was sending to take Seth across the border. Not a man. A woman. He should have been told if there was a change. Seth considered calling Freeman and telling him the deal was off, but he was too desperate to see Maggie.

"What does the guy look like?" Seth said.

Rabbi Scott furrowed his brow.

"Short," he said. "Works out. Tight clothes. Red hair. Uses too much gel. Cold blue eyes. Not that I was checking him out or anything."

Seth put his foot on the armrest of the Adirondack chair and attached the ankle holster to his leg. If the guy was who Seth thought he was, he didn't feel safe riding with him without his gun.

They went downstairs. Seth said a final goodbye and stepped outside. On the street in front of the synagogue, Julian Cross leaned against a dusty Jeep. When he saw Seth, he grinned.

"Been a long time," he said.

"Deacon Wingard sent you?" Seth said.

"Sure did."

"He should have told me."

"He has more important things to do. Empty your pockets."

Seth rolled his eyes. He pulled out his pockets. His right pocket was empty. He held out the blue-and-red wood sculpture that was in his left pocket.

"Is that a bird?" Julian said.

"It belongs to my wife," Seth said. "I'm looking forward to giving it back to her. Can we go now?"

They climbed into Julian's Jeep. Instead of driving north toward the U.S.-Mexico border gate, Julian headed west into the desert.

"Aren't we going the wrong way?" Seth said.

"I'm not one of Freeman's missioners," Julian said. "I have to smuggle you across. Don't worry. We'll get there soon enough. There's a trail I use all the time. I call it the Carpool Lane."

Julian drove fast. The Jeep's headlights barely illuminated the path ahead, but he seemed familiar enough with the road to avoid all the dips and bumps.

"I didn't know Hedge Patrol had an undercover unit," Seth said. "Makes sense. You pose as a coyote, get a truck-full of illegal immigrants, and then pretend to get busted by a passing patrol unit."

Julian cut his eyes at Seth.

"I don't work for the Hedge Clippers."

"Really? Since when do coyotes smuggle people back into the United States for Deacon Wingard?"

Julian took his hands off the wheel, cracked his knuckles, and then grabbed the wheel again. "I bet you went to Harvard," he said.

"Yale," Seth said.

"You Ivy Leaguers think you're so fucking smart."

"I doubt Judy Cross's son went to public school."

"I got kicked out of better private schools than you ever went to."

Seth couldn't help but laugh. It was a funny comment.

"If you don't work for the Hedge Clippers, then why aren't you in a Savior Camp?" Seth asked.

"I have no idea what the hell you're talking about," Julian said.

"The night Hedge Patrol caught us crossing the border. They sent my wife to a Savior Camp, but not you."

"That was a special deal. Deacon Wingard wanted his Hedge Clippers to catch the American Judas, so I arranged for them to meet us in the desert. But then everything turned to shit, and you got away."

Seth thought back to that night in the desert. Hedge Patrol's arrival had brought gunfire, frightened people fleeing in all directions, Seth's fleeting glimpse of Maggie, and Jerry with a big hole next to his eye.

"All those people in the truck were arrested or died because of me?" he said.

"I never thought of it that way before, but yeah, it's your fault," Julian said.

Julian slammed on the Jeep's brakes. Ahead of them, Julian's moving truck was parked next to a large boulder. Men pissing on it were caught in the glare of the Jeep's headlights. They panicked and quickly ran to the back of the truck.

"Welcome to Piss Rock," Julian said.

He turned off the engine but left the headlights on as he climbed out of the Jeep. Seth reluctantly followed him. He'd been here before. This was where it had happened. This was where Jerry Hays had died. It was the last place he'd seen Maggie. They approached the truck and stopped a few feet away, hearing whispers in the dark. The sharp tang of urine hung in the air.

"Dewey?" Julian shouted.

A voice in the dark called back. "Is that you, Julian?"

"Yeah, it's me."

Dewey came out from behind the truck with his hand shielding his eyes. Seth recognized Julian's assistant as the man who had collected everyone's bullets the night he and Maggie had tried to cross the border. He held a handgun in the ready position. Once he recognized Julian, Dewey put the handgun in his belt holster and swaggered over to the two men. He narrowed his eyes at Seth.

"Is that Ginsberg?" Dewey said.

"The American Judas in the flesh," Julian said.

"That beard is a fucking joke." Dewey put his hands on his hips. "I was hoping I might run into you tonight."

Seth wished they would wrap up their chitchat so that they could get moving again.

"Why?" Julian said. "There a problem?"

"No," Dewey said. "I wanted to thank you for giving me your operation."

"Don't screw it up. I worked my ass off to build it into a moneymaker."

Dewey shook Julian's hand and sauntered back toward the truck.

"You're quitting the smuggling business?" Seth said.

Julian spit in the sand.

"Yeah," he said. "It's time to move on."

Seth and Julian climbed back into the Jeep, but Julian didn't start the engine. He stared at Dewey's truck. He slammed his fist on the steering wheel, jumped out of the Jeep, and marched toward the moving truck. Seth groaned as he got out of the vehicle and followed Julian to the back of the truck. The rear door was open. Julian turned on his Mag-lite and aimed the light on the scared, dirty faces of the immigrants huddled inside.

"Try and run away and I'll put a bullet in your head," he said.

He headed toward the front of the truck. Seth hesitated. A woman and a girl came to the opening but didn't get out. With their mismatched clothes and scrawny frames, they looked like two scarecrows.

"Are we still going to Mexico?" the woman said.

"I'm not with them," Seth said.

"We have to get to Mexico."

Seth understood. He'd been inside one of these trucks. He knew that if she didn't make it to Mexico, she would lose her child.

"It's going to be okay," he said, though he was in no position to offer assurance.

Seth hurried to join Julian. He and Dewey stood in the space between the truck and the Jeep. Dewey was taller than Julian, but the shorter man completely dominated him. Dewey's shoulders were slumped forward, and he stared at the ground.

"What the hell was I thinking?" Julian said. "I worked too hard to build this business for someone else to reap the profits."

"You just gave it to me, man," Dewey said. "No take backs."

"Who said anything about taking it back?"

Seth looked up at the stars. Turning himself in shouldn't be this hard. He wanted to see Maggie sooner rather than later.

"We have to go," he said. "They're waiting for us in Tucson."

Julian pulled up his shirt to reveal his concealed holster. He whipped out his handgun and pointed it at Seth.

"I'll decide when we leave," Julian said.

Seth held up his hands reflexively. Julian turned the gun toward Dewey. The big man flinched.

"Give me your gun," Julian said.

"Come on, man," Dewey said. "Don't do this."

"Either hand it over or I'll pick it off your dead body."

Dewey removed his gun from his belt holster and handed it to Julian. He tossed it into the desert.

"I loved that gun," Dewey said.

Julian dug his cellphone out of his pocket.

"I'm calling the Hedge Clippers," he said. "I'm having them arrest these people. This is the last trip on the Carpool Lane."

"Don't do this, Julian," Seth said.

"Don't tell me what I can or cannot do. If I want to blow this operation up, I'll do it."

Seth knew what he had to do. He prayed Maggie would forgive him. "I can't allow you to do that," he said. "I refuse to have any more lives ruined because of me."

Julian squinted at Seth. "Like I give a fuck," he said.

Seth squatted and pulled his gun out of its holster. He held the gun in both hands and pointed the muzzle toward the ground.

"Don't make that call."

Dewey and Julian stared at the gun as if Seth had pulled a magic trick.

"I knew I should have frisked you," Julian said.

The three men between the Jeep and the truck did a little dance. Seth and Julian moved like gunfighters, mirroring each other's steps and positioning themselves so that neither man had the Jeep's headlights in his eyes. Dewey backed slowly toward the truck.

"Put the gun down before you hurt yourself," Julian said.

Seth thumbed off the safety and breached the gun. His palms were so sweaty that he was afraid that the gun would slip out of his hands. Stumbling slightly, he felt as if the earth was spinning too quickly, that he might be tossed off the globe into outer space if he wasn't careful.

To calm himself, Seth thought back to all the things he learned in target practice about what to do if he were in a life-threatening situation. Keep the gun down and never put your finger on the trigger before you shoot. Once you decided to shoot, draw up, follow through, and fire. Aim for the chest with at least two rounds, a double tap.

"We don't have to do this, Julian," Seth said. "Let Dewey take these people to Mexico. You and I can go on to Tucson. Everybody will get what they want."

Julian held his gun by his side and sneered. Pride was the deadliest sin, and Seth could see that Julian's wouldn't let him back down.

"Hey, Ginsberg," Julian said. "How does it feel knowing you're going to hell?"

"I don't know," Seth said. "Let's talk about it about when we get there."

Chapter 52

Pastor Graves greeted Deacon Wingard at the front gate. He held his hat in his hands and stared at his feet.

"I don't likely know how to tell you this, Deacon," Pastor Graves said. "But Maggie Ginsberg is missing."

Freeman glared at the pastor. First, he had lost Chip Randall and now Margaret Ginsberg. When Freeman got back to Washington, he would find a replacement for Graves.

"How did you manage to lose a pregnant woman?"

"We neglected Maternity Barracks because we didn't expect the women to go anywhere," Pastor Graves said, "considering their delicate condition."

Freeman had been briefed about Margaret Ginsberg on the flight to Montana. Hedge Protection kept detailed records on all Savior Camp residents. By the time his government jet landed, he knew everything about Margaret, including when she was due and the name of the family that would adopt her baby.

"I'll have my missioners conduct a search," Freeman said. "The woman is seven months pregnant. She shouldn't be that hard to find."

"How can I help?" Pastor Graves said.

"Go to your office and wait for me," Freeman said.

Pastor Graves hurried away. Freeman headed toward Hedge Protection's Mobile Command Center and paused at the entrance. The gate was open. NCTV crew members walked in and out of the open gate. Some headed for the network's remote truck, while others went to the idle train that would take them back to Washington. The guards posted at the gate made no attempt to check for identification. Freeman approached one of them.

"How do you tell the television people from the campers?" Freeman said.

"NCTV actors and crew members are wearing wristbands or name tags," the guard said.

"Where's the security camera central monitoring station?"

"Follow me, sir."

As they passed a barracks by the front gate, Freeman flashed back to Chip Randall dangling from the crossbeam inside that barracks. He shook his head, as if to dislodge the memory.

In the monitoring station, Freeman sat next to the guard on duty. He called the missioner in charge of tonight's security detail and instructed him to assign a group of his missioners to find Margaret Ginsberg. Then, he scanned the security-camera monitors.

"Come on and show yourself, Mrs. Ginsberg," Freeman said. 'Your husband is waiting."

CHAPTER 53

As the months of her pregnancy dragged by, Maggie had sunk into a dark pit of depression. She had lost track of time. Her mind had become clouded, and she moved through her days on autopilot. Her personality was about to submerge permanently when Judy Cross showed up out of nowhere. She gave Maggie a reason to feel something other than despair. Love was better than hate but hate had its purpose. Maggie had used her hatred of Judy to pull herself back to reality. Lying to Judy about Julian had been delicious revenge. She never dreamed that her little lie would backfire so badly. Now, Maggie prayed for her mind to become clouded again. She was back in the shed, the location of her nightmares.

"Please let me go," she said as she struggled against her restraints. "It's not Julian's baby. I was lying. Make me memorize the entire Bible, but please let me go."

Judy paced in front of Maggie, tapping the tip of a branding iron against her palm. She had taken off the jacket of her purple pantsuit and rolled up her sleeves.

"Can you tell that I've gained a few pounds since we last saw each other?"

Maggie forced herself to focus on Judy's body. The elastic on Judy's pants were stretched to the limit.

"The jacket hid it well," Maggie said. "Purple's a good color for you."

"I used to be a stick. Sure, my metabolism changed as I got older, but I blame you and Amy for this fat." Judy squeezed her side. "You two seduced me into eating snacks."

"Everything we made was low-fat."

"Yes, and when you left, the Devil tempted me with junk food, and I was too weak to fight him."

"If you let me go, I'll make you whatever food you want."

Judy whacked the iron against the side of the chair, inches from Maggie's face. The stench of burnt flesh clung to the walls.

"Julian is a good boy," Judy said, "but Jezebels lay traps for him. They seduce him and then claim he raped them to blackmail me into paying them not to spread their malicious lies."

She pressed the tip of the iron against Maggie's stomach. The pressure was slight, but it was enough to cause her to shake with fear.

"Don't hurt the baby!" Maggie screamed. "You don't believe in murdering babies. You've spent your whole life saying it's a sin."

Judy pulled the iron away and Maggie almost fainted with relief. Judy moved in close to her and raised her hand. Maggie flinched, but Judy gently pulled back the strands of hair that had fallen over her face.

"Julian's father was the true American Judas," Judy said. "He wanted to corrupt Julian, but my faith was stronger. I showed Julian the light. You live in darkness. This baby is a curse on Julian, on me, and everyone who comes near it. For the sake of all that's good in this world, this baby must not be born."

Judy raised the iron like a baseball player at bat. The sharp smell of urine filled the room as Maggie peed her pants in anticipation of the pain.

Before Judy could swing the iron, Tiffany Unklesby moved quickly behind her and smacked the back of her head with a wooden club. The dull thwack was sickening. Judy staggered around to see what had hit her. Tiffany swung the club again and whacked Judy on the side of her head. Judy fell to the floor. Tiffany shook the club at her.

"And to think I used to believe you were a good Christian woman!" she said. "Mom watches your show all the time."

"Is she dead?" Maggie said

Tiffany tossed the club aside, kneeled down, and pulled Judy over onto her back. Judy moaned, but her eyes stayed closed and her body was limp. A lump was already forming on her forehead.

"She's going to have a terrible headache when she wakes up,"

Tiffany said.

She unbuckled Maggie's restraints.

"Why are you here?" Maggie asked.

"Bobbi Sue is something else on stage," Tiffany said. "Counselor Stu got to watching her and forgot all about me. I hightailed it back to Maternity Barracks. Got there just as they were taking you away. I think Jesus led me here to save you."

Maggie grabbed Tiffany in a fierce hug.

"Judy was right about one thing," Maggie said. "Only God could have created Tiffany Unklesby."

They untangled and looked down at Judy.

"Do you think she knows that I hit her?" Tiffany asked.

"I don't think we should stick around to find out," Maggie said. "I was leaving tonight anyway. You better come with me."

"What about your brother?"

"Don't worry about Kenny. He may be a guard, but I'm still his big sister."

Maggie began undressing Judy.

"Why are you taking her clothes off?" Tiffany said.

"I can't get out in my camp clothes," Maggie said. "In Judy's clothes, I should be able to get past the front gate."

Tiffany helped Maggie strip off Judy's pantsuit. Together they hoisted Judy into the chair and strapped her in. Maggie used her discarded clothes to clean herself off. Even with the elastic band, Judy's pants fit snugly over Maggie's pregnant stomach. Her feet were too swollen to fit into Judy's shoes, so she kept her camp sneakers. The last thing Maggie put on was Judy's nametag.

They closed the metal door behind them and left the shed. They joined the throng of people involved with the live television event. Finally, they could see the gate itself.

"Just a little farther," Maggie said.

They got behind a small cluster of crew members. Maggie thought she recognized some of them. They were about to walk through the front gate to freedom, when a tall man with broad shoulders and white hair in a military buzz cut stepped in their path. He held up an official identification card.

"Margaret Ginsberg," he said. "I am Federal Deacon Freeman Wingard of Hedge Protection. You are now in my custody."

CHAPTER 54

Freeman drummed his fingers on the monitoring station console. His frustration was mounting. His missioners had been searching for the missing Margaret Ginsberg for over an hour. He couldn't understand a word his missioner in the fellowship hall was saying because of the Bobbi Sue Sunshine concert.

"Speak up, I can't hear you!" Freeman shouted.

"Sorry, sir," the missioner said. "But I can't hardly hear myself."

"Update me later."

"Sorry sir, what were your orders?"

"Later! Later!"

He hung up and studied the security camera monitors. TV crew members hurried from the concert to the remote truck parked outside the front gate. Freeman had never realized that a live production required so many people and entailed this level of frenzied activity. It reminded him of a Hedge Protection tactical operation.

Slumping in his chair, Freeman wondered why he was here. He had dozens of qualified men in his command that he could have sent to pick up the pregnant camper. There was no reason for him to go to this much trouble, to travel to this sad little camp of lost souls for Seth Ginsberg, the least-dangerous man on Hedge Protection's most-wanted list.

The answer was that this was personal.

Every day, the country sank deeper into a repressive theocracy. More and more women were losing their jobs. If Freeman didn't have complete authority over his department, Grace Lim would have been let go by now. The witch hunt masquerading as the Committee on Immoral Activities justified its existence by sending innocent people to Savior Camps. Freeman felt helpless to stop any of it. His influence had been compromised by the American Judas.

Freeman believed that once Seth Ginsberg was in chains, then the American people would trust Hedge Protection again, and he could use his authority to steer the country back onto the right track.

He nudged the guard sitting next to him and pointed at the monitor trained on the camp's entrance. "Why are there so many people going in and out of the front gate?"

"The television crew needs to move quickly from inside the camp to the remote truck to keep the show on the air. Pastor Graves gave them blanket authorization to move freely about the camp," the guard said. "But don't worry. The guards are on the lookout for a pregnant woman in camp clothes."

"Did you tell the guards to also be on the lookout for a pregnant woman not wearing camp clothes?" Freeman said. The guard stared at him blankly. "If the Ginsberg woman got her hands on a crew member's clothes, she could walk right out without anybody noticing her."

"She'd still need a name tag," the guard said.

"If she could get clothes, she could get a name tag."

"I'll alert the guards immediately."

Freeman stood and put his hand on the guard's shoulder. "I'll tell them myself. It's too stuffy in here. I need to move around."

He left the monitoring station and walked swiftly to the front gate. The night air felt good on his face. The guards at the gate stood at attention. He warned them that Margaret Ginsberg might not be dressed as a camper. Freeman decided not to return to the monitoring station. He needed to be doing something more active, and watching people enter and exit the camp made him feel more useful.

A half hour later, she arrived.

He wouldn't have noticed her except for the royal-purple pantsuit. It was the kind of outfit an older woman would wear, not this young woman. The clothes did an excellent job of covering her advanced pregnancy, but he recognized Margaret Ginsberg from her arrest photos.

Freeman was impressed. Ginsberg and her blonde friend kept their cool and didn't glance about nervously. Margaret even smiled.

Freeman stood in front of her and held up his official identification card.

"Margaret Ginsberg," he said. "I am Federal Deacon Freeman Wingard of Hedge Protection. You are now in my custody."

A look more of sadness than panic crossed her face as she turned and hurried back the way she came. The guards began to give chase, but Freeman held up his hand.

"Stay here," he ordered. "I'll get her myself."

It was like following a turtle. No amount of adrenaline could help Margaret propel her pregnant body fast enough to get away. Freeman followed her at an easy pace.

"Can't you see how futile this is?" he said. "Even if you could run, where would you go? I'm the head of Hedge Protection. The guards, the missioners, the counselors, they all work for me. Make it easy on yourself and give up."

"Fuck you!" Margaret shouted.

She stumbled into the barracks closest to the front gate. Freeman followed her in. It was dark inside. He felt around for the switch and flipped on the light. A large table littered with papers and videotapes sat in the middle of the room. Freeman's throat tightened. He didn't need to see the cots to know that he had chased the woman into the men's barracks where Chip Randall had hanged himself.

Not wishing to risk shooting an unborn child, Freeman was glad that he wasn't carrying a weapon. He walked slowly to the table, bending down to peer under it.

The door to the latrine swung open. Maggie rushed out and slammed into Freeman. He fell on the floor, but he was stronger than she guessed. He got back on his feet and grabbed her before she could get away. As he dragged Maggie toward him, she kicked his shin. He howled in pain but didn't let go. She kicked and scratched him while letting loose a stream of obscenities.

"Fucking shithead bastard son of a bitch eat shit and die!"

Freeman had enough of this harlot. He grabbed the lapels of her jacket and shook her as hard as he could, but she still scratched at his hands and face. He reached for her throat but got hold of her shirt instead. The buttons flew off, and the shirt came open, exposing her chest.

He stopped shaking Maggie and stared at her.

"Who did this to you?"

He pointed at the cross-shaped brand above her left breast.

"Who did this to you?" he repeated.

Margaret glared at him. "You said they worked for you, so I guess that means you did."

"I never authorized this."

"And all the other shit I lived through is okay? What the hell did you think was going on here? What the fuck do you care? As long as you can sleep at night believing that all the pastors out there are doing God's work. Isn't this what you wanted? Isn't this the Christian nation you prayed for?"

Freeman looked around the barracks and realized that their fight had carried them next to where Chip's bed had been. He gazed at the crossbeam above them. It was clean, but Freeman could still see Chip swinging, his bloated face staring down. He could see the words Chip had written in his own blood.

If we say we have no sin, we deceive ourselves, and the truth is not in us. John 1:8.

He released his hold on Maggie, who scooted away from him and covered herself as best she could. She eyed him suspiciously.

"Forgive me," Freeman said. "I have sinned against you."

"What the hell?" she said. "You were trying to kill me a minute ago."

He picked up a chair they had knocked over and sat wearily.

"I once was blind but now I see. And what I see fills me with shame." Freeman stood and held out his hand. "Come with me, Margaret Ginsberg. Your husband is waiting for you."

CHAPTER 55

Maggie pressed her nose against the window like a child on her first airplane ride. This was her first time in a United States Government Jet, and probably her last. It was still dark when the jet took off from Yellowstone Regional Airport, but now the early sun illuminated the earth below. To Maggie, it seemed more like a giant topographical map than a place where people lived. She wanted to see as much as she could before she left America forever.

Maggie could feel the baby kicking her bladder. She tore her attention away from the window and looked around the cabin in search of the lavatory. The missioner sitting in the seat across from her stopped reading his Bible and turned his attention to her.

"Do you need something, Mrs. Ginsberg?" he asked.

"Where's the bathroom?"

"Rear of the plane. Do you need assistance?"

"No, I can make it on my own."

She made her way through the executive jet. Every seat was a comfortable first-class seat. A widescreen monitor was tuned to the National News Network. The bathroom was not the typical cramped room on a commercial plane; it was gleaming and spacious, with a padded toilet seat and cloth towels instead of paper.

The baby began kicking again. Maggie wasn't sure if this had been happening more since she'd left the camp, or if she'd just started noticing it. She felt like she'd woken from a long sleep and was still disoriented.

Maggie waited until the baby quieted down before returning to her seat. The missioner's seat was empty, and she had the cabin to herself. Freeman had disappeared into the jet's private office the moment they boarded. He hadn't come out since. Maggie didn't completely trust Freeman. He had switched from enemy to savior so quickly that this whole thing could still be some kind of an elaborate trap.

Before leaving Camp Glorious Rebirth, Freeman had the scratches on his arm tended to and he had his missioners find a new shirt for Maggie. No one asked her where she'd gotten the clothes she was wearing, and she didn't offer to tell them. They would find out soon enough.

Maggie put her hand on her belly and smiled. "I have a name picked out for you, but I want to check with Seth first."

Seth. Maggie had bounced between accepting that he had died in the desert and believing that he had survived but that she'd never see him again. She lightly touched her chest. The scar carried a constant memory of scalding pain. Maggie had changed so much since she'd last seen Seth. She yearned to be with him, but worried that he wouldn't want the person she'd become.

The missioner returned and sat down in his seat.

"We'll be landing soon," he said as he buckled his seat belt. "Best you buckle up, too."

"How far is Tucson Hedge Patrol from the airport?"

"There's been a change of plan. We're going to the police station instead."

Maggie gasped.

"Deacon Wingard promised me that he'd let me go free."

The missioner shook his head.

"Don't worry. We're not sending you back," he said.

Maggie could think of only one other reason why they might be going to a police station.

"Is Seth okay?"

"Deacon Wingard will discuss the matter with you personally on the way to the station."

Maggie desperately wanted more answers, but she was at their mercy. She buckled her seatbelt. She didn't look out the window but stared straight ahead.

CHAPTER 56

The policemen and Hedge Patrol agents milling about the lobby of the Tucson Police Station tried to pretend that it was no big deal that Federal Deacon Freeman Wingard had just walked through the door. They failed miserably. They gawked, grinned, and nudged one another. It wasn't every day that the leader of the third largest department of the U.S. government and its highest-ranking officer came to their far-flung corner of the country. The officials still weren't sure why he had taken control of this murder investigation. The pregnant woman in a purple pantsuit who arrived with him added to the mystery.

Freeman ignored all of them and walked across the lobby's cracked linoleum floor to where Missioner Lim waited for him.

"You were right, Grace," Freeman said. "I should have prayed to Jesus again so that he could have told me that sending Julian was a bad idea."

Missioner Lim almost smiled.

"Who would you like to see first, sir?" she said.

"I want to see the body first and then our person of interest."

"The morgue is standing by. The person of interest is waiting in an interrogation room."

Freeman glanced back at the officers crowding the lobby. They stood ready to serve.

"Have any of these morons talked to him?" he said.

"Luckily, we were able to get to him first, but since we have two competing law-enforcement departments here eager to impress you, it might be best to have a missioner keep him company until you're ready to speak to him."

Freeman gathered his missioners. He assigned one of them to watch their guest. He noticed that Maggie had taken a seat in the waiting room. He instructed another missioner to make sure she was comfortable and to find her something decent to eat. He remembered how often Mary got hungry when she was pregnant. Then, Freeman had Missioner Lim lead him to the morgue.

The chief medical examiner uncovered the dead body. The harsh overhead light amplified its pale, lifeless complexion. There were two bullet holes close together in the victim's chest.

"Double tap," Freeman said absently.

"The close proximity of the two wounds in this area of the victim shows that the shooter was an experienced marksman," the chief medical examiner said. "One bullet went straight through the heart. Victim was dead before he hit the ground."

"If you don't mind, Missioner Lim and I would like to examine the body alone."

The chief medical examiner couldn't hide his disappointment, but he mumbled a goodbye and left the room. Freeman studied Julian Cross's face. Even in death, he looked angry.

"What do we know at this time about the circumstances of Julian's death?" Freeman asked.

"Ginsberg shot Cross. The only question is whether it was pre-meditated, or if he did it on impulse."

"Ginsberg plotted to kill Julian? What was his motivation?"

"That's the preliminary analysis. The investigation is evolving."

Freeman walked around the table. He pulled a pair of latex gloves from a nearby dispenser and carefully examined Julian's hands. He drummed his fingers on the edge of the table.

"What are your thoughts, Grace? Please be as candid as possible."

Missioner Lim shrugged. "Ginsberg wanted desperately to re-unite with his wife," she said. "He would need a very compelling reason to kill Cross to jeopardize that."

Freeman took off his latex gloves and tossed them on the table.

"Are you really going to free Mrs. Ginsberg?" Lim asked.

Freeman stared at Julian's body.

"Ever since Chip Randall died, the Bible verse that he left behind has haunted me. If we say we have no sin, we deceive ourselves, and the truth is not in us. John 1:8. First, I thought he meant it for himself. He had sinned, and his shame was too great for him to bear." Freeman reached out to touch Julian's cheek, but pulled back. "But then God revealed the truth to me. Chip wrote that quote for all of us. I thought I could erase my sin by saving Chip's son. I see now that Julian couldn't be saved."

Freeman walked toward the door, his footsteps echoing off the walls. Missioner Lim stayed by the table.

"And what about Mrs. Ginsberg?" she called after him. "Are you now trying to save her?"

He stopped and turned back to her.

"Yes," Freeman said. "Her. You. Seth Ginsberg. And anybody else I can save. The mistake I made was in forgetting the truth inside all of us. We're supposed to try and help everyone who touches our lives."

MAGGIE YAWNED, STRETCHED HER ARMS, AND CHECKED THE CLOCK ON the wall. She'd been in the waiting room for four hours. Across from her, Missioner Lim slept on a couch. The smell of burnt coffee hung in the room, but Maggie poured herself a cup anyway. The coffee tasted as bad as it smelled.

"How can you drink that vile stuff?" Missioner Lim said.

"I didn't mean to wake you up," Maggie said.

"You didn't."

"Do you know if he's talked yet?"

"Dewey talked hours ago. He avoided any self-incriminating details, but he told us enough to get a clear picture of what took place in the desert between Julian and your husband."

"I need some air. I'm going to step outside."

"Mind if I join you?"

Maggie cocked her head at Lim.

"Sure," she said. "The company will be nice."

The two women left the station and stood in the parking lot. It was a hot day, but the sun felt good after so many hours of frigid air conditioning.

"That's a lovely outfit you have on," Lim said. "Purple's a good color for you."

"Thanks," Maggie said. "It's just something I threw on in a hurry."

A procession of lawmen exited the police station. In the middle was Julian Cross's former partner, Dewey Dukes. Dewey was escorted to the back of a squad car. The car drove away.

"You don't remember me, do you?" Maggie said.

"We've met before?" Lim said.

"When Amy Bird died. You questioned me for hours to tell you the name of the doctor who butchered her."

"That was you?"

"Are they sure Seth killed Julian?"

"Yes."

Maggie was relieved that Lim didn't hesitate to answer.

"Why?"

"Does it matter? Dewey swears that Seth drew his weapon first. Seth can't claim that he shot Julian in self-defense. The fact that he ran back to Mexico makes him look guilty."

Maggie's eyes welled up.

"I need to know why he's not here with me right now."

Missioner Lim told Maggie the story that Dewey had told the missioners about how Julian, Seth, Dewey, and a truck-full of immigrants had come together in the desert.

"Dewey claims Seth shot Julian to save a mother and daughter from being arrested," Lim said. "If that's true, then I suppose Seth thought about how similar they were to his own pregnant wife and unborn child and felt he had to protect them."

Maggie wiped away the tears rolling down her cheeks.

"Seth doesn't know I'm pregnant," she said.

"He doesn't?" Lim said. "Then I have no idea why he killed Julian."

"I do," Maggie said. "Seth loves kids. Always has."

CHAPTER 57

Seth parked the moving truck in an alley. The emaciated mother and her equally thin daughter sat next to him in the cab. The three of them climbed out and Seth opened the truck's rear door. The immigrants inside didn't move.

"You can come out now," Seth said. "We're in Mexico."

Still, nobody moved.

"He's telling the truth," the woman said. "We passed some casinos. I think this here's Nogales."

The immigrants poured out of the truck, blinking at the early-morning sun. The men shook Seth's hand and the women hugged him.

"Is anybody hungry?" Seth said.

Hands raised. Seth decided not to point out that this wasn't a classroom.

The immigrants followed Seth the few blocks to Bnai Ma'abarot. Nobody on the street seemed to notice or care about the group of disheveled people. When they reached the synagogue, Seth asked the immigrants to wait outside. He found Rabbi Scott in his office. The rabbi stared at him as if he were a ghost.

"Aren't you supposed to be in a Savior Camp?" Rabbi Scott said.

"It's a long story," Seth said. "There are some tired and hungry people outside. I don't think any of them are Jewish. If it's okay with you, I'd like to give them a warm meal before they go on their way."

Rabbi Scott hugged Seth. "I'm glad to see you again," he said. "Need I remind you that ma'abarot means refugee camp? I'll help you serve."

While Seth prepared the food, Rabbi Scott gave the immigrants advice on where they might find work and a place to live. He helped Seth serve them mushroom-barley soup, potato knishes, and brisket tacos. As they wolfed down their meal, Seth told Rabbi Scott about what had happened in the desert. Rabbi Scott hugged Seth again.

Seth looked around and realized that the mother and daughter were missing.

"They didn't come with us," a man said. "We all followed you and they took off in the opposite direction."

After the meal, the immigrants went their separate ways, each thanking Seth and Rabbi Scott before leaving to begin their new lives. One immigrant thanked Rabbi Scott for his "Christian kindness." The rabbi snorted but didn't correct him.

As Seth carried dirty dishes to the kitchen sink, Rabbi Scott took out two wine glasses from a cabinet and a bottle of white wine from the refrigerator.

"Leave the dishes," he said. "Let's talk on the roof."

There, Rabbi Scott opened the bottle and poured them both a generous amount of wine. It was midday, too hot to be on the roof, but there they were. Seth held the wine glass but didn't drink. He stared off into the middle distance.

"What will you do now?" asked Rabbi Scott.

"I can never go back to the United States," Seth said. "I committed a murder."

"You saved those people."

"That doesn't change the fact that I'll never see Maggie again."

Rabbi Scott drank his wine. He made sure Seth drank some too.

"I believe God will forgive me for killing Julian," Seth said. "Do you think Maggie will?"

Rabbi Scott squinted at the sun.

"Only Maggie can answer that question," he said. "Tonight is Erev Shabbat."

"I completely forgot," Seth said.

"Come to services tonight. Let God ease your burden. I have to go downstairs and prepare for the service. I'll leave the bottle with you."

The rabbi downed his wine and retreated downstairs. Seth put his wine glass down. He would probably get stinking drunk sometime soon, but not today. He reached into his left pants pocket and took out Maggie's wooden bird, and took his gun out of its holster, too. He held the two objects in his hands and compared their weight. The bird was much lighter. He wondered why he hadn't left the gun in the desert. Maybe so he could put a hole in his head to match the one in his heart. That was a question he'd ask God tonight.

CHAPTER 58

The sun was setting when a black town car with a New Glory flag and a U.S. government license plate parked across the street from Bnai Ma'abarot. Maggie rolled down the window and gazed up at the neon-blue Star of David. Missioner Lim sat next to her in the back seat. She leaned forward so that she could see the star as well.

"Are you sure he's here?" Maggie said.

"This was the address he gave us," Missioner Lim replied. "Even if he's not here, they might know where he is."

Maggie leaned back in the seat. Now that she was here, she was afraid to get out.

"If he's in there," she said, "are you going to arrest him?"

"Even if I wanted to, I couldn't," Lim said. "I don't have jurisdiction here."

Maggie rubbed her belly.

"You've already done so much for me," she said.

Lim put her hand on Maggie's shoulder.

"I'll wait for you here," she said. "If he's not inside, then we'll keep looking until we find him."

Maggie ran her hand through her hair. She couldn't remember the last time she had washed it. "Why are you doing this for me?"

"Something Deacon Wingard told me," Lim said. "About truth and helping people. I'm doing it because I can."

Maggie nodded. She couldn't wait any longer. She got out of the car and crossed the street. She realized that she'd never been in a synagogue before.

NORMALLY, SETH ENJOYED THE SABBATH SERVICE. HE HAD ARRIVED LATE and slipped into the last pew so that he wouldn't have to talk to the other congregants. He placed his tallis over his head and held his siddur close to his face. He picked a page at random and began reciting prayers in a low voice.

He couldn't concentrate on his prayer book, so he put it aside. He took Maggie's wooden bird out of his pocket and held it in his hands as if it were a gun. He spoke directly to God.

"Why did you put me in that position? Why did you take her away from me?"

He sensed someone sit next to him but ignored them until they pulled his tallis off his head. Seth turned.

"Maggie?"

She ran her fingers through his curly hair, knocking his yarmulke off. He didn't bother to put it back on.

"I didn't know it was you until I saw the bird," Maggie said. "I wondered what happened to Sidney."

It really was her. His Maggie.

"You grew a beard," she said, touching his beard.

"You grew a baby," Seth said, touching her belly.

He wrapped his arms around her. She sobbed into his chest. Soon she was wailing loudly. Seth cried with her. He was vaguely aware that people in the congregation were glancing back at them, but he didn't care. He thanked God for bringing his Maggie back to him. He would never let her go again.

CHAPTER 59

Reggie sat alone at the boarding gate. His bags had been loaded onto the private jet, but he wasn't allowed to board until Roy arrived. They were supposed to have departed two hours ago, but Roy was running late. No explanation was given. He moved according to his own schedule, and the world waited until he was ready, just as the gleaming jet waited on the tarmac.

Reggie understood why Roy decided to fly out of Dulles Airport instead of Reagan. Dulles was more isolated and more deserted. Roy only wanted a small circle of people to know of his travel plans. With international flights restricted to those with government-approved passports, the number of people flying overseas had dwindled to a privileged few. Several American airlines had gone out of business. Reggie wondered how long before airports started closing. He hoped that Dulles would survive. He loved its swooping design, which reminded him of Fred Flintstone's brontosaurus ribs.

Roy decided that he wasn't going to tell Reggie their itinerary until after takeoff. Reggie had no idea where in the world he was going or how long he would be away from home.

Admit it, Reggie told himself, *I'm homeless. And I didn't just become homeless today, either.*

Reggie had lost his home the day Congress made homosexuality a crime. The United States had kicked gays out of its house. He'd only been pretending that he still belonged.

He should have been happy. He was leaving a country that didn't want him. He might even find a place out there that welcomed him. He might find a home.

"Reggie!" shouted Roy. "There's my boy. You ready for the most glorious adventure of your life?"

Roy pranced toward the gate. Reggie glanced outside and saw the crew packing a stack of suitcases into the jet. Roy slapped him on the back.

"I can't wait to tell you about all the places we'll be going," Roy said. "But not until we're in the air. Don't want to spoil the surprise."

"Not even a hint?" Reggie asked, forcing a smile. He was getting better at the fake smiles.

"Only this. We'll be doing the Lord's work by spreading the power of Jesus around the globe. Soon, the world will obey Jesus, as it should, as the Gospels demand."

That told Reggie absolutely nothing. Disappointment showed on his face before he could hide it. Roy wrapped his arm around his shoulder.

"I think I know what's wrong," Roy said, as if he were consoling a child. "You're worried about leaving home and losing all your friends. Don't worry. Just remember that no matter where you go in this big ole world, Jesus and I will be right there with you."

CHAPTER 60

Despite the sweltering heat, Maggie wore turtleneck pullovers. She even slept in them. When she bathed, she locked the door, something she had never done before. Other than the emotional embrace Maggie and Seth had shared when they were first reunited, she avoided any intimate contact. Seth yearned to press his hands on his wife's swollen belly and feel the baby kick, but Maggie flinched at his touch. He felt a sharp sting in his chest every time she moved away from him.

Maggie refused to talk about Camp Glorious Rebirth other than to say it was the worst experience in her life and the sooner she forgot about it, the better. Seth worried that she might never get over Savior Camp. He had a recurring nightmare that he would wake up one morning to find her transformed into a complete Jesus Zombie, unable to communicate in any way other than reciting Bible verses.

What worried him even more was that it wasn't Maggie's experience at the Savior Camp that was tearing them apart. He had abandoned her, twice. Seth feared that he had destroyed her ability to trust him.

A month had passed since Maggie's return. So much had changed in that short amount of time. Seth had accepted Irby Belsky's offer to run the Belsky Foundation, the human-rights organization dedicated to restoring America's democracy. Irby had agreed to let Seth wait to start until after the baby was born.

Seth and Maggie had a spacious apartment in the Santa Fe neighborhood in Mexico City. They found an OB/GYN that they both liked. Seth had shaved off his beard and kept it off. They should have been happy, but instead they were drifting apart.

Seth spent many nights at a local bar watching soccer. What he needed was a synagogue like Bnai Ma'abarot, but he hadn't liked the ones he'd visited so far.

He was at the bar one night, about to order a cerveza when he was overcome by an urgent need to get through to Maggie, and he didn't want alcohol to blur his thoughts. He had to know if they had a future together.

Seth rushed home and entered their bedroom. Maggie had taken a bath. Her hair was wet, and all she wore was a terrycloth robe. She jumped when she saw him. She pulled the robe tightly around her and backed into a corner.

"What do you want?" Maggie said.

"I live here," Seth said. "Remember?"

He regretted his sharp retort as soon as he said it, but he was hurt by Maggie's reaction. Maybe he should have stayed at the bar.

"Could you leave for a little while?" she said. "I want to get dressed."

"But I'm your husband," Seth said.

"And the Lord God made for Adam and his wife garments of skins and clothed them. Genesis 3:21."

Seth cringed. She was reciting more and more Bible verses lately.

Seth meant to do as she asked, but his legs wouldn't move. He knew he needed to be patient. There was no time limit on how long it took a person to recover from the shit she'd gone through, but damn it, he wanted his wife back.

"I understand that you need time," Seth said, "but I have to know."

Maggie clutched the top of the robe. Her face was white with fear.

"You're leaving me," she said.

"No," Seth said, taking a step forward. Maggie pressed harder against the wall. "But I need to know if you still love me."

"I do," Maggie said.

"Do you? You aren't angry at me?"

"It's not you. It's me."

"Then talk to me. Why can't I touch you?"

Tears ran down her face as she slowly pulled her robe open. Seth looked at his wife's naked body for the first time in over half a year. He wanted to gaze at her gloriously pregnant stomach, but something forced his eyes upward. Above her left breast, the skin was reddish brown and puckered around the edges.

Seth stared at the cross that had been branded onto Maggie, and for the first time he began to understand the suffering she had endured.

"They made me ugly," Maggie said.

Seth walked over and gently kissed her wound.

"They tried," he said, "but they failed."

He put his arms around her and held her. She put her arms around him. She screamed but didn't let go. He didn't run away from her screams. He didn't let go. They huddled under the covers as if they were hiding from demons. Words poured out of her, interrupted by hiccups and wiping her nose as she told the story of her time in the camp. They slept in each other's arms.

As the days went by, Seth did his best to soothe her fear and she did her best to ease his guilt. Neither was miraculously cured, but it was a beginning. Maggie still hid her scar from the world, but not from Seth. Finally, after weeks of patient cuddling, Maggie wanted to try having sex again.

Seth looked online for the best positions for pregnant women. They decided on the position where they laid on their side facing each other and formed a V. Seth tried to enter Maggie, but the position didn't work well. They switched to Maggie on top. That worked really well. Seth liked feeling the weight of her swollen belly on him.

"Are you going to say it?" Maggie said.

"Say what?" Seth said.

"Whenever you put it inside me, you say you're home."

Seth rubbed Maggie's stomach.

"We're home," he said.

CHAPTER 61

FRANK WILLIAMS: Wake up sleepyheads. It's 8:30 a.m., and you're listening to Radio Free America or as we like to call it around here, Christian Free America. I'm Frank Williams, and I'll be your host this lovely morning. My guest today is Seth Ginsberg. He's joining us here in our studios in an undisclosed location south of the border. Glad you could join us, Seth.

SETH GINSBERG: Thank you for having me on your show, Frank.

WILLIAMS: Are you kidding? The pleasure is all mine. You're a folk hero and a symbol for religious freedom.

GINSBERG: I don't know about that. There are people on the other side of the border who still call me the American Judas.

WILLIAMS: I'm afraid there will always be people who will call you that, Seth, even after the United States comes to its senses. Because of the efforts of organizations like the Belsky Foundation, we're making progress. It wasn't that long ago when the United States government blocked the signal from underground stations like Radio Free America, but now Americans are free to listen to what we have to say.

GINSBERG: There's still a long, hard road ahead. Abortion, homosexuality, and science are still illegal. But marriage for procreation only has been rescinded and women retained their right to vote. I believe the American people are slowly beginning to realize that the country went too far, especially after global pressure forced the United States to allow the International Red

Cross to inspect the Savior Camps. Their report on the humanitarian abuses in the camps went a long way in convincing many Americans that they need to consider restoring the rights that were lost due to the CHRIST Act.

WILLIAMS: I still can't understand why people weren't marching in the streets after that report came out.

GINSBERG: I'm sure a lot of people bought the government's claim that the IRC's report was a lie created by non-believers. Even now when it's obvious that America is no longer a super power and their economy is crashing, the majority of Americans still believe that the United States is on top and the rest of the world is jealous of their religious purity.

WILLIAMS: How do you keep from being frustrated?

GINSBERG: In my travels, I've met so many people from other countries who are praying for America to return to the great nation it once was. And through back channels, I've talked to a number of Americans who have realized that to be a good Christian and a good American means rejecting the present theocracy in power. They're the ones who will eventually dismantle the National Church and bring America back to being a great and free nation to all people of all religions, living equally together.

WILLIAMS: Do you think people like you and me will be able to return to America in our lifetime?

GINSBERG: I have a Mexican passport that allows me to travel anywhere in the world, except the United States. But even if America changed back to a full democracy tomorrow, I can never return home unless I want to spend the rest of my life in jail. But I pray someday my children can.

WILLIAMS: Speaking of children, I forgot your little girl's name?

GINSBERG: Amy Leah Ginsberg. She's eighteen-months old this week.

WILLIAMS: Now, I understand that you're Jewish and your wife is Catholic.

GINSBERG: That's right.

WILLIAMS: Which religion are you going to raise your daughter?

GINSBERG: Both.

WILLIAMS: But Seth, that's so confusing. The poor girl is going to be completely screwed up about religion.

GINSBERG: I know. Isn't it wonderful?

ACKNOWLEDGMENTS

My thanks to Gabriella Burman, Mindy Dawn Friedman, Gabriela Martin Sanchez Guerrero, Sheri Joseph, Andisheh Nouraee, Dee Perez, Ginger Pinholster, Megan Volpert, Susan Rebecca White, and Neil White for their valuable comments on early drafts. Thank you to my agent Jill Marr of Sandra Dijkstra Literary Agency for her patience and belief in this story. Much gratitude to Steve McCondichie, April Ford, Eleanor Burden, and all the folks at Southern Fried Karma Press for their guidance and encouragement. *Jesus Land: A Memoir* by Julia Scheeres and *The Family: The Secret Fundamentalism at the Heart of American Power* by Jeff Sharlet were major influences.

This book never would have happened without the love and support of my wife, Jessica Handler. As soon as I finished a chapter, I read it to her. Her feedback and insight were invaluable.

About the Author

What matters most toMickey Dubrow is that the reader is never bored. Mickey is passionate about telling stories that offer fresh perspectives while also being entertaining, and he want sreaders to feel excitement, sympathy, amusement, joy, and maybe even a little anxiety when they read his work. In college, he wrote and drew a cartoon strip before moving on to work in television for thirty years. But even with his extensive experience and success, he didn't believe he had talent for writing fiction...so he decided to write a novel for the fun of it, and he's been hooked ever since. In *American Judas*, Mickey explores, among other possibilities, lost faith in America and what this might mean for the freedoms we cherish so much. He holds a BFA from the University of Tennessee, Knoxville. As a freelance writer and producer for television, his clients include CNN, Turner South, Cartoon Network Marketing, HGTV, and SRA/McGraw Hill.

Share Your Thoughts

Want to help spread the word about *American Judas*? Consider leaving an honest review on Goodreads. It is our priority at SFK Press to publish books for readers to enjoy, and our authors would love to hear from you!

Do You Know About Our Weekly Zine?

Would you like your unpublished prose, poetry, or visual art featured in SFK Press's weekly online literary publication, *The New Southern Fugitives*? A zine that's free to readers and subscribers, and pays contributors:

$60 per book review, essay & short story
$25 per photograph & piece of visual art
$25 per poem

Visit **NewSouthernFugitives.com/Submit** for more information!